Meet Raina and Teague.
Two people thrown together on one desperate mission,
sworn to be enemies, destined to be lovers.
Their story began long ago in
THE KNOWING CRYSTAL.
Now it continues in

FIRESTORM

His abrupt changes in mood confused Raina. One moment Teague was cold, withdrawn, then angry, then he acted the possessive man, and then the next . . . ? She pondered that for a moment, the first inklings of his possible motivation slowly permeating her mind. He acted as if . . . as if he'd realized he was revealing too much . . . as if he *cared*.

A curious, melting gladness filled Raina. She scooted close and laid a hand on his. "There's no reason to beg pardon, Teague. We are partners. It's good that we're concerned about what may happen to each other."

He glanced up warily, a haunted expression in his eyes. "Is it, Raina? I'm not so certain."

His words gave her pause. There was something, some underlying, unspoken message there. If she dared press further, she risked . . .

Exactly what *did* she risk?

Taking her heart in hand, Raina dared words she never thought she'd utter to a man. "I cannot speak for you, but it seems, whether I wish it or not," she forced herself to say before she lost her newly found courage, "I cannot help but care for you. You've saved my life twice now. As much as I distrust and loathe most men, I cannot continue to view you in such a negative light. Though I find it most unsettling, it is the truth and I must face it."

KATHLEEN MORGAN

FIRESTORM

PINNACLE BOOKS
KENSINGTON PUBLISHING CORP.

PINNACLE BOOKS are published by

Kensington Publishing Corp.
850 Third Avenue
New York, NY 10022

First Printing: September, 1995

Printed in the United States of America

To my family—my husband, John, and my two sons, Brad and Sean. I couldn't have done it without the meals you cooked, and clothes you washed, and the house you cleaned while I was in the final throes of this book's deadline. You guys did such a good job, I'm seriously considering letting you keep on doing all the work indefinitely.

Not in the clamour of the crowded street,
Not in the shouts and plaudits of the throng,
But in ourselves, are triumph and defeat.

Longfellow, "The Poets"

The Prophecy

The son must suffer,
Die to himself and the world,
Before the taint can be exorcised,
Before the evil is overthrown.

But woe to any who harm him.
His is the right to search,
To plumb the secrets within.
His is the right to choose.

A living death or life
Of fire and light.
A firestorm of obliteration.
Or triumph.

One

"My ears must be failing me, Brother Tremayne. Did you just say you will not do as I ask? *Surely* I heard wrong."

King Falkan, ruler of the system of planets known as the Imperium, leaned forward on his throne and cocked a graying black brow. His scathing glance slid down the form of the hooded man standing before him. A tall, broad-shouldered man swathed from head to sandaled feet in a long-sleeved, dark gray robe and floor-length black sleeveless overtunic.

"It is as you heard it, Imperial Majesty." Teague Tremayne, warrior monk of the famed Monastery of Exsul, made a long, slow bow, his hands hidden deep within the cavernous sleeves of his simple robe. "I tender you my deepest regrets, but I cannot do as you ask."

"Indeed?" the king inquired silkily, the rustling movement of his purple serica-cloth raiment the only sound in the stone-silent reception chamber. "Pray, rise and tell me why *is* that, Brother Tremayne?"

Teague squared his shoulders and straightened. Here it comes, he thought. He'd hoped that the questions were over. It seemed now they would never be.

He forced himself to step closer to the ornately gilded, raised dais. Though the effort to lower his gaze and bow humbly once more to the most mighty and formidable ruler of their galaxy was hard, even after all these cycles of monastic training and brutal self-discipline, Teague did it. As always, the act of submitting his will to the will of others soothed his tormented soul.

A familiar wave of peace and tranquillity washed over him. It was for the best, he reminded himself. No good ever came of anger, in times of peace *or* war. *A cool head, a clear intent, a heart calm and gentle,* he intoned the first lines of an ancient, monastic saying to himself, *prevail over all things, at all times . . .*

"I beg pardon for my disrespect, Imperial Majesty," Teague replied, once more meeting the hard, glittering glance of King Falkan, "but I am exiled from my home, have been these past nineteen cycles. Even if it were possible now to pass through Incendra's electromagnetic field alive, my monastic honor would not allow me to break the vow I made never to return."

"And who can demand more of you than I?" Falkan stood, took two steps, and halted at the edge of the dais, glaring down at Teague with all the authority of his formidable position. "What man, be he even a king of his own meager planet, has more power, more right, to ask this than I?"

Once again, Teague lowered his head briefly in humble obeisance. "None, Majesty. But I will not do this, even if, in the refusal, it costs me my life."

"Will not?" Falkan's squarely chiseled jaw clenched. White lines of tension bracketed his mouth. *"Will not?"*

Will not? Teague thought bitterly. When had it *ever,* since that horrible day, come down to an act of will, one way or another? There was no volition left within him when it came to Incendra, no confidence it could have been any different, even if he'd known what to do or how to do it, no need, save the need to just . . .

forget. But to tell the king now that he would not go to Incendra was a lie, and he never lied. *"Can not,* Majesty," he said instead. "I simply cannot."

At that moment an errant beam of light from the midday sun pierced the room, striking the mosaic floor between Teague and the royal dais. For a fleeting instant, the gray- and black-garbed monk allowed himself to study the intricate design of the tiny pieces of colored stone, the scene of a land engulfed in a fiery inferno. Incendra, he thought with a shattering realization. Whether the mosaic had been meant to represent and remind him of his home planet or not, it did. His home, not only a place dotted by the firestorm-shrouded caves, but a land torn apart in the fiery torment of failed responsibilities, usurped throne, and devastated people.

"Er, pardon, if you will, Uncle." A new, deeply resonant voice intruded on the heavy tension building in the room. "Perhaps if Brother Tremayne knew of the Volan spy ship and the reasons we ask this of him . . . ?"

With a superhuman wrenching of forbidden thoughts and desires from what could never again be, Teague lifted his gaze to the tall, dark-haired man standing to the left of the dais. Cool gray eyes locked with his. Lord Teran Ardane, nephew of the king and royal ambassador, smiled. Teague eyed him closely, perceived the honest intent of the man, then shuttered his brief surge of gratitude behind a mask of monastic tranquillity.

It served him well, this dearly acquired facade of monkish calm and control . . . served to hide his true thoughts and emotions not only from others, but from himself. Yes, it served him well indeed. He didn't know how he would have survived all these cycles without it.

"I would hear those reasons, Imperial Majesty,"

Teague said, turning back to King Falkan. "I owe you that courtesy, if nothing else."

"You owe me more than courtesy, Teague Tremayne," the king growled. At the warning clearing of a throat, he shot his nephew a questioning glance, then sighed and turned back to Teague. "But Teran is right. Our reasons notwithstanding, the journey back through Incendra's electromagnetic storm is danger enough. You have the right to know why we ask what we do of you."

"The now deadly force field surrounding my planet was never my motive for refusing you, as treacherous and surely fatal a journey as it would be. The warrior monks of Exsul are sworn to die in the service of the Imperium." The big monk shifted his legs slightly, his stance widening. His hands fell from his sleeves, swinging 'round to knot behind his back. "My reasons for refusing you are not Exsul's, but my own."

Falkan's mouth quirked in irritation. "Gods, but you're one of the most infuriating—!"

He inhaled a steadying breath, then gave a wry chuckle. "But then, why should I be surprised?" the king continued, half to himself. "The kind of men I call on for these kinds of missions are never easily intimidated or short on stubborn pride. Not Teran, or his brother Brace, or their friend Gage Bardwin."

A grudging respect gleamed in the king's eyes. He turned, walked back to his chair, and sat. "Yes, Teran, Brace and Bardwin have served me well, in truth, been the most resourceful and steadfast of allies in this rapidly worsening battle against the mind-slaving alien invaders. But now I desperately need you to be that same kind of ally. *Desperately,* do you hear me?"

"I hear you, Majesty."

Falkan nodded crisply. "Then listen well, Tremayne,

before telling me you cannot do as I ask." He hesitated a moment, then forged on. "We are at war, fighting for our lives against the most deadly enemy the Imperium has ever faced. The Volans from the Abessian galaxy are slowly but surely, and in the most insidious of ways, infiltrating our planets and enslaving the minds of our people."

Teague frowned. "The Volans? In all the hundreds of cycles they've roamed the universe, they've never once come the way of the Imperium. Why now?"

"Because the Knowing Crystal is no more," Teran Ardane offered, moving close to stand between Teague and the king.

He was a big man, Teague realized, as he met him eye-to-eye. As big and fit as any warrior. His gaze glanced off his, but not before the steely determination glinting in Teran's eyes left its indelible impression on the monk. Teague smiled inwardly. The bearded, ebony-haired man would be a formidable enemy. The wiser course, if it were at all possible, was not to make him one.

Teague sighed and pulled back his cowl, settling its coarse gray cloth upon his shoulders. "I'd heard tales—who hasn't?—of your discovery and return of that stone of power after its theft hundreds of cycles ago, as well as how your brother destroyed it in the pools of Cambrai. It was an evil thing, no matter how the people revered it. But now you say the approach of the Volans and the Knowing Crystal's destruction are somehow linked?"

"So it seems."

Teran studied the monk. Without the shadowy concealment of his monastic cowl, the man's features came into better view. He was strikingly handsome in a masculine sort of way, with thick, low-set brows, a long, straight nose, thin but well-curved lips, and eyes a striking silver-blue. Eyes as cold and clear as an icy mountain stream, Teran thought. And just as inaccessible.

His tumble of sun-streaked dark blond hair cascaded to his shoulders. Its lack of styling or care, save for the rough hand he raked through to drag the long strands back from his face, told Teran all he needed to know. The monk was not only peacefully composed, but so piously detached he seemed altogether heedless of the trappings of a normal life and the superficialities others found all but essential.

Yet for all his outward semblance of indifference and serenity, there was still something about Teague Tremayne that plucked at Teran, stirring uneasy thoughts and wary questions. Something sad . . . haunted . . . and at great odds with the initial impression of monastic calm and steely self-discipline.

That consideration troubled the king's ambassador but failed to sway him from his mission. Despite all the doubts and questions a closer look at the monk had stirred, Tremayne was still the only man for the job. His fame as a warrior monk was renowned. He had served the Imperium faithfully and brilliantly in countless diplomatic and battle missions in the past. His credentials for this mission were impeccable.

Most important of all, though, he was an Incendarian, and off-planet Incendarians were as rare as the feathers of the nearly extinct Cygnian weaver bird. Yet only an Incendarian—actually, *two* of them, to be exact—had any chance of making it through the deadly electromagnetic shield now encircling the planet, much less had any hope of succeeding on the mission.

Two Incendarians. Teran smiled to himself. Obtaining

the consent of the second person chosen for the job was another problem in itself. A problem better dealt with after they had gained Tremayne's cooperation.

The captured Volan spy ship they hoped to use for the journey to Incendra was best handled by two pilots. With his reputation for calm logic and ferocious courage, Tremayne was one of the obvious choices. There was little time to seek out other Incendarians at any rate. The situation was simply that grave.

"I've still to hear the reason you need me to return to Incendra," the warrior monk prodded gently, piercing Teran's jumble of thoughts. "Or what it has to do with the Volans."

"Do you know much about them?"

"Volans?" Teague shrugged. "No more than most, I'd wager. They enter peoples' minds and take over their bodies, totally enslaving them to their bidding. Unfortunately, the higher metabolic rate demanded by their alien entities shortens their slave's lifespan. They are soon forced to move on to other victims."

"They're the scourge of the universe and will soon be the destruction of the Imperium!" King Falkan cried. "As one of the Imperial planets, isolated though it is by its deadly storms, Incendra will fall, sooner or later. If for no other reason than loyalty to your own kind, you must help us, Tremayne."

"Help you do what?" The first glimmer of anger darkened Teague's mood. In an almost reflexive response, he quashed the forbidden emotion and swung back to the king. "Discount my personal beliefs and desires in this matter?" he continued, in a more well-modulated, monkish tone. "My deepest thanks, Imperial Majesty, but I must decline."

Falkan's eyes narrowed dangerously. "You make it

sound like this is all beneath you," he snarled, his face growing red. "Like . . . like this is all some game we play here. I warn you, Tremayne. I—"

"If you will, Uncle." Teran gripped Teague's arm.

Ever so slowly, the monk turned to meet Teran's gaze, then looked down to where the other man held him. A muscle jumped fleetingly in his jaw, then stilled. "Release me." Teague looked up, locking glances with the bearded man. "No one lays a hand on a monk of Exsul without severe consequences. Even one who intends no harm."

For the briefest instant, a look of defiance, of anger, flared in the king's ambassador's eyes. Teague tensed, readying himself for an attack.

Then, with a wry smile, Teran released him. "My apologies. I meant nothing by the act, save to finish my tale."

The big monk slid his hand back into his sleeves. "Then do so," he said quietly. "Nothing is served by prolonging this meeting."

"No, nothing is served," Teran agreed, "if we cannot come to a meeting of minds and hearts and wills." He glanced up at the king. "Perhaps more would be accomplished if we adjourned to the comfort of your private library?"

Falkan nodded his assent. Teran glanced back at Teague. "A goblet of uva wine and some sweet cakes might be the perfect solution to our rapidly fraying tempers. If that would be acceptable to Brother Tremayne?"

Teague eyed him closely. What was the man's game? If he thought to ply him with liquor until his tongue loosened . . . "The library is acceptable. The wine is not. We are not permitted to indulge in such libations."

"Then perhaps a cup of unfermented uva juice or some Umarian spice tea?"

"The tea would be acceptable."

The king's ambassador gestured toward the door at the other end of the hall. "Come, then, Brother Tremayne. The day draws on even as we speak. And there is still much left to discuss."

The monk cocked a dark blond brow. "Indeed?"

Teran nodded, his mouth tightening in a resolute smile. "Indeed."

The sweat cave was hot, hotter than he'd ever endured, but the heat and scorching mist that rose every time he emptied a ladle of water over the superheated stones did little to ease his unsettled state of mind. With a soul-deep sigh, Teague rocked back on his heels, his fingers gouging into the sweat-slick flesh of his tautly muscled thighs.

He'd been in the sweat cave a half hour now, squatting naked in the dark, searingly hot chamber of stone, willing the chaotic tumult in his mind to calm. It had always—*always*—worked before. But not this day. And perhaps never again.

His thoughts slipped back to the meeting in the king's private library. A grim smile twisted the monk's lips. Teran Ardane was a clever man, his mind more swift and agile than a fleet cerva startled out of hiding.

He had known better than to threaten or browbeat, techniques for which his uncle, the king, was famous. No, Teran Ardane hadn't done anything more than state the facts. Facts that included the unexpected capture of a Volan spy ship with state-of-the-art technology, technology that appeared capable of shielding travelers from

Incendra's intensified electromagnetic field. Facts that included the Imperium's need for a special stone found only on Incendra. A stone they desperately required to push the Volans back and keep them, once more, out of the Imperium. And only Teague, as one of the few Incendarians caught off planet when the force field had suddenly intensified, had any hope of going back and retrieving it for them.

With a low groan, the monk flung back his head, his eyes clenching shut. What was he to do? *What was he to do?* He breathed deeply, raggedly, inhaling a suffocating cloud of steam. It made him cough and choke.

Teague fought for a moment to regain his breath, then forced his thoughts back to the problem at hand. Indeed, what *was* he to do? According to the Ardanes, the Imperium had begun the development of a device to divert the mind-slaving aliens from the Imperium and keep them, once more, at bay. If the prototype was successful—and the special Incendarian stone was a crucial element to its success—the plan was to build a transmission plant on each Imperial planet to protect it.

Only one obstacle to the king's scheme remained. He needed pilots to navigate the Volan spy ship—pilots capable of surviving Incendra's harsh climate, who knew the land and the language. Pilots who *must* be Incendarians. It was why they wanted him. Why he must go. The fate of the entire Imperium could well depend on him—an Imperium he had sworn to serve when he'd taken his monastic vows.

Yet even knowing that, the decision to refuse or accept the king's offer was made no easier.

Maintaining his thigh-punishing crouch, Teague shifted from one foot to the other. The soles of his feet stung from the hot stone he squatted upon. His chest ached from the brief, shallow breaths he took to avoid singeing his lungs. He opened his eyes. Sweat dripped into them. Still, he remained in the sweltering cocoon of stone.

Teague welcomed the discomfort. Pain was an integral part of his monastic training. Pain disciplined the flesh and tempered the mind. It focused one on the immediate, the here-and-now, and cleared the head for the work still to be done.

And there was indeed work to be done—*if* he chose to return to Incendra. Nothing more could be accomplished, however, until the Ardanes found a second Incendarian. Teague half wished they'd never find another one.

The big monk smiled grimly. That desire wasn't as farfetched as it might initially have appeared. Even before the increase in the force of the electromagnetic field had effectively halted all interplanetary travel, few Incendarians had ever chosen to journey off planet.

In an attempt to control the people by limiting the technological advances offered by other planets, his father, and fathers before him, had seen to that. Yet now, Volan ship or not, Teague tempted an agonizing death in flying back through the storms. As did any other one foolish enough to accompany him.

Foolish . . . A fool . . . You're such a disappointment . . .

Stirred by the memories evoked by those words, for a fleeting instant Teague's thoughts flew backward, into a past he struggled every day of his life to forget. He turned the soul-searing phrases over and over in his mind.

His father had spoken those words and worse to him many times as a lad. Those times when he'd hesitated to try some warrior's task his sire had set him, or when his father had taken the measure of his son's small, skinny stature. Those times when he'd been discovered hiding in some leafy bower with his sketchbook and drawing tools, instead of out on the sun-drenched practice field, wielding one of the cumbersome Vastita cudgels so prized by that particular desert tribe.

Prized, as well, by his big, hearty, warrior-king father.

His father had always been right. He *had* been a fool, and a weakling and a coward. Had been unworthy to claim the right as son and heir to the kingdom of Farsala, one of the largest continents on Incendra and realm of the seafarers and rocky coasts, of the mountain peoples and lands wherein lay the capital, of the inhabitants of the vast lake districts, and of the twelve desert tribes. And in that failure, that worthlessness, he'd betrayed not only his family, but his people and his land.

The strong, smooth muscles of Teague's thighs screamed in agony, twisting in spasms from the low crouch he doggedly maintained on the floor. Let them burn, let them hurt, he thought with a fierce, almost jubilant resolve. It was worth it if the pain would sear through the tumult of anguished thoughts and memories, the rising fear. He needed desperately to forget . . . before the *forbidden* forced its way past his mental defenses.

Before he must face what he never wished to face again.

Teague clenched his eyes shut, blocking out the dimly lit chamber with its crude stone benches and pile of glowing red stones, the simple wooden water bucket and ladle sitting nearby. His shoulders hunched. His head dipped in anguish.

It wasn't working. Not this time. The first fingers of

panic plucked at his gut. No matter the long cycles of monastic training, no matter the iron-willed discipline that had brought him to such an exalted position in his own order, Teague still couldn't contain the terror that surged through him at even the slightest consideration of returning to Incendra.

He stood to lose everything. Everything—his honor, his renewed sense of purpose, his dearly bought and even more dearly held self-control, and . . . and something even more elemental—the essence of what he now was, what he'd overcome, and *become*.

Ah, gods, Teague thought, his fingers digging deep into his thighs. He couldn't *bear* the thought of reverting back to the terrified, tormented, mangled boy he'd been when the monks of Exsul had first taken him in! Couldn't bear reliving that soul-shattering sense of failure and worthlessness!

By the five moons of Bellator, the Ardanes didn't know what they asked of him! Incendra was his land, ran in his blood for generations untold. Yet once he set foot back on its precious soil, he didn't know what primal forces—forces he might not be able to contain—would once again be loosed within him.

He *had* to protect the tenuous control he'd regained by dint of much effort and suffering from the clutches of his father and the man who'd killed him. To lose that again . . .

His life had been thrust into total chaos and disruption when Malam Vorax had overthrown his father. His existence, or at least all he'd ever known as the only son and heir at thirteen, had been brutally shredded before his very eyes. And it could all be destroyed in the space of a few days or weeks back on Incendra.

Destroyed . . . if Vorax found him, if he was once

more forced to face his people and relive his failure, his shame.

What would become of him then?

It was selfish, Teague well knew, to think only of his own needs and desires. It was cowardly to consider his own petty fears of greater worth than the plight of an entire Imperium of people. In the end, what he was, who he'd become, should be of little import. What *should* matter was the good of many. Yet who else but he would heed what happened to him?

His family was gone; his people surely cared little for what had become of the king's heir. Small reason for any to concern himself with a Royal House whose internal weaknesses and failings had ultimately led to its downfall. That particular truth, above all else, had been drummed into him over and over again by Vorax's exquisitely talented torturers.

No one. There was no one who cared or would ever care again what happened to him.

Terror sucked at the monk, clawing at him with talons of remorselessness until it threatened to drag him down into that all-too-familiar sticky, suffocating morass of mindless oblivion. His heart pounded in his chest. He gasped; he shuddered. He fought for breath.

Survival . . . the most primal instinct of all. He *must* survive.

Head bowed, fists clenched, Teague shoved unsteadily to his feet, grasping frantically at the only crutch left him—the mind control that his beloved monastic training and cycles of strict discipline had given him. He began desperately, fervently, to recite the sacred, healing Litany of Union.

Time is not linear but circular, he mentally intoned.

The universe has always existed and will continue to exist.

Even as he repeated the soul-healing phrases, his breathing began to steady, his pulse to slow. *Anything born into this life has lived before. Any being who dies creates the cause for the rebirth of a new being. One's petty concerns are as naught. One's fears are groundless. All that matters is the unceasing flow of the universe.*

As always, the litany stirred him to the deepest recesses of his being. Renewed strength filled Teague. The tension eased from his body. Peace washed over him in mind- and spirit-soothing waves.

After a time he lifted his head, a smile of serene acceptance on his lips. His fear was gone, buried beneath the weight of a greater truth, a higher calling. His own existence meant nothing, save to serve the unceasing flow of the universe. He must never forget that, or cease to let it guide him. In the end, it was all he could ever hope to depend on.

Whatever fate awaited him on Incendra, perhaps it was his to meet. In the infinite, cyclical way of things, perhaps there was yet something undone that needed doing. And perhaps, just perhaps, the time had come to do it.

The monk threw back his shoulders, strode across the cave, and flung open the door. Steam ejected from the stone chamber with a hiss and a roiling white cloud. As the mist gradually cleared, the first glimmers of stars in the rapidly darkening sky came into view.

Teague grabbed a cloth and wrapped it about his hips. One hand securely clutching the meager bit of homespun, he stepped outside.

The cooling night air wafted over him, setting his

overheated and sensitized flesh to tingling. A shudder vibrated through his sweat-sheened body. With an impatient motion, he tossed back the long hanks of sodden hair that had fallen into his face and glanced around.

Perched on a rocky mountainside several kilometers from the Bellatorian capital of Rector, the sweat cave sat beside a small, beehive-shaped hermitage that monks of Exsul were required to use whenever they visited the royal city. Behind the hermitage was a high-walled exercise enclosure guarded by a locked door. In the deepening dusk, Teague could barely make out the center of the city that lay below, or the palace situated there with its gray walls and turreted buildings stacked one atop the other.

Just as well, he thought. It was past time to get on with what remained of the monastic day. There were meditations to be completed, a simple meal to be eaten, and later, a long-overdue ritual still to be performed.

And on the morrow? Well, Teran Ardane and the king would expect their answer on the morrow.

Teague glanced toward the hermitage. For once, it didn't beckon as it always had before, that cool stone sanctuary of countless monks of Exsul, that precious haven from the cares and tribulations of the outside world. And it wouldn't, not this night or any night for a long while to come.

Monastic discipline or no, he hadn't bested the dark terrors that had coiled around and embedded themselves in his heart this eve, terrors stirred anew for the first time since so many cycles ago. Terrors he'd thought he'd banished and now found he hadn't.

Once again, Teague felt thirteen cycles old. Confusion flooded him, a sense of overwhelming vulnerability and helplessness. *A fool . . . Disappointed in you . . .*

Surely those were the most painful words a child could ever hear from his parent. And because of those words, and his failure to save his family from their final destruction, those terrors might well destroy him someday. But for this moment in time, he must hold them at bay.

Peace flooded Teague once more. There was victory enough to be had in that. There had to be. He could only live one moment, one day at a time. Meanwhile, life must go on as it always had—until it became necessary for it to change once more.

All that mattered was the unceasing flow of the universe . . .

Two

Marissa Ardane glanced at her husband and nervously wet her lips. "I don't know if I'm up to this, Brace. I thought I was, but now I'm not so sure. It's one thing to ask a friend for a favor. It's entirely another to ask her to risk her life."

Brace Ardane, nephew to King Falkan and younger brother of his royal ambassador, cocked a dark brow and smiled. He stroked a finger tenderly along his wife's cheek. "She's the only one for the job, sweet one, and you know it."

The movement of one of the three transport technicians slanting a furtive glance their way caught his eye. Brace shot the man a quelling look across the large room of computer terminals, control panels, and a large transport platform enclosed in a transparent shield. The inquisitive technician had the good grace to blush and avert his gaze. "This discussion is moot at any rate." Brace then continued in a lower voice. "A discussion best reserved for a more private time, after Raina's arrival."

His wife caught the subtle movement of his head in the transport technician's direction and nodded. "As always, you're right." She shrugged the tension from her neck and shoulders and shot him a mischievous grin. "It must be difficult for you."

"Hmmm?" Brace asked distractedly, engrossed, once again, in watching the movements of the three men as they completed the final preparations for receiving an interspace transport. "What's that?"

"Being so infernally perfect all the time."

Her husband's head swiveled around. "What?" He stared down at her for a moment, then chuckled. "Now that you mention it, it *is* difficult. But not any more difficult than handling a she-cat like you."

"Or our four daughters?"

He rolled his eyes. "You had to remind me, didn't you? I thought this trip to Rector was to be a brief if glorious respite from our two sets of toddling twins?"

Marissa smiled archly. "Oh, it *will* be, beloved. Just as soon as Raina arrives and we've had time to convey Falkan's request and—"

"And you've had five or six hours to talk and renew old acquaintances," Brace finished for her wryly.

"Five or six hours!"

"I know you, Marissa. You haven't seen Raina since before our first set of twins were born. Shall we lay a wager on how long it takes you two to catch up on the past three years?"

"No, you'd win, and you know it." Marissa's gaze dropped for a flicker of an instant, then lifted to meet his. Mischief sparkled in her eyes. "Would you care to join us? I remember how well you and Raina got along when you first met."

He gave a snort of disbelief. "She didn't like me then, and I doubt we'd share more than a wary respect even now. You, sweet one, are the only thing that binds Raina and me. She tolerates me because of that." His mouth twitched. *"And* just as long as I treat you well, too, if I recall correctly."

Marissa's eyes darkened with distant memories. "Raina has good reason to distrust men. She won't be happy to hear she must now work with one on such a dangerous mission."

"From what little you've told me of her past she won't be happy to hear she's being asked to return to her former home, either."

"No," Marissa sighed, "she won't." For a moment, her glance strayed toward the technician who was taking his place at one of the control panels. As she watched, he shoved the power lever forward. Marissa turned back to her husband. "But as you already said, she's the only one for the job." Her mouth quirked sadly. "Besides that strange monk, of course."

A curious buzzing filled the room. Marissa's heart commenced a wild pounding. Her hands rose, clenched over her heart. Raina, she thought. Raina would be here any moment now.

In a shimmering flurry of color and light, the slender form of a red-haired, green-eyed woman gradually materialized. "Raina," Marissa breathed, and shot her husband an eager, questioning glance.

"Go to her, sweet one," Brace urged, a smile of loving understanding glimmering on his lips. "It all depends on you, at any rate."

For an instant, she stared back at him. Then, Marissa gave an unsteady laugh. "It's been a while since I was involved in the salvation of the Imperium. I'm afraid I might be out of practice."

His hand settled in the curve of her lower back and he gave her a gentle shove forward. "Trust me. It'll come back. It always does."

Marissa tossed her long mane of chestnut brown hair and walked over to stand before Raina. Her friend smiled in greeting and, as the transparent shield around her lifted, she stepped off the transport platform.

"Marissa!" she exclaimed, and strode over to her. Though her heart leaped with excitement, Raina refused to reveal her emotions before the men gathered in the room. She motioned to Brace, standing near the door. "I see you brought your husband. Must I endure a requisite social hour with him before we're permitted some time alone?"

Marissa had opened her mouth to protest when Raina laughed and grabbed her hand, giving it a quick squeeze. "I was only joking, sweeting. Come, let's leave this place. I cannot bear the prying eyes of these other men."

Leading the way, Raina headed across the room, halting only when she stood opposite Brace. As tall a man as he was, she lifted her gaze only slightly to meet his. Her glance was steady, direct. "You want something of me, Ardane. Let's find a private place and finish the unpleasant business quickly, so I may then spend the rest of my time here visiting with Marissa."

"An excellent suggestion, domina," Brace agreed equably, using the ultimate feminine term of respect. "Is the palace garden suitable?"

Raina's eyes narrowed. "Domina, is it now? You must *really* need a favor to address me thusly." She shot Marissa an amused glance. "He's become quite the diplomat, hasn't he? And yes," she continued, looking back at Brace. "The garden is quite suitable."

Brace laughed. "And *she* hasn't changed a whit, has she, sweet one? I like that." He indicated the door with a motion of his head. "Shall we go, then, Raina? The day draws on and we've less than a half hour left before the sun sets."

The red-haired woman nodded. "Most assuredly, Ardane."

The journey through the halls of the palace's aux-
iliary building housing one of the city's two transport
stations was silent save for the clap of their footsteps
on the smooth stone floors and the polite greetings
exchanged with any they passed. The late spring wind
buffeted the windows, but the heat of the sun that had
beaten in all day warmed the corridors nicely, prom-
ising an equally pleasant if brief interlude outdoors
before nightfall.

As they walked, Raina glanced outside. The gardens
skirting that side of the building were large and arranged
in the ancient Umarian manner, a popular technique long
revered as one of the cornerstones of Imperial gardening.
A half kilometer square, the garden included myriad herb
beds, a small orchard of cerosa and pirum trees covered
in snowy white and delicate pink blossoms, and long, intricately interconnected beds of arosa bushes and various
exotic flowers imported from all over the Imperium.

But another self-aggrandizing display of the long-
reaching arm of the mighty warrior planet Bellator,
Raina thought bitterly, riveting her gaze back to the long
hall before her. And of a king whose summons none
dared refuse.

She shot Marissa a sideways glance. Her friend seemed
genuinely happy to see her, but their greeting, however
warm it had been considering the circumstances, had
been overlaid with a certain tension. It didn't originate
from her husband's presence, or from any undue influence on his part, though.

Marissa wouldn't have agreed to any of this if she
hadn't felt the need was great. Indeed, so great and of
so much import that even a secured interspace commu-

nications link wasn't worth the risk of it being inter-
cepted and decoded. What needed to be said had to be
said in person.

That, even more than Marissa's anxious reserve just
a few minutes ago, worried Raina, setting her warrior's
instincts on edge. A pleasant possibility filtered into her
mind. Perhaps this mystery involved some mission in
which she and Marissa could join forces. Just like old
times . . .

Brace triggered the portal to open at the end of the
long hall, then stepped aside and motioned the two
women through. Raina allowed Marissa to go before her,
then followed, halting beside her husband. "Not coming
with us, are you?"

"I thought you two feminas could use some time
alone." He grinned down at her. "Disappointed?"

Raina's mouth quirked. "Hardly, but you already
knew that, Ardane. You've never been a stupid man."

His grin widened and he chuckled softly. "Careful
now. You border on the complimentary."

She cocked her head as if in sudden consideration.
"Do I? I must be growing soft, then." Raina stepped
through the doorway and cast a sardonic look over her
shoulder. "But if you believe that, Ardane, watch your
back, for I may well be there when you least expect
it."

Brace threw back his head and gave a shout of laughter. Then, without another word, he withdrew into the
building and sent the portal sliding shut before him.

Raina turned, her glance meeting the frowning one
of Marissa's. "I meant no harm, sweeting," she hastened
to explain, misinterpreting the emotions behind her
friend's frown. "He really isn't bad—for a man, that
is."

"Oh, I know that." Marissa made a distracted, dismissing movement of her hand. "Both you and Brace revel in the verbal battle. But I know you see him for the good man he is, too." She paused, wetting her lips. "It's . . . something else."

"Something like the reason why you invited me—no, *insisted*—I come to Bellator, after three cycles apart?"

Marissa flushed. "I asked you to visit many times in the past. If you recall, it was you who had some excuse or another."

"Yes, that I did," the auburn-haired woman admitted gravely. "The Sodalitas needed me. You, on the other hand . . ."

"Didn't need you anymore?" her friend finished for her. Marissa smiled sadly. "Whether I need you or not, you'll always be my dearest friend, Raina. You just didn't want to share me with Brace, or with our children. I think it would've made you . . . uncomfortable, too."

Raina eyed her closely for the space of an inhaled breath. "Perhaps." She shrugged. "One way or another, I'm here now. What is it you want of me?"

The chestnut-haired woman laughed. "Always the take-charge leader, always right to the point. Have you no need to hear first how the cycles have gone for me, or, for that matter, to permit me to ask the same of you?"

"I'll ask those questions soon enough. First, let's get the less savory business completed. Then we'll have time to renew old acquaintances and truly enjoy each other's company."

Marissa nodded. "Fine." She indicated the path that lay before them. "Let's walk out farther into the garden, where none may overhear. A woman will soon join us

whom I want you to meet. Brace has gone even now
to fetch her. What we have to say to you bears no eaves-
dropping. The future of the Imperium may well depend
on this mission."

"Indeed?" Raina fell into step beside Marissa. "I'd
an inkling it was something like that." They made their
way down the flagstone path, skirting raised beds where
the bright green, sprightly shoots of what looked to be
Cygnian bellflowers and Moracan silver torches already
grew in dense profusion, before taking a path to the
left, past a variety of herb plots, to where a cunning
little bower of uva vines stood. There, Marissa indicated
that they should sit.

The buds of the uva leaves had yet to open and fill
the spaces between the entwined vines. Thus, though
the bower gave them some semblance of privacy, the
lack of foliage also afforded Raina and Marissa an un-
impaired view of the garden from all directions.

Raina smiled inwardly. Wife and mother that her
friend might now be, she still retained the essence of
their Sodalitas warrior's training and innate vigilance.
No man, not even one of the caliber of Brace Ardane,
would ever take that from her. She was still her own
person, and that was good.

Light from the setting sun streamed through the
skeletal framework of the bower. It flickered off Raina's
hair, setting it aflame with glints of deep bronze, vivid
copper, and crimson. For a fleeting instant, Marissa was
caught up in the fiery beauty of her friend's vibrantly
red tresses. As always, Raina wore her long hair pulled
severely off her face and high up onto the back of her
head, where it was then braided to hang down to the
middle of her back.

Not one for feminine adornments of any kind, Raina's

only concession to a visit to her best friend was, instead of her usual warrior garb, a cerulean blue long-sleeved overblouse of shimmering serica cloth with black breeches tucked into knee-high black boots. The requisite Sodalitas long dagger was strapped to her left thigh. It was, for the occasion, however, housed in an ornamental sheath of finest black domare hide encrusted with sparkling azurite gems that exactly matched Raina's overblouse.

She truly was a magnificent woman, Marissa thought in loving admiration, from her sparkling green eyes and flawlessly fair skin with its disconcerting sprinkling of freckles across the bridge of her nose, to her slender, whipcord-hard, but still femininely curved body. A woman whom many men had looked on with a desire that had never been reciprocated. A woman who most likely would never know or want the affection or devotion of a man.

The realization saddened Marissa deeply, especially in the past few years since she'd come to know and love Brace, bear his children, and raise their family together. If only Raina would open herself to the possibility of there being a man out there whom she might be able to trust and love. If only . . .

"Are you going to sit there all day and stare at me, or get on with the purpose of this meeting?"

Raina's dry inquiry pierced Marissa's romantic haze. The wind, whipping in and out of the vine-twisted bower, plucked at the wavy tendrils of hair softly framing Raina's face, blowing one curling lock loose and into her eyes. With an irritated motion, she brushed it away.

"Well? I'm waiting, Marissa."

Marissa swept aside an old, dried uva leaf that had

drifted down onto the lap of her gown and sighed. "Yes, I suppose it would be the best—to get it over with, I mean. But where to begin?" She paused, pursed her lips thoughtfully, then plunged in. "We need you to return to Incendra."

Raina's head jerked around. She went pale. "What did you say? Surely I misheard."

"Oh, I knew I'd make a muddle of this!" Her friend threw back her head and closed her eyes. Then she exhaled a deep breath and riveted her gaze on Raina. "The Volans. We need a stone from Incendra that we think can be used to keep them away. And two Incendarians must go back to Incendra to retrieve a supply of that stone. You are one, and the other . . ."

"Go on," Raina urged sharply, when her friend's voice faded. This scenario was taking an unexpected and most distressing turn. "Who is the other?"

Marissa nervously glanced away.

"Marissa, who is the other?"

"A monk," the chestnut-haired woman sighed. "A monk of Exsul, to be specific. He, too, is an exile from Incendra."

"A monk?" Raina gave a disparaging laugh. "A man? Gods, Marissa, you know how I feel about men, much less some puling monk!"

"I'd hardly call a fifth-degree Grandmaster warrior monk 'puling'! And especially not one such as Teague Tremayne. Surely even you've heard of him?"

"Yes, I've heard of him," Raina muttered. "But I still don't care if Grandmasters of the fifth degree *are* said to possess unusual powers." Her mouth twisted in disgust. "All those tales are but a crock of barsa dung, I say."

"They're said to be capable, in the proper meditative

state, of invulnerability to pain and injury," Marissa offered, beginning to grasp at anything to convince her friend of the monk's worth. "A talent that could well be an invaluable asset."

"And a lot of good that'll do me if we're set upon and I have to wait for him to go into his meditative state." Raina sighed and shook her head. "Face it, Marissa. We'll be long dead before he becomes invulnerable, much less wakes out of his trance to help me."

"Well, there are also rumors of his mental powers," Marissa added disgruntedly. "Like mind reading, for one, and some not so savory, like—"

"An ability to coerce or destroy minds that don't bow to his will?" Raina gave a snort of disbelief. "It's all monkish boasting, I say, and meant to intimidate and control. For all their exalted principles, these monks are no different than any other man. Liars, manipulators, hypocrites!"

"He *is* a strange one," her friend admitted, "even for a monk. But one way or another, they are bound by rules that forbid doing harm to further their own needs or desires."

"How reassuring. Not only is he a man, but a strange one, at that."

Marissa frowned. "I don't quite know how to explain it. There's just something . . . different . . . about him. Not that he doesn't seem a good and brave and fair man," she hastened to explain when Raina cast her a skeptical look, "it's just that he seems rather sad. Perhaps he, too, left Incendra under tragic circumstances."

"What have you told them about me?" Panic tautened Raina's voice and filled her heart. "You vowed never to tell anyone why I left Incendra. It's no one's business, and I mean for it to stay that way!"

"Oh, no, Raina. Never." Marissa took the red-haired woman's hand. "I never told anyone—not even Brace—about what happened to you. And I never will!"

"Fine." Raina withdrew her hand and leaned back. "I couldn't bear the shame of other . . . men . . . knowing that about me. I hate them all as it is. If they began to look at me . . . that way . . . I swear I'd cut out each and every one of their hearts!"

"Brace wouldn't do that," Marissa hastened to her husband's defense. "He'd—"

"Pity me?" Raina laughed, the sound raw and ragged. "I couldn't bear that, either. I want nothing from men, Marissa, save to be left alone to live my life as I wish."

"Well, at least you'll get neither lust nor pity from this monk. He is forsworn to keep himself apart from women." She cocked her head. "In fact, I couldn't imagine a more perfect partner for you, if you must be forced to take a man for a partner. He doesn't want you and you don't want him, yet you're both trained warriors and Incendarians in the bargain."

"I never said I agreed to this mission," Raina growled. "You presume too much, even for our—"

"Ah, there, here she comes now!" Marissa exclaimed in relief, noting the approach of the woman she'd been expecting. As the woman walked up and halted before her, Marissa stood and extended her hand. "Come, Cyra. Allow me to introduce you to Raina."

Raina rose and eyed the other woman warily. She was small and delicately boned, her piquant face and shoulders framed by a cloud of pale blond hair. If her simple garb of white overtunic and long blue skirt covered by a three-quarters'-length light gray open coat hadn't proclaimed her to be of the scientific bent, the sweep of her dark brown eyes as she scanned Raina did. The look had been sharply assessing and analytical. For all the outward semblance of delicate femininity, the warrior woman realized, this was not some submissive or ignorant female.

"Raina," Marissa intruded into her friend's thoughts, "this is Cyra Husam al Nur. She is one of Bellator's— and the Imperium's—most brilliant geophysicists. Cyra is also the person who developed the hypothesis for the device that might well be the Imperium's salvation."

"Then you're a woman worth knowing," Raina said, extending her hand to the blond woman. "I'm a Sodalitas."

Cyra took Raina by the arm and clasped her hand-to-elbow in the traditional Imperial greeting. "I've heard of you, Raina. Your exploits as leader of that warrior women society have preceded you. I couldn't be more pleased that you've agreed to this mission. It's dangerous enough without sending some inexperienced—"

"I've agreed to nothing."

The scientist paused and cast Marissa a quizzical look. "But I thought—"

"Raina is correct," Marissa hurried to explain. "She hasn't accepted the mission as yet. We had only just begun to discuss this." She motioned to where two cushioned, brown-and-white mottled marmor stone benches sat at right angles to each other beside a large, copiously spewing fountain. "Come, let's move over there, where we can all talk in more comfort."

They followed her in silence, settled themselves on the benches, then looked up expectantly at Marissa, who still stood before them. Behind Raina and Cyra, the water burbled and splashed as it tumbled from the gaping mouth of a stylized stone rapax looming on its stone pedestal high above the large, circular base of the fountain. In the fading warmth of the dying sun, a cool breeze slid over their skin. Marissa repressed a tiny shiver, glanced from one woman to the other, and swallowed hard.

"Cyra was part of a scientific expedition to Incendra about six cycles ago," she began, focusing her gaze on Raina. "The ruler of the kingdom of Farsala requested the Imperium's help in locating a deep vein of precious aureum that reputedly ran through the vast Ar Rimal desert. While there, she made the acquaintance of the leader of one of the desert tribes"—she slanted Cyra an enigmatic look—"who led her to some caves at the base of the Barakah Mountains. These caves are quite unique in that they are—"

"Guarded by firestorms," Raina dryly supplied. "I don't need a geography lesson on my own planet, even if I did leave when I was but fifteen cycles old. Just get on with explaining what Cyra has to do with this little quest to Incendra."

"Fine," Marissa muttered, flushing in anger. "I intend to do just that, if you wouldn't be so impatient."

"Sorry," muttered Raina in return. "This is making me very uncomfortable, that's all. The sooner we get to the end of it, the better."

"Yes, perhaps it would be best to get this over with," Cyra briskly interjected. "I found some very interesting crystalline formations within those caves," she said, picking up the thread of the discussion. "A rare form of a high-frequency resonating type of stone, to be exact. The only other kind I've ever encountered were at the pools of Cambrai."

"The pools of Cambrai?" Her interest finally piqued, Raina leaned forward, her forearms coming to rest on her outspread thighs. "But that's where the stone for the Knowing Crystal was mined. Are you saying this Incendarian stone is made of the same kind of crystal?"

"Not *exactly* the same kind of crystal," Cyra admitted, "but very similar. It's why we need it. The theory is that the Knowing Crystal kept the Volans at bay all these hundreds of cycles while they roamed the universe, seeking out and decimating other galaxies. It seems too great a coincidence that the Volans never once encroached on the Imperium until about four cycles ago, when Marissa and Brace managed to destroy the Knowing Crystal in the pools of Cambrai. We now think the stone of power must have been instrumental in keeping the Volans out of the Imperium."

"So now you want to create another Knowing Crystal." Raina slowly shook her head. "I'm not so sure that's wise."

"We're designing a device that'll utilize only what we believe are the neurologically disruptive aspects of the stone while screening out the other, potentially more troublesome properties. And since the two forms of crystal are different in many ways, from their hardness, color, and transparency to their specific gravity, electrical properties, and magnetism, we hope to avoid re-creating the same problems we encountered with the Knowing Crystal . . ."

"A very nice theory," Raina agreed, "with us, once again, the unwitting test cases."

"There seem few other choices, Raina." Her hands locked behind her back, Marissa began to pace to and fro. "The Volans aren't going to wait around for us to sort through all our options. We have to make the best decision we can with the time and resources available."

"And what of the electromagnetic storm about Incendra?" Raina rose and strode over to confront her. "I

won't be much good to you if I arrive on Incendra
dead."

"We've a Volan spy ship specifically designed to
carry the occupants through the field safely. It seems
strange that they possess such a craft, almost as if they,
too, were planning on infiltrating Incendra."

"Or had their own purpose for the crystal in the
firestorm caves," Cyra supplied from behind them.

Raina wheeled. "If that's the case, time is of the essence."

The blond woman nodded. "Exactly. And why we
want two Incendarians to go. As natives, you'll both be
more easily able to blend into the population. You know
the land and language, and have a vested interest in
preventing the Volans from succeeding with whatever
nefarious plan they might have in mind for Incendra."

Raina laughed bitterly. "A vested interest? In that
you're mistaken, Cyra. I don't care what happens to Incendra. When I left it fifteen cycles ago, I left nothing
of value behind. Nothing, do you hear me?"

The scientist glanced questioningly at Marissa. "Then
perhaps we must look further for another to accompany
Brother Tremayne. I know it'll be difficult, finding another Incendarian quickly, but if she's unwilling—"

"I said I was unwilling to help Incendra," Raina
snapped, a fierce resolve forming within her. "I didn't
say I was unwilling to help the Imperium. Moraca is
part of the Imperium, and my sister Sodalitas live on
Moraca. If I truly am so vital to the success of this
mission, I'll do it for them—and for Marissa and her
family—but never, ever, for Incendra."

Cyra eyed her intently, then nodded. "Whatever your
motive, I respect it." She offered her hand. "And I wish
you success."

Raina took her hand and shook it. "When do we depart?"

Marissa and Cyra exchanged hooded looks. "Within the week, if all goes as planned. We still await the monk's decision."

"He hasn't decided yet?" Raina's mouth twisted derisively. "His purported courage and altruism are *most* inspiring."

"Brother Tremayne arrived earlier today," Marissa explained. "He requested a short time to consider all aspects. He'll give us his decision on the morrow."

"Oh, he will, will he?" Raina's hands clenched at her sides and her chin lifted a notch. She, who had suffered unspeakable degradation and the cruelest of betrayals at the hands of Incendarians, was willing to go, yet this monk hesitated? "Perhaps I just might be able to hasten his journey through his terrible dilemma a bit."

She turned to Marissa. "Where is this indecisive holy man to be found?"

Marissa glanced toward the mountains towering over Rector. Already they were swathed in shadow. "Up there," she said, gesturing toward a tiny point of white illuminated by flickering light high on the mountainside. "Monks of Exsul never remain within the walls of a city after nightfall. They are forbidden to sleep among the laity. And it is also forbidden," she added, with a quelling look at Raina, "that any woman disturb a monk once he sequesters himself for the night."

Raina's gaze lifted to the mountains. "And when, sweeting," she asked with a taut, secret smile, "have I ever cared a whit for the laws of men?"

Three

The wind whipped down from the mountains, setting the perpetual light torches on the four corners of the exercise enclosure to fluttering wildly. The erratic undulations of the blue-violet flames plunged the hard-packed dirt yard alternately into flickering, demented shadows, then eerie, otherworldly light. Teague stepped through the solid robur-wood door and locked it shut behind him. He set down the heavy orichal metal brazier of charcoal and the sheathed ceremonial dagger and glanced up at the heavens.

High in the cloud-strewn firmament, three of Bellator's five moons gleamed in the blackened sky. Star clusters twinkled. Tangy woodsmoke from his dying cookfire assailed Teague's nostrils, followed closely by the pungent scent of the evergreen sempervivus trees that surrounded the monastic grounds on three sides.

A pleasant eve to be snugly ensconced in a hermitage, Teague thought, with a small pang of longing, the wail of the wind and sounds of the night rising around him. But the time for the Grandmaster blade ritual was long overdue. And perhaps, just perhaps, the ancient ceremony—known only to the highest members of his order—would finally afford him the peace of mind and strength to face the morrow. It had always sustained him before.

With one final glance at the star-studded heavens,
Teague turned to his disrobing. He removed his long,
sleeveless black overtunic, carefully folded it, and placed
it before the door. Next came his gray homespun robe
and black breeches and boots, until he stood clad only in
the simple red loincloth of the Brotherhood. Teague retrieved the brazier and long dagger and strode to the center of the exercise yard.

Once more he laid the dagger beside the brazier and
squatted before them. A small tinderbox hung from a
red cord tied to one of the brazier's handles. Teague
opened it and removed the stone, a piece of metal, and
a bit of dried grass. He soon had a small fire burning
in the pile of charcoal.

The sharp fragrance of aromatic wood gum from the
sacred cedra tree filled the air. Teague inhaled deeply,
mentally visualizing the incense filling not only his
body but his mind, consecrating him, cleansing him.

Purify me, he solemnly intoned the opening words of
the sacred blade ritual. *Open me, heart and soul, to the
cleansing odor of righteousness. Guide me so that I may
soar to the highest regions of the mind. Free me, if only
for a brief moment in time, from a body constrained by
base urges and the sordid corruptions of the flesh.*

Teague reached inside the narrow band of cloth that
covered him and withdrew a small vial of oily fluid.
Unstopping it, he poured a generous amount into his
palm, touched his fingers to the liquid, then began to
rub it onto his body. The peppery scent of sacred herbs,
overlaid with the heavier odor of musk, rose on the
freshened breeze. The brazier blazed hot and bright now,
warming Teague's flesh and the ceremonial oils.

His fingers glided over the swell of his chest, then
down the length of his arms, then back over his chest

again and down his belly. Teague's skin began to tingle. A fire flared to life, searing deep into Teague's bone and muscle and sinew. Strength such as he'd never experienced, save in these rare moments of consecration, surged through him.

Teague closed his eyes, willed himself to breathe slower and slower. Willed his pulse to slacken. With long, languorous strokes, he smoothed the remainder of the oil over his thighs and down his calves. Even as he did, he felt the power swell within him. It was time for the first, most intricate movements of the blade ritual.

He rose, the sheathed dagger in his hand. With a firm motion, Teague crossed his left arm over his body, grasped the dagger's hilt, and sharply withdrew it. Lunging forward on his left leg, he gave a guttural cry and thrust the dagger to the sky. For long minutes he stood there, every muscle in his body taut and straining.

The wind gusted down, tossing his long, tawny hair into his face and across his shoulders, the strands clinging to the oil coating his body. Teague paid it little heed. In an effortless flow of powerful muscles, he leaped back, then wheeled, sweeping the blade through the air with a sharp, slicing motion.

Changing direction with catlike swiftness, he spun about once more. His hands moved in unison with his legs, slashing and kicking. He swung first to the right, then to the left, over and over and over, until his muscles began to burn and clench with spasms.

Yet still Teague forced himself on, the sweat beading and sliding down his body to mingle with the sacred oils. There was no surer way to reach the heights of self-renunciation, no surer way to drive the demons from his flesh and heart. The night was young, and only in the pinnacle of his torment would he at last be free.

Free . . . to attain the final purification—and earn the right to take the ultimate test of all . . .

Gusts of wind slammed down the mountain, buffeting Raina, impeding the determined progress she made toward the hermitage and her meeting with the monk named Teague Tremayne. It had already taken her over an hour to make the trip from the royal palace, through the city, and up the road that led into the foothills of the Carus Mountains. Though she could now easily make out the perpetual light torches at the four corners of some stone enclosure beside the monk's beehive-shaped hut, the increasing steepness of the trail and the encumbrance of the wind would lengthen the remainder of the journey yet another hour.

Nonetheless, she was determined this very night to meet with the indecisive monk. The Volan threat would only worsen with each passing day. Raina needed to ascertain as soon as possible if the monk, warrior though he might be, was a fit partner for the mission.

In her cycles as leader of the Sodalitas, she'd seen plenty of so-called warriors who, when it came down to the requisite skills, were more bluff than ability. Yet though she needed a partner in this undertaking, if for nothing else than to take the crystal back to Bellator, she didn't need one she couldn't depend on.

Incendra held nothing for her. Let the planet and all its people rot, for all she cared. But she'd do anything for the Sodalitas. If they truly were threatened by the Volans—and she had no reason to doubt the truth of Marissa's words—it was her duty as their leader to do whatever was necessary to protect them. If that meant journeying back to Incendra, then so be it.

However, once the mission to retrieve the special crystal was completed and the fate of the Imperium secured, Raina meant to stay behind on Incendra. She had left there fifteen cycles ago an emotionally and physically ravaged girl with no ability to avenge herself. She'd return this time a warrior, skilled in battle and the hunt. Return this time to track down the men who had betrayed her, track them down and kill them, even if, in so doing, she died. Her honor, long besmirched, demanded no less.

First, though, she must survive the journey through the electromagnetic field, then the rigors and dangers of finding and harvesting the crystal and getting it back to the spacecraft. For that, Raina needed a skilled, intelligent partner. Yet for all the tales of the magnificent prowess of Exsul's warrior monks, Raina had grave doubts that any were up to her exacting standards. Few men ever were.

The whitewashed walls of the enclosure and conical hermitage gleamed in the moonlight. Though the perpetual torches burned brightly, the small windows of the monk's dwelling place were dark. Raina frowned. There was yet an hour or two before midnight. Was the monk already abed?

A soft man, to be sure, fettered by his personal needs and creature comforts. A man who'd find the hardships of Incendra a rude awakening. A man who would also have to be continually coddled and prodded.

At long last, she crowned the final incline and headed across the small plateau toward the hermitage. Pulling up outside, Raina listened for sound of movement or life within the small stone hut. There were none.

Stepping up to the door, she had lifted her hand to knock when a guttural cry pierced the air. Raina wheeled, one hand darting to the dagger strapped to her thigh. The wind howled and wailed as it streamed through the tree-strewn ravine. For an instant, she wondered if she hadn't mistaken the wind for a human voice. Yet the sound seemed to have come from the walled enclosure.

Raina hesitated a moment more, then rapped on the door of the hermitage. There was no answer. She knocked harder. Still no answer.

"Brother Tremayne?" The wind snatched the words away and spirited them off into the night. "Brother Tremayne, are you in there?" she asked again, more loudly this time, and moved to peer into one of the darkened windows. There was no sound or movement from within.

Squaring her shoulders, Raina turned on her heel and strode across the short expanse of stone and dirt toward the walled compound. Obviously the monk wasn't abed after all. It seemed more and more likely that he was in the enclosure instead. The door opening onto the interior, however, was locked.

"Be damned!" she muttered under her breath. She put her ear to the door, listening for any sound of movement within. The whistling wind swallowed any noise that the thick door and stone walls didn't mute.

Raina leaned back. The walls were over three meters high and half a meter thick. Even with a running jump, she couldn't reach the top. She crept close and ran her hand over the texture of the wall, searching for hand- and footholds. There was a small overhang just beyond the height of her head.

She examined it and found it deep enough for a foothold. But was there another above to grab onto? None that she could find in the flickering light of the perpetual torch burning nearby. Cursing softly, Raina began to walk the perimeter.

Luck was with her. On the far side of the enclosure, lush sempervivus trees grew. She eyed them critically, finally settling on one particularly stout one in the middle. It looked sturdy enough to bear her weight and certainly was tall enough, towering over the walls by a good five or six more meters. It would also, she realized, give her shelter once she topped the walls. The monk, if he were inside, need never know of her presence until she chose to reveal it.

She grabbed hold of a branch above her head, swung up into the tree, and began to climb. The pitch oozing from the rough bark was sticky. The sempervivus needles pricked at her face and hands. The tree's pungent odor made her want to sneeze.

A fine way to spend one's evening, Raina silently groused. Curse the monk for making things so difficult! Already she didn't like the man.

The scent of incense wafted by. The red-gold light of a fire caught the corner of her eye through the tree boughs, then a fleeting glimpse of bare skin and movement. Shoving the branches aside, Raina turned and positioned herself for a better view.

In her shock, she nearly lost her grip on the tree trunk and toppled over backward. A man, long of hair and scant of clothing, his hard-muscled body glistening in the torch light, stood below. In his hands he clenched a long ceremonial dagger. Before him on the ground burned a coal-stoked brazier. For the space of an inhaled breath, he remained totally still. Then, with a harsh cry, the man wheeled and executed an intricate series of thrusts and parries, followed swiftly by a seemingly endless, athletically fluid repetition of front and side kicks.

Raina couldn't take her eyes off him. Was this truly the warrior monk Teague Tremayne? He was one of the biggest, most powerful men she'd ever seen. Few men intimidated her, even in height, but this man—this monk—was magnificent in every way.

He wore a narrow red loincloth that left his muscularly rounded buttocks bare and covered him only briefly in front with two strips of cloth that came together in a large knot over the swell of his manhood before falling to mid-thigh. The smooth planes of his bulging chest were ritualistically tattooed with huge bird talons reaching down across his pectoral muscles nearly to his nipples, and a mythical bird of prey twisting in flight down each of his upper arms.

Raina had heard tales that the warrior monks of Exsul received such tattoos upon gaining the exalted status of a Grandmaster, but she'd never seen them until tonight. With his long mane of dark gold hair tumbling down in his face, his superbly fit, all but naked body glistening in the firelight, and the long, lethally tipped dagger in his hands, the monk appeared some primally potent and dangerous animal.

She had thought to come here tonight and shame or intimidate this man into agreeing to go with her to Incendra, if he seemed even half the man she needed as her partner. Now, after seeing him, Raina knew she would do neither. Indeed, even the sight of him filled her with unease and set off a primitive warning vibrating deep in her gut. She didn't know why. She just felt it.

Yet, even knowing this, Raina couldn't take her eyes from him. He was strength and beauty and sleek, gleaming perfection. His stamina, as he executed one flawless battle maneuver after another, was breathtaking. Would he never tire, never quit, until the night burned away to dawn?

At that moment, with a low groan, he sank to his knees on the dirt floor. His head lowered until it touched his chest. His body shook, suddenly wracked with tremors. Then he went still.

Nothing moved but his hands. He lifted the dagger and brought the tip to rest against the middle of his tautly muscled abdomen. The monk took a deep breath and exhaled it slowly. Then his forearms bulged, flexed. In a blinding movement, he drove the blade into his belly.

Raina choked back a horrified cry. Her nails gouged into the rough tree bark and she maintained her position by sheer animal reflex. A wave of nausea washed over her, then dizziness. But never once did she take her gaze from the man kneeling below.

She waited for the blood to spurt and drench the ground before him, waited for the death rattle, for him to fall. Waited, and saw nothing but him kneeling there, head bowed, dagger clasped to his belly.

The seconds pounded by, each marked by the crazed thud of her heart and the rush of blood in her ears. The world spun, whirling about her until she was caught up in a deafening vortex of light and sound. And, at its center, knelt the monk. A man who, with one violently irrational act, had become the focus of her heretofore uncomplicated universe.

The tension built, plucking at her already strained nerves and perceptions, until Raina thought she'd scream from the pain. Then the monk moved. With a low groan, he wrenched the dagger from him—a dagger as immaculate as it had been when he'd first plunged it into himself. He picked up the dagger sheath lying beside him and rose, turning to face the three moons shining now just above the mountain and trees where Raina hid. With a smooth, supple movement, he brought the dagger up to his lips.

Once more, Raina choked back a gasp. She saw his face fully now, and its sweat-slick planes were bathed in such terrible, anguished beauty. Unconsciously, she reached out a hand to him, then caught herself in the uncharacteristic, shocking act.

It didn't matter. He had already lowered the dagger and, in a sharp, ceremonial move, resheathed it. Then he turned and strode over to his clothes. Gathering them up in his arms, he unlatched the door, opened it, and strode out into the suddenly calm, eerily silent night.

Behind him, in the center of the dirt-packed ground, the fiery coals in the brazier slowly died and a thin wisp of scented smoke curled to the sky.

"I tell you true, Marissa," Raina said the next morning, as they made their way through the palace corridors to the meeting with King Falkan, "I cannot work with the monk. It's as simple as that, no more, no less."

"And *I* say again," her friend persisted, shooting her a worried glance, "it's *not* that simple. You agreed yesterday to work with him." She grabbed Raina by the arm and pulled her to a halt. "Exactly what happened between the two of you last night? Did he say something to offend you?"

"He said nothing to offend me. And the matter of last night is closed. Do you hear me, Marissa? Closed!"

Raina jerked her arm from Marissa's grasp and glanced out the long window that faced onto the huge palace courtyard. People bustled about, some hurrying to household tasks, others self-importantly climbing the bank of steps that led up to the entry hall, intent on some sort of royal business.

All so normal, so commonplace, Raina mused, like it had been yesterday and in all the days before. But nothing would be normal or commonplace to her anymore. Not after what she'd seen and experienced last night.

The confirmation of the rumors about Tremayne's supposedly unnatural powers was unsettling, but Raina had traveled the Imperium and could adapt to unusual beings and their unique abilities. She didn't particularly like teaming up with a man who might well be her better in warrior skills, but in time she would find some way around even his greater powers.

No, it wasn't his prowess with the blade that unsettled her and led to her sudden change of heart regarding joining him on the mission to Incendra. It was the strange and frightening emotions he'd stirred. Emotions like concern, protectiveness, and, worst of all, attraction.

Raina shuddered in revulsion. Attraction? For a man? Perhaps she'd misinterpreted her feelings. Perhaps it was but an admiration for a perfectly honed and superbly healthy body. She was a warrior, trained to respect her enemy, to assess him for his weaknesses as well as strengths so as to assure her own eventual triumph over him. And the monk Teague Tremayne, as exposed as nearly every millimeter of his body had been to her, was magnificent in every way.

Perhaps admiration was indeed all it truly was. But then why had she almost cried out in distress when he'd stabbed himself? And why had she reached out to him when he'd finally turned his face to her and she'd seen the terrible pain etched there?

Those questions, more than anything else, haunted Raina. She'd felt his pain, recognized it as so very similar to her own. The kind she'd carried deep inside ever since—

With a vicious wrench, Raina recalled her thoughts to the present. Nothing was served by wallowing in a morass of self-pity or regret. She'd finally taken control of that seething sense of impotence when she'd made the decision yesterday to return to Incendra and set the injustice to rest at last. But she *could not* return with this monk.

There was a greater danger in Teague Tremayne than in continuing to live with the memories of Incendra. Raina didn't know why she knew it; she just did.

She forced a smile. "Forgive me if I seemed a bit harsh a few seconds ago," she said, instantly remorseful for the hurt she'd most evidently caused her friend. "I-I just don't want to . . . talk . . . about last night. Not quite yet, anyway. There's still too much to sort through."

"He didn't touch or hurt you, did he? That's all I want to know."

"Do you imagine me gone soft and helpless in the past few cycles?" Raina tossed her long braid off her shoulder and laughed. "No, sweeting, he didn't touch or hurt me." *Not physically, at any rate,* she added silently, torn once again by her conflicting emotions. "We didn't even meet, if the truth be told. I just . . . saw him."

Marissa's sudden look of interest gave Raina warning of how her words could well be misconstrued. She flushed. "It's not what you think," she muttered.

The chestnut-haired woman cocked her head, a teasing glint dancing in her eyes. "And how do you know what I'm thinking?"

"Never mind." Raina made an impatient motion with her hand. "King Falkan awaits us. We should be going."

"Indeed, we should." Marissa strode out. "Brother Tremayne should be there, too." She cast Raina a surreptitious look. "He must give the king his answer this morn."

She had known she must meet the monk sooner or later, but suddenly Raina fervently wished it was later. *Much* later. No good was served, however, in revealing her reluctance to her already too perceptive friend. Though Raina could be as inscrutable as a stone statue when it suited her, she'd spent too many cycles in close friendship with Marissa to hide much from her for long.

"It matters not to me," she replied tersely as she walked along. "I told you before that I won't work with the monk. The king will have to take either him or me, and find another Incendarian to fill the second position."

Marissa shrugged. "Have it your way. I learned long ago not to argue with you when you get that obstinate look on your face."

"Obstinate? I'm never obstinate," Raina cried, outraged. "I just know my own—" Her voice faded as they rounded a corner and she noted the monk standing but fifteen meters away, outside the closed doors of the royal reception hall. A stout doorman, garbed in the shimmering finery of his office, guarded the portals.

Raina's steps slowed. The monk, alerted to their presence by the sound of their footsteps, lifted his gaze from what looked to be an intent inspection of the tiled floor. Raina's breath caught once more in her throat.

Ice-blue eyes the color of a clear mountain stream locked with hers—eyes that assessed her dispassionately, then lowered once more to the floor. A surge of irra-

tional anger filled Raina. How *dared* he discount her
so quickly and with such lack of interest, when even
the most fleeting memory of him last night set her own
pulse to racing!

She was a warrior, curse it all! She deserved respect
and consideration for that, if for nothing else. "The arrogant slime worm," she muttered under her breath.

"What did you say?" Marissa glanced at her. "I
could've sworn I heard—"

"It doesn't matter. I can handle him."

Marissa shot her a disbelieving look. "Do you want
me to introduce you, since you've supposedly never
met?"

"No." Raina's reply was swift and terse. "There's no
need for you to stay. You said Brace awaited you. I'm
quite capable of dealing with this monk *and* the king."

"Er, maybe I'd better stay." Marissa drew to a halt.
"There are times when your blunt approach tends
to . . ." Her words died and she looked decidedly uncomfortable.

"Tends to offend, to anger, and irritate?" her friend
smilingly supplied.

"Yes, if you must know the truth."

Raina chuckled. "Have no fear, sweeting. I haven't
been leader of the Sodalitas for the past eight cycles
without learning the proper time and place for my blunt-
ness. I find, though, that a straightforward approach
generally works well with males. They're not particularly known for their ability to perceive subtleties."

Marissa's mouth quirked wryly. "Well, be that as it
may, have a care with the king. According to Brace,
he's none too tolerant of rebellious or uncooperative
subjects of late."

"No, I'd imagine not," Raina admitted. "And, as little

as I think of the man personally, he has good reason to be concerned. The Volans are a grave peril to us all." Her friend took her hand and gave it a quick, reassuring squeeze. "I know you'll make the right decision."

Raina smiled grimly. "Yes, I will. You can be certain of that." She squeezed Marissa's hand briefly, then pulled away. "Go. Your husband awaits, and I've a monk to make the acquaintance of."

Marissa nodded and stepped away. "Good fortune," she silently mouthed, before turning and striding back the way they'd come. Raina watched until she disappeared around the corner. Then, squaring her shoulders and lifting her chin, she turned and walked over to Teague Tremayne.

Teague watched her approach. Curiosity, for a moment, overcame his monkish discipline. The woman was quite tall and slender, and she moved with a sure, athletic grace. A warrior woman, if he wasn't mistaken.

His glance slid down her body once more, taking in her dark auburn hair in its severe braid, her sparkling green eyes, her fair skin, and the sprinkling of freckles across her nose. Teague found the freckles endearing, softening her in some inexplicable way. She wouldn't like to know that, though, he realized with a surprising surge of insight. She would pride herself on her warrior's prowess and presence.

He didn't know how he knew this about her, or why he even cared, but the certainty of the knowledge unsettled him. Teague had never let anyone get too close to him in any way, not even his fellow monks, save for the former abbot who'd died five cycles ago, carrying Teague's secret to the grave. And he certainly had no desire whatsoever to become attached to a female.

She pulled up before him, dressed in a belted green,

long-sleeved tunic, black knee-high boots, and black breeches. The scent of her wafted to him on an eddy of air. Teague's nostrils flared, unconsciously inhaling her unsettling essence of fresh spring breezes and the hauntingly sweet valleria flower.

His instinctive, primal response startled him. In all the cycles since he'd left Incendra, he'd never felt any stirrings toward a female. True, he'd found many attractive, but no more so than a beautiful animal or an exquisitely wrought sculpture or a glorious sunset. But this female . . .

Well, there was just something about her.

She extended her arm in an Imperial greeting. "My name is Raina, leader of the Sodalitas of the planet Moraca. I'm supposedly the other half of this little twosome headed to Incendra."

He glanced down at her outstretched arm and buried his hands even deeper within the folds of his sleeves. "Please forgive what may seem to be my rudeness, but it isn't permitted for me to touch flesh with you. I have taken a vow of perpetual—"

"Chastity." Raina finished the sentence for him and let her hand fall to her side. "Nonetheless, it was but a common courtesy, not meant as an initial overture of seduction," she continued dryly. "You monks are rather full of yourselves, if you imagine every woman schemes to take you to bed."

"I am sorry if you see it so." Teague clamped down on his exasperation and forced a bland smile to his lips. Yes, there was *definitely* something about this female, and he wasn't so sure he liked whatever it was. "I meant no discourtesy."

"No," Raina muttered, "I don't imagine you did. It matters little, at any rate. I cannot work with you on this mission. Either you must give it up, or I. One way or another, I'm not the partner for you."

Her refusal intrigued him. He didn't want to work with her, either, but preferred that the rejection had come from him. He arched a dark blond brow. "Indeed? And why not?"

"Isn't that obvious?" Raina's mouth twisted. "I'm a Sodalitas. I don't particularly like, and definitely don't trust, men."

He smiled. "It seems our needs run parallel. I cannot work with females. It goes against my vows."

"Fine." Raina nodded her agreement. "Then all that's left is to inform King Falkan of our decision."

At that moment, the doorman, signaled by the loud, sonorous clang of a gong, turned and swung open the two tall doors. The intricately carved robur-wood panels parted to reveal the cavernous depths of the royal reception hall and the dais whereupon sat the king. Beside him stood Teran Ardane.

Teague glanced down at Raina, who, even at her unusual height, was still a head shorter than he. "Shall we go, femina? The king awaits."

Raina nodded and, not even pausing for him to join her, headed out. Teague eyed her retreating back for an instant, then hurried after her. *A cool head, a clear intent, a heart calm and gentle,* he grimly intoned, *prevail over all things, at all times . . .*

This time, however, the ancient saying failed to ease the rising irritation stirring within him. What was wrong with him that a complete stranger, one he'd met but a few minutes ago, could unsettle him so easily? Perhaps he was more distraught over his dilemma regarding Incendra than he'd first imagined.

They drew up together before the royal throne and

bowed. "Rise," King Falkan said. "I await the outcome of your decisions. Even now, time is passing, and each day we squander brings the Volans further and further into the Imperium."

His gaze shifted to Teague. "Well, Brother Tremayne? Have you decided to join the mission?"

"If you have need of me, Majesty, then yes, I will go to Incendra." Teague took a step forward. "But I cannot travel with a female. I have taken a vow to shun them and I cannot break it."

Falkan smiled. "In most cases, I would never ask such a sacrilege of you, though I must admit," he said, his gaze skimming Raina, "that a femina as fetching as this one would tempt any man, be he vowed or not. But this is one case where an exception must be made. Step closer, Brother Tremayne. I have something to show you."

He pulled a small scriptura pad from his sleeve and handed it to Teague. "I anticipated just such a problem and contacted Abbot Leone of the Monastery of Exsul. He has granted you a temporary dispensation from all your vows. He has also," Falkan added slyly, "ordered you to cooperate with me to the fullest extent."

Teague accepted the metal pad with the computer generated-message from his abbot, a cold fear gripping his heart. There was no way out of it, then. He must obey, or risk disobeying not only the king, but his abbot—breaking his sacred vow of obedience to him. But to travel and live and work in close quarters with a female for weeks, maybe months!

What had Abbot Leone told him about vows? That their true worth was revealed only by a test of significant magnitude, a test most frequently fought out in the world, not in the safe, secure confines of a monastery.

Reluctantly, Teague lifted his glance from the scriptura pad and met that of Raina. She stared back, her striking green eyes gleaming with understanding—and an unexpected, most startling compassion.

"It seems," he softly said, "the decision is yours. I have no choice now but to obey." With that, he lowered his head and shoved his hands deep into his sleeves.

Did he want her to decline the king's request? Raina wondered, bemused by his sudden physical and emotional withdrawal. There was no abbot to command her. True, she still risked Falkan's anger if she refused him, but she doubted he'd put her to death because of it. And her refusal would certainly ease the monk's personal turmoil. But suddenly, she wasn't so sure she wanted that.

It wasn't a vindictive need to get back at him for his monastic arrogance. Neither was it some perverse desire to punish herself, though agreeing to join forces with Tremayne might well result in that. No, it was something else . . . something deeper and oh, so very bewildering and illogical. Something that sprang from the heart, not the head.

She shouldn't do it. Shouldn't follow where she'd never gone before, into that nebulous, uncharted realm of emotions, rather than remain on the path of clearheaded logic. But that look on his face last night . . . and the abject fear that had emanated from him when he'd held the scriptura pad in his hands and read the fateful words of his abbot . . .

He was trapped, forced to do what he'd no wish to do, and Raina knew now, with a surety that startled her, that he didn't shy from the mission out of cowardice or indolence. No, it was something far deeper, something ingrained in the man that drove him. Something that had happened to him long ago . . . perhaps even on Incendra.

The realization filled her with a curious sense of one-ness, of empathy, of partnership with the enigmatic monk. She shouldn't let such maudlin emotions color her decision—she never had before—but for once, she did. Perhaps there was a certain twisted destiny in it all—a monk who shunned women and a woman who hated men, both Incendarian exiles, both with unre-solved issues they'd thought they'd left behind that still needed resolution. And though the kindest act might well be to spare the monk the pain of her presence, her needs must ultimately prevail over his.

Raina shook the overly sentimental musings aside. The king awaited her decision. "Brother Tremayne," she softly said. He lifted his gaze to hers, his eyes shim-mering pits of agony. "It seems," she forced herself to continue, "that I have little other choice, either."

She turned back to Falkan then, unnerved and unwill-ing to face the monk's torment a moment longer. "I will go, Imperial Majesty. I'm not naive enough to imagine you can so easily or quickly find another Incendarian to replace me at any rate. The monk and I will just have to work out our differences between ourselves."

King Falkan leaned back in his throne and smiled. "Good, I was hoping you'd both see the wisdom of my decision."

"When is the proposed departure?"

"In a week," the king said. "You must have time to gather your things, learn the intricacies of piloting a Volan ship, and be briefed on the caves and the proper technique for extracting and transporting the crystal back to us." He shot his nephew—who until now had stood silently nearby—a questioning look. "Do you want to tell them about the third passenger, or should I?"

"A third passenger?" Raina glanced from one man to the other, suspicion narrowing her gaze. "There was nothing ever mentioned about a third Incendarian. If so, you have the two you need and I retract my offer—"

Teran held up a silencing hand. "A moment, femina. You misunderstand. The third passenger isn't an Incendarian; he isn't even of the humanoid species. In fact," he continued, shooting the king an amused look, "he doesn't even possess a body."

Raina graced the monk with an irritated glance. "I think we're being manipulated here, Tremayne."

"Perhaps," he agreed, his monastic facade once more in place. "And perhaps not. Let us give them a chance to explain, femina."

"Fine," Raina gritted, her glance riveting back on Teran Ardane. "Pray explain."

"We need a way of identifying the specific resonating crystal from caves with myriad forms of stones," Teran said, stepping forward to the edge of the dais. "We don't have time, though, to fashion a device sensitive enough to do that. So instead of a machine, we've decided to use a living entity. An entity whose neural sensitivities are already aligned with the precise form of crystal we need for the deterrent device."

A niggling suspicion formed in Raina's breast and wound its way up until it lodged in her throat. She gave an unsteady laugh. "And exactly what kind of entity would that be? A Volan, perhaps?"

Teran nodded, his solemn gaze locking with hers. "Exactly, femina. A Volan."

Four

For a long moment, Raina and Teague exchanged startled looks. The big monk turned back to gaze up at Teran. "A Volan? Surely you jest. The mission is perilous enough without taking the enemy with us."

Teran smiled. "As difficult as it may be for you to believe, this Volan is not our enemy. Already he has helped us in countless ways in our battle to find some solution to this distressing problem."

"So, he's a traitor to his own kind, then?" Raina interjected with a contemptuous sneer. "I find that equally distasteful."

"Rand's not a traitor," Teran quietly replied. "He truly has the best interests of the Volans at heart. But he realizes as well that his people cannot continue on the path they have chosen. He wishes to work with us to find some honorable way out of this dilemma—a way that will be satisfactory to all."

"An honorable Volan?" Raina gave a disparaging laugh. "I find that hard to believe."

"Well, we've little time to discuss the morality of the issue just now." Teran stepped down from the dais. "You'll have to accept him on our word that he's trustworthy and vital to the mission."

Raina turned to Teague. "And what have you to say, Tremayne? Are you willing to passively accept this?"

He eyed her, a muscle ticking along his jaw. "I accept nothing passively, femina. But I also choose to make my decisions based on adequate information. I say we learn more of this Volan." He glanced at Teran. "In the meanwhile, are there any more surprises in store for us? I'd prefer to know them all now."

The king's ambassador smiled. "No. I think you've had enough for one day."

"How kind of you to notice," Raina muttered. She squared her shoulders and met Teran's gaze. "As the monk said, we need to learn more of this Volan. When can we meet him?"

"Now, if that suits you." Teran indicated a door behind the throne. "The Volan—Rand—currently resides in one of the laboratories. As he is once more without a body, he is connected to a life support system."

"A Volan without a body?" Raina frowned. "Then how are we to take him with us, much less to make much use of him?"

"All that will be revealed in due time." Teran lifted his hand toward the door. "Shall we go?"

Raina gave a disgruntled snort, then fell into step behind the bearded man. Teague followed silently in their wake, his hands tucked in his sleeves, a thoughtful expression on his face. The trio made their way down the long corridors, outside across the gardens, and finally back into a low-slung set of buildings that sprawled, like the spokes of a wheel, out in every direction. Yet another series of stark hallways pierced by occasional closed portals were traversed, before Teran finally drew up before a door with a small sign before it.

The sign read "Biosystem Research." For some reason, Raina didn't like the implications of that particular designation. It smacked of sordid experimentation and secretive plans, all involving the lives and bodies of living things. She knew she shouldn't be so negative about scientific research, but the horrors, the atrocities she'd seen on Incendra, after Malam Vorax had come to power . . .

With a tiny shudder, Raina directed her attention back to the issue at hand—one that was disconcerting enough in its own right. Teran ran a flat card through the key control beside the door. The portal slid open. Inhaling a fortifying breath, Raina followed the big Bellatorian inside.

The room was typical of most laboratories. Large, pristine, and sunlit, it had walls lined with cabinets filled with jars of various solutions and specimens or clearly delineated areas of stasis fields. Long metal tables equipped with various computerized machinery filled its center. A few scientists worked at the tables or bustled to and fro from cabinets or the stasis fields to retrieve some specimen or solution.

Teague drew up beside Raina. "Very interesting, Lord Ardane," he remarked dryly, glancing about him. "But where is the Volan?"

Teran indicated yet another door across the room. "Rand resides in there. He isn't an object of general interest or titillation, as bizarre as his current condition may be. And I expect the same consideration and respect for him as I would for any other living being."

"You truly care for this alien, don't you?" Teague asked.

"He sacrificed much for us, finally even willingly leaving the body of one of our people who he'd been inhabiting. Such a thing is unheard of in a Volan. And Rand dearly loved having a body again." He shot Raina, who glared back at him disbelievingly, an amused glance. "They once possessed bodies of their own, you know, until their increased metabolic rates finally burned them out."

"I've heard the tales," the warrior woman snapped. "It still doesn't justify their enslavement of unwilling victims."

"No, it doesn't," Teran gravely admitted. "But who's to say what we would have done in the same situation? The survival instinct is powerful, perhaps the most powerful driving force of all."

"Sometimes, though," Teague quietly offered, "it compels us into shameful, ignoble acts, when death would've been far more honorable."

Raina jerked her gaze to the monk. Though his expression was hooded and all but inscrutable, she could've sworn she caught a fleeting shadow of pain in his voice. Did he speak from personal experience, perhaps? She shoved the consideration aside. She didn't want to know any more about the man than was absolutely necessary.

"An ethical dilemma, to be sure," Teran agreed. "But, come, the day draws on, and you've still to learn the rudiments of piloting the Volan spy ship. We've a mockup of the actual one that remains in orbit around Bellator for you to practice on just a few doors down."

"I can't wait," Raina mumbled under her breath.

Teran and Teague must have heard her, for they exchanged an amused glance. She stared back, refusing to allow either man to intimidate or silence her. When they stepped out once more, however, she followed them across the room without comment or protest. No further purpose was served in grumbling, Raina decided. They'd committed to the mission and any and all eventualities it might entail.

The room they entered was dimly lit by a luminescent green sphere suspended from various tubes in one corner. A faint humming from some machine connected to the tubes completed the eerie scene. Uneasiness prickled down Raina's spine. There was definitely the feel of an alien presence in the room yet, at the same time, the presence seemed benevolent, almost eager for their company.

Teran closed the door behind them and walked over to the machine. He adjusted some levers and depressed a few digitalized buttons, then turned back to Teague and Raina. "With the assistance of this dual life support and communications device, Rand can both survive and talk with you. We're working on miniaturizing all the components to ease bulkiness on the mission. The prototype should be ready within the next few days."

"How small will you be able to make the device?" Teague walked over to examine the machine more closely. "We need to bring as few extra items across Incendra as possible."

The Bellatorian shrugged. "The biosphere that Rand must reside in cannot be made any smaller, but we hope to reduce his life support and communications device to tiny packs that'll fit onto the sides of his shielding receptacle. That receptacle should be no more than about a fifteen-by-fifteen-millimeter cube, just large enough to enclose his biosphere and fit easily into a carrying pack."

"Why is this shielding receptacle necessary?" Raina demanded.

Teran grinned and gestured toward the glowing green sphere. "Why don't you let Rand explain? His communications device is functional. Rand?"

A soft, mellifluous voice rose out of the dimness

where the machine sat. "Would it first be possible, Lord Ardane, to make the acquaintance of my other visitors? I heard a male and a female. Are these the two people I must travel to Incendra with?"

Teran chuckled. "My apologies, Rand. They are indeed your new partners. The female is Raina, the male, the monk, Teague Tremayne."

"Raina. Teague," the disembodied voice said. "I'm very pleased to meet you at last. I look forward to getting to know you and—"

"I've no inclination whatsoever to get to know you better, Volan!" Raina cut him off. "There's little enough about this mission that suits me, but it never has nor ever will be anything more than business. And I certainly have no intention of making friends with either you *or* Tremayne."

There was a long pause before the machine transmitted the Volan's thoughts again. "I can understand your hesitation in dealing with me. I'm the enemy, after all. Or at least, that's the only way you can view me right now. But a good warrior knows as well that the greater the knowledge of the enemy, the greater the potential advantage."

"True enough," Raina agreed, willing to concede this . . . this machine that much. She was working from too emotional a base here, she reluctantly admitted, and that was never wise when it came to matters of life and death. It was just hard enough dealing with the unsettling presence of Teague Tremayne on this mission, much less a Volan in a box. "We'll have ample time, though, for further acquaintance while on the mission. For the moment, I merely want to know why you need a shielding receptacle."

"For two reasons, Raina," Rand softly replied. "First,

to protect my biosphere. It has but a thick, membranous exterior that can be penetrated with a sharp object and willful intent. If that happens, my entity, which dwells within, will die. I'd prefer for that not to happen."

"And the second reason?" Raina prompted.

"To protect my highly sensitized response to Incendra's electromagnetic field and to the crystal's effects until it is necessary for me temporarily to be exposed to the correct stones to determine which is the one needed. Teran tells me I'm the best determinant of the proper crystal in caves lined with myriad forms of crystals."

"And the only reason we seem to need you on this trip," the warrior woman added grimly.

"I don't care to be exposed to unnecessary danger any more than you do, femina," Rand said. "In my current state, I'm extremely vulnerable."

"Then why not give him a body?" Teague demanded, turning to Teran. "He could still be sensitive to the type of stone we need, and perhaps be of some physical use in the bargain."

"A fine idea," the Bellatorian sardonically agreed, "but there seems to be a dearth of volunteers of late willing to give up their bodies."

"Then what about a clone?" the monk persisted. "They are mindless, but this Volan seems to have the mental faculties necessary to fill that void. And even a clone is human enough to help us."

"We've given some thought to that issue," Teran said, "but it takes time to grow a clone. Even with the new acceleration process that forces the clone cells to mature to an adult form in just two cycles rather than in the normal developmental lifespan, it still takes two cycles.

And Rand would be little help to you save in an adult body."

"I concede that would be the wisest course."

"There's also the additional issue," Teran continued, "of the strain his Volan entity would put on the donor body. Drugs that might slow or even eliminate the problem are in the formative stages, but they aren't ready yet."

Teran sighed and shook his head. "We are working on this problem and its solutions as quickly as we can, not only to provide a viable resolution to our dilemma, but to those of the Volans as well. But as I've said before, there isn't time right now for a body for Rand or the procurement of other Incendarians who might better suit either of your personal tastes. The Volans might not accept our offer of clone bodies even when they are ready. We've got to protect ourselves, in the meantime, as best we can. Hence, the deterrent device. What we offer as the best solution to the current situation *is* the best one at the moment. And what you must accept and work with."

"I thank you for your patience with my questions," the monk said, rendering him a respectful bow. "I will accept and work with what is currently feasible. I just wished to more fully understand . . ."

"And I beg pardon if I seemed a bit peevish there." The Bellatorian rendered him a courteous nod in reply. "The stress of planning this mission begins to wear thin." He smiled. "It's been over two months since I last saw my wife and children. The separation grows overlong."

Teague met his gaze. "Loved ones are important. I am happy that you find support and comfort in yours."

"Then, the sooner this mission is over, the better,"

Raina remarked with a twinge of irritation. "Is there anything else that we need to know about this Volan—at least, anything vital to the mission?"

"There is one thing more, one last purpose of the shielding receptacle." Teran glanced briefly in the biosphere's direction. "Volans are commanded by a higher presence, one that emanates from the Volan Mother Ship, the apparent source of all our problems since its excursion into the Imperium. Volans are born and bred to obey, to follow the collective mind of the hive ship. Until Rand was cut off from the Mother Ship's unceasing directives while he was secretly assigned to the planet Tenua a few months ago, he functioned as mindlessly as the rest of his kind. The shielding receptacle is also designed to protect him from further directives of the Mother Ship if, for some reason, its influence can and does ever extend to Incendra. Rand knows this and so should you, in case you ever decide to remove him from the shielding receptacle."

"Are you saying that the Volan could turn on us if his Mother Ship began to influence him again?" Raina took a step toward Teran, all her warrior's instincts once more at the ready.

"Yes, that's a distinct possibility," the king's ambassador admitted. "Though Rand insists he would fight the hive directives with all his might, now that he has come to realize their destructive intent, neither of us is certain whether he could resist them for long."

Raina fought the anger that swelled once again within her. "I don't like this. Don't like it at all."

"I must agree with the femina on this." Teague exhaled a long, considering breath. "This mission is danger-fraught enough, and now you say the Volan isn't to be trusted? You add more and more until you make it all but impossible for us to succeed."

"I never said this would be easy, Brother Tremayne. We seriously doubt, though, that the Volan Mother Ship's transmissions will be able to pierce Incendra's electromagnetic field. The planet sends out emissions that seem as neurologically disrupting as that of the special crystal we seek. In fact," Teran added, a worried frown plucking at his brow, "there are some studies being conducted right now that suggest the increased planetary electromagnetic radiation might even arise from those firestorm-guarded caves."

"And what might be the significance of that?"

The king's ambassador shrugged and shook his head. "We don't know. It might be of the greatest significance or not. One way or another, we haven't the time to hold up the mission awaiting results." He gestured toward the glowing biosphere. "Have you further questions of Rand?"

Teague shook his head. "No." He glanced at Raina. "Have you any questions, femina?"

Raina eyed the biosphere for a long moment, then shook her head. "No. But I reserve the right to question the Volan at a later time."

"You have that right and I'll gladly answer," Rand's voice rose, once more, out of the darkness. "The opportunity for all of us to get to know each other better will be ample during our journey."

"You possess an obsessive need to learn more about the humanoid species," Raina remarked, eyeing the biosphere suspiciously. "Why is that, Volan?"

A soft chuckle emanated from the communications device. "Not for any subversive reasons, to be sure. I simply wish . . . to understand . . . your kind. You are a fascinatingly complex species. Yet in many ways, you are more like us than dissimilar." He paused, and when he spoke again, his voice seemed tinged with a wistful sadness. "It may sound unbelievable, but I hope to learn more of myself in learning more of you. And perhaps, in the learning, regain a part of me that has long been lost."

Raina stood there in the dimly lit room, momentarily overcome with the most bittersweet realization that this mission might not just be for the successful acquisition of a stone. It might well also be a mission of self-discovery and the fulfillment of personal goals. It certainly was for her, even if, in the fulfillment, others must die. It seemed to be one of the Volan's personal goals as well.

And the monk? He had secrets long buried, that much was certain. Whether he chose to examine them remained to be seen. Raina smiled. One way or another, the wisest course was to discover and remain cognizant of the personal agendas of all the players. It would give her the upper hand and assure the success of her own desires.

In the end, that was all that could ever be permitted to matter. She had learned that cycles ago. She must not allow anything else to come before it. Not if she wished to survive.

"A most admirable goal, Volan," Raina forced herself to reply. "If one can truly believe it."

"Only time will prove the truth, one way or another."

"Yes," she bitterly admitted. "Whatever that truth may really be."

Seven days later, all preparations complete, Teague stood in the transport chamber, awaiting Raina's arrival and final preparations for transport to the Volan spy ship. Rand, in his shielding receptacle now complete with compact communications device and life support system, hung from a carrying pack on the monk's back.

"This is quite an adventure we're embarking upon," the Volan commented, masking his excitement with difficulty. "I only wish I had a body so as to experience it in every way."

"Enjoy a torrid sun beating down, sucking every last bit of moisture from your body, do you?" Teague wryly inquired. "Or the frigid nights, or the choking desert dust that gets into everything, including your clothes and food? Not to mention the arduous journey on foot, so as not to call undue attention to our presence?"

"I am sorry." Rand's voice took on an apologetic tone. "I know you and the femina bear the brunt of the mission, especially the physical aspects. But after months confined to the narrow world of a room, even my limited participation in this mission is a welcome change."

Teague chuckled. "I didn't mean to berate you for your lack of participation. I suppose I just don't see this as an adventure. And be forewarned, neither does the femina."

"But you both return to your home planet after cycles of exile," Rand sounded puzzled. "Doesn't that at least please you?"

"I left for a reason," the monk tersely replied. "I've no wish to return, not now or ever."

"And Raina? How does she feel about it?"

"Why don't you ask her? Her reasons are her own, and none of my affair." With that, Teague reached over and flipped off the communications device, effectively silencing the increasingly inquisitive Volan. There was some comfort in the knowledge he could distance himself whenever he wished from at least one member of his party. Unfortunately, it was the least unsettling member of the two.

He shrugged out of the heavy pack that, besides Rand's special carrying case, included a month's supply of dehydrated food, a water purification system, a stunner, a blaster, two changes of typical Incendarian desert garb, a small mining pick and drill, and special shielded transport sacks for the stone. Rand's pack was entirely self-contained and included a power source and nutrient system sufficient for a good six months. He and Raina, on the other hand, if their foray on Incendra lasted longer than a month, would be forced to live off the land.

This was his last chance to back out of the expedition. Once on the Volan ship, there was no turning back. For a brief instant, Teague contemplated simply walking from the transport chamber and palace, never looking back until he'd traversed the Carus Mountains and reached Exsul. But no welcome would await him there. Abbot Leone had commanded that he cooperate with the king in whatever he wished.

A sense of futility swamped Teague, overwhelming in its intensity. There was no way out, no matter where he turned. And that, if nothing else, should reassure him that he truly *was* on the path he was destined for. Yet why did some part of him—the weak, cowardly part, to be sure—still fear this journey? Why couldn't he just . . . accept . . . and find his dearly desired peace in that?

Yet that peace continued to elude him, no matter what formerly tried-and-true monastic rituals he performed. The memories of Incendra failed to fade this time. The horrors of that day, the shattering sense of betrayal and shame and failure he'd felt, returned again and again. And there seemed nothing—absolutely nothing—he could do to blot them out anymore.

It didn't help that thoughts of the Sodalitas he must join with kept creeping unbidden into his mind. He'd heard it said, even as a lad, that Incendarians were potent only with their own kind, that they were physically attracted solely to their planet's opposite sex. He wondered if that might possibly now be affecting his response to her.

Over the cycles, Teague had given little thought to the fact that, though he might find a particular female beautiful, he had never once felt the stirrings of desire. He had viewed it instead as a blessing in his particular calling. Then, he'd promptly forgotten about it.

Yet still the niggling worry ate at him. Though Abbot Leone had granted him a temporary dispensation from all his vows for the course of the mission, Teague now wondered if there had been a subtle message behind that surprising indulgence. Did the old monk know of the potential temptations that lay ahead? Had Teague, in effect, been given permission to break his vows without impunity?

The consideration angered him. Did the abbot seriously imagine that a fifth-level Grandmaster was so weak as to succumb to the sordid clamorings of the flesh, just because a particularly alluring female was forced upon him? The rest of the monks had fought the carnality inherent within all males—and they fought it every day of their life. He could do no less—and still hope ever to feel worthy to stand among them again.

A sense of anticipation, of eagerness for the battles ahead, filled him. He'd been spared such temptations all these cycles. Now, at long last, he would battle those as well. Battle them and prove, once and for all, that he truly *had* earned his rightful place—in every way—in the Brotherhood of Exsul. That he truly belonged *somewhere* in this vast cosmos. Not like on Incendra . . . where all he'd ever been was an unworthy son and heir.

The portal of the transport chamber slid open. In walked King Falkan and Teran Ardane. A hush settled over the room.

Teague strode over to greet the two men, a fierce excitement pumping through his veins. It was all so clear now. Incendra beckoned, a land no longer just his home, but rather a testing place, a living cauldron of fire and pain wherein he would at long last fully die to himself and the world. Wherein, at long last, he'd be purified.

Wherein he'd finally be found worthy . . .

"What do you mean, you 'might not be coming back'?" Marissa demanded, as she waited for her friend to finish her final preparations before they departed her room for the transport chamber.

Raina looked up from the sheath she was strapping to her left thigh. She cocked her head, a bemused smile on her lips. "And exactly what about my statement didn't you understand?"

"The part about you telling me you might not return to Bellator once you and the monk retrieve the crystal, that's what!" The chestnut-haired woman strode over to confront her. "What in the heavens do you plan, Raina? You know the spy ship requires two pilots."

"No, it doesn't, actually." She finished fastening the sheath and slipped her prized Nadrygean dagger into it.

Light sparkled and shimmered off the fine, nearly indestructible metal as it slid within its molded jacket of black domare hide, filling Raina with a grim sense of possession. She'd worked long and hard to purchase such a weapon and now, at long last, it might serve her in the most soul-satisfying of ways.

She lifted her gaze to calmly meet Marissa's. "I learned a lot about that spy ship in the past few days. I learned one person can pilot it. The process is more difficult, but the Volan computers on board can be programmed to autopilot with just a bit of ingenuity. Long enough, at any rate, for the pilot to catch several hours' sleep from time to time. After all, the journey to Incendra, thanks to the speed of the new planetary drivers, takes only five days."

"Then why did Falkan insist on two pilots?"

Raina shrugged. "Most likely to assure a backup, not only in flight, but on Incendra as well. It was the wisest course, in case something happened to one of us. But on the return trip, the only issue is the flight itself."

"It still doesn't explain why you might not return."

Green eyes locked with blue. "It's all quite simple, sweeting. I mean to tie up some loose ends, ends left hanging for a very long time. Loose ends," Raina added grimly, "that I should've taken care of long ago."

Marissa's eyes narrowed. "You never mentioned that as a reason for going before. You mean to avenge yourself, don't you?"

"No, I didn't mention it before," Raina admitted matter-of-factly. "But the longer I thought about it, the more it began to appeal to me. My revenge is long overdue."

"Raina, you could die in the attempt. Malam Vorax alone will be a difficult man to kill, *if* you can even get close enough to do it. He's now ruler of Farsala, the most powerful kingdom on Incendra."

"I've spent the last fifteen cycles training as a warrior." Raina smiled bitterly. "And now, thanks to this Volan ship, I have the chance to return to Incendra. I've thought long and hard over this in the past days. It's my destiny, Marissa. I'm meant to go back not only for the sake of the Imperium, but for my own sake, too."

"But what of your life on Moraca?" her friend cried, throwing up her hands in exasperation. "What of the Sodalitas?"

"I've given my all to them and never once have I asked for anything in return. But now . . ."

Raina paused, searching for words to describe her feelings. For a fleeting instant, speech failed her. How could one ever explain the yearning, the hunger, the impotent anger that had seethed within her all this time, begging for its own chance for release? How could one make someone else—even Marissa—truly understand?

"But now," she finally forced herself to continue, "it's my time at last. The Sodalitas will just have to choose a new leader. They've done it before. They can do it again."

"And what of you, Raina?" Marissa pleaded. "Will you throw it all away? All the progress you've made, the successes you've achieved? For what? To make the lives—and deaths—of two already miserable men just a little more miserable? *You* are what counts, not them. Killing them won't heal you. Only *you* can do that."

"No, you are wrong in that," Raina quietly replied. "I cannot be fully whole again until they are dead. Malam Vorax and . . . my father."

With a fierce shake of her head, she flung the sudden swell of anguish aside. Yes, her father would die, too.

Neither he nor Vorax deserved to live after what each, in his own self-serving way, had done to her. Done to her then, and over and over again in her heart and soul for the past fifteen cycles. But now, just when they thought they were safe from retribution, she would return. Return . . . and avenge herself at last.

Raina smiled a savage, secret smile. The plan was sound, the decision firm. And the anticipation of the vengeance to come so very, very sweet . . .

Five

Raina halted at the door to the transport chamber. She inhaled a ragged breath, then squared her shoulders and activated the key control. The portal slid open to reveal a large room in cool green hues. Teague Tremayne stood to one side, deep in conversation with King Falkan and Teran Ardane. At the other side of the room, near the transport consoles and technicians, stood Cyra Husam al Nur.

She motioned Raina over. Ignoring the curious glances of the monk and his two companions, the warrior woman headed across the transport chamber to Cyra. The petite scientist shot her a grateful glance.

"I know this isn't the best time to ask this of you," Cyra began, "but if you could spare me a moment?"

Raina nodded. "Something further you wish to add about the crystal?"

"No." Cyra sent a furtive glance in the direction of Teague Tremayne, her gaze momentarily snagging on the carrying pack hanging from his shoulder. He was once more deep in discussion with the others. "The Volan," she said. "Beware of him. Though he's essential to the success of this mission, he's not to be trusted."

"Isn't that stating the obvious?"

"No, you don't understand." Cyra stepped closer, her voice dropping. "I've worked with subjects who were

Volan enslaved. Driven by their Volan masters, they are deadly, devious, and cold-hearted. They are also very intelligent and manipulative. This Rand may be physically limited by the confines of his biosphere, but he's still a Volan."

She shuddered. "I loathe them and all that they represent. I can't help it, but I do."

"Your concern is noted." Raina cocked an inquiring brow. "Is there anything more? The king awaits."

"Yes, there is one thing more." The blond woman hesitated, then lifted her chin and forged on. "You'll have to travel through the Ar Rimal desert to reach the firestorm caves. This may seem pointless and potentially futile, but there's a man, a leader of one of the desert tribes . . ."

"The same one who led you to the caves?"

Cyra looked away. "Yes. That one. His tribe roams that area of the Ar Rimal. If you should happen to meet him . . ." She riveted her gaze back on Raina. "There's a message I'd have you give him."

"The Ar Rimal is vast. The odds are great we won't—"

"I know," the blond woman hastened to interject. "I know, but it's the last chance I may ever have of communicating with him and there are . . . things . . . things I need to say. I'd at least like to know I tried."

She suffers deeply because of this man, Raina realized, noting the tears glistening in Cyra's eyes and her taut, strained expression. Compassion filled her. "Tell me your message and I'll do my best to get it to him. I can't promise anything, though, as it might jeopardize the mission, but I'll—"

"Thank you!" Cyra grabbed Raina's hand and gave it a quick squeeze. "I know. I understand." She paused then.

"Well, the message and the man's name?" Raina prodded, when no further information was forthcoming.

The blond woman swallowed convulsively. "I wish you to tell him that, in spite of it all, I love him still"—she flushed crimson—"and always will."

Raina frowned in puzzlement. "If you love him so, then why are you—"

"It's too long a story to tell." Cyra managed a wobbly smile. "And far too complicated to belabor. You've a transport awaiting you. Just . . . give him my message, if you will."

She released Raina's hand and had made a move to step back and walk away when Raina halted her. "His name. What's this man's name?"

Once more, Cyra's eyes filled with tears, this time overflowing to trickle down her face. "Bahir. Bahir Husam al Nur," she whispered achingly. "My husband." Then, without another word, she turned and fled the room.

Raina watched her leave, even more confused than she'd been before. Her husband? Then why—

She let that question die the death it deserved. It was none of her concern what had transpired between Cyra and this Bahir. He'd most likely betrayed her in some way, as men were wont to do.

The real tragedy was that Cyra persisted in loving him. Raina wished heartily that she hadn't agreed to carry the message. The last thing she wanted was to involve herself in the middle of someone else's romantic predicament, or be responsible for fanning the flames of what was apparently a doomed love.

Turning, she strode over to stand before the king, rendering him a formal bow. "I am at your command, Imperial Majesty."

Falkan's gaze swept over her, then he nodded. "All is in readiness." He looked at Teague. "And you, Brother Tremayne? Are you ready as well?"

"Yes, Majesty."

With a sweeping gesture, the king indicated the transport platform. Raina and Teague silently mounted it.

"The fate of the entire Imperium may well rest in your hands," Falkan then said. "May your journey be a successful one."

As he spoke, the transport shield lowered with a muted whir. The king and Teran Ardane stepped back. Across the room, one of the technicians shoved down a lever. A buzzing filled the air.

Inexplicably, panic flooded Raina. She couldn't go. It was all a mistake. A terrible, tragic mistake.

Savagely, she squashed the shameful thoughts. It *wasn't* a mistake. It was her *destiny*. And she *would* see it through—for the sake of the Imperium, for herself.

"It *is* frightening, is it not?" the monk softly asked beside her. "Even if you know in your heart it must be."

Startled, Raina turned toward Teague. Her lips moved, but no sound escaped. Even as she tried to speak, he began to disappear. Then, in a flurry of bright, sharp light, the transport chamber dissolved before her eyes.

"Onboard systems are all functional," Raina intoned, as she made one last check of the cockpit console.

Lights of all hues blinked and glowed from the computer terminal that lay before them. Teague looked up from the other seat of the small, cramped cockpit of the Volan spy ship, pausing in the programming of the coordinates for the refueling station on Cygnus, their one and only stop in the five-day space flight to Incendra.

"I suppose there's no further reason for delay, then." His glance locked with hers. "Is the Volan lashed down securely? The initial acceleration as we pull out of Bellator's orbit will be a bit rough."

"He's fine." Raina checked the security of her own seat harness one last time. "Let's get on with it, shall we?"

Teague bit back a smile. The Sodalitas was as unhappy with this mission as he was. That was good. She'd be highly motivated to hasten the mission's completion. Just as highly motivated as he was, it seemed.

He grasped the yoke firmly in both hands. "Navigation program engaged," he instructed the computer. "Initiate orbit departure sequence."

"Orbit departure sequence initiated," the flat, mechanical voice of the flight computer responded.

With a rumble and a lurch forward, the thrusters fired. The spy ship broke orbit and soared off, away from Bellator and toward the stars. Display panel lights flashed in a crazed multicolored succession. The small craft shook with the driving force of its powerful engines.

Teague was flung back into his seat. His hands tightened about the flight yoke, more for support than to maintain a direction already controlled by the flight computer. He liked the idea, nonetheless, that the secondary guidance system of the yoke was in place. He'd never totally trusted computers.

After what seemed an interminable time, the turbulence finally ceased. "Now free of Bellatorian orbit," the flight computer droned.

Teague programmed in the autopilot, then released his

grip on the yoke. Relieved to have successfully completed takeoff, he momentarily forgot his monastic presence and grinned over at Raina. "Have you noticed that even the dialogue of Volan computers is sparse and monotonous? I've never heard a more emotionless voice."

"What did you expect from a species that believes in total mindless conformity? Scintillating discourse?" Raina shot him a scornful glance. "It's but a machine, after all."

He scowled back. "My apologies for what was apparently an inane remark on my part. I was only trying to make some pleasant conversation." Stung by the female's reply, Teague choked down a disparaging comment or two of his own about her lack of manners. "Neither of us may wish to be here, but there's little purpose served in going for each other's throat at every opportunity. We have to work together, after all."

"Correct me if I'm wrong, Brother Tremayne." Raina arched a mocking brow. "Aren't you required to avoid females at all cost? I but wonder at your motives now in attempting pleasantries with me."

"They were nothing more than an effort to make an already unendurable journey a bit more bearable," he gritted, suddenly aggravated to the limits of his control. "However, since you obviously find my conversational attempts offensive, be assured I'll refrain from further 'pleasantries' in the future."

"Just stick to the mission, Tremayne. That's all I've wanted, or will ever want, from you."

"Fine," he rasped, and turned his gaze toward the view screen. "That's just fine with me."

They sped through an ebony vastness, tiny bits of starlight the only apparent signs of life in an otherwise lifeless space. Neither spoke for a long while, content to stare out the view screen at the impressively infinite blackness. Then, from behind them, a third voice spoke.

"You seem to have a strong antipathy for each other," Rand said, quite evidently puzzled. "Why is that?"

Raina and Teague's glances met. "Do you want to turn him off, or should I?" she demanded.

"I've no problem with his question," the monk replied mildly. "I don't hate you, after all. I'm just not permitted close involvement with you."

"Well, I don't appreciate nor will I tolerate him prying where he has no right to go." Raina released the safety clasps on her harness and shoved out of her seat. "As far as I'm concerned, there's no reason to have to listen to him again until we near the caves. Until then, there's no need for him at all."

Teague grabbed her arm as she made a move to walk past him. Raina froze, then looked down to where he clasped her. His fingers were long and tapering, the span of his hand wide. His nails were clean and neatly trimmed.

A derisive smile twisted her lips. Definitely the hands of a pampered man, she thought. Incendarian by birth or not, this time he'd tolerate the hardships poorly.

"Release me, I say." She glared down at him. "Now."

Instead, the monk's grip tightened. "The Volan, potential enemy though he might be, is a living being. He has done nothing to deserve this derisive treatment from you. Rather than turning his communications device off, I think you owe him an apology."

"Be damned!" Raina jerked free with a vicious twist of her arm. "I'll not apologize to some alien entity in a box. And I won't be dictated to by you, either." She strode over to where Rand's carrying pack sat strapped to the floor. Squatting, she began to fumble with the pocket housing the communications device.

"There's no reason to turn me off," the Volan said. "I but meant to get to know you better, and ease the animosity—"

With a snap of her wrist, Raina flipped off the audio controls. Once more, silence permeated the cockpit. A grim satisfaction filled her. In one quick and simple demonstration, she'd showed the Volan *and* Tremayne that she'd not be coerced or intimidated into following their desires. Let this one lesson suffice. It would save them all a lot of misery if it did.

She rose and walked over to stand beside Tremayne. He slowly lifted his gaze to her, his expression calm, shuttered. "Wish to turn me off now, too, do you?" he drawled, the challenge glinting in his eyes belying his lazy manner. "How unfortunate for you I have no control switch."

"Unfortunate, indeed." Raina subjected him to a cool, appraising look. "But there are other ways to shut you out for a time. If you've no objection, I'd like to make use of the sleeping cabin. There's no sense in both of us staying awake. Besides," she added sweetly, "if we take turns sleeping, we minimize the amount of time we must spend together in close quarters."

"A wise idea." The monk turned back to the view screen. "Sleep as long as you like and, when you're done, I'll take my turn. Oh, by the way," he added, as she turned to leave, "flip the Volan's communications device back on, will you? I find myself desiring some pleasant conversation for a change."

"Do it yourself, Tremayne," Raina snapped and, without another word, stalked out of the cockpit and down the short corridor to the ship's single sleeping chamber.

* * *

The five-day trip passed uneventfully. The refueling at Cygnus went without a hitch. Raina and Teague managed to avoid each other most of the day by carefully planning their sleeping schedules around each other, and spending the rest of their free time with one in the cockpit and the other in the equally cramped galley.

Teague had never realized how miserable the confines of a spacecraft could be when one was trying to avoid someone. Especially someone who, for all her irritating, high-handed ways, was still the most sexually alluring female he'd ever known. Curse the Incendarian attraction! Curse his lack of experience in curbing his response to it!

He knew they couldn't go on like this indefinitely, if for no other reason than that it would severely hamper if not sidetrack their mission. But he also knew it wasn't an issue easily solved or one best dealt with just yet.

Raggedly, Teague shoved a hand through his hair, exhaled a deep breath, and leaned back in his seat. He simply wasn't trained or knowledgeable when it came to dealing with females. If things had gone differently, if he hadn't been on his way to Incendra on a difficult and potentially dangerous mission, he wouldn't have had to.

"You are disturbed."

Teague twisted in his seat and flung a look in the direction of the Volan's carrying pack and receptacle. In the past days, as much to learn more of the alien as to distract himself from his rising tension and sexual stirrings, he'd spent many hours talking with Rand.

It was surprising how much information, scientific, philosophical, and literary, the Volan had accumulated in the months after his return to his biosphere. There had been little else for him to do to pass the days, Rand had informed him, and, the more he learned via the store of audio recordings Teran Ardane had provided him, the more it whetted his appetite to learn.

Teague chuckled. "Has anyone ever told you that you're extremely inquisitive? Most humanoids don't appreciate being questioned about their private thoughts."

"I've noted that," Rand said. "But I've also noted that most humanoids also aren't all that adept at working through their problems without verbalizing them, either."

Teague turned to gaze out through the view screen. The cloud-obscured orb of Incendra gleamed like some warm, welcome beacon in the vast blackness of space. They'd be entering its gravitational pull soon. The plan was to decelerate by plunging into the planet's upper atmosphere, where air friction would slow the spacecraft down, then climb out again into the desired orbit. Once orbit was obtained and all systems restabilized, they'd descend once more, this time to land. No, Teague thought, it wouldn't be long now before the mission began in earnest.

"I press too much, don't I?"

The Volan's voice jerked Teague from his contemplation of the hours ahead. "What?" He smiled. Above all else, Rand seemed to possess the most all-consuming need to understand the functionings of the human heart. Though Raina attributed his actions to sinister motives, meant ultimately to be used against them, Teague wasn't so sure.

The monk sighed and shook his head. "I don't mind, really, but I'm also not accustomed to sharing my thoughts and feelings, either."

"Could you at least tell me why the femina is so . . .

er . . . antagonistic toward you? I understand her reasons in my regard. She sees me as an enemy. But you . . . you are a fellow humanoid."

"I'm also a male," Teague replied, "and, for some reason, Raina doesn't trust or like men. She's a member of a warrior society of women called the Sodalitas. They live in their own city on the planet Moraca, shun men save for the necessary procreative purposes, and raise only the female babes they bear. Though some of them hire out as mercenaries to help support the Sodalitas who stay behind to run the city, they never willingly seek out or desire the company of men."

"She's been hurt by some man, then?"

"Most likely. Marissa once mentioned that Raina wasn't born into that warrior society. She joined them of her own accord."

"Then you must prove to her you are no danger to her. She needs to learn that or she'll never have any hope of happiness."

Once more, Teague twisted in his seat to glance behind him. "What, by the five moons, are you talking about?"

"I don't understand." Puzzlement tinged Rand's voice. "Why do you care if Raina finds happiness or not?"

"Isn't that what all humanoids seek? A close and long-lasting bonding—especially between a male and a female?"

"Some may wish for that," Teague growled, "but not I, nor, it seems, Raina."

"You are a monk. I think I understand the laws you must abide by. What I don't understand is why you would choose such a lonely life of renunciation over that of companionship and love." Rand hesitated. "If it wouldn't be an imposition, could you at least explain that to me?"

Teague smiled and shook his head. The Volan was persistent if nothing else. "Men embrace the monastic life for different reasons. One way or another, it's chosen in the hope of finding fulfillment or answers or peace. All of which," Teague added dryly, "could be viewed as a form of happiness."

"And why did you choose it?"

Once more, the monk turned to gaze out the view screen. "I chose it for many reasons," he said softly, the memories flooding him with surprising force. "In the beginning, it chose me, when the brothers took me in. I was lost, confused . . . barely even sane. They gave me shelter, protection, and the most compassionate understanding. I don't know what I would've done without them.

"Later, I remained out of a sense of obligation, that I owed them recompense for all they'd done for me. And, little by little, I began to see how their way suited me, how I could finally be of some use to others, and how living this kind of life could give me back what I had lost. So I stayed, took my vows, and strove to become the best monk I could."

"Your exploits are legendary. I'd say you succeeded."

Teague's mouth quirked wryly. "Some might well say that."

"And you?" Rand persisted. "What do you say?"

"It's hard to judge until one's life is over and one can look back. I'm content, though. I've achieved some of my goals. Others"—he shrugged—"I've yet to achieve."

"Perhaps the mission to Incendra will provide you with yet another measure of success. I hope to—"

The entry proximity warning buzzer went off. "Approaching the planet Incendra," the flight computer droned. "Transmit new directives."

Teague swiftly programmed in the atmospheric deceleration commands, then depressed the intercom button to the sleeping chambers. "Femina?"

"What?" came a voice rusty with sleep.

"We're nearing Incendarian orbit. I need you in the cockpit immediately."

There was a rustle of bed clothes, the soft thud of feet hitting the floor, and then the sound of a huge yawn. "I'll be there in five minutes."

Teague released the intercom button and went back to delivering further instructions to the computer. Raina, true to her word, stepped through the corridor hatchway exactly five minutes later. She hurriedly covered the short distance and swung down into her seat.

"What do you need help with?" she demanded tersely as she strapped herself into her safety harness.

"Keep a close eye on the hull temperatures and structural stability as we decelerate into the upper atmosphere," Teague said, without taking his eyes off the computer panel. "I'll have my hands full making certain the ship maintains the proper angle of descent. As good a heat and electromagnetic protective shielding as this craft has, nothing can withstand the friction of too steep an atmospheric reentry."

"I think I can manage that," the warrior woman muttered. "It's just these three lights, isn't it?" she asked, pointing to the upper right corner of the computer panel that stood before her. "I wouldn't want to bungle such a complex assignment, you know?"

"Entering Incendarian atmosphere in five seconds," the flight computer said.

Exasperated by her barely contained sarcasm, Teague shot Raina a piercing look, then turned back to the job at hand.

"Entering Incendarian atmosphere in three seconds, two seconds, one second . . ."

With a mighty jolt, the ship struck the planet's upper atmosphere. The layers of air shivered over the spacecraft in turbulent waves, bucking it to and fro. Raina held onto her safety harness with both hands, her gaze never leaving the three panel lights that were her charge. The lights held steady for a time, then one began to flicker erratically.

Quickly, she programmed in a diagnostic search for the source of the difficulty and found it in the rear starboard protective shield, which appeared not to be functioning adequately.

"I need to go aft and check out the rear starboard panel," Raina shouted over the deafening sound of the thrusters straining in reverse as they fired in an attempt to slow the craft's descent.

"What?" Teague roared back, jerking his head up to look at her.

"The rear starboard shields!" Raina screamed, pointing to the flickering light on the computer panel. She unfastened her safety harness and, with great difficulty in the rocking ship, climbed to her feet.

Teague eyed her, then the panel, comprehension finally dawning. "Check it out as fast as you can, then get back here. This descent isn't going well."

Raina nodded and turned, making her way toward the hatch corridor by lurching forward bit by bit, grabbing whatever she could for support. The roar of the thrusters lessened somewhat once she worked her way down the corridor, only to be replaced by a new noise. Her heart sank. It sounded like . . . like a loose panel.

Slamming her fist down on the button of the wall intercom situated nearby, Raina yelled for Tremayne.

"What?" his deep voice came. "What's wrong?"

"I think the rear starboard shield is loose," Raina cried. "I'm going in through the hold to check it out!"

"No!" the monk roared. "It's too dangerous. If the panel's loose or damaged, the heat, not to mention the electromagnetic radiation, can get in. It could kill you!"

"And so will burning up in the atmosphere if I don't fix it," Raina shouted back. "We don't have any choice in this, Tremayne, and you know it. I'm here and you're not."

"Don't!" Teague bellowed. "Don't do it!"

Raina hesitated an instant longer, then released the intercom button. Turning, she made her unsteady way down to the end of the corridor and the floor panel that opened into the hold.

Six

The computer panel flashed in a dizzying array of colors. Monitors sounded alarms. A terminal exploded, filling the cockpit with the scent of smoke and melting wires. Teague swore a most unmonastic oath under his breath.

Something had gone awry in the atmospheric deceleration. Whether it was the loose protective shield or some equipment malfunction, perhaps overstressed by the unexpected turbulence of Incendra's atmosphere, Teague didn't know. It mattered little. Repairs could be made and a computer diagnostic run later—if they survived.

His thoughts turned fleetingly to Raina. What would she find in the hold where the rear starboard panel was? He didn't want her there—the danger was indeed great—but there was no other choice. He couldn't leave the helm. There was nothing more he could do but attempt to break their downward trajectory and achieve a stable gliding pattern in the upper atmosphere. It was too late to continue with their original plan. Too late, and pointless, at any rate.

Teague only prayed that Raina could make the repairs quickly. If there truly was a radiation leak into the hold, the less exposure she suffered, the better. He only hoped the shields had held well enough to prevent any kind of leak.

The severe downward angle of the ship's nose failed to respond to the flight computer. They plummeted toward the ground, the heat sensors clanging in alarm. Desperately, Teague programmed an override command. The secondary guidance system took over. Grasping the yoke, the monk hauled back with all his strength.

For the longest, most sickening span of seconds, nothing happened. The spy ship continued on its fatal course, the overloaded forward thrusters screaming in protest. Then, miraculously, the bedlam seemed to change in tone, lessen in volume and intensity. Just as miraculously, the ship's steep angle of descent began to level out.

The monk maintained his death grip on the yoke, unwilling to believe what his flight computer was telling him. "Angle of descent eighty degrees nose low . . . seventy-five . . . sixty . . . forty-five . . . thirty . . . fifteen . . .

"Zero."

With a groan, Teague pushed the yoke forward to maintain a level course before they headed back upward. The craft steadied, straightened. He shut down the forward thrusters, checked the control panel for signs of any significant damage. Blessedly, there was little. The navigation system appeared to have suffered the most destruction.

Thanks to the damaged navigation system, though, the autopilot was now nonfunctional. Teague programmed an override control lock to maintain steady flight, released his safety harness, and stood. His knees wobbled as relief made him momentarily lightheaded.

They'd barely survived, that Teague well knew, but

they *had* survived. Or at least, *he* had. He'd yet to see how Raina had fared.

He quickly headed through the cockpit hatch and down the corridor. The hold's floor panel had slammed shut, probably during all the turbulence. It was probably for the best. If there'd been a radiation leak, it had remained contained in the hold.

Teague halted at the computerized wall panel and programmed a demagnetization command. The lights flashed, ran through the sequence, then extinguished.

"Demagnetization sequence completed," the computer informed him.

Teague moved to the hold's floor panel, knelt, and lifted the small door until it locked in place. Steep metal stairs led down to the subfloor and the ship's hull. "Raina?" he called down into the hold. "Are you all right?"

There was no answer. Filled with rising dread, Teague climbed down the stairs. The small hold looked as it had before lift-off, sectioned off into neat, shelved compartments stocked with shielded receptacles designed to carry the Incendarian crystal back to Bellator. Strapped firmly onto their shelves, they'd suffered no damage from the rough ride down.

"Raina?"

Teague headed toward the rear starboard section, its back wall blocked from view by the ceiling-high shelved compartments. As he made his way around the compartment fronting the starboard wall, a low groan emanated from directly behind him. He wheeled and found the Sodalitas crumpled in a corner behind yet another shelved compartment.

His heart pounding, he raced over and knelt before her. "Raina? Femina? What happened?"

Her dark auburn lashes fluttered open. "The panel . . .

it was loose. I managed . . . to seal it shut . . . but it took a long while." She attempted to lever herself to one elbow and failed. "Ah, curse it all," she whispered. "I'm so weak."

Teague reached out and brushed aside a long, curling lock that had worked free of her braid. "The electro-magnetic radiation?"

Raina grimaced, then nodded. "That, and exposure to some high levels of heat, I'm afraid. Guess it'll soon be a mission of two once more."

"Don't count on that just yet. You're too stubborn to give up easily. Besides, are you really willing to admit I was right in ordering you not to come down here?"

"Hardly, Tremayne. You know better than that." With a superhuman effort, Raina offered her hand. "Help me get out of here, will you?"

He scooted close, pulled her gently to a sitting position, and lifted her over his shoulder. Backing out of the narrow space, Teague hefted Raina more securely in place, then stood. The climb up the stairs with the additional weight of his human burden was a challenge, but he made it and soon had her lying on the narrow bunk in the sleeping chamber. He slid a pillow beneath her head and covered her with a blanket.

"I'll be back in a few minutes." Teague's glance skimmed over her. She was pale, her skin clammy, and she could barely keep her eyes open. It was vital that he get the necessary injections from the med kit into her, a med kit they'd been as thoroughly instructed in the use of as they had the piloting of the spy ship and collection of the crystal.

Teague ran from the sleeping chamber and down the hall to the galley where the kit was kept. He all but ripped it off the wall and raced out of the room, back down the corridor, and into the sleeping chamber. His hands trembled as he laid the box on the small table and opened it.

What had Cyra said? First give the antiradiation drug to decrease the effective amount of rads from a new radiation exposure and prevent further damage. Then the torpine, to put the patient into a healing trance for the next twenty-four hours. Between the two, one hoped to be able to minimize the damage. Later, after meds to treat specific side effects like nausea and vomiting, and healing ointments for any skin damage, there was an ample supply of narcotics for pain.

He looked back at Raina. She lay there unmoving, apparently having drifted into unconsciousness. It was for the best, Teague told himself. She'd been through enough trauma without having now to endure his fumbling efforts to heal her . . . if he *could* heal her. There was no telling how much radiation exposure she'd received. He would never know. She would either live or die, and the final answers would lie in that.

He gave her the injections. Then, after removing Raina's boots and loosening her clothing, Teague covered her with several more blankets to keep her warm. He lingered there a moment more, gazing down at her.

At the sight of Raina lying there so pale and quiet, his stomach clenched and his throat went dry. She had risked her life to save him and Rand and the mission, a mission she'd very reluctantly embarked upon—with an alien and a man she despised. Yet she had done it, nonetheless.

A grudging admiration for Raina's courage filled Teague. Not only was she beautiful and infinitely desirable, but now, on top of everything else, he found he respected her. Whatever had happened to her at the hands of others, Raina still lived by the most honorable of precepts.

The admission of his esteem for her, however, didn't ease any of Teague's rising torment. If anything, it only intensified it. And now, to make matters even worse, he would have to care for her, to touch her.

Choking back an agonized groan, Teague turned and exited the sleeping chamber. Raina would be safe enough for now, and he had more pressing matters to attend to. Matters like landing the ship as soon as possible, before something else malfunctioned.

"How is the femina?" Rand immediately asked, when Teague reentered the cockpit.

The monk halted and glanced down at the Volan's pack. "She suffered radiation and heat exposure while repairing the rear starboard panel."

"I was afraid of that. If I can be of assistance . . ." Rand paused, then gave a self-disparaging laugh. "Rather ludicrous of me, isn't it, offering my assistance? Without a body, I'm not much use to anyone."

Compassion for the Volan's frustration filled Teague. He took his own body so much for granted. What must it be like not to have one, to be totally helpless and dependent on others even just to survive? "No, you're not much use without a body," the monk replied honestly. "At least, not in any physical sense. But your store of knowledge is indeed valuable and, with Raina ill, I'll require all the assistance and advice I can get."

"Whatever I can do to help, I will do gladly."

Teague smiled. "I know that, Rand, and it's deeply appreciated." He walked over to his seat, sat, and strapped himself back in. A quick check of the control panel revealed nothing further had happened to the ship in his absence. The navigation system was indeed non-

functional, Teague discovered, as he attempted to recon-
firm the landing coordinates, but aside from that, all
seemed in order. He'd just have to manually pilot the
ship down to the ground.

"We may not be landing in exactly the location we'd
originally planned," he called back to Rand. "A minor
detail, though, in the total scheme of things."

"And what scheme of things were you alluding to?"
Rand shouted back.

"Survival, Volan," Teague replied, a grim smile twisting his lips. He disengaged the control lock, manually
fired the rear thrusters, then shoved the yoke forward.
"The only thing that truly matters in the end, wouldn't
you say?"

An evening breeze swept across the hot sands, cooling
the desert. The sun dipped below the distant, rock-strewn
land and wind-carved, misshapen cliffs, exploding at last
in an inferno of fiery crimsons, deep ochres, and golds.
Save for the occasional howl of some wild desert canus,
it was silent. The soft silence of the wilderness, the land
of the nomads and desert tribes. The Ar Rimal.

Teague watched as the sun's dying glory peaked, then
faded, his heart and mind beset with a confusing jumble
of emotions. He was safely on Incendra, the Volan ship
landed. Raina, still in the throes of the healing stupor,
slept on, no worse save for a slight reddish flush to her
skin that had appeared a few hours ago.

Even with the aid of the antiradiation drug, it was
now evident that she'd experienced at least some of the
milder symptoms of the sickness. If only she didn't
worsen. But he didn't know, wouldn't know, for at least
several more days.

In the meantime, though they had arrived in the Ar Rimal desert, Teague had no idea of their exact coordinates. Tonight he'd try and reorient himself by the stars. The onboard computer could plot their exact location once Teague had made a few measurements and calculations. The navigation system, however, would need major repair work.

Indeed, there was quite a bit of work to be accomplished in the next few days. Besides Raina's nursing, the ship needed to be hidden and the necessary repairs completed. Once they set out for the caves, they needed a fully functional ship for their eventual return. A quick escape off planet might be essential.

He turned from the scene of sand and sky and headed back to the Volan ship. It would be cold soon. The lack of cloud cover that was the curse of the desert on hot, sunny days also prevented the retention of heat at night. Though they must conserve fuel for takeoff when they departed Incendra, Teague calculated they could spare a small amount each night to heat one room on the ship. And that room would be the sleeping chamber.

There was adequate space for Rand and his pack under the bunk. Teague could make a simple pallet on the floor beside the bed. Sharing the same room with Raina served many purposes—fuel conservation, as well as his being available to her in the night. Not that he liked the idea, necessity though it might be. No, he didn't like it at all.

But she was helpless and ill, and he owed her whatever aid he could offer. His monkish qualms about sleeping so close to a female were of little concern now. His monkish qualms, it was beginning to seem, would hold little weight for the entire mission.

Teague sealed the front hatch, made one last check

of the cockpit, then headed down the corridor to the sleeping chamber. Raina lay on the bunk just as he'd left her an hour ago, quiet, unmoving. He checked her and found her skin hot, her breathing a bit labored, but otherwise, her condition was unchanged. She'd awaken near midday on the morrow, when the effects of the torpine had worn off.

He lowered the light source to a soothing dimness, then laid out several blankets and a pillow on the floor. Though disinclined to sleep just yet, Teague settled down on his makeshift pallet nonetheless. As he rolled over onto his back and bunched the pillow beneath his head, Rand's voice rose out of the darkness.

"How was it outside?" the Volan asked. "Could you see the sun and sky and land? What did they look like?"

The wistfulness in the alien's voice plucked at Teague. "Yes, I saw it all," he replied softly. "The sun was just setting, and it was glorious. I'd forgotten how unique the sunsets are over the Ar Rimal. There's just something about that clear, dry air that seems to intensify everything, especially the colors. And the scents and sounds." Teague exhaled a contented breath. "They carry for such distances in the desert."

"I used to love seeing the day end," Rand murmured. "There was such a sense of completion to it all, and the setting sun just seemed the crowning glory to one's accomplishments."

"There is much in life to be appreciated and savored, isn't there?" Teague asked thoughtfully. "You make me reexamine a lot of things. Things I've taken for granted until they began to seem inconsequential. I wonder . . ."

"Wonder what?" Rand prodded, when Teague paused.

"I wonder . . . if I haven't been missing a lot of the simpler, more elemental aspects of life. Aspects that are far more essential to our hearts and minds and souls than some of the complex truths we are always striving to attain."

"I've wondered that myself. Wondered that perhaps I shouldn't just be content with my predestined fate—however limited it may finally be."

Teague cocked his head to glance in the Volan's direction. "Perhaps. But your dilemma, and its solution, will of necessity be much harder than mine. Mine is simply that I'm not certain I know *how* to begin anew. Or if I even have sufficient courage to change."

"Life is an endless series of rebirths and renewals, I think. It's also a myriad of little deaths. But isn't the true victory found ultimately within ourselves, and how we face each triumph and defeat?"

"You're waxing eloquent tonight, Volan."

"Am I?" Rand chuckled. "Perhaps you just bring it out in me."

A heavy drowsiness crept up on Teague. His lids lowered. Sleep wouldn't be as elusive as he'd first imagined, he thought. He turned on his side and shoved his pillow more comfortably beneath him. "Perhaps I do indeed," he said. "But I think as well that you give as much as you take, Volan."

"I thank you for that." There was a long pause, then Rand's mellifluous voice once again pierced the heavy silence of the night. "Sleep well, Teague Tremayne."

"Sleep well . . . Rand."

"Curse it all!" Teague threw down the big view light and began to dig frantically in the damp sand beneath the part of the spy ship where the water storage tanks were located.

"What's wrong?" Rand called, ensconced nearby in the shade of a tarp the monk had fashioned into an awning across the front of the ship.

"The water storage tanks," Teague shouted back, his voice now muffled from beneath the belly of the ship. "We landed atop some rocks that punctured both tanks. It looks like half the water has leaked out already, and I need to get the holes sealed or we'll lose it all."

He scooted out and, climbing to his feet, ran for the repair kit. What else could go wrong? he thought angrily. First the navigation system, then Raina, and now their water.

Teague shot a quick glance over his shoulder just before reentering the ship. Even now, the sun was rising to its zenith, blindingly hot in a sky bleached of color and devoid of life. They wouldn't last many days in this heat without water.

Grabbing the repair kit, Teague hurried back down the corridor. As he passed the sleeping chamber's portal, he hesitated. He made a quick decision and keyed the door to open. Raina lay on the bunk, moving restlessly.

She'd waken soon, Teague thought. And be in pain, no doubt. But his first priority, for all their sakes, must be the water tanks. Grasping the kit firmly, he headed back outside.

Two hours later, Teague had the leaks plugged. Unfortunately, half the water supplies were gone. They had a week's worth of water left, if that much.

"Not good, eh?" Rand asked, when the monk had climbed back out from beneath the ship.

Teague shoved a hand through his sweat-damp hair and brushed as much sand as he could from his bare chest and breeches. "Let's just say we need to head out of this desert as soon as possible."

"Where are we exactly, anyway?"

"According to my calculations, a good three hundred kilometers off course. Where we'd planned to land only a day's journey from the firestorm caves, we now face over a week's trek across the desert to reach the m. *If* we make good time and *if* our water holds out long enough for us to reach the nearest oasis."

"How soon will the femina be ready to travel?"

Teague shrugged and walked over to squat beside Rand. "I haven't any idea. It'll all depend on how ill she really is, and I won't know that until she wakens."

"And if she's too ill to travel for several days, or if she's dying, what then?"

He shot the Volan a sharp look. "What are you getting at?"

"The mission is more important than any one of us."

"So I should just leave her here to fend for herself as she can," Teague rasped, his anger rising, "and set off with you? Is that it?"

"It would seem the most logical thing to do. The fate of an entire Imperium might well rest on the success of this mission."

"Getting rather cold-blooded here, aren't you? Is that how Volans deal with their problems? Just turn and walk away?"

"The welfare of the hive is what counts," Rand calmly replied, "not that of any one individual."

"Well, I don't particularly care for that approach, or for you right now, for that matter."

"Yet you did the same thing in agreeing to this mission," the Volan persisted earnestly. "For the good of the Imperium, you sacrificed your own desires."

"My desires are one thing," Teague snapped, climbing

to his feet. "I am vowed to serve the Imperium. Raina's life is quite another."

A low chuckle emanated from the carrying pack.

"What's so amusing?" the monk demanded, his anger once more on the rise.

"Nothing, really. I was right about you, though. You *are* a moral man and will do the right thing, no matter your prior training or commitment to the Imperium."

Teague's eyes narrowed. "So, this was just a little test, was it?"

"In a sense, yes. I needed to know where your heart was in this. Now, I do."

"Rand . . ." Teague hesitated, struggling with his exasperation, even as he realized why this issue was so important to the Volan. He, too, had gone against his training and commitment to his own kind because it was the moral thing to do.

"Yes, Teague?"

"Nothing. From now on, just ask me outright if you have a question. I much prefer the direct approach." He wheeled and headed for the main hatch.

Behind him, Rand's reply carried clearly in the dry desert air. "As do I, my friend. As do I."

The relative coolness of the ship's shaded interior was a welcome relief from the blistering heat of the desert. Teague savored the cooling eddies of air his passage through the ship made on his overheated body. He desperately craved a swallow or two of water, but decided the water conservation must begin immediately. Perhaps in another hour he'd quench his thirst, but not just yet.

When he entered, Raina was tossing and turning on her bunk, mumbling incoherent phrases. Teague sat on the edge of the bed and pressed the back of his hand to her forehead. Her skin was hot, damp, and rosy pink. He took her by the shoulder and gently shook her.

"Raina? Femina? Wake up."

Ever so slowly, her long, dark auburn lashes lifted. Rich green eyes, bleary and confused, gazed up at him. "What . . . where . . . where am I?"

"You're in the spy ship." Teague wet a cloth and wiped the sweat from her forehead and face. "We landed safely on Incendra and are in the Ar Rimal desert."

Puzzlement furrowed her brow and she licked her lips. "What happened . . . to me? I feel so . . . bad, so thirsty."

"You were exposed to radiation when we came through the atmosphere. Don't you remember?"

Her eyes clouded in thought, then she nodded. "Yes. How long . . . have I been sleeping?"

"Twenty-four hours." Teague tossed the cloth back into its basin of water and rose. "I gave you an antirad drug and some torpine to put you into a healing sleep. And now, I'm going to fetch you some water to drink. It'll help the rest of your meds go down easier."

"Tremayne. Wait." Raina lifted a trembling hand.

"What is it, femina?" He glanced down at her, concern for her welling anew.

Somehow, the sight of Raina's hand, shaking with weakness, pierced Teague to his very soul. For all her exasperating qualities when she was well, he found he much preferred her that way. Whole and healthy, he could view her as an adversary to be overcome. Weak and helpless, she stirred in him surprising emotions of compassion and protectiveness—emotions he had no right to feel.

"How . . . bad . . . is it?"

For an instant, he was confused by her query. Then Teague realized she meant her condition. He sighed and shook his head. "I don't know, femina. You tell me."

She plucked at her tunic, attempting to open the neckline further. "Hot . . . I feel so hot. Like my insides are burning up."

"Would you like me to help you undress? I could cover you with a light sheet for modesty."

"No!" Raina shoved to her elbows, lingered there a moment, then fell back in exhaustion. "I'll . . . I'll do it myself."

"Suit yourself," he said, inexplicably relieved that she hadn't taken him up on his impulsive offer. He stared down at her for a long moment. "Anything else?" Teague asked. "If not, I'll go for the water."

"No," she mumbled, already fumbling with the fastenings of her sleeves. "Just give me a few minutes of privacy before . . . before you return."

Teague nodded. "As you wish." He turned and left the room.

He fetched a carafe and cup from the galley, then filled the carafe half-full with water from the spigot near the sink. From it, he poured himself a cupful and downed its contents, then set the cup over the mouth of the carafe to cover it. The rest would be Raina's, until she finished it. In her condition, she would need far more water than he.

The unexpected sound of a thud and soft cry jerked his head around. The carafe in his hand, Teague raced out of the galley and down the corridor to the sleeping chamber. Raina, bare from the waist up, sprawled face-down on the floor.

His heart in his throat, Teague paused in the doorway. If he came to her aid, he must touch her bare flesh, see her nakedness. Even the thought set his blood to pulsing wildly through his veins—and his sex to fill and harden. He bit back an anguished curse. There was no help for it. She could do little more than lie there, moaning softly.

He stepped in, placed the carafe on an inset wall shelf, then opened the cabinet and took out a sheet. Kneeling, he laid the thin cloth over her, then gathered her up into it and his arms. She must not have heard his entrance for, when the sheet touched her and she felt herself picked up, she gasped.

"Hush, femina," he crooned. "I mean no offense to you. I but wish to help you back to bed."

She turned, grimacing as her tender flesh rubbed against the cloth and the firm support of his arms. "I . . . tried to remove my breeches . . . and fell out of bed." She managed a weak smile. "I sound like a helpless old woman, don't I?"

"No, you don't," Teague rasped, unaccountably touched by her courage. "You've suffered a grave trauma to your body. It'll take time for you to heal."

"Ever been nursemaid to a woman before, Tremayne?"

He flushed. "No, but it cannot be much different than caring for a male."

"And you've nursed a fair number of males, then, have you?" She eyed him closely.

"No, not many," Teague admitted. By the five moons, he thought, why did she have to stare at him in such a way? It was bad enough she lay in his arms, so soft, so close, so desirable . . .

With a start, he realized he was standing in the middle of the sleeping chamber, still holding Raina when he could have put her back in bed minutes ago. He swallowed hard, took the two steps to the edge of the bunk, and sat, laying her down. The sheet had fallen back, exposing one silky shoulder and her upper chest. Teague quickly flipped the cloth up to cover her.

"Do you still want your breeches off?" he asked, forcing the question past a strangely dry throat.

Raina glanced down, then nodded. "Yes, of course."

He motioned to the sheet covering her. "With your permission, I could tug the breeches off if you can manage to get them down past your hips. The sheet would maintain your decency."

She considered that for a moment. "It seems the best course." Reaching beneath the sheet, she began to pull at her breeches. After a few minutes of near futile struggle, Raina fell back on the bed, exhausted. "I'm sorry. I can't seem to manage . . ."

Teague dragged in a deep breath, then gingerly grasped hold of the lower legs of her breeches and pulled. She was able to offer little assistance but, bit by bit, he managed to tug her breeches down. Despite his care, there was no way to avoid occasional contact with her skin.

Her skin . . . as smooth and silken as he'd imagined it would be in those moments when his overstimulated imagination had pierced his iron self-discipline and he'd thought, however briefly, of her. The touch of that skin, warm with fever, vibrant with life, sent an astounding sense of recognition shuddering through him, a recognition of his maleness and her femininity, of the need to join with her, to make her his in the most primal way.

Fire seared through him. Teague found he couldn't speak. His body flushed hot, then cold, then hot again. And through it all, his sex grew harder, throbbed, ached.

With a fierce tug, Teague wrenched the breeches free

of Raina's legs and flung them aside. His breath came hard and fast. His head lowered as he fought to regain control. His long hair tumbled down into his face. For once, he was thankful for its shielding cover.

"What . . . what's wrong?" Raina whispered, puzzlement threading her voice. "What have I done—?"

At her strangled cry, Teague's head jerked up. Her horrified gaze was riveted on his lap, wherein the hard evidence of his desire strained against his breeches. He flushed even hotter. "I-I'm sorry. I didn't mean—"

"Get out!" Raina cried, levering to her elbows and scooting away. "I should've known you'd be like all the rest—just another sordid, lecherous male! Get out of here before I—"

With a frustrated groan, she fell back, panting from her sudden exertion. She turned her face to the wall, refusing to look at him. "Just get out, will you?" she whispered.

Teague shoved unsteadily to his feet and stood there, shamed beyond belief at his carnal desires. He glanced down at himself, at the erection, huge and straining and so totally foreign, that remained even now. Nausea filled him. Self-loathing.

"It's not what you think," he rasped hoarsely. "It's just the . . . the natural attraction . . ." His voice faded in frustration. He shot one more beseeching glance at Raina, but she'd rolled onto her side, huddling against the wall, shutting him out. Teague turned and staggered from the room, utterly and totally devastated.

Seven

For a long while, Teague leaned against the wall outside the sleeping chamber, dragging in deep, unsteady breaths. He couldn't go back in and face her just now, though he knew she'd soon need pain meds. He doubted she wished to see him, either.

Straightening, Teague turned and headed outside. A few minutes more or less wouldn't matter, and he desperately needed a more logical perspective on the matter. Funny, he thought, as he strode down the corridor and through the cockpit to the main hatch door, how quickly he was coming to value the Volan's companionship, as strange a relationship as it might be. He smiled and shook his head. He must be starved for a sympathetic ear, or just be growing a bit odd after all these cycles.

A blast of oppressively hot air struck him as he exited the ship. Before him, rising from the desert floor, undulated shimmering waves of heat. Teague shoved a hand through his hair, brushing it back from his face. If it weren't for Raina's presence, he'd have been tempted to strip down to his loincloth.

With a weary sigh, he lowered himself upon a cargo box he'd brought out to use as a makeshift seat. He tugged off his boots and set them aside.

"Problems with the femina?" Rand casually—too casually—asked.

"Yes. Does that surprise you?"

"As a matter of fact, no, it doesn't." The Volan paused. "If I may be so bold to ask, what happened this time?"

Teague leaned back against the shaded side of the ship. "She fell out of bed trying to undress herself. When I helped her finish her . . . er . . . disrobing, I found myself unexpectedly . . . stimulated."

"This grows intriguing. What happened then?"

Teague shot the Volan a narrow look. "She didn't take too kindly to that, of course. Would you have expected any other reaction from Raina?"

"No. And how did you feel about that?" Rand's question was as carefully tempered as his voice.

Teague could feel the flush rise, once again, to his face. "She was quite justified in her response. My behavior was dishonorable and shameful." He lowered his head and burrowed his bare toes into the sand. It was warm and dry, no matter how deeply he dug.

"Dishonorable and shameful?" Rand repeated, puzzled. "What? Your natural response to a woman, I've been told by Teran, is quite beautiful. I may not be well versed in humanoid mating practices, but when I was last in a male body, I, too, felt some stirrings toward a female. I can only imagine how much more powerful and consuming it must be for your species."

"You don't understand." Teague glanced up. "I'm a monk, vowed to shun such desires. And I thought I had, until I met Raina." He shot the Volan an anguished look. "But now I find not only do I have these . . . these feelings, but I can't even control my body's responses."

He slammed down his fist on his thigh. "Curse it all! I thought I was strong enough to control them."

"So don't control them. What can be wrong in following your natural impulses?"

"Don't control—" Teague paused, then rolled his eyes and shook his head in exasperation. "You seem to have missed one minor point here. I'm a monk vowed to chastity. I don't want a mate and neither, it seems, does Raina."

"Correct me if I err here, but don't life matings frequently begin in this way?"

"I don't want a life mating," Teague gritted. "I like my life as it is."

"Well, be that as it may, it certainly appears your body does."

There was no convincing Rand to the contrary, it seemed. Teague rose. He might as well go back and confront Raina. It couldn't be much worse than what he was now facing.

"My body isn't being consulted in this," he ground out. "I make my decisions based on logic, not emotions or physical cravings. I'm a monk of Exsul and intend always to remain one. My life is consecrated to the service of my Order and the Imperium, not to my own whims or desires. Now, if you don't mind, I need to get back to the femina."

"And what if you respond to her again?" Rand called after him, as he turned and strode away. "Will you add that guilt to all the other burdens you already bear? I say instead, don't learn to despise *that* part of yourself as well, my friend."

Teague climbed into the ship, stalked back through the cockpit, and down the corridor. He drew up, however, when he reached the sleeping chamber's portal. *Don't despise that part of yourself* . . . What had Rand meant by that? he wondered. He didn't despise . . .

Harking back to his reaction to his physical response to Raina, Teague knew that he *had* despised himself. Yet the Brotherhood had never taught that the natural mating urge was sordid or immoral. It had but suggested that it was better if a monk renounced it in order to achieve a higher state of discipline and inner peace. The self-loathing he'd experienced with Raina had been his own.

With a shuddering sigh, Teague placed the palms of his hands against the door and pressed his forehead to it. It was his fear rising to the surface again. It encompassed so much, he now realized. His fear of failing, of unworthiness, of his inherent weakness and inability to remain true to his vows.

His vows . . . Gods, would he fail even in that, after all these cycles, after all the sacrifice and discipline and striving? Would he ultimately fail in everything, then?

Little fool . . . disappointed in you . . .

Like wraiths conjured from the mists of time, memories flooded Teague. Of that day, when he was thirteen and discovered the ancient passage behind the huge tapestry hanging in the royal library. Of how he'd taken his sketch book and box of charcoal styluses and explored the long, torturous, web-strewn tunnel, coming out at last on a hidden opening at the back of the mountain upon which the fortified royal city perched.

Teague, long fascinated with architecture and intricate structures, had added the majestically rocky face of that mountain to his collection of drawings, entitling the sketch "The Tapestry Passage." He was very proud of that particular drawing, and had carried it in his dark green domare-hide folder with the rest of his finest artistic endeavors. Carried it until the day his father, the king, had found him on the forward ramparts, sketching the army of Malam Vorax as he'd laid siege to the fortress—and the throne.

In a fit of anger and frustration, no doubt exacerbated by the stresses of the long siege, his father had knocked Teague's portfolio to the parapet's stone floor. "You sit here like some pampered child," he'd raged, "while around you your people suffer and die to protect your birthright. Gods, what did I ever do to deserve a son like you? You puling little fool! I'm so disappointed in you!"

Shamed to the marrow of his bones, Teague had done little more than sit there mutely, as several of his drawings, caught on a freshened breeze, had floated up into the air and over the wall. The sheets of paper had soared across the land, gently dropping until they disappeared far below. His father had stormed away then, leaving Teague to gather what was left of his sketches and stuff them back into his folder.

After that day, he'd never drawn again.

Even now, standing in the corridor outside the sleeping chamber, Teague fought the old pain, struggling to deal with wounds that had been wrought at one of the most vulnerable, traumatic times of his life. If only his father had lived to see him now. Now, as tall and powerfully built as his father had been. Now, a warrior monk and fifth-degree Grandmaster. Perhaps now, his father would've at last been proud, would've understood.

If only his father had lived.

But there was nothing more that could be done for that, either. Teague pushed off from the wall and straightened, dropping his hands back to his side. Time for self-pity was a luxury he lacked today.

Raina lay inside, most likely in pain. He must enter, swallow his pride, and beg her forgiveness for what had happened earlier, then withdraw once again behind that monkish, impenetrable facade that had always served him so well. The mission was what mattered, not their personal issues. And especially not ones of a more sexual nature.

The portal swung open at his command. Teague stepped inside.

At the sound of his bare footsteps, slapping against the metal floor, Raina turned. Earlier, she'd adjusted the ceiling light to full intensity. Now, in the glare, she had to squint to see his face.

"What do you want?" she snarled. "Come back for more depraved titillation, have you?"

The monk's mouth went tight. He flushed. "I came back for two reasons. First, to apologize. Second, to see to your needs." He took two steps closer. "Are you in pain, femina?"

She was, but Raina was damned if she'd admit it to him. It'd been bad enough that he'd become so aroused by her seminudity. But it was intolerable that the blatant evidence of that arousal had excited her as well.

Gods, she didn't know how she'd react to him anymore! And Raina didn't like that. Men were the enemy. They must always remain that way.

"You came in here to apologize," she said, deciding it safest to divert the subject back to him. "Are you still of a mind to do so, or not?"

Teague heaved a deep sigh. "I'm sorry if my physical reaction to helping you undress seemed rather, er, prurient. I didn't mean it as such. It's just that I have no experience in such . . . things . . . and I just . . ." His voice faded and he averted his gaze.

"Just what, Tremayne?" A dark flush spread up his neck and face. Interested in spite of herself, Raina shoved upright in bed and propped herself against the wall.

He didn't answer immediately, finding sudden interest in a scattering of sand that had matted to the hairs of his forearm. Raina's eyes followed as his long, tapered fingers brushed lightly at the sand, sending it showering to the floor in a flurry of glittering granules.

Her breath caught in her throat. His skin was so tan, the dense hairs on his forearms glinted gold in contrast. Her gaze followed as he pulled his hand away. She watched it slide across the rippling ridges of his abdomen to drop at his side. Then her glance returned to his torso.

His chest was solid, bulging with muscle, his skin smooth, his nipples broad and flat. The exotic tattoos seemed to gain a life of their own as he moved, the mythical birds leaping out when he flexed his arms in any way, the huge claws across his pectorals appearing to curve inward and grasp. Symbols of power and battle engraved on living flesh, they fascinated Raina in a way no mere painting could. She wanted to reach out, to touch them, to run her—

With a start, she realized that the monk was no longer looking down, but was now staring straight at her. Raina swallowed hard, cursing the brightness of the room that hid nothing. She grasped at the first thought that entered her mind. "Your tattoos. Did they hurt . . . when they pricked you, I mean?"

Puzzlement darkened his eyes. "My tattoos?" he mumbled. "Well, yes, I suppose they did. But the honor of the marking was well worth the temporary pain."

Raina gazed up at him for a long moment. When he said nothing more, she forced the conversation back to more neutral grounds. "I accept your apology, Tremayne."

"That's it?" he asked, surprise in his voice. "I never finished telling you—"

"And what good would it serve, save perhaps to embroil us in yet another argument?"

Raina didn't think she could bear it if he claimed even a momentary sexual attraction or passing stimulation when he touched her. Combined with his awkward, embarrassed response earlier when he'd tried to explain his actions, one thing was perfectly clear. The monk, Teague Tremayne, was both unsullied and untutored when it came to matters of the flesh. And those kind of men could be the most dangerous when their lust was finally stirred.

It was her lust, though, startling and unnerving as it was, that truly unsettled her. She despised men. How could she change so suddenly, just because she'd seen him perform some perverse monkish blade ceremony? It made no sense. It wasn't as if they were fated to meet and fall in love, just because they were—

Incendarians! Raina choked back an anguished groan. She'd forgotten about her people's exclusive mating urges. Urges and potency they were said to experience exclusively with their own kind. She was drawn to the monk because he was Incendarian!

Relief made her feel almost giddy. That was all it was, a long-denied surge of primal response. All she had to do was ride it out and, sooner or later, it would fade back to a more controllable level. A level Raina felt confident she could manage until she and Tremayne finally parted company.

"You are right, of course," the monk said. "Further explanations would serve no purpose. Better that I con-

cern myself with giving you something for the pain and
an ointment for your burnt flesh."

Her pain. She'd forgotten about it in the intensity of
the past few moments. And her skin did burn.

Gratitude for his consideration filled her. Then Raina
reminded herself that the mission's success could well
hinge on her rapid recovery. That was Tremayne's motive in the offer, and none other.

She nodded, the old cynicism snuffing out the strange
new wave of budding comradeship. "Yes, something for
the pain would be nice. I, however, will apply the ointment."

The faintest glimmer of a smile hovered on Teague's
thin, well-curved lips. "A wise plan, femina. A wise
plan indeed."

As he turned to fetch the med kit, Raina could've
sworn she saw relief glimmering in his silver-blue eyes.
Relief that he'd not be required to touch her again. The
same relief that she felt, that *he* wouldn't touch her,
recalling him helping her undress . . . and the sensuous
stroke of his fingers against her flesh.

Despite the drugs and ointments, Raina's illness continued to worsen. She became nauseated; she couldn't
keep any food or liquid down, and soon became dehydrated and feverish. Teague was forced to insert an intravenous line just to keep fluids in her but, despite all
his efforts, Raina didn't get better. He began to despair
for her life.

Though she refused to let him touch her, every time
she fell into a delirium, he sponged her down. Day and
night, Teague worked over Raina. He barely ate or slept,
yet nothing he did seemed to help. She'd be lucid but

weak for hours, then all but unconscious and consumed with fever. Then she would finally waken once again before the cycle began anew.

"You will make yourself ill, too, if you continue this way," Rand stated flatly one evening two days later, as they prepared for bed in the sleeping chamber, Raina once more in a stupor. "I say again. There is little more you can do for the femina. She will either live or die, and meanwhile we sit here, vulnerable and losing valuable time."

"Don't you think I know that?" Teague growled. He swiped a trickle of sweat from his brow. The heat had grown oppressive as the day had waned. Dark, heavy clouds had built on the horizon, threatening rain. He fervently wished it *would* rain, if for nothing else than to replenish their dwindling water supplies.

"Yes, I know you know that," the Volan replied. "But I also think, in the process of fighting to save her, you've lost sight of our true purpose here."

Teague shot him a seething glance. "That again." He brushed a damp lock of hair from his bare shoulder. "Well, I haven't forgotten, despite what you may think. But I cannot leave Raina while she still lives. She sacrificed herself to save us. Or have you conveniently forgotten that?"

"No, I haven't forgotten," Rand calmly said. "But you have to make a decision, my friend."

"Easy enough for you to say," Teague snarled, at the end of his patience. "You can sit there in your little box, totally helpless and useless save for your mind, and force the most odious of decisions on me. Yet in the end, you'll come out of this as untouched as you came into it."

Rand was silent for a long moment. "Do you think

I'm grateful for the fate that keeps me trapped in this box? Think that it frees me of moral obligations and responsibilities? Well, you are wrong, my friend. I *hate* this existence! I yearn for a body, a *real* life. But I cannot have one. Yet though I'm spared the gut-wrenching choices that only you who possess form and substance have to make, I won't turn from what I know to be right. I offer what I can, what I feel to be truth. And I'll continue to do so, whether you like it or not!"

"He's . . . he's right, Tremayne," a weak and weary voice whispered.

Teague wheeled and looked down at the bunk. Raina stared up at him, bleary-eyed, but awake once more.

"I-I thought you were . . . asleep. I didn't mean for you to hear . . ." Frustrated and at a loss for words, Teague's voice faded.

"I know." Raina managed a tremulous smile. "But the Volan is right this time. We came here to complete a mission. The longer you linger here caring for me, the more you endanger not only yourselves, but the success of the mission as well. You must go, Teague. You must leave me."

"No." Teague strode over and sank to one knee beside her bunk. "I won't. I can't."

"Why?" she whispered. "Why do you persist in this, when you know in your heart that the Volan and I are right?"

Teague hesitated, puzzlement furrowing his brow. "Why? I don't know. Perhaps because you were willing to risk your life for me. Perhaps because we're of the same planet. Or perhaps, just perhaps, because you've suffered enough at the hands of men."

She went rigid. The old pride and panic—that anyone should guess her shameful secret—flooded her. "You know nothing—*nothing*—of what I've suffered. And it doesn't matter anyway. It's my burden to bear, not yours."

The monk leaned back with a sigh. "No, I don't know what happened to you, but I sense it was horrible. Your hatred of men . . . well, it had to arise from some terrible betrayal. And I won't be party to adding to that betrayal." A concerned, considering look flared in his eyes. "Did some man rape you, Raina? Is that what happened?"

Horror, then fury, shuddered through her. How *could* he know? How dared he even ask? "And why should it matter, one way or another?" she snapped. "What happened to me is my own affair." Her mouth tightened and a grim look burned in her eyes. "I don't pry into your sordid, secret past, do I?"

Teague went very still. "No, you don't."

"Then let it be, Tremayne. The issue here isn't me, it's the mission."

"She's right, of course."

His anger rising, Teague turned toward Rand's pack. "Keep out of this, Volan. This is between Raina and me."

"Ah, so it's like that, is it? I'm permitted to speak only when I don't contradict you?"

Teague took a threatening step toward Rand, his fists clenched, before he realized the absurdity of his actions. What had he thought to do? Attack a box? He exhaled a deep breath and turned back to Raina. A tiny smile lifted the corners of her mouth.

"It doesn't matter what either of you says." He forced himself to continue in a more modulated tone, once again in control. "My mind is made. I'll do what I think is right in this matter."

Raina stared up at him. They locked gazes. As he watched, all the anger, all the wary defensiveness, all the antagonism faded from her eyes. Confusion crept in, and fear. Then she shuttered her gaze.

"Fine," she said at last. "Suit yourself. But know this as well: if the situations were reversed, I'd leave you if you threatened the mission. Remember that, Tremayne, in case that day ever comes."

Her terse admission startled him. He would give her *his* loyalty, but she would not give hers? Yet she'd risked her life for him. It made no sense, but Teague wisely decided not to delve further.

He smiled. "I'll remember, femina." He rose to his feet. "Now, go to sleep. You'll need all the rest you can get if you're soon to be back to your old vigor."

She glared up at him but said not another word. He checked her intravenous infusion one last time, then dimmed the light and walked over to his pallet on the floor. Lying down, Teague pillowed his head beneath his hands, pondering Raina's words and his strange response to her.

Thunder boomed overhead; rain pounded against the ship's metal shell. Teague jerked awake and lay in the dark, momentarily disoriented. Where was he? Back in his own bed in his cell in the Monastery of Exsul?

A thrashing and incoherent mumbling in the bunk above him wrenched him back to reality. Teague levered to one elbow and glanced toward Raina. She tossed and turned, consumed once more in the throes of a fever.

"Don't!" she cried. "Don't do it! I-I don't want you. Get away from me!"

For an instant, he imagined she was talking to him.

Gods, did she loathe him so deeply that it even permeated her dreams? Just because once he had inadvertently revealed his desire?

"Ah, gods," she breathed, her hands lifting before her in a protective motion. "I don't want to life mate, Malam. Get away. Ah, get away from me!"

Teague froze. *Malam?* Did she speak of Malam Vorax? Surely not. It would be too much of a coincidence that both their lives had crossed paths with that depraved and evil man's.

"No!" Raina screamed, arching from the bed. "Get off me. *No! No! No!*"

Teague shoved to his knees beside the bunk. "Raina? Femina?" He made a move to stroke back the hair from her sweat-drenched forehead, hesitated, then pulled away. She moaned and threw her head to and fro, but didn't open her eyes.

Wetting a cloth from the bowl of water he kept on the floor by her bed, Teague pressed it to her forehead. She was burning with fever. He jerked back. "Gods, Raina!"

He leaped to his feet, strode over to the light, and turned it up. Her intravenous line had run dry. It didn't matter; they were out of the special sterile fluid anyway. Teague quickly discontinued the line and gathered her up into his arms.

He hefted her close to him, clutching her sheet-swathed body against his bare chest. She was so hot. He must get her outside, into the rain, and cool her.

Triggering the door panel to open, Teague strode out into the corridor and through the cockpit. Raina began to writhe in his arms. Her hands crept up and around his neck, her nails clenching, scoring his flesh.

"Let me go," she whimpered. "Don't hurt me . . . *please,* don't hurt me . . ."

At her plaintive entreaty, memories flooded Teague, of a night etched in his soul, of the crude and perverted tortures Malam Vorax had ordered inflicted upon him. And now, to his utter dismay, he must relive it again, only this time through Raina's memories, memories so horribly vivid that they pierced even the roiling mists of her feverish mind.

The main hatch slid open at his command. A gust of chill, damp air surged in. Rain clattered on the attached tarp and ship, hard little needles of frigid moisture.

Teague inhaled a fortifying breath and stepped outside. A few long strides and he stood in the rain. The wind, free of any further encumbrances, whirled around him, battering him, soaking him to the skin in but a few seconds. The thin sheet wrapped about Raina became drenched, clinging to her, molding to her every curve. She began to shiver.

"Cold, so cold," she moaned. "Don't put me in that cold, dark, horrible hole. Please, Malam. Please . . ."

A shudder coursed through Teague. That horrible hole . . . the torture caverns of Ksathra. The memories her words stirred! He didn't know if he could bear much more.

He cradled her head to his breast and stroked her tangled red mane. "Hush, sweet femina," he soothed, frantically searching for the right words to put an end to her fever-induced nightmares. He groped for something, anything, to say, uttering the first declaration that entered his mind.

"It's over now and you're safe. I won't let anything happen to you."

"Don't leave me."

She stirred restlessly against him. A soft breast and chill-hardened nipple brushed his chest. Teague choked back an anguished groan. By the five moons, first she stirred his heart with her terrible revelation, and then she reawakened his body—again. He didn't know how much more he could take.

The rain poured from the sky. The wind howled. The night suddenly grew black as the depths of perdition. Standing there on the sodden desert sand, Teague closed his eyes and fervently, desperately, began to recite a series of soul-easing litanies. *A cool head . . . a heart calm and gentle . . .*

Please, please, help me. Help me to be what I must be . . . His fervid prayers gradually transformed to despairing pleas. *Give me strength where I have none. Please . . . before it's too late.*

Yet still the peace wouldn't come. The frustration, the hunger, the searing need remained. Desolation swamped him. After all these cycles, he didn't even have the support of his monastic beliefs. What had happened? And why? Gods, what would become of him now?

With an agonized groan, Teague sank to his knees on the saturated land. Water sloshed up around him; sand splattered his breeches. The wind, swirling about with frigid blasts, chilled him to the marrow of his bones. But it was the looming blackness, fetid and suffocating, that commanded his panic-stricken attention.

He couldn't catch his breath. He was dying. Dying. From his smothering, relentless, all-consuming fear.

It had defeated him at last.

"Gods," he whispered. "I can't take anymore. I just . . . can't take . . . any more."

"Hush," Raina's voice, weak but suddenly coherent, rose above the crazed tumult of the storm. "I'm here. You're safe. I won't let anything happen to you."

Teague's eyes snapped open. He glanced down. Raina

gazed up at him, her striking green eyes clear and lucid
once more.

Embarrassment, then shame flooded Teague. He hadn't
meant for her to see him in his fear and defeat. Already,
Raina held a frightening power over him. He didn't dare
surrender any more. Not if he wished to remain the man
he had been.

He swallowed hard, then forced a wan smile. "Your
fever—it seems to have abated." Awkwardly, on legs still
rubbery from the aftermath of his terror, Teague climbed
to his feet. But stand he did, to prevail against the terror
one time more. There was triumph enough in that.

She shifted slightly in his arms and nodded. "Yes, so
it has." Water spattered her face, trickled into her eyes.
Raina released her grip about Teague's neck and wiped
her face. With the action, she inadvertently nudged her
sheet down, exposing a breast. As one, their gazes lowered to the ivory-hued mound of flesh.

Teague's glance lifted to hers. This time, if only for
a fleeting moment in the midst of a storm, there was
no fear, no anger, no outrage in Raina's eyes. Calm acceptance and trust burned there instead.

She would regret it, rage at him again on the morrow
in her old inimitable way, but it didn't matter. Something
had changed irrevocably between them this night. The
realization, frightening as it was, nearly sent him back
to his knees.

He reached up and, with one hand, awkwardly flipped
the sheet over to cover her. "It grows cold out here,"
Teague rasped thickly. "It's past time we went back inside."

"Yes," was her simple, heartfelt reply.

Eight

"Er, may I ask you something?" Raina said the next morning, as Teague rolled up his bedding and stuffed it beneath the bunk.

She levered to one elbow, feeling better than she had in days. The fever seemed finally to have run its course. Her skin was healing. Her appetite had returned—with a vengeance. She would live and, because she would live, there were now some unresolved issues between them. Issues they would *have* to resolve.

The monk lifted a wary pair of silver-blue eyes to hers. "What exactly did you wish to know?"

After last night, she knew he was as uncomfortable with her as she was with him. Last night, their reluctant alliance had reached a crossroads. How they approached this day, and the ensuing days, would determine the future course of their relationship. Whatever that relationship was.

Raina approached that particular issue with great care and even greater hesitation. But she couldn't ignore the facts any longer. She owed Teague Tremayne her life. He could have, *should* have, left her and gone on with the mission. But he hadn't.

He'd also, in the course of the past days, learned more than she'd ever dare let anyone—save Marissa—know.

That realization angered her. Exactly how much she'd revealed in her delirium Raina now wished to discern.

Though she doubted the monk was the kind to use it against her, she had to know what he knew. His special knowledge of her put her at a disadvantage. What she'd inadvertently revealed she couldn't retract, but she could protect herself against it.

Raina's glance strayed to Rand's pack in the corner. "Is he able to hear what we say?"

"His communications device isn't turned off, if that's what you're asking."

"I'd prefer," she said, her gaze locking once more with his, "if it was. What I have to say to you is private."

Teague shrugged. "As you wish." He rose, walked over to the pack, found the audio switch, and flipped it off. Then, like a man going to his execution, he returned to the bunk.

As she gazed up at him, a sudden realization struck Raina. *He's as unsure and as unwilling as I to broach the subject of last night.* She hardened herself to that knowledge. For her sake, at least, they must talk.

She scooted over, then indicated a spot on the edge of the bed. "Sit, if you will. It's difficult conversing with a man towering over you."

"Indeed?" A faint smile quirked his mouth. "Don't care for the psychological disadvantage it puts you in, do you?"

Raina gave a disparaging snort and rolled her eyes. "That, and it puts a crick in my neck. Now sit, Tremayne."

He did as she'd asked. The bunk creaked, then sagged under his greater weight. Raina experienced a momentary surge of panic at his nearness, at his hip touching her thigh, then firmly tamped it down. *She* had invited him into such close proximity. It hadn't been of his own choosing.

In the coolness of the early morn, he'd donned his tunic over his breeches, though he'd neglected to close the deep neckline. As he sat there, expectantly awaiting her next words, his scent, of damp clothes and man, filled her. She caught a glimpse of the swell of his chest and the outline of the tattooed claws on his bulging pectorals. No matter how many times she saw it, the ritualistic markings never failed to send a tiny shiver of excitement coursing through her.

Raina shook her unnerving response aside as quickly as it struck her. She needed to discover how much he knew of her, not dwell on their undeniable and rising physical attraction. That was another problem in itself, and best not addressed. To do so would force the problem out into the open, perhaps even compel them to face and deal with it. And Raina knew she couldn't do that, at least not yet.

"I said . . . certain things . . . while I was ill," she made herself begin. Her glance slid away, careening into the muscled expanse of his thigh. The leg rippled with his slightest shift in position. Her mouth went dry, but she couldn't find the courage to meet his gaze. Curse this damned attraction, she thought.

"Yes, you did," Teague agreed carefully. "But they were the usual ravings of a fever-muddled mind. I thought little of them."

He was hiding something, Raina thought. But what?

She forced her gaze back up to his. "How much did I tell you about my past, and what happened to me when I was last on Incendra?"

His nostrils flared, his eyes widened but, aside from

that the monk's expression didn't change. "I told you. You made little sense. I paid no heed to what you said."

"And I say you lie, Tremayne." Even more on edge than before, Raina eased up straighter in bed. "If you think to spare me by pretending not to possess a knowledge you have, think again. I'd rather know the truth than wonder."

His mouth went grim. He looked away. "I'd have indeed spared you. You are proud, Raina. I am aware you'd not like for me . . . to know."

"Know what? Tell me, Tremayne."

Teague turned, subjecting her to a cool, direct look. "That a man named Malam wanted to life-mate with you, and when you rejected him, he raped you."

She could feel the blood draining from her face. Gods, he *did* know, at least part of it. Her worst fears had come true. Raina dragged in a deep breath. "You must have misunderstood. It . . . it didn't happen that way at all."

He frowned. "You don't have to lie to me, either, femina. I don't think less of you for what happened."

"And do you think I care, one way or another, what you think of me?" She leaned forward, her anger flaring. "You . . . you insufferable, self-righteous holy man!"

Puzzlement furrowed his brow. "Insufferable? Self-righteous? Because I'm sorry about what happened to you?"

"I don't want or need your pity, Tremayne!"

The monk considered that for a moment. "No, I don't suppose you do. But I'm sorry nonetheless. No female deserves such treatment at the hands of a male."

"He'll pay. You can be certain of that." *As will my father,* she silently added.

There was something, perhaps the hard conviction underlying her simply spoken words, that appeared to give the monk pause. "What do you mean to do?" he demanded suspiciously. "We're on a mission to retrieve the Incendarian stone, not to carry out some vendetta."

"I'm well aware of what our primary purpose here is," Raina gritted, his barely veiled warning setting her nerves on edge. "But once it's completed, well, we'll just have to see how things go then."

"This Malam," Teague said, suddenly seeming to change tack. "Is he perhaps the usurper, Malam Vorax?"

"What if he is? What concern is it of yours?"

Teague gave a disbelieving laugh. "What concern? You talk of going up against the most powerful man on the planet, then have the audacity to ask what concern it is of mine? Think again, femina. We're partners now. What one does affects the other."

"No." She vehemently shook her head. "We're partners for this mission, and that's all. You'll never command or control me, no matter what debt I now owe you for my life. And when this is all over, *if* we survive, we'll once more go our separate ways. Won't we, Tremayne?"

He shoved to his feet and stared down at her for the longest time, anger, frustration, then confusion flashing through his eyes. Finally, a look of calm—monkish calm—settled over his face. "You know the answer to that as well as I, femina." With that, he turned on his heel and left the room.

Raina stared at the open door Teague had left in his wake, her own emotions a confusing, upsetting jumble. *Did* she know the answer? she thought, suddenly awash in a storm-tossed sea of apprehension like none she'd ever experienced. And did he, when all the subterfuge was over and the games they played with each other were done?

Those were indeed the yet unanswered questions. In the meantime, there *was* one thing she was certain of. Despite his now familiar and predictable retreat behind his monastic facade, she had seen the truth as surely as he. The monk hadn't been any more certain of the answers than she.

They set out across the Ar Rimal four days later, already a week behind schedule but, thanks to the heavy rains, at least their water supplies were fully replenished. Though Raina insisted she was ready for the journey, both Teague and Rand had their doubts. They finally agreed to her demands, with the proviso that the first day's travel be short, and only half the distance they hoped to travel each day.

The terrain was bleak, the sand little more than a fine gravel that lay in wind-layered ripples. Steep-sided gullies gouged deep tracks where the rainstorm runoff had flowed across the parched land. A few scraggly glasswort bushes grew at wide intervals to maximize their absorption of water, the windblown sand collecting around their bases.

From time to time they passed grotesque rock formations rising from the desert floor, wide and capped at the tops, narrow at the base from the shearing effects of the wind that bounced along most times only a meter or so from the ground. A few desert birds nested high in the rock crevices. Small rodents scurried hither and yon from holes carved out at the bases. Once they saw a huge, long-fanged sand cat, its small, slender ears tipped with dark tufts, staring down at them from its rocky perch high overhead.

Even from the relatively safe distance of fifty meters away, Raina couldn't help a small shudder. Tales of the Incendarian sand cat had filled her growing years, as it had all children living in or near the vast Ar Rimal desert. No beast was more vicious or a more lethal hunter, taking most victims unawares and swiftly and efficiently slashing them to death with only a few swipes of its long, curved claws. Though both she and Teague carried stunners and blasters, Raina still felt strangely vulnerable beneath the animal's predatory stare as they skirted its vantage point and continued their trek across the desert.

The first day passed uneventfully, the blowing sand and oppressive heat the main discomforts. Yet even with the slower pace Teague had insisted they set to spare her, as the hours passed and the sun began to dip from its zenith, Raina found herself longing for the end of the day's journey. She gazed off in the distance, gauging what stand of rocks might suit them best for a campsite. As she did, a fresh flurry of sand, heading straight toward them, caught her eye.

She stared at the strange cloud of dust, attempting to ascertain if it were but another wind devil or not. There was something about it, however, that didn't appear—

Raina grabbed Teague's arm, jerking him to a halt.

He turned a sand- and sweat-coated face to her. He wore the traditional desert garb of long white tunic over his boots and breeches, sleeveless brown cloak, and distinctive headcloth wound about his head and face and tucked up so that only the upper half of his face showed. Despite the protective garb, however, it was evident that

he, too, was having difficulty readapting to the sweltering heat.

"What is it, Raina?" Teague asked, struggling to keep
the weary irritation from his voice. "We just took a rest
stop an hour ago. It's too soon for another—"

"Riders, Tremayne," she said, cutting him off. "See,
there on the horizon? There must be four or five, on
equs, and headed straight toward us. What do you suggest we do?"

He frowned, then glanced about him. They'd left the
last set of rock formations an hour ago and were once
more out in the open. "Well, there's nowhere to hide,
is there?" he inquired mildly. "I'd recommend an atti-
tude of friendly caution. If we're truly fortunate, they
may offer us traditional desert hospitality and take us
back to their camp."

His grimy face broke into a grin. "I don't know about
you, but I used to love the sweet mentha tea and the
thin pancakes the desert nomads frequently made for
breakfast."

"Just like a male, to be led to the slaughter by his
stomach," Raina muttered. "I suggest, instead, we keep
our stunners ready and the blasters charged. Just in case
they've other plans for us than the usual desert hospitality."

"A wise precaution," Teague equably agreed. "We've
both been gone many cycles and customs could've
changed in the interim."

They set their stunners, charged their blasters, and
hung them off their shoulders for easy accessibility, just
in case they'd be needed. The group of nomads grew
closer, the pounding of their big, heavy equs' hooves
setting the ground to trembling the nearer they came.

The riders were dressed in desert garb and wore the traditional red and black colors of the Kateb tribe.

Teague and Raina exchanged guarded looks. The Katebs had never been well known for their hospitality, nor for their honesty, preferring to acquire wealth and whatever else they might need through raids and thievery. They were also not averse to murder, if it were necessary to gain their objectives.

"Great, just great," Raina muttered softly. "Of all the twelve tribes, the first one we had to encounter was the Katebs."

The men reined in their mounts in a cloud of dust, making a great show of settling their ample cloaks in place about them and checking the long, curved daggers hanging at their sides.

"Easy, femina," the monk whispered out of the corner of his mouth. "The battle isn't lost yet."

Raina smiled grimly. "Indeed. I hardly think four Katebs are much challenge to us. You *are* current on your warrior skills, aren't you?"

One of the nomads, vaulting down lithely from his big, heavy-bodied equs, cut short further discussion. The man sauntered over, eyed Raina's cloaked form briefly, then turned to Teague.

"I'm Fazir, leader of the Katebs of the Quadir oasis." He made a deprecatory motion toward Raina. "How much for the female?"

"I'm not for sale at any price, you son of a slimy, thieving—"

The monk swiftly and surreptitiously grasped her hand, giving it a sharp, warning squeeze. "What the femina was trying to say," he smoothly interjected, "was that she's not for sale *because* she's already taken."

Fazir glanced disbelievingly from Teague to Raina,

and back. "She's yours? Then why doesn't she maintain the proper respectful distance behind you? And why was she permitted to speak to a stranger?" He shook his head. "No, I don't think she's yours."

"We come from another land, far from Farsala and across the Great Sea. Our customs," Teague smilingly explained, "are somewhat different from yours."

"Across the Great Sea, eh?" The Kateb leader shot a smirking glance at his men. "Then that makes you not of our kind." He turned back to Teague, his hand moving to the dagger hanging at his side. "And requires no hospitality or consideration of your customs *or* your right to the female."

In the next instant, Fazir, dagger drawn, went for Teague. He slashed downward toward the monk's chest even as he leaped. Teague didn't have time to fire the stunner clenched in his hand, nor to swing his blaster into position. Both men fell to the sand, grappling wildly for the dagger.

Fazir's three compatriots jumped down from their equs and slowly fanned out in a half-circle before Raina. She stepped back. They advanced. She swung the blaster up into position.

"Stay back, if you value your filthy, thieving lives," she snarled.

"Now, is that any way to talk to your new masters, sweet one?" The fattest and dirtiest of the three gestured toward the blaster. "Give the pretty stick up now, and we'll promise not to hurt you. Well, not too much, anyway," he said with a lewd chuckle, glancing at his two cronies.

Then, in a lightning-swift move surprising for a man of his size, he flung himself at her. Raina fired, spraying him with a fiery blast. He screamed, then fell.

The other two men leaped at her. She took out one before the other struck her, knocking her to the ground. He grabbed for her throat. She didn't bother to stop him.

An instant later, her Nadrygean dagger was in her hand. A second more, and it sliced across her attacker's throat.

With a gurgle, he fell atop her, his lifeblood spurting from the severed artery in his neck. Raina shoved him aside and rose, searching for Teague and his opponent. Even then, the big monk was climbing to his feet, brushing the sand from his robe. Fazir lay writhing on the ground in death's last throes, his own dagger protruding from his chest.

Teague's eyes widened when he took in Raina's bloodstained clothes. "Are you all right, femina?"

Her mouth quirked wryly and she nodded. "Quite fine, actually. I just wish I wasn't wearing the blood of my enemy. I should stink like a pile of offal in another few hours and with no extra water to spare . . ."

"The Blandira oasis is less than a half day's journey from here. At this time of day I'd wager the Katebs, who aren't known to travel too far from a water source, weren't all that far from their camp *and* water. With the aid of these fine equs," he added, walking over to capture two by their reins, "I think we, too, will now make short work of the trek to the next oasis."

"Good." Raina strode over to take up the reins of one of the equs. "Let's get on with it. Already, I'm beginning to reek."

"A few minutes more, femina. We need to bury these men."

Raina eyed him in surprise. "You'd give men who meant to kill you the respect of a burial? I say, rather, leave them to fry on this desert until the carrion eaters find them."

Teague shrugged. "Do what you wish, but I cannot leave any man without a burial and the appropriate prayers said over his grave." He shed his cloak, rolled up his tunic sleeves, and walked over to stand beside Fazir. The man was finally dead.

With the butt of his blaster, the monk began to hack out a shallow grave in the sand. Raina watched him for a few minutes, then gave a snort of disgust and, taking her own blaster, stalked over to help him.

The campfire illuminated the night, casting a warm, red-gold light over Teague and Raina as they huddled by it for warmth in the rapidly chilling desert. Motes of fire and ash rose on the air, flaring briefly in incandescent glory before dissipating far out in the darkness. Wood sap heated, snapping and popping in sporadic bursts, the only sound of life in the heavy, desert silence.

Supper had been finished several hours before, a simple repast of journey bread, dried meat sticks, and a handful of sweet, succulent palmas fruit that Teague had managed to shake loose from one of the tall, narrow trees growing in abundance around the small oasis. He'd been correct in his supposition that the Katebs hadn't strayed far from the nearest source of water, Raina thought, staring at him through the smoke and shimmering heat of the fire. He'd been right about a lot of things.

They'd worked well together today, she and Teague, fighting the Katebs when his initial attempt to divert the nomads' interest in her had failed. His claim to be her life mate had flowed surprisingly easily from his lips. Surprisingly easily, for a monk.

He sat there, seemingly absorbed in the task of polishing the Kateb dagger he'd appropriated from one of the dead men. Fascinated, Raina watched as he slid the cloth he grasped in his long, strong fingers up and down the gleaming length of the curved blade, his actions so smooth, so sure, so gentle. Would his hands move as expertly over a woman's body . . . *her* body?

More and more frequently of late, since the lingering effects of the radiation sickness had finally left her, Raina thought of Teague. Countless questions filled her mind, of what manner of man he truly was, hidden beneath the protective facade of his monkish demeanor, of why he'd left Incendra and when, and of what had turned him from the life of a normal man to that of a monk.

So many questions, so few answers, and no right to ask, either. It surprised her that she even cared to know. She'd never had any desire to pry into anyone's past before, and certainly no man's.

Yet this strange monk with his tormenting secrets intrigued her. But why? Was she still so confused and needy, after all these cycles, that the first man who tossed her even the smallest crumbs of kindness and concern could turn her head?

She'd almost succumbed to the charm of a man once. Brace Ardane, Marissa's husband, had treated her with respect and kindness from the moment they'd met. He had treated her with courtesy even after she'd tossed him into a cell when he'd brought her dying friend to the fortified city of the Sodalitas. Always, Brace had comported himself with dignity and courage, until even she couldn't help but find him admirable, in both spirit and body.

But he was Marissa's even then. Because of that, Raina had kept her distance with cutting words and a threatening banter all these cycles, and never thought or desired to find another like him. Never. . until she'd met the monk Teague Tremayne.

Raina inwardly winced at the irony of it all. She, who had long ago vowed never to trust or desire a man, now trusted and desired a man she couldn't have. A monk . . . a man who had taken perpetual vows of chastity, whose path must always follow a different course than hers. She should be thankful that once again fate had protected her from herself, from her rare if foolish inconstancies of the heart. As she would continue to do herself, once this mission was over and they parted forever.

"You both seem unusually quiet and pensive tonight," Rand's voice unexpectedly pierced the silence. "I must admit to the anticipation of a slightly more entertaining evening than sitting here listening to the wind blow and the fire burn."

"And since when did we agree to provide your entertainment, Volan?" Raina demanded, irritated by his intrusion into her bittersweet thoughts. "After all that time in that biosphere, you should've long ago adapted to the silence."

"Raina, there's no reason to be cruel." Teague laid down the polishing cloth and the dagger. "I can't imagine any being ever getting accustomed to an existence limited to the confines of a biosphere."

"Fine," she muttered, picking up a twig and twirling it in her fingers in an attempt to avoid meeting his reproachful gaze. "Then let him provide the topic of conversation. I'm fresh out of them at present."

The monk turned to the carrying pack. "Well, Rand? Any suggestions?"

The Volan chuckled. "Quite a few, you can be sure. For starters, though, I'm very interested in learning why you left Incendra."

Teague gave a start, opened his mouth, then clamped it shut.

Raina laughed in disbelief. The Volan had asked one of the exact questions she'd been thinking just a few minutes ago. A question she'd never have asked in a millennium, no matter how badly she'd wished to know the answers. If nothing else, Raina had always respected another's right to his privacy. But now that someone else had asked the question, she found herself leaning forward in expectation, eager to hear Teague Tremayne's reply.

He must have seen the change in her body, must have felt the palpable aura of anticipation filling the air. He glared over at Raina. "Did you set him up to this?"

She reared back in surprise. "What? No, I didn't, though I'll admit to a certain interest in hearing your answer. It's only fair, after all. You know a lot more about me than I wished to share."

"Fair, is it?" Teague considered that for a moment, then shoved a hand through his hair and sighed. "Well, I'm not so certain what fairness has to do with this. My reasons for leaving Incendra, however, are my own. I'll not share the details with anyone."

"Anything you care to reveal will be accepted with the greatest respect and interest," Rand said. "It's past time we began to know each other better."

"And what will you share in return, Volan?" Raina

snapped. "You, who are so full of questions yet reveal so little about yourself?"

"Ask me anything you wish to know. If I have the answers, I'll tell you," he replied. "If you truly *care* to know."

That offer took Raina aback. "Well, I'll be sure and do that, if and when I *am* interested."

A low chuckle drifted over from across the fire. Raina's gaze jerked up, meeting the faintly amused Teague's. "And what's so funny, Tremayne?"

"You've a most amazing way of doing battle," the monk said. "First you threaten and scold. Then, when you finally get what you want, you leap back like some child surprised that she really got what she asked for, and not at all certain what she'll do with it now that she has it."

Raina scowled. She slapped the stick smartly and repeatedly against her leg. "It's not like that at all. You misconstrue my motives."

He shrugged. "Perhaps. I suppose you'll just bear closer study."

"Which was exactly my point to begin with," the Volan interjected triumphantly. "All of us getting to know each other better. Now, tell us what you care to of your story, my friend. I grow impatient."

The monk graced the Volan with a wry smile. Raina had never been so glad for the reprieve his action gave her from his unrelenting stare. What had he meant, that she'd "just bear closer study?" Was he as curious about her as she was about him? Raina shrugged aside that unsettling consideration and its potential implications. She wasn't so sure she wanted to know why the monk might be interested in her.

"Why did I leave Incendra?" Teague began. A pensive, considering expression darkened his eyes, then he lowered them to stare into the fire. "Because I had nothing to keep me here, no home, no family, no name, and no hope. The monks of Exsul took me in, gave me a new home and life and self-concept. I owed them everything in return."

"Even to the sacrifice of your personal freedom?" Raina asked. "I can't see ever owing a debt that would deserve such a sacrifice."

He glanced up, pinning her with a relentless gaze. "And I say we all sacrifice our freedom in some form or another, sooner or later. As long as we consider it well spent, what harm is there in it?"

"None, I suppose," Raina admitted. She began to sketch aimlessly in the sand with her twig. "But when it's a choice made to avoid one's responsibilities, or to flee from oneself, I don't see it as one well spent."

"And what choice did *you* make, all those cycles ago?" Teague asked quietly. "To flee *your* past, perhaps, and never face it?"

Raina's jaw went taut, but she refused to look up. "I don't know what you're talking about."

"Don't you? You blame all men for what one did to you, and vow to live the rest of your life punishing them for the actions of one. In the process, you turn your anger within as well as without, inexorably destroying yourself. And there is nothing—*nothing*—quite so dark or cruel as what we do to ourselves."

"How moral and upright coming from you—you, who always seem to have all the answers!" Raina shoved to her feet. "How glib, how clever you always are, with your monkish platitudes and pronouncements. Well, it won't work this time. You're not going to turn the mistakes of *your* past, *your* feeble reasons for choosing the monastic life to hide behind, against *me*."

She threw down the stick she still clenched in her hand. "Have a very pleasant evening debating this further with the Volan!"

In a spray of sand and righteous indignation, Raina turned and strode away in the direction of the small, spring-fed pool. Teague watched her go, remorse flooding him. He'd been a fool to prod at her so. He didn't know what had possessed him to attack her like that, though he truly believed Raina *had* allowed the anger and bitterness of her rape at the hands of Malam Vorax to twist her perceptions and relationships. Yet it wasn't his right to involve himself into her personal affairs. He wasn't her life mate, after all.

"You touched on a raw nerve there, my friend," the Volan offered, gently piercing the tumult of emotions roiling in Teague's mind. "Was she, perhaps, striking too close to your own doubts and fears?"

Anger rose within him. "Think what you want. You always do anyway."

"You are two of a kind. Did you know that? Both wounded, both fighting as hard as you can not to bleed to death from that wound, yet bleeding nonetheless. Have you ever considered," Rand quietly persisted, "that perhaps you could help heal each other? It seems the way of your kind."

"I need no one's help," Teague growled. "I have my vows to sustain me."

"Vows that sustain but don't cure. The cure, I think, can only come from within oneself. And, sometimes, one cannot do that without the help of one's friends— and lovers."

"Lovers?" Teague gave a disbelieving laugh. "You

grow dangerous, Volan. Now, you'd have me renounce my vows, give up all I've worked so hard to attain, and take a lover."

"If the vows no longer serve, then they're of no further use. Did the femina speak true when she claimed you hide behind them to flee from yourself?"

"You know nothing of me or why I do what I do!"

"No, I don't know the details, it's true. But I can guess, from the little you've shared this night and all the days and nights we talked while the femina was ill, that you've suffered some horrible wounding of the spirit. A wounding you've spent all these cycles attempting to sublimate in a monastic life. And you've done quite well at it, too, haven't you? A fifth-degree Grandmaster with special powers few others possess. Few can ever hope to attain such exalted heights of self-avoidance."

Teague rose. "Your words are hard, Volan, unfair, after all the time we've shared together. And, for all your study of our ways, there's still much you don't understand. Perhaps will never be able to understand."

"True enough," Rand admitted. "But I try. I truly try."

"I know you do." Teague ran his hand through his hair. "I'm weary. Perhaps another time we'll talk more of this, but not tonight."

"Honestly spoken, my friend," the Volan agreed. "But what of the femina? Don't you owe her at least as honest an admission?"

Though he didn't want to acknowledge it, Teague knew Rand was right. He just felt so vulnerable, so unstable right now. To seek Raina out . . .

"You're right, of course." He sighed his reluctant acquiescence. "I do owe her an apology."

With that, he turned on his heel. In a few, quick

strides, Teague had left the circle of light and headed out into the darkness shrouding the oasis. A chill breeze stroked his face. Teague shivered, grateful now for the long tunic and cloak. With the addition of the thick lana-cloth blankets and a well-stoked fire, though, they should sleep warmly this night.

As he walked along, he made a mental note to gather more wood to sustain the fire through the night, just as soon as he made his brief apologies to Raina and returned to the camp. A good night's sleep would renew them all for the hard day of travel ahead. Even with the welcome addition of the equs, the journey was still—

He stopped short, every nerve instantly on edge. Be it an unusual sound or sudden premonition, something had triggered his well-honed warrior's instincts. There was danger close by, out there in the darkness.

A low growl floated by on the breeze; the gamy, distinctive scent of a desert sand cat followed swiftly in its wake. He recognized it at once. All it took was one time, the memory of just one encounter . . .

Then he saw Raina move in the moonlight, slowly inching her way backward. She was about five meters ahead and slightly to his left. Until then, she'd blended so well with the trees that he hadn't seen her. Her dagger was clenched in her hand but, other than that, she was weaponless.

A dagger was little use against a sand cat. And there was little time to make it back to the blasters. Even now, the sand cat loomed from its hiding place in the tree above her, his long fangs bared, snarling in warning. The beast was sure to spring at any moment.

"Raina," Teague called softly. "I'm directly behind you, about five meters back. I want you, on my command, to turn and run to me. Hand me your dagger as you pass, then keep going until you reach camp. Come back as quickly as you can with a blaster. I'm sure you'll know what to do with it."

"And why not run back to camp and return with the blaster yourself, Tremayne?" she tautly shot back. "You're five meters closer than I."

"Because I'm bigger and stronger than you and can hold off the sand cat longer, that's why!" he hissed. "Now, no more of this. The cat will attack while we stand here arguing."

She hesitated an instant longer, then nodded. "Suit yourself, Tremayne. At your command."

He inhaled a deep breath. "Now!"

Raina wheeled and ran, her dagger at her side. From behind her, the sand cat roared, outraged that his prey should take him by surprise. The huge beast leaped from the tree and bounded after her. Teague ran toward her.

As they passed, Raina shoved the dagger into his hand. A quick look, then she was gone, racing for the camp. Teague dug in his heels and lowered himself into a fighting stance.

"Purify me," he solemnly intoned the opening words of the sacred blade ritual. "Open me . . . guide me . . . free me . . ." He dragged in slow, deep breaths, willing his pulse to slacken, his body to relax, to accept, to soar . . . To prepare and protect him from the sand cat's claws . . .

Then the beast was upon him. Teague took the brunt of the weight of the huge animal before falling to strike the ground hard. For an instant, as the cat sank his claws into his chest, he thought the blade ritual had prepared him.

Then the pain came, sharp, shattering, agonizing. He cried out, his roar of bewilderment and despair swallowed in the triumphant scream of the sand cat.

Nine

Her heart thundering in her breast, Raina raced through the palmas trees toward the dim light of the campfire. She ran as fast as she could, knowing, even as she did, that there was little likelihood of making it back to Teague in time. The desert sand cat was just that powerful, just that efficient.

She reached the campsite, snatched up a blaster, then wheeled and raced back. As she did, a cry, swiftly followed by an animalistic scream, filled the air. Teague. Ah, gods, Teague! she thought, the fear and panic twisting her heart into a tight little knot.

Her legs pounded down the hard-packed path, her mind reeling with the sudden, horrific change the night had taken. A few minutes ago, it had been a perfect eve for repose, for contented contemplation of the day past. Now, it was filled with the terrible sounds of battle. A battle wherein a man rendered a fearsome sacrifice . . . just so she might live.

Teague, oh Teague, she thought. *Why? Why?*

Raina found the two, man and cat, rolling in a deadly embrace on the ground. The stench of the beast mingled with the sharp tang of fresh blood. Teague's blood.

She set the blaster mechanism to fire, aimed, and awaited the first opportunity to shoot the cat without killing the monk. It came when Teague, with what must have been a superhuman effort, flung the sand cat off and away from him.

The huge beast immediately gained his footing and, turning, sprang for him once again. In that instant, Raina fired. Fire spewed forth, a sizzling, crackling blast that briefly illuminated the darkness before striking the sand cat fully in the chest.

The animal screamed in agony. He writhed and twisted in the air as he plummeted to the ground. Raina slung the blaster across her chest and ran for Teague. She didn't need to waste time checking if the cat was dead. The blaster was a killing weapon.

The monk lay there, unmoving, drenched in blood. Raina slid to a halt at his head and dropped to her knees. She shoved her hands beneath his back and clasped him by the shoulders. Without even a pause to see if he was conscious, she began dragging him back to where there was light and safety.

"G-gods, Raina," he groaned, as she pulled him along. "Could you try to avoid as many rocks as you c-can? I don't need the rest of my b-body ripped open."

The sound of his voice, weak and pain-laden as it was, heartened Raina. He was still alive. Perhaps there *was* hope.

As they neared camp, the fire threw tongues of undulating light upon them, revealing the horrifying extent of Teague's injuries. Raina bit back a despairing groan. He was covered in blood, his tunic and cloak rent with crimson slashes staining darker and wetter by the second. Gods, how had he survived this long without bleeding to death?

Dragging the monk close to the fire, Raina hurriedly shoved a rolled-up blanket beneath his head, then scrambled over to the pile of packs to retrieve the med kit.

She carried the kit over, dug into it, and retrieved the thin laser cautery.

It was then that she saw her bloodied dagger, still clenched in his fist. Laying the cautery aside, Raina pried the weapon free and tossed it to the ground by his head. Then she turned and, grasping the front of his long tunic, ripped it asunder.

His torso bore countless deep gashes, all oozing blood. She took up the laser cautery, flipped it on, then paused. "This will hurt, but I can't spare the time to give you a narcotic. You could well bleed to death if I don't hurry."

He nodded his acquiescence and managed a weak smile. Raina inhaled a deep breath, then aimed the cautery tip toward his most copiously bleeding wound. With a sizzle, it seared the bleeder shut. Teague gasped, gouged his fingers into the sand, and shuddered.

Raina swung quickly to the next gash, cauterized that one, and moved on. Though it pained her to cause him such torment, she'd not a moment to spare. His life came first, his comfort second.

Teague groaned softly now, his big body jerking beneath her relentless care. Sweat broke out on his face. He bit his lip until it bled.

After a time, she couldn't tell which wounds she'd cauterized and which she hadn't, so profuse was the bleeding from the yet untreated wounds. Rearing back, Raina grabbed for the water bag, twisted the cap open, and poured a generous amount of fluid over Teague's chest. The monk hissed in pain and arched up, his body rigid and taut.

"G-gods, Raina," he moaned. "Wh-what are you doing?"

"Flushing the blood away so I can see what bleeders

are left," she replied tersely. "Hold on. We're almost done."

"You're a s-savage nurse. B-best you remain a warrior."

Though she heard the faint tinge of teasing in his words, she spared him not a glance. Time later to chastise him, if he lived. Time later to ease his pain. But now . . . now all that mattered was saving his life, conserving each and every precious drop of blood he had left.

Finally, blessedly, Teague lost consciousness. Raina spread out a clean blanket, unceremoniously rolled him over, and began to work on his back. The sand cat had been viciously thorough. Hardly any part of his body, save his hands, booted feet, and face, had escaped unscathed.

At long last, she finished with his back and legs. After cleansing the wounds anew with water, Raina slathered a healing ointment on them, laid a clean cloth over his back and each of his legs, then carefully flipped Teague onto his back.

As she worked to cleanse and apply ointment now to his chest and arms, one of their equs whinnied. The other soon followed suit. From out in the darkness, came the answering whinnies of several other equs. Raina went still. The sound of hoofbeats, of squeaking leather and clinking metal, filled the air.

Instinctively, she grabbed up her dagger, brandishing it before her. Then the realization of the futility of the action permeated her mind. The dagger was of no real use to her if the sounds were any indication of the size of the group that approached.

An impulse to grab a blaster and hide in the darkness filled her. One glance at Teague lying there helpless and wounded dispelled that notion. A fierce protectiveness swelled within her. She wouldn't leave him. She'd sooner die fighting at his side.

Quickly, Raina resheathed her dagger beneath her robe, then covered Teague with a clean cloth and a blanket to protect him from the night chill. She threw the last few sticks of wood on the fire, then stood, walked over to where she'd thrown down the blaster in her haste, and picked it up. Making her way back to where Teague lay, Raina sat once more, placing the ready-to-fire weapon across her lap.

"How is the monk?" Rand asked. "From your comments when you returned with him, I could tell there was a battle with some animal and that he was wounded."

"I managed to stop his bleeding," Raina muttered. "The rest will be up to him. In the meantime, we have visitors."

"The equs calling out. They were calling to others."

"Exactly."

"I would help you in any way I can."

She glanced at his carrying pack. "My thanks, but there's little you can do at present. Best you stay silent. Incendarians, for all their exposure to some of the Imperium's advanced technology, most likely haven't had much experience with a talking box. I don't know what effect it would have on them."

"A wise plan."

Men's voices—many of them—rose on the night air. Raina checked Teague one last time. He was still unconscious, and his freshly cauterized wounds looked stable. If they were to die this night, at least he wouldn't suffer. It wasn't much, but it was all the consolation she could find in such a dismal fate.

The equs halted at the edge of the small oasis. The

riders dismounted. There was a brief, low interchange. Then four tall men entered the circle of light cast by the fire.

All were dressed in long, flowing white robes that covered their bodies from their high-collared necks to their booted feet. Over the robes, they wore thick, do-mare-hide belts with long, curved, sheathed daggers shoved beneath them and bright blue sleeveless cloaks that fell to their feet. Their heads were covered by flowing white headcloths, the ends of which they wrapped around their faces.

Typical desert garb and the colors of the Tuaret tribe, Raina thought, gazing up at them—a large, strong tribe known for its fairness and hospitality. Some of the tension eased from her. They most likely wouldn't die this night, after all.

The tallest of the men eyed her, then Teague. "We track some thieving Katebs and find instead a *mirah* and a man who looks," he paused to study Teague more closely, "like he just fought a sand cat."

"Which is exactly what he did," Raina responded dryly, pointedly ignoring his attempt at gallantry in his use of the desert term for a beautiful woman. "If you're looking for the Katebs, they lie buried in the sand about four hours' ride east of here."

The man arched a dark brow. Thanks to the headcloth pulled across his face and the dim light of the fire, Raina could make out little more of the man's features than his amber-colored eyes and bronzed skin.

"Am I to understand that you and your friend encountered them earlier?" he asked, when she failed to elaborate.

She met his sharp, assessing gaze squarely. "Yes. Not that they lived long enough to enjoy our company." She laid the blaster aside, but within easy reach, and began to sort through the contents of the med kit. "Now, if your curiosity has been sufficiently appeased, I really must get back to my friend. The rest of his wounds need tending."

"And do you refuse us the hospitality of your fire?"

Raina froze. The unwritten law of the desert demanded that she not turn away any who asked to share her fire. Though Raina had been born and raised near the royal city of Ksathra, she was well versed in desert customs. The Ar Rimal spanned too great a portion of Farsala not to have had many aspects of its unique heritage permeate all parts of the kingdom. She couldn't, in all good conscience, turn them away.

"You know it's forbidden to deny another the comforts of one's fire." Raina stood and, walking over, gathered up their remaining packs and carried them back to the side of the fire where Teague lay. "You may take your rest there," she said, gesturing to the now cleared area. "Our food supplies are meager, but we will share them if you've—"

"We've adequate supplies of our own," he said impatiently, cutting her off with an imperious wave of his hand. "The water of the oasis and a spot at your fire is all we require."

"Fine." Raina nodded stiffly. "Suit yourself." She sat and began pulling out the medical supplies she needed.

"A moment more, *mirah*."

Raina glanced up, once again wary. "Yes?"

"Are you life-mated to this man?"

"What is it to you, one way or another?"

He shrugged and let the headcloth fall free of his face. Raina gave a start of surprise. His was a face of aggressive virility, with dark, high-bred features, firm and sensually molded lips, and a blade of a nose that had apparently been broken once. It was, she noted, the only flaw in a flawlessly rugged, handsome countenance.

"What is it to me?" he repeated slowly. "Nothing, for I am mated. But most of my men,"—he gestured to the group of fifteen Tuaret warriors beginning to file in behind him—"are without life mates. If you are unmated, I would know it now. You are far too lovely to remained unclaimed."

Anger and indignation flooded Raina. Why, the unbridled arrogance of the man! Yet even in her outrage, she recalled the desert customs well enough to know he could give her over to one of his men and suffer no consequences, if she dared admit she were unmated.

Teague would back her again. She was certain of that, if nothing else. And common sense told her she needed once more to claim what she wasn't—a mated woman.

"Of course he's my life mate," she lied smoothly. "Who else would fight a sand cat to protect me? Why else would I be working so hard now to save his life?"

"Indeed." He walked over and took his place across the fire from her. "And what are you called, *mirah?* I would know whose camp I share."

"My name is Raina."

"And your mate's name?"

"Teague Tremayne."

There was an expectant pause as Raina awaited a return of the courtesy. It wasn't forthcoming. In the eyes of the desert, she was but a woman, after all. Her rights and privileges were few, save those she gained from her mate.

"And your name?" she asked finally, meeting his bold gaze with an equally bold one of her own. "If you would deign to share it with me? In the name of my unconscious mate?"

He smiled thinly. Raina could tell he wasn't particularly pleased with her lack of customary subservience, but she didn't care. It was her fire, curse it all, and her offer of hospitality.

"In the name of your mate, then," the Tuaret leader softly agreed. "I am called Bahir. Bahir Husam al Nur, leader of the Tuarets. Or rather," he added, as a bitter afterthought, "what is left of the tribe, after Malam Vorax declared most of us outlaws."

He watched her as she worked on her mate—if the man lying unconscious beside the fire truly *was* her mate. Despite her words to the contrary, Bahir wasn't so sure the *mirah* was claimed by the man she nursed so solicitously. There was something about her manner, not to mention the look in her eyes whenever she'd spoken to him. It was not the look of a woman who had sworn to be the dutiful, subservient spouse.

She vaguely reminded him, in her demeanor, at least, of his first mate, Cyra. He wondered what tribe this woman claimed, to be so bold, so forthright in her dealings with men. Perhaps she wasn't even of the desert, though she dressed that way.

Suspicion plucked at him. Bahir continued to study her as his men prepared their evening meal, struggling with the tattered remnants of old, time-faded memories. Had he seen her somewhere before? If so, where? Was she, along with her "mate," a spy, sent by Malam Vorax or one of the desert tribes still loyal to him?

The *mirah* definitely bore close watching. There might well be more to her and her comrade's presence here than he had first imagined. If there was, Bahir meant to gain the upper hand as swiftly as possible. He hadn't kept his people alive for the past four cycles by waiting for opportunity to fall into his lap.

He'd no intention of changing his tactics now . . . no intention of ever allowing himself to be betrayed again.

Teague remained unconscious for another hour, long enough for Raina to complete the care and bandaging of his wounds, repack the med supplies in the kit, then furtively study the actions of the Tuarets and their leader. The men seemed as all others, eager to cleanse the grime from their bodies in the pool, then settle down for a tasty meal. Afterward, they sat or lounged about the fire, telling tales, laughing, joking, and covertly watching her.

Their covetous, hungry glances she could handle in the way she'd always done before—by ignoring them. But the vigilant gaze of their leader was much more difficult to discount. Though there was a certain amount of open admiration in his inspection, it was the deeper, almost predatory scrutiny that worried Raina. He didn't trust her. That meant he most likely doubted her claim to a life mating, as well. Exactly what else he suspected, she didn't know, but if it endangered their mission . . .

When she'd heard his name, her first reaction, after surprise, had been a wild surge of hope that she could use him to protect and escort them to the firestorm caves in the Barakah Mountains. He was Cyra, the Bellatorian geophysicist's husband, after all, and was said to roam that area of the Ar Rimal. If he and his men were perhaps headed back in that direction . . .

But if he had other plans for them, or decided to stand in their way, well, they still had the blasters and stunners. So far, neither Bahir nor his men had chosen to ask about or examine the weapons. She doubted they were totally ignorant of the blasters' true function, though. Until Incendra's electromagnetic field had intensified just four cycles ago, the planet had permitted limited contact with the rest of the Imperium. Bahir had met Cyra when she was on a scientific expedition, after all.

But thankfully, desert courtesy precluded taking such liberties as touching what wasn't theirs. The owner was expected to be the first to offer. And Raina didn't have any intention of offering her weapons to them.

In the meantime, though, it was best to pretend to a friendly camaraderie and hope, if the nomads truly were heading in the direction of the Barakah Mountains, that they'd offer to take them along. *If* Teague survived his injuries.

Fleetingly, Raina wondered what the Tuaret leader would do if the monk died. She brushed that unsettling consideration aside almost as swiftly as it had entered her mind. Just as swiftly as she'd brushed aside the notion of giving Bahir Cyra's message.

It could serve as a potential advantage over him in the future. No, until she knew more of this man and his possible plans for them, she'd not share his wife's communication. One problem at a time and—

Teague stirred, moaned softly. His eyes opened. Raina's heart gave a great, joyous leap. She leaned close, her breath so close to his they met and melded.

"We've guests, Tremayne," she whispered. "Have a care what you say."

"Wh-what?" With a painful effort, he turned toward

the fire. His glance locked with that of the Tuaret leader, staring straight at them through the flames. "Wh-who is he?"

Raina shot the man a furtive glance. "His name is Bahir. He's the leader of an outlaw Tuaret tribe." On impulse, she kissed Teague on the cheek.

He gave a small start and looked at her in astonishment. "What was that for?"

"Bahir doesn't believe we are life mates. I but wished to demonstrate my undying affection for you."

Teague's mouth quirked wearily. "I'd wager he's not the only one who doesn't believe it, but my thanks for sharing that with me. You had a reason for this sudden life mating, I assume?"

"Of course. I'm not in the habit of taking monks for husbands. Bahir wanted to give me to one of his men."

"Then I'm especially honored to be of service to you." Teague tried to lever to one elbow and failed. He gasped, then grimaced in pain and fell back.

"Oh, the narcotic!" Raina exclaimed. "I'd forgotten. Would you like an injection? I could give you one for pain, as well as the torpine."

He considered that for a moment, then shook his head. "I'll take the narcotic, but not the torpine. With these nomads here, I don't think it'd be wise to leave you, if only in a healing sleep, for twenty-four hours."

"They seem trustworthy enough," she said, digging in the med kit for the injectors. She palmed the two in her hand so no one could see them. Little purpose was served drawing undue attention to the fact that they possessed unusual and potentially off-planet technology.

"Trustworthy enough as far as respecting the laws of the desert, at any rate," Raina finally continued. "I think I'll be safe enough for the time being, and the torpine should have quite a favorable effect on external wounds like yours."

"No doubt. Give them both to me, then. The sooner I'm healed, the sooner we'll be free of these men." Teague smiled wanly. "Rand. How does he fare?"

"So far, they haven't discovered his presence. I hope to keep it that way as long as possible." Raina paused expectantly. "Ready for the injections?"

"Yes. More than ready."

Still covering the devices, she lowered first one, then the other small disposable air-jet injector to his neck, pushed the activating mechanism, and delivered the medications directly through his skin into the jugular vein. Several seconds passed, then Teague's pain-tautened expression began to ease. A minute later, and he had drifted off to sleep.

Raina threw the injectors back into the med kit. Then, in as casual a manner as she could, she lifted her gaze to scan the men gathered about the fire. Some had already begun to doze where they lay. Others talked while brewing a small, long-handled pot of water to make mentha tea. But the rebel leader remained where he sat, neither dozing nor talking, his piercing gaze fixed on her.

She wondered how much he'd seen, how much he suspected. Did he guess they were in fact not from Farsala, but from Incendra itself? She didn't like the man, Raina decided with firm conviction. He was too arrogant, too domineering, and too clever for comfort. He'd not be easily fooled or manipulated.

Well, formidable adversary that he might be, Raina reassured herself, she'd faced men such as him before and triumphed. She'd do so again; she had to. Teague and Rand depended on her. So did the mission. And she wouldn't fail.

Raina leaned down toward the unconscious Teague, pausing just millimeters from his mouth. She glanced over at Bahir and smiled. At her unspoken challenge, anger flared in the Tuaret's eyes. Triumph swelled in Raina's breast.

It was nothing, however, to the sudden, soaring pleasure and fierce sense of tenderness that swamped her when her lips touched Teague's. Her heart jolted. Her mouth went dry. In spite of herself, Raina jerked back as if burnt.

Bahir smiled, triumph gleaming in his eyes.

Ten

Teague slept through the rest of the night. Only the guard Bahir had set to the first watch remained vigilant, but still it wasn't fear that one of the men would catch her unawares in an attack that kept Raina awake. It was all the thoughts and realizations that continued to bombard her.

The attack of the sand cat, the first frantic efforts to save Teague from bleeding to death, then the arrival of the Tuarets and their unsettling, suspicious leader had been turmoil enough. But when all that was compounded by her burgeoning emotions for the monk, Raina found that her usually unshakable composure teetered on the edge of shattering.

That loss of composure was disconcerting enough. But the hunger, the sheer magnitude of her reaction, when she'd kissed Teague that second time . . . well, it terrified her.

She wanted him, his heart as well as his body, and she didn't know what to do about it. It was foolish, crazy, and surely fated to thrust her life into total chaos and her pride into a shambles. And that was if she were lucky and the monk spurned her. If he didn't . . .

Raina shivered in dread. If he didn't, if they mated . . .

Ah, gods, she thought in an agony of confusion. How could she possibly even consider lying with a man, after the humiliation and pain of the last time? She must be mad. She *was* mad to lie here, thinking of such a thing, wanting it.

Her need for Teague was also a total waste of time, a distraction from what truly mattered—the successful completion of the mission. Only then could she be free to pursue her own objectives, finally to avenge herself. There was no time for the accommodation of some frivolous urgings of the flesh. There never had been before and there certainly wasn't now.

There was no getting past it. She'd just have to maintain a rigid self-discipline until the mission was over. She'd done it before; she could well do it again. What other choice did she really have?

Despite Raina's renewed determination, the night passed fitfully. Dawn found her unrested and on edge. It didn't help when Bahir lost no time confronting her.

"Your mate," he said, squatting before her as Raina sat and shoved the tousled remnants of her braid back in place. "Will he recover or not?"

Her head snapped up. "How am I to know that? He was injured only last night. Besides, what is it to you?"

Bahir's jaw went taut, his eyes hard and flat. "You are singularly impertinent for a woman. I must have a talk with your mate—if he recovers."

"And if he doesn't, you or one of your men will see to my chastisement yourselves," she taunted, realizing even as she did that it was unwise, but wanting to know what he had in store for her. Quite frequently, men admitted more in anger than when calm. "Is that it?"

"Something like that," the Tuaret muttered. "That isn't why I asked you about your mate, though. We'd like to journey on soon, but I won't leave you two here alone. There are more Katebs roaming about. You and your mate didn't kill all of them, you can be sure. After a raid, they tend to move in small groups." He smiled grimly. "They think it makes it harder for their pursuers to catch them. They're wrong, however."

"I'm quite capable of taking care of myself."

"Most certainly." Once again, Bahir eyed her admiringly. "You don't strike me as the helpless type. A *mirah* in desperate need of taming, to be sure, but never helpless. The Katebs, however, have no honor. And you *are* only one person."

"So, what are you offering?" Anticipation fluttered in Raina's breast. "I won't leave Teague."

"And I wouldn't ask you to." He leaned back on his haunches, his gaze careful, considering. "Where were you headed before the sand cat attacked?"

She hesitated but a moment, then seized the opportunity presented her. "To the Barakah Mountains. I have family there." It wasn't really a lie, Raina thought. Her father most likely still lived in the royal city of Ksathra, still the endlessly ingratiating, obedient minion of Malam Vorax. And Ksathra was in the Barakah Mountains. "We've been gone many cycles,"—also not a lie—"and I've a wish to visit my father before he dies."

"We travel in that direction, too, once we've caught and punished the rest of the thieving Katebs. I would offer you the safety of our escort when that task is completed. In the meantime, this oasis is as good a headquarters for our forays to punish the rest of the Katebs." He arched a dark brow. "If, of course, you've no objection to our presence for a few more days?"

Raina gave a wry laugh. "I'd be a fool to object. You offer us both protection while Teague regains his strength *and* safe escort where we intended to travel anyway. In the name of my mate," she added quickly, thinking it politic to make more effort at appeasing his overbearingly masculine need for feminine subservience, "I accept your offer."

"Good." The Tuaret leader stood. "I'm pleased you've the sense to see the wisdom of my plan. You are headstrong and proud, but not an unintelligent woman."

"Careful, Bahir," Raina gritted, struggling with yet another surge of exasperation at his patronizing manner. "Your extravagant praise will turn my head."

"It was most certainly not meant to," he said, frowning. "Such intimacies are your mate's, and only his. It would be unseemly and dishonorable to trifle with another man's possession." With that, Bahir turned and walked away.

She shot a furious look at his retreating back. *I'm no man's possession,* she silently replied, *you arrogant son of a desert viper. Nor will I ever be.*

Yet wasn't that exactly what her overwrought emotions for Teague were leading her to? a tiny voice asked. Wasn't that what desire, what love, did to a woman's heart and mind?

Taken aback, Raina stopped short. True, she'd seen that happen with most women, especially those on Incendra. Especially those mated to men of the desert tribes.

But then there were Marissa and Brace. Brace had never dominated his mate, never tried to, so far as Raina could tell. Her friend wouldn't have put up with it if he had.

Yet he seemed quite content with her, as she was with him. For all purposes, they appeared to have a relationship of equals. The way it should be between a man and a woman.

Her glance lowered to where Teague lay, still held peacefully in the throes of the torpine. What kind of mate would he have been, if things had been different? If he hadn't been a monk, if she hadn't grown into the kind of woman fate had forced her to become? Could they have had a chance at a life and love like Marissa and Brace's?

The equs snorted. One stomped a great cloven hoof. Men's voices, rising in anticipation as they prepared a quick breakfast before setting out on the day's search for Katebs, intruded on her poignant musings.

With a start, Raina recalled herself to the present. Curse it all. Once more she'd allowed herself to slip back into that sweet, lovesick dreaming. Curse Teague for being so brave, so self-sacrificing, so solicitous of her! And, she added, as her gaze swept from his beautiful, strong-featured face down the long, powerful length of his body, so superbly, magnificently made. If only he'd been mean, as so many men were, or at least ugly . . .

But he wasn't, and therein lay the problem. With a deep sigh, Raina took up the water bag and rose. Nothing would be served by mooning after a man she couldn't have and, if she'd a shred of sense, shouldn't want. Better to fill the time with action. Better to do anything but passively sit here and yearn and lust and dream.

The forays the next two days were spent apprehending the rest of the Katebs. After pulling five men to stay behind and guard the oasis each day, Bahir split the rest into two groups. He led one, and a big, bluff, burly Tuaret named Aban ben Farran led the other.

They rode out soon after breakfast and didn't return until sunset. From the extra equs they brought back both days and the look of the booty the animals carried, Raina surmised that the expeditions had been productive. Bahir soon apprised her of just that fact on the eve of the second day—they had "punished" all the raiders and could begin the journey to the Barakah Mountains on the morrow.

Teague woke late that first night, took several swallows of water and a few spoonfuls of broth Raina had concocted from dried meat sticks and seasonings, then promptly fell back asleep. She was heartened, however, by the heightened color in his cheeks and the fact that his wounds hadn't festered. Her quick response in cauterizing, cleansing, and applying the healing ointment must have worked. Now, if only the torpine had truly hastened his healing process . . .

He slept most of the next day, waking at intervals only long enough to take more water and broth. The next morning, however, his restless movements woke her. She pushed to one elbow, shoved the hair from her eyes, and glanced over at him. He stared back, quite alert and animated for a man so recently and seriously wounded.

"Good morning, femina."

"Good morning, Tremayne." Raina smiled tentatively, suddenly uncomfortable with him and her newly awakened emotions. "You look well. How do you feel?"

"Much better, thank you." He attempted to roll onto his side and failed. "Well," he admitted wryly, "I feel greatly improved, at any rate. Could you help me to sit? I tire of this helpless position on my back."

She looked at him with some misgiving. "I could get you up, but I'm not certain you could remain sitting for very long." Raina glanced about, searching for something to prop him up with, when Bahir strode over.

"Could I perhaps be of assistance, *mirah?*" he asked.

Raina shot Teague a quick glance. At the Tuaret's admiring term, his mouth had gone tight. "Er, yes, that would be appreciated," she muttered. "Teague, this is Bahir Husam al Nur, the leader of the Tuarets. Bahir," she continued, meeting his watchful gaze, "this is my mate, Teague Tremayne."

The amber-eyed nomad nodded. "I am pleased to cross paths with you," he said in the traditional desert greeting.

The monk tersely returned the appropriate response. "And may our paths always be ones of hospitality and friendship, Bahir Husam al Nur."

"What do you wish my help for?" Bahir asked without further preamble.

"To sit for a while. I grow weary of lying flat on my back."

The Tuaret chuckled. "Good. Your healing progresses." He turned, strode away, and soon returned with a saddle. "Fetch a blanket to cover this, *mirah,* and your mate will have the finest back support in the desert."

At his imperious tone, Raina bit back a stinging invective. How dared he order her about! And she was past weary of being addressed as a beautiful possession rather than as the person she was. Yet she also knew to attempt a debate with him over those issues was a lost cause.

In the kingdom of Farsala and especially in the desert, men had total power. It was why she'd left fifteen cycles ago, why she'd dreaded returning. And why she'd finally avenge herself against the two men who symbolized, thanks to the pervading customs of the land, her victimization.

"As you wish," Raina bit out the reply, slanting Teague a darkly mutinous look. Bahir's behavior notwithstanding, the monk had better not get the idea that she'd submit to this any longer than it took to free themselves of the Tuaret and his men. Teague's mouth quirked in sympathetic understanding. Then, as if remembering himself, his jaw went taut.

Startled, Raina frowned in bemusement and busied herself settling the blanket over the saddle. Once that task was complete, she helped Bahir lift Teague to a sitting position and drag him back to rest upon the upright saddle. "Comfortable?" she asked the monk.

"Quite. My thanks, femina, and,"—he looked up at Bahir—"for your assistance as well."

There was a pause. Finally, Bahir glanced from Teague to Raina. "Have you discussed with him the possibility of departing the oasis on the morrow?"

Raina shook her head. "No. Teague just now woke and we were trying to decide how to get him up when you walked over."

Bahir cocked a dark brow. "Well, now seems an appropriate time, *mirah*."

"Perhaps he'd like a few minutes to clean up first, have a drink of water," she hedged. She needed to talk with Teague alone, fill him in on all she'd told Bahir. The Tuaret leader was too quick and would pick up on any inconsistencies in their stories.

"And perhaps, most of all," Teague drawled, irritation threading his voice, "I'd appreciate not being talked about as if I'm not here."

Two pairs of eyes turned to him. Bahir's glinted in

amusement. Raina's widened in surprise, then she flushed.

"I'm sorry," she hastened to say. "I didn't mean—"

Teague didn't like how angry and resentful she seemed in the Tuaret's presence. What was there between them? The nomad leader's masculine appreciation of Raina was more than evident. The basis for Raina's reaction, on the other hand, he wasn't so sure of.

A strange emotion flared within him. It made him uncomfortable, uneasy. He didn't like the feeling. It smacked too much like possessiveness, like . . . like jealousy!

Heat rose in Teague's face. Jealousy? *Jealousy?* He'd no claim on Raina, and didn't ever want one. Yet the feeling remained nonetheless, clenching about his gut.

Fool, he silently berated himself. How much are you willing to sacrifice because of this female? How much more than you've already lost?

A fleeting memory of the sand cat's attack slashed through him—a memory of the pain, of the sharp, pungent scent of his blood, but even more appallingly, the shock that he should *feel* the pain, that he should *bleed*.

Somehow, some way, in the course of the past few weeks, he'd lost his powers. Powers that had taken cycles of grindingly hard work and unstinting, unrelenting discipline to achieve. Powers whose attainment had finally elevated him to a fifth-degree Grandmaster and gained for him, at last, the respect and approval he'd labored so long to secure.

Yet now . . . now his powers were all but gone, eliminated as easily as one snuffs out a candle, leaving only a thin, mocking trail of smoke as feeble reminder of the power and glory that had once been the flame's. Agony seared through Teague. Ah, better never to have gained such powers, never to have felt the soaring, exultant triumph of rebirth and renewal, than to have had them and then squandered them! Squandered them, and all because of his unholy desire for a woman.

What had happened had happened, he grimly told himself, and no amount of impotent mourning would bring them back. Only action could do that. And that action, he now knew, was to shut Raina out of his heart and mind as quickly and irrevocably as possible.

She was the cause of it all, or rather, the cause was his weakness in resisting her charms. There was no other explanation. And no other solution.

"An apology isn't necessary." His voice congested with anger and frustration, he forced himself back to the matter at hand. "Just include me from now on, if you will, in whatever plans you two have made."

"Bahir offered to escort us to the Barakah Mountains. He and his men are headed back in that direction themselves."

Teague eyed the other man, weighing the possible cost of taking him up on his offer versus the dearly desired buffer he and his men might place between him and Raina. "A most generous proposition," he slowly replied. "I fear, however, that I'll still not be able to travel on the morrow. Yet it seems unfair to keep you and your men waiting here for my convenience."

The Tuaret smiled and squatted to put them at a more equitable eye level. "We've equs aplenty, thanks to the extra ones we, er, appropriated today from some ill-fated Katebs. It'll be an easy enough task to cut down a few palmas trees and fashion a litter to sling between two equs. Until, of course," he graciously added, "you're in better condition to ride . . ."

The monk considered Bahir's offer, and knew it for

the practical solution that it was—to many problems.
"It sounds reasonable enough. I, too, wish to reach the
Barakah Mountains as soon as possible."

"You've pressing business there, then?"

"I already told you we go to visit my family," Raina
hurriedly interjected. "Neither Teague nor I have seen
them in many cycles. That seems pressing enough to
us."

Bahir locked glances. "So you've told me. But I was
speaking to your mate, not you."

She glared back at him, but withheld further comment.

Teague watched the interchange, puzzled at Raina's
unusual reticence. She wasn't the type to take such overt
dominance lightly.

"Well?" the Tuaret asked, casually turning his attention back to Teague. "Is it only family you visit?"

"And why would you have reason to doubt my mate's
words?" Teague countered. There was something about
the nomad's manner that sent a warning vibrating
through him. But since he hadn't been party to most of
what had gone on between Bahir and Raina, he knew
he had to tread carefully here or risk contradicting what
she might already have said. A diversionary offense
seemed the best tactic. "Has she done something to
raise your suspicions that what she told you isn't true?"

Bahir's mouth twitched. "If I implied such a thing, I
beg pardon. I meant no insult to your mate. I but meant
to offer what other services you might require in the
journey. And, to do that, I needed to know your plans."

Teague smiled benignly. "And you do. If they change
in the meantime, I'll be certain to share them with you."

"That is all anyone can ask." Bahir gave Teague a
courteous nod. "I'm certain you have things you wish

to discuss with your mate. I'll not detain you any longer. But if you would, I'd invite you to our supper this eve. The Katebs recently slaughtered two of the small herd capras they'd stolen from us. We plan a modest feast to make use of their meat."

"A most generous invitation," Teague said, knowing to refuse the offer would be to tender grave insult. "One Raina and I will gladly accept."

"Until this eve, then." Bahir rose and walked away.

Teague waited until he was out of earshot. The rest of the Tuarets, save the guard standing at the edge of the oasis, were bathing at the pool in preparation for breakfast. There was no danger of being overheard by them. "What exactly did you tell him?" He turned back to Raina. "I think it best we both agree upon the same story as soon as possible. The man is no fool."

"No, he isn't." Raina shifted uncomfortably. "I told him little, though, save that we were life mates and were going to visit my family in the Barakah Mountains. You did well in how you handled him."

"He seems inordinately interested in you."

She gave a start. "What does that have to do with anything?"

"You said he wanted to give you to one of his men. I think he may want you for himself instead."

"He has a wife."

"And can't men of the desert tribes take more than one wife? It's certainly an accepted practice as far north as the royal city."

Her uneasiness began to grow. "Yes, you know they can. But I don't think . . ."

"Go on," Teague prompted silkily.

"I think his interest was more in the truth of my words, then specifically in me."

"And if it *is* in you, what will you do?"

She frowned in puzzlement, taken aback. Where was he headed with this? "What do you mean, what will I do? I already told him we were life mates. What more do you *want* me to do?"

Suddenly, Teague flushed and averted his gaze. "Nothing," he muttered angrily. "I was wrong to press you so. It's none of my concern, nor right, to question what you do with another male. I . . . I beg pardon."

His abrupt changes in mood confused Raina. One moment he was cold, withdrawn, then angry, then he acted the possessive man, and then the next . . . ? She pondered that for a moment, the first inklings of his possible motivation slowly permeating her mind. He acted as if . . . as if he'd realized he was revealing too much . . . as if he *cared*.

A curious melting gladness filled Raina. She scooted close and laid a hand on his. "There's no reason to beg pardon, Teague. We are partners. It's good that we're concerned about what may happen to each other."

He glanced up warily, a haunted expression in his eyes. "Is it, Raina? I'm not so certain."

His words gave her pause. There was something, some underlying, unspoken message there. If she dared press further, she risked . . .

Exactly what *did* she risk?

Taking her heart in hand, Raina dared words she never thought she'd utter to a man. "I cannot speak for you, but it seems, whether I wish it or not," she forced herself to say before she lost her newly found courage, "I cannot help but care for you. You've saved my life twice now. As much as I distrust and loathe most men, I cannot continue to view you in such a negative light.

Though I find it most unsettling, it is the truth, and I must face it."

"You are far more courageous than I, then." Teague lowered his gaze and shook his head. "But the real truth of our situations lies before us, whether we like it or not." His features twisted in a mask of anguish, but he forced himself to look up at her and forge on. "I'm a monk, Raina. I'm vowed to shun females and I must. Let it lie, whatever there is growing between us. For my sake, if not for yours."

She stared at him, sick, stunned. She'd offered him her friendship and perhaps more, and he'd spurned it, however kindly. Bitterness filled her. She should have known, should never have opened her heart to him. He was, in the end, a man, and the nature of a man was to cause hurt, one way or another.

"I meant nothing forward in my offer of friendship," she tautly replied, "but if you are forsworn even to refuse that, so be it. I must admit, though, that I cannot help but feel sorry for you and your monkish laws. They prevent you, I think, from living life as it was meant to be lived."

"You may see it so, but I view them as the means to a higher, purer path," he slowly replied, gazing up at her with considerable reluctance. "And, one way or another, they're all I have, femina. Don't begrudge me the one solace and support I have in life."

"I begrudge you nothing, Teague Tremayne. I just pity your loss."

He smiled sadly, thoughtfully fingering the blanket covering him. "The night of the sand cat's attack, Rand said some hard things to me. He said my vows might no longer serve me, might no longer be of further use.

He also agreed with you that I used them to flee from myself."

Raina laughed in surprise, the pain of his rejection already beginning to ease. "The Volan thought I'd said something of import? He actually *agreed* with me?"

"Yes," Teague said, glancing back up, "he did."

"Yet you'll still cling to those vows, won't you?"

"I've no other options, femina. The world I rebuilt after my world here on Incendra was destroyed is now threatening to collapse. And it was a good world. I served the Imperium well." With a shuddering breath the monk appeared to master himself, withdraw once again behind his monastic mask. "But my personal concerns aren't, and have never been, the issue here," he continued briskly. "We've a mission to complete."

"You're wrong, Teague Tremayne." Raina released his hand and leaned back, knowing the time for honest expression of one's feelings had drawn to a close, but determined that the monk would know it all. "Your concerns *are* an issue, are of importance. No monastic mouthings will ever change that. But this is neither the time nor place to delve deeper, or wear our hearts upon our sleeves. In time, though, when the proper opportunity presents itself, I'd be honored if we talked more about this."

"Why, Raina?" A wondering look flared in his eyes. "Why should it matter so much to you?"

"For many reasons," she said, "only the first of which is the fact that I begin to think our problems, our terrible secrets, aren't all so very different. Perhaps, just perhaps, we can help each other in this."

"Rand said that very same thing." He chuckled. "I begin to think he knows us better than we know ourselves."

"An unnerving consideration," Raina muttered uneasily, "that a Volan might know us better than we know ourselves. What does that say for us? For the survival of the Imperium?"

Teague pondered that a moment. "I'm not certain, but I'm also no longer so troubled it'll be to our detriment—one way or another."

"Aban. I need a word with you. Privately. Now."

The swarthy, dark-haired Tuaret shot his leader a questioning glance. "Now, Bahir? Cannot it wait at least until I finish saddling my equs? We ride out in but a half hour."

"No," Bahir tersely said. "It can't." Aban was a loyal compatriot and a fearless fighter, but he lacked, and would always lack, a certain sensitivity to the nuances of leadership or a mind quick enough to grasp complex concepts easily. It was why Bahir had chosen another to rule the tribe when he was gone.

The Tuaret leader gestured in the direction of the spring. With a huge sigh, Aban dragged off the saddle he'd just placed on the back of his equs and laid it on the ground. Without another word, he followed Bahir into the trees.

It was silent at the spring save for the murmured conversation of a few men standing across from the gently agitated waters, filling sewn capra-hide bags for the journey ahead. Bahir eyed them briefly, decided they were well out of earshot, and turned to his friend. "The woman and her mate. They've weapons that they cannot be allowed to keep. I want you to take those weapons while I talk with them."

Aban cocked his head, one bushy black brow arched

in surprise. "But to steal from one's host is forbidden
in the name of hospitality. And they seem friendly
enough."

Bahir stooped, picked up a flat pebble, and skimmed
it across the surface of the spring. In a series of low,
almost parallel skips, the stone flew across the water,
sending out silvery ripples in its wake. "Perhaps, but
then again, perhaps not," he softly replied. "What matters to me is that a weapon of great devastation, a
weapon none of us has ever been allowed to possess,
killed that sand cat. You saw the terrible hole seared
through the beast. Do you want to risk facing such a
weapon?"

"No." The other man vehemently shook his head.
"With even one of those weapons, they could hold all
of us at bay, and kill many before we could overpower
them."

"And they have two."

Aban nodded. "Yes."

"There's more, Aban."

"More?"

"The woman, Raina, used healing tools that produced
an amazing recovery in her mate. I saw his wounds this
morning when she cleansed and put fresh bandages on
them. They're almost healed, after only three days, and
from a sand cat attack, no less."

"I marveled that he even survived the attack. No one
ever lives more than a few hours, if that long, and this
man . . . well, he not only lives, but now you say he
is almost healed?"

"Exactly." Bahir turned to him. "She said they came
from far away, but her family lived in the Barakah
Mountains. I know of no land that possesses such advanced technology, save Farsala, and that only as Malam

Vorax permits. If such weapons existed on Incendra, Malam Vorax would have them."

Aban scratched the large, black mole peeking through the beard on the left side of his jaw. It was a nervous gesture Bahir had grown used to seeing whenever the big, burly man fell into any sort of deep, convoluted thought. "Perhaps he soon will," Aban said, "if these people journey to visit him, rather than some relatives, as the woman claims."

Bahir smiled grimly. "You see my point then, about the weapons. It becomes more than just protecting the men. Gaining possession of these weapons may well determine our eventual fate as a tribe. And if they should somehow fall into Vorax's hands . . ."

At the terrible implications of that possibility, Aban's eyes widened. His hands instinctively fell to his curved dagger. "Taking the weapons is the easy part," he agreed, finally warming to the task at hand. "How will you discover their true intent?"

The Tuaret leader sighed and shook his head. "I don't know yet. But they now journey with us and, though they may think they're free to come and go, that's no more than an illusion. For all practical purposes, they're our captives until I decide otherwise."

He moved close and grasped his compatriot's arm. "I want no one to know what we've discussed here, but the two strangers must be watched at all times, surreptitiously, of course, until I get the answers I need. Set the appropriate men to that task."

Aban bowed. "It will be as you ask, lord." The Tuaret leader released him. Aban turned and strode away.

Bahir lingered at the spring, contemplating the next few minutes to come. He loathed treating people who'd offered him and his men hospitality, however reluctantly, in such a hostile manner. But the longer he was with them, the greater his suspicions grew. They weren't of Farsala, despite their facility with the language and knowledge of the customs. Their motives for being here weren't honest, either.

The woman especially disturbed him. Even when he discounted her impertinent manner, there was something about her. The first time he'd met her, she'd immediately reminded him of Cyra. He'd thought at the time it was her fiery temper, her lack of proper respect. He knew now it was more than that—far, far more.

She reminded him so strongly of Cyra, Bahir now realized, because, like Cyra, she wasn't of Incendra. Neither, he added grimly, was her companion. And that consideration, with its disturbing implications and potential problems, was the most worrisome one of all.

Eleven

Raina finished fastening the neckline of Teague's long robe and helped him slip into the loose, sleeveless cloak. She then placed the headcloth atop his long, blond hair and tied the ends up to cover the lower half of his face.

Already, though the day burned bright and hot on the desert, the winds blew strong, whirling heavy curtains of sand into the air. They would all need the headcloth this day, Raina thought, not only to protect them from the sun, but to keep the sand out of their noses and mouths.

"There," she said finally, leaning back to survey her work. "I think you're ready for the journey."

Teague scowled. "I feel like a fool, cosseted and dressed by you, carried along by others on a litter like some babe. I may be a monk, but I admit to the failing of possessing some small amount of pride."

" 'Some small amount'?" She grinned. "I hate to dis-illusion you, Teague Tremayne, but you possess more than just a small amount. Not that I find that offensive in a person," she hastened to add, when his scowl deep-ened to a thunderous glower. "I just find it amusing that you seem to view yourself as the typical humble monk."

That pronouncement didn't seem to sit well with him,

either. "My monastic bearing isn't an acceptable topic of discussion," he growled.

Raina considered that for a moment, then laughed. Ever since their talk yesterday, he'd become extremely prickly about certain things. Well, though she'd agreed to accede to his requests not to press their friendship further, she wasn't about to minutely examine every word that left her mouth.

"Yes, perhaps you're right," she conceded. "I meant no harm or insult in what I said, though tact has never been one of my particular gifts. You'll have to get used to it, however. I don't plan to instigate too many changes just to suit you. You certainly aren't trying too hard to suit me."

At her wry self-assessment and pointed, if gently couched, jab at him, Teague's mood appeared to lighten. "No, I'm certainly not," he admitted. "I also, it appears, don't make a very good patient. I beg pardon for my ill humor."

Her smile faded. "I understand. Truly I do." She glanced up and saw Aban watching them. Raina waved him over.

"Yes, femina?" Unlike his more arrogant leader, Aban always treated her with the utmost respect.

"My mate is ready for the litter. Could you find some men to help him to it?"

"It will be as you ask." The bearded man signaled two men. "Assist our honored friend to the litter," he directed his compatriots.

They helped Teague to his feet, then, with each one supporting him on a side, guided him over to where two equs stood patiently, nose to tail, the litter slung between them. Raina paused to position the furry cerva-hide pillow into a more comfortable spot on the tautly stretched blankets before advising the two men on the least stressful way to lift Teague onto the litter. The whole process went surprisingly smoothly.

The monk glanced up from his supine position. "My thanks,"—he smiled at the two Tuarets—"for all your—"

Abruptly, he stopped speaking. "Raina," Teague rasped, "Aban is taking the blasters."

She wheeled and, to her horror, saw the burly Tuaret walking away with their two blasters in hand. She raced over. "Aban. Wait."

He halted and turned, a mild look of inquiry in his eyes. "Yes, femina?"

"Those two pieces of, er, equipment." Raina gestured to the blasters. "They're part of our possessions. I want them back." As she spoke, she extended her hand. "Now, please."

"No, femina." He graced her with an apologetic smile, but stood his ground. "I've been instructed to appropriate these weapons."

"Appropriate? Weapons?" Raina struggled to contain her anger. "And who would—?" She stopped short. She knew the answer to that question even as the words fell from her lips. *Bahir.* Curse his conniving, suspicious mind!

She stalked over to where Bahir stood, giving final instructions to some of his men. "Bahir," Raina called to him without even breaking stride, "I must speak with you."

He didn't turn or reply, but only continued talking with his men. His stance altered imperceptibly, though. Raina knew he'd heard her. As she approached, his men nodded their understanding of his directives and walked away. She stomped around to stand before him.

"Why did you give Aban orders to take some of our

equipment?" she demanded, her hands fisting on her hips. "The laws of the desert and hospitality—"

"Are superseded by the need to ensure the continued welfare of my people," he curtly cut her off. "The equipment Aban confiscated were weapons. You know it, and so do I, so play no further games with me."

Fleetingly, Raina considered pulling out the stunner she kept with her at all times and taking the Tuaret leader hostage in return for her weapons. That thought, however, quickly died an ignominious death. Teague lay helpless on the litter, too far away to protect. Besides, Bahir had made no open threat, but only wished to take their blasters. And the stunner, along with the dagger strapped to her left thigh beneath her long robe, might later come in handy at a more opportune moment.

"We wished you no harm. The blasters were but for our own protection, if we ever needed them."

"Well, you don't need them against us." He studied her thoughtfully. "As reluctant as I am to order this, we must also examine your other belongings. In the event, you must surely realize, that there are additional weapons hidden within them."

Raina dragged in a steadying breath. "Of course. What other choice do you have, considering the circumstances?"

Bahir frowned, not at all pleased by her undertone of sarcasm. Well, he couldn't really blame her for being angry and defiant, no matter how well she'd managed to contain the hostile emotions. Women had their fair share of temper, to be sure. Even his gentle Najirah . . .

"None, *mirah*," he said. "I have no other choice, considering the circumstances." He motioned to several of his men. "Search their belongings for any other weapons."

As Raina watched, the nomads carefully but thoroughly went through their supply packs. They found the other stunner and tossed it over to Bahir, who examined it closely. He shot Raina a searing glance.

"I've seen one of these before. It's a stunner, isn't it?"

She considered lying, fabricating some story, but suspected the Tuaret leader was wily enough to try it out on her or Teague if her explanation didn't suit him. She decided honesty, at least to a limited extent, was the best policy. "Yes. It won't kill, though."

"I'm well aware of its function," he said tersely. "Do you have any more of these hidden elsewhere? Perhaps even on your person?"

It was too much to give up the second stunner without some sort of fight. And no desert man—at least, not one with a shred of honor—would lay a hand on her to check her. "No," she lied, "that's the only one."

Bahir scowled. "I suppose I must take you at your word for the time being. Or at least until we reach our main camp and one of our women can examine you."

"It won't be necessary even then," Raina snapped. "I told you before. We wish you no harm."

His men finished with the supply packs. One of them turned to Rand's carrying pack. Raina's breath caught in her throat. If they should open it, the strange and complex equipment would surely give away the secret of where they truly came from. No such technology as Rand's communications device and life support system existed on Incendra.

Yet there was no way to stop the nomads from opening Rand's pack and searching it. Frantically, Raina considered all possible options and cast aside each of them save one. Bahir would have to be told the truth. But unless he decided otherwise, there would be no purpose served in the rest of his men knowing. The more people aware of the true intent of their mission, the greater the risk.

Bahir." Raina gripped his arm. "That pack,"—she gestured to Rand's carrying pack—"contains some very delicate scientific equipment. I would prefer to open it myself, in your presence."

Recalling Cyra's tale that she'd met the Tuaret leader while on a scientific expedition, Raina gambled that Bahir would respect the need for care in examining the pack. Her gamble paid off.

Bahir hesitated but a moment, then nodded. "So be it." He motioned for his men to stop their search.

She leaned toward him. "In private, please."

His eyes narrowed. "And why is that?"

Raina expelled a deep breath. "Because the pack holds equipment that I doubt either you or any of your men have ever seen before. And I'm not so certain, once *you* hear the explanation, that you'll want them to know the truth about its contents."

"Another, even more fearsome weapon, perhaps?" he drawled silkily. "One that you could use to overpower or even kill me with?"

She met his skeptical gaze fully. "No. I swear it. Besides, what purpose would be served in killing you, when you now have our blasters and Teague lies at the mercy of your men?"

"None, it would seem. But at every turn I discover further lies and deception. When will it end?"

"I've no reason to trust you, either," she retorted hotly. "Though your motives may spring from a well-intentioned need to protect your people, ours rise from an even greater cause."

"And that is?" he prodded.

"Nothing that will serve Malam Vorax or threaten you, you can be sure."

"I can be sure of nothing until I know fully what you and your mate intend to do." He glanced in Teague's direction. "Must I go to him to get the truth? He watches us with great concern. Would he tell me what I require if I threatened to hurt you? Or perhaps if I threatened him?"

Raina looked over at Teague. He'd propped himself up on his elbows, his big chest straining against the ropes that now bound him to the litter. Apprehension—and frustration at his helplessness—gleamed in his eyes.

She managed a taut little smile of reassurance and turned back to Bahir. "There's no need to speak of torture," Raina muttered, her mind made. "Permit me but a moment to talk with Teague."

"No, I think not." A hard, implacable look settled over the Tuaret's darkly handsome features. "The more you bargain and hedge, the more suspicious I become. You wished to speak with me privately about the contents of this pack and the real purpose of your journey to the Barakah Mountains. Do so now, or suffer the consequences."

"Fine." She made an irritated motion. "Come. Take the pack and let's go to the spring. It'll be private enough there."

He followed behind her, Rand's carrying pack slung over his shoulder. When they reached the spring, Raina stopped and sank to the grass. Bahir hesitated.

"Sit," she urged, a sardonic cast to her mouth. "I won't attack you."

Bahir did as she'd asked, taking great care to maintain a proper distance. "I know that." Nonetheless, he flushed darkly. "I'm just not in the habit of lounging about with another man's mate."

"It's nice to know you have some scruples."

"And what exactly is that supposed to mean?"

"Nothing." Raina waved away his angry demand with a casual movement of her hand. "You wanted to know what was in that carrying pack. It's the life support and communications system for an alien being."

His eyes widened. *"What?"*

She sighed and gestured toward the pack. "Open it. Look inside. You'll see a box, and within that box is a biosphere containing a Volan named Rand."

"And how am I to know what it truly is? Already, I see your technology is far superior to ours."

Raina shrugged. "Would you like me to open the pack, lift out the box, and introduce you to Rand? I can do little more than that to prove the truth of my words."

"There's a lot more you can do." His amber-colored eyes glittered as hard as jewels. "Like telling me where you're really from."

If she told him the truth, she might eventually have to kill him if he betrayed or threatened their mission. Yet if she didn't, they might never make it to the Barakah Mountains. Raina sighed. "Though Teague and I are Incendarians, we haven't lived on Incendra for many cycles. We both left when we were young and have never returned until now."

Satisfaction gleamed in the Tuaret's eyes. "I thought as much. Why did you come back?"

"The Imperium is threatened by the invasion of Volans, an alien race of mind-slavers. Teague and I came to Incendra to retrieve a special stone found in the firestorm caves."

"Indeed?" Bahir lounged back on his elbows, his

long legs stretched out before him. "Yet you bring a Volan—the enemy—with you in this special pack. Once again, I find your whole story hard to believe."

"Then what *will* it take to convince you, Nomad?" Rand's voice rose, unexpectedly, from the pack. "Raina has told you the truth. There is nothing left for you to do now but help her and Teague in their mission."

The Tuaret leader jerked upright. Startled, he looked from the carrying pack to Raina. "How did you do that? Without your lips moving, I mean?"

Raina rolled her eyes and shook her head. "I didn't do it. That's Rand speaking." She shot the pack a wry grin. "You're not doing a very good job of convincing him, Rand."

"Then he's not a very intelligent man," the Volan countered. "The facts of my existence are indisputable."

"Are they, now?" Bahir quickly opened the carrying pack and found that there was indeed a metal box within. He hauled it out. "How do I see this . . . this biosphere? How do I truly know if there's some life form within it?"

"Flip open the locks. Inside you'll find a membranous sphere. Shake it and you'll see a green luminescence appear. Those are the temeritas. They maintain Rand's Volan entity through a biochemical process similar to that in the neural network of a Volan host."

"Host? The Volans need hosts?"

Raina nodded. "They burned out their own bodies long ago. Now they travel through the universe in search of new bodies. That's why we need that special Incendarian stone. It's to be used to keep the Volans out of the Imperium."

"We've seen no Volans on Incendra."

Gods, Raina thought. Must she give lessons to the

man now? "They're almost impossible to detect once they've entered a body. And once they're within, they rapidly burn out their host and kill him. Hence their insatiable need for new hosts."

A pained expression stole across Bahir's face. He set aside the box and began to rub his temples. "Not so fast," he mumbled. "You're going too fast."

Raina paused, cocked her head, and eyed him curiously. "I beg pardon. I suppose this is all quite overwhelming for you, as isolated as Incendarians now are from the rest of the Imperium."

Bahir shot her an irritated look. "I'm neither slow nor stupid. I just . . . suddenly have a . . . a terrible headache."

"I'm sorry." Raina felt inane saying that, but she didn't know what else to say. "Is there something more you'd like explained?"

He sat there a long moment, a puzzled expression on his face, as if he couldn't quite work through a reply. "No," the Tuaret leader finally replied. "Aban. I . . . need . . . Aban."

"I suggest you go and get this Aban, femina," Rand said. "Our friend here sounds ill."

Muttering, "he's not our friend, Rand," Raina shoved to her feet, shot one last glance at Bahir, who had begun rocking back and forth, a blank expression on his face, and turned and ran back to the camp. "Aban," she cried, motioning him to her side. "Bahir. I-I don't know what's wrong with him, but he appears to be very ill."

The big Tuaret shot her a disbelieving glance, then headed for the trees, Raina at his side. "What have you done to him? I swear, if you've harmed him in any way—"

"I've done nothing!" Raina said fiercely. "One moment we were talking, and the next, he said he had a headache. Then he became increasingly confused."

A stricken expression twisted Aban's swarthy face. "By the firestorms, not again! It's too soon. They're coming too close together now!"

"What? What's coming too close together?"

He shook his head, his mouth gone tight. "Nothing. It's none of your affair."

She couldn't get another word out of him after that. They reached the spring and the spot where she'd left Bahir and Rand. Aban's gaze took in the open pack and the metal box, then swung to where his leader sat, rocking to and fro.

"Bahir," he softly said, dropping to his knees on the grass beside his friend. "It's Aban. I'm here to take you back to camp." As he spoke, he reached up and stroked Bahir's head.

Raina couldn't believe her eyes. Aban was treating the proud Tuaret leader as if he were a child or a doddering old man. She walked over and squatted beside Aban. "What's wrong with him?"

"Nothing. Nothing's wrong with him." The denial came out in a strained, choked voice. "Just help me, if you will, to get him to stand. He can walk back, if we can just get him up."

She moved to Bahir's left, grasped his arm with one hand and, with the other, slid it across his back to clasp his other side. Aban did the same on the right. Together, they managed to get the powerful Tuaret leader to his feet. In a slow, halting procession, they led him back through the trees.

"Aban," Raina tried again, "I don't mean to pry, but if I knew what was wrong with Bahir, I might have some medications that could help him. Our medical technology, where we come from, is quite advanced, and—"

"There's nothing that can help him!" the big nomad cried in a tear-choked voice, pulling Bahir to a halt. "Nothing, no cure, no hope. Let it be. Let us deal with this in our own way."

Taken aback, Raina flushed, then nodded. "Of course. I beg pardon. I meant no harm."

"I know you didn't, femina. But just . . . let it be."

The Tuarets fashioned another litter, strapped it in place between two more equs, and laid Bahir on it. Then, after tying Rand's carrying pack to the back of Raina's saddle and packing the remaining supplies, the little caravan set out across the Ar Rimal, heading west, in the direction of the Barakah Mountains. They traveled all day, halting for several hours in the noonday heat to rest and take a light meal. As the sun finally began to sink toward the distant horizon, Aban called once more for them to head out.

Both Teague and Bahir slept a good portion of the day. When Bahir was awake, he rocked to and fro within the confines of the straps that bound him securely in his litter. Teague, whose equs walked alongside those of the Tuaret leader's, watched him, a concerned, thoughtful expression on his face.

Twilight blanketed the desert before Aban finally called a halt for the night within a steep-sided gully that meandered across the land. Wildflowers and hardy desert grasses grew in profusion along the rocky floor. Though the rush of water from the last rainfall had long ago been sucked into the earth, there was at least enough forage for the hungry equs.

Raina immediately swung down from her equs, her muscles, not used to the strain of riding, screaming in protest. She walked stiffly over to check on Teague. He was awake.

"How do you feel?"

He shot her a wry glance. "Coated in sand and baked to a crisp. Aside from that, as good as can be expected. I'm giving serious consideration to riding on the morrow."

Raina gave a disbelieving snort. "A bit premature, don't you think?"

He shrugged. "Thanks to your expert care and the torpine, my wounds are sore, but healed. And, more to the point, I tire of being an invalid."

She untied the ropes binding him to the litter, then stepped back and motioned to him. "Then climb down and show me how healed you really are."

"Is that some joke?" Teague shoved to a sitting position and eyed the considerable distance to the ground with misgiving.

"No." Raina cocked her head. "The distance to the ground is the same height as climbing up onto the back of an equs, only a lot easier. If you can't make it down on your own, how can you expect to make it up the same way?"

"I see your point," he muttered. Teague swung his legs over the side of the litter and, grasping the pole for support, gingerly lowered himself down. The sudden demands on his abused muscles nearly sent him to his knees. As it was, his legs buckled and he gasped in pain.

Raina quickly strode over to assist him. Though he tolerated her hands on him because he needed her help, the look he sent her was anything but grateful. With

slow, halting steps, they made their way across the gully
to where a campfire was already being laid. Raina
helped Teague to the ground, then ran back, unsaddled
her equs, grabbed the water bag, and brought it and the
saddle back to Teague.

"Is there anything else you need just now?" she
asked, once she'd gotten the saddle propped comfortably
behind him.

"You're not my nursemaid," he gritted. "I can manage
without you for a time, I suppose."

"Just like *I* managed without you when *I* was ill."
She handed him the water bag. "Here, drink some
water. You're probably just irritable from dehydration.
I'll take care of my equs in the meanwhile."

Teague glowered up at her but accepted the bag and
unstoppered it. He took a long, deep swallow of the
water, then lowered the bag and wiped his mouth with
the back of his hand. "Satisfied?"

In the dying rays of the sun, a soft rose color washed
the desert, reflecting off the high rock walls of the gully
and Teague's face. Rugged strength was carved into
every plane of his increasingly sun-bronzed features,
from his thick, dark brows to his long, straight nose
and strong mouth. But it was his eyes, little more than
glinting silver shards in his narrowed gaze, that caught
and held Raina's regard.

A guarded antagonism, a barely contained anguish,
gleamed there. The contradictory emotions puzzled
Raina. It was as if . . . as if he hated her, yet didn't
want to, all at the same time.

The realization filled her with a startling surge of
compassion. She wanted to sit beside him, take him into
her arms, and comfort him. He was a good man—she
knew that now with every fiber of her being—but a

terribly tormented one. And he didn't deserve to suffer so.

There was little, however, that she *could* do about it, or, if the truth be told, *dared* do about it. Though Teague might believe he risked his soul in taking her as friend, she risked just as much. It was a risk Raina realized now she'd willingly take, but she wouldn't and couldn't force that same decision on him. It wasn't right, wasn't fair, and it would be a poor show of gratitude for all he'd done for her.

"Yes, I'm satisfied," she said softly, knowing that to linger there an instant longer might be their undoing. Wordlessly, she turned and walked back to the equs.

Teague watched her retreating form, a painful knot forming in the middle of his chest. Gods, but she was so beautiful, so kind to him, so caring. She didn't deserve the way he'd treated her just now, or for the past few days. He was being intentionally cruel, and it sickened him.

Yet what choice had he? He had to drive her away in any way he could, or lose everything. Everything . . .

Once more the panic swelled within him. His breath grew ragged. His heart pounded. Clenching his eyes shut, Teague began the old, familiar litanies. Over and over he mentally intoned them, drawing on them for comfort, for support, for sustenance in a time in which he found himself drowning, bereft, lost.

And like the blade ritual powers he'd forfeited in his unholy desire for her, the litanies and the sacred teachings failed to give him surcease. Teague's hands fisted, his nails scoring his palms. Tears of pain and sheer terror welled in his eyes.

Gone . . . everything was gone. Crazed, irrational thoughts whirled through his mind. He had nothing.

Nothing . . . and it was all Raina's fault. Gods, how he regretted agreeing to come on this quest, regretted ever meeting her! Yet he had, and now she was slowly but surely destroying him.

Anger filled him. She would take it all, then walk away untouched, unaware of what she'd done, unconcerned and uncaring. More than anything, her lack of concern over what she'd wrought infuriated him. She would take everything from him and leave him a quivering, impotent, needy specter of the man he'd worked so hard to become—and never know or care.

He hated her for that most of all.

Twelve

Bahir woke from his illness—whatever it was—shortly before dawn. Until then, Raina hadn't been allowed near him. The Tuaret leader was cared for by his men in a gentle, solicitous manner that surprised her. She hadn't thought men capable of such tender concern.

It was also evident from their protectiveness and care that Bahir elicited great loyalty and affection from his followers. Though she found him overbearing and arrogant to a fault, Raina was also astute enough to know these were traits most men would find admirable. They'd see them, instead, as signs of self-confidence and forceful leadership, invaluable attributes in a leader. Strange, she mused, how the same qualities men found commendable in each other could be turned against women to control and intimidate.

After a quick breakfast of journey bread, last night's leftover mentha tea, and more dried fruit, they began to break camp. Teague, now even more taciturn and disagreeable than the eve before, stubbornly insisted on riding today.

"One more day of rest," Raina pleaded. "Just give your wounds *and* your strength one more day. If you push yourself too hard too fast, you'll lose all the headway you've made."

"Let it be," he gritted, struggling to stand. His gaze

never met hers as he straightened his cloak and head-cloth, then brushed the sand away. "I've told you before, you're not my nursemaid. It's past time you began to listen."

Stung, Raina struck back in the only way she could. "You didn't reject my nursing after you were attacked by the sand cat. You thought my judgment and care was good enough then."

"And if you hadn't stomped off in a snit," he retorted, riveting a pair of blazing ice-blue eyes on her, "I'd never have had to fight the sand cat at all. They fear fire. They'd never have come near our camp. So let's just say we're even and leave it at that."

"Why, you ungrateful crock of—"

A throat cleared loudly behind them. As one, Teague and Raina wheeled, ready to pounce on anyone fool-hardy enough to intrude on their self-absorbed dispute. It was Bahir, quite recovered.

His piercing gaze swept over them. He smiled a small, secret smile. "A lover's spat, I gather?"

"It's nothing like that." Teague inhaled a steadying breath and forced his tension to ease. No purpose was served by his and Raina's argument anyway, save to stir his frustration and fury to greater heights.

He managed a tight smile in Bahir's direction. "I'm glad to see you've recovered from your illness. What can we do for you?"

"You look like you're recovering well from your recent injuries, too," the Tuaret leader replied, obviously choosing not to elaborate about what had recently befallen him. "Are you yet ready to ride?"

"No, he isn't," Raina said.

"Yes, I *am,*" Teague ground out, casting her an icy glare.

Bahir's lips twitched. "Good. I'd like you to ride with me, then. There are things I need to discuss with you."

It was evident from the look the Tuaret sent Raina that he hadn't included her in the invitation. Satisfaction, albeit admittedly childish, filled the monk. "As would I with you, Bahir." He glanced over to where all the equs were tethered. "I'll need a mount of my own."

Bahir nodded. He took Teague by the arm. "Then come. There are several to choose from, depending on your level of riding expertise. Have you ridden much, or . . ."

As they walked away, their voices faded. Raina stood there, gazing after them, seething at their overt snubbing of her. Curse Bahir, she raged. And most of all, curse Teague Tremayne!

She had half a mind to follow after them and remind them both that she was an equal partner in all this. But that smacked too much of a child begging to be allowed to play with the older children, and she'd never beg. Let them think they'd gained the upper hand. They'd soon see the error of that. No man—save one—had ever bested her before.

No man ever would again.

"Your mate revealed some very interesting news yesterday," Bahir began a short while later, as they rode out across the desert once more. He'd taken great care, Teague noted, to distance their equs from all the others. It was obvious he didn't want what they said to be overheard.

"Regarding the carrying pack you walked off with toward the spring?" Teague carefully replied. Raina had had little opportunity to speak to him in private yesterday. All he knew was that she'd told Bahir about Rand and the purpose of their mission.

"Yes. It seems there's an alien residing in a biosphere within it."

"True enough."

"She also told me that both of you came from a planet other than Incendra and are on a mission to retrieve some stone in the firestorm caves. A stone you mean to use against the Volan invasion."

"Also true."

Bahir looked over at him. As he did, an errant breeze blew a loose end of his headcloth across his eyes. He grabbed the flapping fabric and tucked it firmly back beneath the rest of the cloth twisted about his neck. "You're fortunate that I found you before Malam Vorax did."

"Indeed?" Teague cocked a dark brow. "And why is that?"

"How long have you been gone from Incendra?"

Teague hesitated. "Nineteen cycles."

The Tuaret leader did a swift mental calculation. "You were here, then, when Vorax usurped the throne. How old were you?"

"Old enough to know what happened," Teague hedged.

Bahir shot him a sharp, appraising look. "Did your family support his cause?"

"No, but what does it matter? Vorax is still in power. Obviously, he rules and rules well."

"There are some who would contest that assertion."

The Tuaret leader was quite evidently one of them, if the low, hard-edged tone of his voice was any indication, Teague thought. But where was all this leading? He shifted in his saddle to ease the ache in his right hip. He really should have taken Raina's advice and used the litter one more day.

"Contesting it is one thing," Teague replied, forcing his attention back to the conversation and away from his discomfort. "Succeeding in his overthrow is another."

"I am only one man, my tribe only one of twelve," Bahir snarled. "I cannot defeat Vorax alone."

"No, you can't." Teague's sense of unease began to curl and twist within him. Was it because this discussion stirred old memories, unresolved issues? He firmly tamped down that consideration, shutting out all emotion, all reaction to Bahir's words. This fight was the Tuarets', not his.

"The two blasters I had confiscated," Bahir picked up the thread of the conversation once more. "Are there more of them on Incendra? With weapons such as those, I could bring the war to a head rather than just harass and inflict only the most minor damage against Vorax and his cause. Perhaps then the tribes who hate Vorax as much as I, but fear his power, would be willing to join with me."

"There are only two blasters, Bahir. I'm sorry." In spite of himself, Teague felt a twinge of sympathy for the man's plight. He fought for a hopeless cause, and he knew it.

"You came here somehow. In a spaceship, perhaps? No one has ever transported here, thanks to our unusual atmosphere."

"Yes, we came on a ship." Teague eyed him warily. "But what has that to do with Vorax?"

"Does your ship perhaps possess weapons? Guns to protect it, to fight with?"

The Tuaret leader was grasping at any possibility now,

but Teague wouldn't willingly turn over the Volan ship to Bahir even if it *had* possessed weapons. The ship was their only way home. Bahir, however, didn't need to know that.

"No. The ship has no weapons," he said. "It's a Volan spy ship. Small, easily maneuverable, but not a fighter. Its only value lies in the fact that its hull is specially designed to protect against Incendra's increased electro-magnetic radiation."

As if plumbing the depths of his soul, Bahir locked gazes with Teague for a long moment, saw the truth in the other man's eyes, and sighed. The Tuaret's shoulders slumped. "I feared as much."

Bahir slammed his fist upon his thigh. "Curse it all. What will they do, once I am gone?" he muttered, half to himself. "Who will carry on the fight? Vorax *cannot* be allowed to continue to rule. He's corrupt, ruthless, and cruel. He's also draining us all dry with his endless taxes. And his son is no better than he."

He shook his head and sighed. "What will become of Farsala? Of Incendra?"

"The old king was said to be a corrupt and foolish ruler as well." Though he knew he trod on dangerous ground in broaching the subject, Teague wanted to put an end to this discussion as quickly as possible. Better that the Tuaret face the truth. He was only exchanging one incompetent ruler for another. "Before you destroy Vorax, perhaps you should find someone else better suited to rule. And if you can't, leave well enough alone."

"Well, it certainly isn't Vorax's son," Bahir gritted. "When it comes to atrocities and perversions, Sinon Vorax has taken up where his father left off."

"Then perhaps you? Frequently the leader of a revolt gains the throne."

The Tuaret leader shot him a searing look. "Do you mock me now, on top of everything else?"

Confused, Teague shook his head. "No. I was serious. You seem an able commander. You care. And you've the courage of your convictions. All necessary attributes of a good ruler."

"It was never meant for me to rule Farsala. I but fight for the rightful heir—the old king's son—until the day he returns."

Teague's breath lodged in his throat. A block of ice formed about his heart and frigid shards of blood shot through his veins. "There is no rightful heir," he finally managed to choke out the words. "He died in the rebellion."

"Did he?" Bahir's gaze turned back toward the desert. "Did he?" he slowly repeated. "No one really knows what happened to the old king's son. There are rumors he escaped, that he's in hiding." He chuckled. "I've even heard one tale that Vorax so greatly feared the prophecy that he sent the son off planet rather than dare kill him."

The Tuaret swung back to Teague. "The prince was thirteen cycles old when his father was overthrown. After these nineteen cycles past, he'd be a mature man now. A man old enough to regain the support of the people, to rule."

"If he truly lives." Teague shifted restlessly in his saddle, his unease growing with each passing second. How had they ever come to this particular topic? How could he turn it aside before it struck too close to home?

"Oh, I think he lives," Bahir said confidently, glancing at Teague. "Do you recall the prophecy?"

When Teague didn't answer, he began to intone the ancient words.

> The son must suffer,
> Die to himself and the world,
> Before the taint can be exorcised,
> Before the evil is overthrown.

> But woe to any who harm him.
> His is the right to search,
> To plumb the secrets within.
> His is the right to choose.

> A living death or life
> Of fire and light.
> A firestorm of obliteration.
> Or triumph."

"And your point in all that?" Teague demanded irritably, when he'd finished. "It's nothing more than some archaic mouthings of some even more archaic Order. And it most likely doesn't even apply to this particular case."

"The prophecy has never been fulfilled in all the hundreds of cycles since it was first proclaimed. And does it not now apply perfectly?" Excitement rose in Bahir's voice and flared in his eyes. "The son lives but must suffer and go into hiding until he can exorcise the taint in his own bloodlines. A taint that ultimately led to the loss of the people's faith and the success of Vorax's rebellion. Vorax certainly believed it applied to the prince. It's why he spared his life. It's the only reason a man as cruel and ambitious as Vorax would've let the young prince go."

"A fine theory," Teague drawled, fighting with all his might to keep his voice calm, his demeanor relaxed and indifferent. "Yet it still all hinges on whether the prince truly survived. Have you found him? Has anyone any proof that he lives?"

Bahir's amber eyes glittered. His mouth went tight. "No. No one has found him or has proof he lives. But I know he does and, until the day I find him, I'll carry on the battle in his name. Someone has to. To continue to live under Vorax's oppressive rule and not stand up to him is unconscionable. There has to be someone, some voice, that cries out against him. Some voice, however weak it may be, that prepares the way for the prince when he finally returns."

A prophet, Teague thought. Bahir saw himself as a warrior prophet. He shut his eyes for a brief moment. Gods, was there any man more difficult to abide than one so idealistic, so unrealistic? He'd had his fill of such men in the monastery. Fanatics, out of touch with the realities of life and living, with people and their shortcomings, their failings. Out-of-touch, foolish dreamers with no idea of the impracticality of their vision or its futility.

Yet without such men to prod and prick at the conscience, the hearts and minds of the masses, a tiny voice deep within him clamored, where would they all be? Without men like Bahir to stand up for what was right, to champion those oppressed by the inequities and injustices, what hope was there? Oftentimes, these men were the guiding lights of humanity, the incessantly vocal irritants that would not be silenced until, at long last, the people couldn't overlook or discount the problems anymore.

But be that as it may, it wasn't *his* problem, Teague

harshly, almost violently, reminded himself. This was an Incendarian problem, and he was no longer Incendarian.

He'd freed himself of that particular encumbrance immediately, just as soon as he'd set foot on Bellator. He'd had to. The burden of his lineage, the shame of his planet, had nearly crushed him. To be free of that was to start anew. To build a new life, a new person, a new heritage—one that could begin afresh in any way he wished.

No, he'd not let himself be drawn back into it all, Teague resolved. Just because he admired Bahir's determination and idealism. Just because he envied the Tuaret's sense of purpose, his dedication to something he believed in deeply. Just because the man possessed what he, in all his cycles and for all his efforts, had still never quite been able to achieve.

Teague sighed and shook his head. "Be that voice then, Bahir. There's nothing, though, that Raina or I can do for you, save give you our blasters when we're finally done with our mission. That, and tender you our admiration for what you attempt to do."

Something—disappointment, perhaps—flickered in the Tuaret leader's eyes. "Then you won't stay, help us fight Vorax? This is your land, your people, too."

"And what additional help would we be?" Teague gave a disparaging laugh. "Very little, I'd say, in the total scheme of things."

Bahir smiled and shrugged. "You're right, of course. But at this point, I take any and all happily. My army grows one by one, but it grows."

"You're a wise and able leader. I wish you good fortune in your endeavors."

"Do you, now?" the Tuaret asked cryptically, then turned once more to gaze out on the shimmering heat that was the desert. The land undulated before them in waves of fine, smooth sand. Here and there a small, scraggly plant broke the unchanging tranquillity but, aside from that, the desert rolled on in endless hills and vales.

It was the bleakest, most barren part of the Ar Rimal, but Bahir loved it nonetheless. He'd been born and raised in the desert, knew no other life save what its harsh dictates demanded, and had never desired or dreamed of another. Never . . . not even when that devotion had threatened his life-mating with Cyra.

Cyra hadn't realized the depth of his commitment to his life and land. Perhaps because of that, their love had been doomed from the start. In the end, it had definitely been the final wedge between them, the death knell of their life-mating, when he'd adamantly refused to leave his people and go with her back to Bellator.

Yet even now, the memory of Cyra filled him with sadness, creating an empty, aching void he knew now would be with him to the end of his days. Perhaps that pain, that endless yearning, was his punishment. As inexplicable, as improbable as it seemed, he had lost his heart to a woman not of Incendra. Lost his heart and broken all biological and cultural taboos to life mate with her.

Bahir's mouth twitched bitterly. Well, at least his days of punishment and suffering were numbered, small consolation though that was.

Not that Cyra would care, if she even knew. She'd fled him and their tender, budding union after only a cycle, turned her back and walked away without remorse or hesitation, with only the most minimal of efforts to try to adapt to the desert and its customs. Left him just after he'd discovered that the dreaded curse of his ancestors had descended upon him as well.

No, there was but one blessing in his impending death sentence, and that was that his yearning for Cyra would at last be over. No more lonely, anguished nights lying under the stars or beneath the shelter of his tent, hungry, aching for her until he thought he'd cry out from the pain. No more frustration, no more anger so intense he thought he'd explode from the tension that had no outlet, no hope of ever finding surcease.

Cyra was gone, living somewhere far away in the heavens, and it was too dangerous to return now even if she wished to. But at least he had his people, his cause, to sustain him in these last days of his life. It was small comfort, Bahir sadly acknowledged, shamed to admit to such selfish, self-pitying thoughts. Yet it was truth nonetheless, and he tried hard to face the truth, no matter how brutal or bitter. Tried so very, very hard.

He only wondered if all his efforts, all his fine plans and aspirations, would accomplish anything of any value in the end.

The journey through the Ar Rimal that day took them across a seemingly endless sea of sand. They camped at sunset in a deep depression between two towering hills that provided some shelter from the wind and reflected back a substantial amount of the campfire's warmth. Teague and Raina spoke little to each other as Raina was still incensed over his willing complicity in Bahir's earlier snub of her.

The next morn dawned bright, cloudless, and warm, heralding yet another long, hot day. The Tuarets, however, were unusually jovial, urging their big equs on at as rapid a pace as the animals could manage. They knew they'd reach home today.

By midday, Raina watched as the land began to change once again, easing into a dry, barren expanse slashed by numerous ravines and rocky, high desert. Large outcroppings of boulders, split and gnarled from the extremes in temperature variations between night and day and the scouring effects of frequent sandstorms, became more and more numerous until she could almost imagine they rode through a forest of stone. Occasional stream beds carved their muddy, meandering way down from the distant mountains.

Gradually, as they moved along, tuberous asphodel bushes and patches of low-growing, spiky glasswort thickets began to fill the terrain. In the deep ravines, desert grass grew profusely where the muddy waters ran. Raina observed it all with a growing sense of wonder. The Ar Rimal had turned, in just a day's journey, from a desolate land into one that could support life.

Near sunset, Bahir sent out two riders. The men galloped off across the now hard-packed desert floor, their huge equs moving with a strangely awkward, yet floating beauty, their hoofbeats pounding a loud staccato in the heavy silence of the dying day. Soon, with a series of wild whoops that pierced the deepening twilight, the two Tuarets returned, accompanied by nine or ten others.

Joyous greetings were exchanged. The pace of the returning Tuarets increased, until all were loping toward a distant stand of craggy rocks and deep ravines. High atop a particularly large hill where there perched a huge formation of stone resembling a fortress, the flickering light of campfires drew them all. As the equs climbed the steep, twisting path among the rocks, voices lifted in excitement could be heard.

Raina glanced back at Teague, riding behind her. "We'll be hard pressed to escape this place," she called to him in a low voice, "if there's ever a need to do so."

His teeth flashed white in the gathering gloom. "I don't plan on staying long. Do you? We've a mission to complete."

She grinned and nodded, then turned back to the trail. Up ahead, in the dimming light, Raina suddenly caught sight of Bahir's tall, broad-shouldered form. Unease threaded through her. The Tuaret leader had studiously avoided her for the past two days, save for one incident this afternoon, when he'd dropped back from his position at the head of the caravan to ride beside her. That visit, however brief, had unsettled her as none other before.

Raina had shot him a disinterested look, then focused her gaze straight ahead. Bahir, however, wasn't to be thwarted in whatever purpose had brought him to her.

"We'll make my camp by nightfall," he'd begun.

"So I've heard." Raina hadn't even bothered to grace his comment with a look.

"As a token of my esteem, you and your mate will have your own tent. After the lack of privacy of the past days, I'm certain you'll enjoy the chance for some secluded time together."

"Yes, I'm quite certain."

"I've many young men in my camp," he'd gone on to tell her, apparently not at all perturbed by her lack of enthusiasm. "You must try, as best you can, to comport yourself with dignity and restraint. Bring no shame upon your mate."

Anger twined about Raina's gut, clenching it tightly. "And how would I bring shame, Bahir?" she demanded, finally meeting his gaze. "Because I've an opinion and a mind of my own? Because I choose to walk among you all as a free woman, rather than hide behind a veil and the confines of a tent?"

His eyes narrowed. "Our women wear no veils, and neither are they confined to a tent. But your opinions aren't appreciated unless requested. And you must defer to your mate in all things."

"And if I don't? What will you do then?"

"I?" He gave a harsh laugh. "I won't have to do anything. But my people will, if and when they begin to question the authenticity of your life-mating. And that can have dire consequences, *mirah*. Consequences you and your mate might not find pleasant. If he *is* truly your mate." With that, the Tuaret leader urged his equs forward, loping up the line until he once more gained its head.

Her worst fears had come to fruition, Raina thought, as she followed the stream of riders toward the firelight beckoning just beyond the next turn of the trail. Bahir, wily man that he was, had always doubted the veracity of their claim to be life mates. And with that veiled warning earlier he'd brought the issue to a head, cautioning her to play the proper mate or risk being given to one of his men as a real mate.

She should be grateful to him for the admonition, she well knew, but she wasn't. It was but his way of "taming" her, as he'd once said she needed. Of intimidating her into acting the proper woman.

Defiance warred with caution as Raina followed the men up the last incline and into a large, open area sheltered on all sides by rock walls. She scanned the enclosure and counted at least fifty black, woven capra-hair tents, staked out in clusters of two or more dwellings.

Family units, Raina realized, making for at least ten to twenty individual clans within the tribe.

Campfires burned before each cluster of tents. Women squatted before the fires, cooking the evening meal. Some wore black headcloths over which red or green scarves trimmed in bits of aureum thread were tied around the top of their heads and brows. Others chose to go uncovered, their dark hair flowing, unbound about their shoulders and down their backs. All were dressed in long, flowing robes of deep blue and black, cinched at the waists by colorful woven belts and decorated with equally colorful stripes sewn in decorative swirls onto the robes.

Children and an assortment of small, yapping canus ran about, wending their way through the equs to welcome the returning riders who'd halted and were beginning to dismount. Raina sat there atop her equs, unsure what to do next. Bahir leaped down from his own mount and strode back to where she and Teague waited.

"Come," he said, extending his hand to her. "I'd introduce you to my family and have you join us for the evening meal, before showing you and your mate where you'll sleep this night."

Raina eyed his proffered hand. Did he think her so helpless, after all she and Teague had been through of late, that she couldn't climb down unaided from her own equs? The answer, however, was obvious. He cared not a whit for her abilities. He but tested her willingness to heed his advice on proper feminine conduct.

She shot him a venomous look, but accepted his hand without protest or comment and slid off her equs. Bahir waited until Teague was off his mount—Rand's carrying case clutched in his hand—then turned and, clasping

Raina's hand firmly in his, escorted her across the camp to the largest and most ornately decorated tent.

A woman who looked to be in her mid-thirties bent over a cook pot before the solitary tent. When she noted their approach she straightened, calmly awaiting them. She was slender, her light brown hair unbound and falling to the middle of her back. The leaping flames of her campfire distorted her features. Still, Raina couldn't help but think she somehow looked familiar.

That sense of familiarity solidified into recognition as Bahir drew up before the woman, Raina's hand still in his. Bright blue eyes in a plain but sweetly feminine face widened as the woman seemed to recognize Raina at the same moment the warrior woman recognized her. It was Najirah, a girlhood friend from her days living in the royal city of Ksathra. Najirah, who now lived the simple life of a Tuaret, instead of in the opulent luxury of the royal city.

"Raina," Bahir said, his mouth quirking in wry amusement as the two women took their shocked fill of each other, "this is Najirah, my second wife. Najirah, this is Raina, a female of great courage and no small amount of independence." He motioned for Teague to step forward. "And this is her mate, Teague Tremayne. They'll be our guests this eve, and for all the days to come that they wish to partake of our hospitality."

Najirah nodded a greeting to Raina, then turned to Teague, a smile of welcome on her lips. As she did she gave a small start. Her eyes widened once more and she paled.

"My lord," she whispered, her voice gone tight and low. "My lord . . ."

Thirteen

Teague froze. His glance locked with Najirah's, hard, piercing, and filled with a veiled warning. Did she know? But how? *How?* He'd been but a lad when he'd left Incendra. Surely he'd changed enough in appearance . . .

But what had his mother once said about women? That they "could look into the hearts and minds of men and see them for who and what they truly were"?

Best to pretend ignorance of the woman's deferential greeting, Teague swiftly decided. Best to take command of the situation before it disintegrated into total chaos. He strode up, slung Rand's carrying pack over his shoulder, and took Najirah's hand in his. "I'm honored finally to make your acquaintance, femina. Though both Raina and myself are simple wayfarers and come from distant lands, your mate and your people have treated us with the utmost kindness and consideration. I accept your hospitality with great pleasure."

As she stared up at him, confusion darkened Najirah's bright blue eyes. She scanned his face intently, her soft, full mouth tightening in deep consideration, then shrugged, as if tossing aside whatever she'd been contemplating. "My husband and I are honored as well that you would accept the simple hospitality of our home," she finally replied in the cool, carefully modulated tones of a woman of breeding.

Gently, she slipped her hand from his and gestured to the large cushions placed on a woven grass mat near the fire. "Please, if you would recline, I will bring you cool water to wash your hands and face. The meal will be ready soon."

Teague nodded and looked over at Bahir. The Tuaret nodded in response to Najirah's invitation, then shed his headcloth and cloak and handed it to his wife. Garbed only in his long white tunic, he walked over, lowered himself to the mat, and leaned upon one of the cushions.

The monk followed suit, removing his own headcloth and cloak. Then, after a moment's hesitation and a gaze that cautioned Raina not to refuse, he handed her his clothing. Setting Rand's case beside another brightly colored cushion, Teague joined Bahir on the mat.

Raina accepted the items with a raised brow, but no protest. Walking over to Najirah, she forced a bright smile. "I'm not familiar with all the nuances of your tribes' customs, but I'd like to help. Pray guide me, if you will."

Najirah, who'd been furtively but unwaveringly watching Teague, jerked her attention back to Raina. "Customs?" Comprehension dawned. "Ah, yes. Come,"—she made a quick motion with her hand—"and I'll show you where to put your mate's things in our tent. Then, if you don't mind, could you help by offering the men the wash water while I finish preparing the meal?"

As she talked, Najirah led Raina into the tent. She didn't stop, however, until they were nearly at the back of the shelter. Then, in a quick move, she stopped, turned, and grabbed Raina by the arm.

"By the firestorms," she whispered, a joyous excitement lighting her eyes and voice. "Is it really you, Raina? I thought never to see you again, after that day I helped smuggle you onto that space freighter leaving Incendra. Why did you come back? And who is that man Bahir claims is your mate? He reminds me of—"

She stopped short and blushed. "I-I beg pardon. My courtesy is lacking, to intrude into your private matters in so forward a manner."

Raina laughed softly and gave her a big hug. "I'm as glad to see you as you are me," she said, finally leaning back and releasing Najirah. "And I came because Teague and I were sent here on a mission of vital importance to the Imperium."

Najirah eyed her. "Indeed?"

"Indeed," Raina smilingly agreed. "But that can be explained further later. Suffice it to say that besides you, Bahir is the only one who knows our true purpose here, and that is how it must remain."

"I understand." The brown-haired woman paused. "This man, the one you call Teague, your mate—how long have you known him?"

Her question sent a ripple of unease through Raina. Why would Najirah care how long she'd known Teague? A little voice warned her to proceed with care. Though she and Najirah had been the closest of friends, that had been over fifteen cycles ago. Much had changed since then. Najirah's loyalties were to Bahir now. And Bahir already knew or suspected more than Raina wished.

"Teague?" She found sudden interest in the fine braid edging his cloak. "Cycles now. We grew up together, or, rather, since the time I arrived on Bellator." She lifted her gaze and met Najirah's squarely. "Why do you ask?"

A troubled look flared in the other woman's eyes.

"He reminds me of someone, a boy who lived in Ksathra, in the royal palace, before you came to live there." She hesitated, then sighed and shook her head. "I'm most likely mistaken, but he looks so much like . . ." Her voice faded.

Something in Najirah's tone, in her words, gave Raina pause. Her gaze narrowed. "Yes, go on," she prodded. "Who does Teague remind you of? Who does he look like?"

Najirah eyed her in puzzlement. "Don't you know? Hasn't he told you? You're his mate, after all."

Exasperation filled Raina. "Even mates have secrets from each other." She decided to risk revealing a tiny bit of what she'd gleaned in the past weeks, if only to encourage Najirah's confidence. "I will admit, though, that Teague's past isn't something he has shared with me. At least, not all of it."

Bahir's wife exhaled a deep breath, nodding in apparent understanding of the vagaries of husbands. "Well, I wouldn't say this to just anyone, for I got the distinct impression he didn't wish anyone to know, but since you're his mate . . ."

"Yes?"

"He reminds me of the crown prince Tarik, of the Royal House of Shatrevar," Najirah whispered in a conspiratorial tone, leaning close, as if fearing she might be overheard. "And he looks just like his father, the old king."

The meal was a surprisingly sumptuous one, consisting of one large hammered metal plate filled with a bed of cooked grain upon which had been placed chunks of roast cerva marinated in herbs and spices, and another upon which sat flat pieces of a traditional circular bread. Nearby, along with a tall, curved pot used to boil the deep, dark, rich faba, sat a smaller plate filled with baka cakes flavored with a sticky mixture of apis honey, syrup, and nuts.

Teague ate well, keeping pace with Bahir as they scooped up mouthfuls of the grain and meat dish with pieces of the flat bread, then washed it down with liberal amounts of cerevisia, a hearty, fermented liquor brewed from the tubers of the asphodel bush. Raina's appetite, on the other hand, thanks to Najirah's startling revelation about Teague, was barely adequate to avoid an outright insult to the Tuaret couple's hospitality.

She entered little into the conversation of the two men, which she imagined pleased at least Bahir. Though Teague sent her occasional questioning glances, she pretended not to notice, concentrating on keeping her eyes cast down as befit a desert wife. After a time, as the consumption of the cerevisia increased, she was left more and more to her own thoughts.

Was it possible? she asked herself over and over. *Was* Teague the son of the old king? She searched her memory for any hint of his past, any nuance or shading in his words.

She recalled the first time she'd seen him, that night at his hermitage, outside the Bellatorian royal city of Rector. Even then, there'd been something special about him, from his magnificent body, his endless stamina and power as he'd carried out the repetitive movements of the strange blade ceremony he performed, to the terrible, anguished beauty of his face. He was a man among men in her eyes, but that didn't make him the king's son.

Yet the sense of a secret torment, a barely contained

fear even that day when he'd reluctantly accepted the
call to go to Incendra, had moved her, plucked at her,
until Raina, too, had agreed to a mission her mind, if
not her heart, told her was foolhardy and potentially
fatal. Even then, her instincts whispered that he shied
from the journey not out of cowardice or indolence, but
something far deeper, something that had happened long
ago . . . perhaps even on Incendra.

There had been other incidents as well, none meaning
much in itself; but when they were woven, bit by bit,
into the tapestry of the past weeks . . . Like his comment that night on the spy ship, after they'd landed and
she was still ill from the effects of the radiation sickness. He'd admitted to guessing she'd been ill treated at
the hands of some man or men. That her hatred of men
had arisen from some horrible experience . . . perhaps
as terrible as his. And when she'd struck out at him in
her anger and shame and accused him of having his
own sordid, secret past, he hadn't denied it.

What Raina remembered most vividly of all, however,
was later that night, when Teague had taken her out into
the thunderstorm to cool her fever. When he'd sunk to
his knees, whispering in an agonized voice that he
couldn't take it anymore. Even then, Raina had wondered what he couldn't take. Wondered what haunted
him so badly that it roused such abject fear in a man
she'd already suspected, even then, to be brave and
strong and good.

The incident in the storm had only corroborated his
later revelation, that night at the oasis before the sand
cat's attack, when Teague had admitted why he'd become a monk. "I had nothing . . . no home, no family,
no name, and no hope . . ." And when he later shared
his conversation with Rand with her, admitting the

world he'd rebuilt as a monk, after his world on Incendra was destroyed, was now threatening to collapse . . .

He'd given her so many hints—inadvertently, she was certain, knowing his fierce pride—but with Najirah's additional revelation, it now all fell into place. Fell into place, when she added her knowledge of what was said to have happened to the royal family once Malam Vorax had seized power.

The queen had been flung from the parapet wall that towered over the valley, screaming in terror all the way down until she struck the sharp rocks below. The princess, four years older than her brother, had been given to the soldiers loyal to Vorax and repeatedly raped until she fled, naked, to the fortress walls and leaped to join her dead mother. The old king, along with his young son, had been forced to watch the atrocities; then the king had been beheaded and his head hung from the main gate.

And then there was the prince, brutalized by what he'd witnessed, alone and at Vorax's mercy. It'd been said afterward that though Vorax had had the lad tortured in a myriad of crude and depraved ways, he'd feared killing him. That in the darkest hours of the night, he'd sent the prince away alive, but never to be seen or heard from again. The ancient prophecy would allow no other fate—not if Vorax, a superstitious man when all was said and done, wished to keep the throne he'd stolen through treachery and deceit.

At long last Raina understood Teague's reluctance to return to Incendra, his fear, his pain. And understood, as well, why he kept it all a tightly guarded secret. He'd suffered enough for the failings of his family, shared enough of their shame. And then, to return to a land that had not only brutally rejected him, but had cast him out . . .

Admiration for his courage swelled in her breast. A fierce desire to aid him, to protect him from further pain. And a need to comfort him, to love him. If only he would let her. If only he dared . . .

Yet it wasn't her right to question him about his heritage. It wasn't her right to pry, or force open the floodgates of his heart. Teague had done the best he could with what a heartless fate had dealt him. It was better if she let the truth of his past be.

He wasn't just a simple monk anymore, though. He was most likely the crown prince, the true heir to the throne of Farsala, the most powerful kingdom on Incendra. He was the greatest threat to Vorax's rule that the evil man had ever known. And because of that, the mission was endangered. Because of that, she had to know the truth. It was the only way they could prepare for all eventualities.

Briefly, Raina considered cornering Najirah this night, before she'd a chance to talk with Bahir and share her suspicions. That idea quickly died an ignominious death. Najirah adored Bahir, was intensely loyal to him. That much, even in the short time she'd spent with her girlhood friend, had been more that evident. No, Najirah would never keep such a momentous secret from her husband.

The dilemma lay in what Bahir would do once he knew. He hated Malam Vorax. He might well try to use Teague as a rallying point for the armies he hoped would join him. She wouldn't put it past the man. He did exactly what he wanted, when he wanted.

She shot a glance in the Tuaret leader's direction. He and Teague had their heads together in slightly tipsy conversation. Their growing inebriation was for the best, Raina thought, at least as far as Bahir was concerned. The drunker he got tonight, the better. Teague, on the other hand, needed as clear a head as possible for their impending discussion.

Raina looked over at Najirah. "Isn't it time we brewed the faba and served the baka cakes? If the men drink much more cerevisia . . ."

The blue-eyed woman smiled. "A wise decision."

She rose and, walking over to where the faba pot and a plate of sweet cakes sat, picked them up and brought them back. Placing the cakes on the mat near the fire, Najirah proceeded to add water, then the faba beans and some rich cardamite spices to the pot. She hung the pot from a tripod over the crackling fire. Rising, Najirah walked back to the tent and soon returned with a small carved box.

A set of fine white pottery cups, their curved outsides painted in the bold swirls of desert language, were stacked carefully within. Najirah took out four and handed one to each of them. "They were our wedding gift from my father," she shyly offered. "They bear Bahir's family name in the old script. 'Husam al Nur' means 'sword of light.' "

"A fitting name for the man who is fated to be the savior of his people." Teague lifted his glass of cerevisia high in salute.

Bahir's mouth twisted wryly. Najirah, however, glanced at Teague in horror. "But that cannot be. Bahir is—"

"Enough, Najirah," her husband sharply cut her off. "Don't shame us by insulting our guest's attempt to honor me. He means no harm, one way or another."

She blushed and lowered her head. "I beg pardon, Teague Tremayne," she murmured. "I meant no insult."

Teague managed a lopsided grin. "No insult was taken, domina."

At that moment the water in the faba pot began to boil. Steam sang from the curved, narrow spout. Najirah closed the carved box, laid it down, and rising, hurried over to the fire. Their cups were soon filled with the thick, strongly flavored faba. The baka cakes were the perfect complement.

Afterward the two men talked a time longer while Raina helped Najirah clean up the remnants of the meal. Though she wished for a few more moments alone with Bahir's wife, the opportunity never arose. At long last, the Tuaret leader yawned, stretched out his arms, and glanced pointedly from Teague to Raina, then back to Teague.

"It's past time you and your mate took your rest. As must Najirah and I. I've been too long without the sweet comfort of a woman, as I'd wager you have, too."

The monk's gaze skittered off Raina's. Both quickly looked away. "Yes, it *has* been too long without the privacy we prefer, er, in order to fully savor the sweet comfort of each other," he finally forced himself to reply. "And I must thank you for that as well."

Bahir rose. "Come. Let me show you your tent. It's just a short distance behind ours."

Teague climbed to his feet, Rand's carrying pack in his hand. Raina stood, both eager and a little nervous about sharing a tent alone with Teague. Eager because she needed desperately to talk with him. Nervous because she didn't know what might happen between them afterward. Wordlessly, she nodded her farewells to Najirah, then followed after the two men.

The black capra-hair tent sat a sufficient distance back and away from Bahir's to ensure privacy, wedged into one corner of the steep, stone-walled enclosure. Raina eyed it with approval. There was no way any could approach the tent and overhear their conversation, save by first passing Bahir's dwelling. And though the possibility remained that the Tuaret leader might spy on them, somehow Raina doubted that. For all his irritating mannerisms, Bahir had never struck her as anything but straightforward.

Bahir paused at the opening of the tent, his glance locking with Teague's. "There are a bag of water and cloths to cleanse yourselves with, as well as a small jug of cerevisia and some fresh palmas fruit, in case you wake later and are hungry. The pallet is large and supplied with soft cushions, in addition to several blankets to protect you from the night's chill.

"Not that you'll most likely need them," he added, his gaze becoming shuttered and unreadable. "A warm, willing *mirah* can take a man's mind off most anything, wouldn't you agree?"

In spite of himself, Teague's blood warmed at the thoughts the Tuaret's words stirred. It seemed he and Raina must sleep together this night whether they wished it or not, or risk stirring Bahir's suspicions even further. He'd provided them the privacy of their own tent for a reason. He wished now to see if they used it as befitted two lovers.

Teague nodded. "I agree." He forced his answer past a throat gone suddenly dry. Dry with anticipation. Dry with fear. He turned to Raina, lifted the tent flap, and motioned her in.

She shot him a narrow-eyed glance, then ducked her head and walked in. Teague, still holding the tent flap in his hand, turned back to Bahir. "My thanks for your hospitality this night. I bid you a safe and most pleasant rest."

"And I you, Teague Tremayne." With that, Bahir wheeled about and strode away.

The monk stood there for a time, gazing after the tall nomad, sorting through all that had happened in the past days, trying to make his way through the complex maze of truths and untruths to pierce the heart of the man, to anticipate the best course to take with him. Minute by minute, it seemed, the mission became more and more complicated. And then there was Raina.

With a low, soughing sigh, Teague turned, leaned down, and stepped into the tent. The flap fell behind him, snapping down with a disconcerting finality. There was no avoiding her this night, or the feelings and desires that ran rampantly through him. Yet this night, like all the rest until the mission was over and he could turn finally from her forever, must be faced, must be endured.

At the sound of the tent flap falling, Raina wheeled about. A small, hanging oil lamp had been lit, bathing the interior—and Raina—in a soft, golden light. She'd unbound her hair, and it cascaded down about her shoulders in a shimmering cloud of russet. Longing twisted within Teague, made his throat tighten, his eyes burn with unshed tears.

Gods, but he was so weary of denying himself, he thought. So tired of having to raise his guard every time he was near Raina, as if . . . as if she were some vile temptation that would corrupt and destroy him. She was but a female, curse it all . . . and he was a man.

A man . . . but also a monk. A fifth-degree Grandmaster. A paragon of virtue and shining example of the heights to which self-discipline and denial could take one in the Order. And he stood to lose it all. All—for just one night of pleasure.

He gestured to the water bag hanging from the center tent pole. "Would you like some privacy so you might wash before bedtime?"

Raina's glance skittered to the bag, then back to Teague's. "I don't need any privacy. I trust you."

The simple statement, and the calm, steady look she sent him as she said it, took Teague's breath away. He managed a taut little smile. "Well, be that as it may, I don't trust myself. I'll return shortly."

At his passing, the tent flap snapped back in place. Raina gazed longingly after him, then sighed and began to remove her tunic. She poured a small amount of water into a large pottery bowl and dipped a cloth into it. As she wrung out the excess water, Rand's voice rose from his carrying pack.

"Your friendship with Teague grows," he said. "That is good."

Raina jerked from the task of washing her face. She flushed and made a move to cover her bare breasts before catching herself and letting her arms fall back to her sides. She gave an unsteady laugh. "How long has your system been turned on?"

"For the past two days of the journey. Teague thought I might overhear something that could be of value when he wasn't around." Rand paused. "I thought you knew. I am sorry if I surprised you."

"Well, I didn't . . . know, that is," she muttered and resumed her washing. "Did you learn anything of interest?"

"Not much, save that Aban is very worried about Bahir. He was discussing it once within range of my communications device."

"And? Did you discover what's wrong with him?"

"No, save that his illness is fatal and beginning to rapidly worsen."

She frowned. "That doesn't bode well for us. We could use his help."

"I thought you didn't like him."

Raina rolled her eyes and shook her head. "I can dislike someone and still see his use."

"I suppose you're right. Is that how you feel about the monk?"

"Teague?" Raina paused in her bath, suddenly wary. "What's it to you, Volan, how I feel about him?"

"He will need your help, your support, in the days to come."

She gave a harsh laugh. "So I'm beginning to realize." She sobered, suddenly awash in a wave of fear and uncertainty. She felt a fool, talking to a box as she was, but for just a moment, she needed to share the terrible burden of Teague's identity with someone. "I'm not so certain I can help him, Volan. Not with what I've just learned about him."

"He cares about you. He trusts you. And you've yet one additional advantage."

Raina eyed him suspiciously. "What's that?"

"You're a female. From what I've gleaned of your species, males find it much easier in most cases to open their hearts and bare their souls to females. Especially one they might care for and desire."

She really shouldn't be surprised that Rand, even within the limitations of his box, had discerned the tension, the need growing between her and Teague. But wanting someone was one thing. Being able to help him, or even knowing how, was another.

"But you don't understand, Volan," she said softly. "I'm not the typical woman. I haven't the time or the skills for such things."

"And that frightens you."

She immediately bristled. "I never said that."

"We all fear what we are unsure of, of wanting too badly, too strongly, what matters most to us. Fear that if we do and it is taken from or denied us or we lose it, we'll be devastated, and more bereft than we were before."

"Is that how it was with you?" Raina asked, her curiosity piqued. "When you gave up your body?"

Rand didn't answer for the longest time. "Yes, it was— and is," he finally said. "Yet even in the loss, I find I would take the chance again. I felt so alive, so whole, so vital in a body. The ability to feel, and experience, and live was so much more intense—and so much more natural. And yet . . . I knew there was still something lacking. As if I wasn't quite whole yet. As if a part of me was still missing. As if . . . as if . . ."

He sighed. "Well, it's not something I'll find the answer to soon or easily. And it doesn't matter this night. You and Teague are what matter."

"You're most confusing. For a Volan, I mean." Raina tossed the wet cloth back into the bowl, quickly dried herself, then grabbed up a clean tunic out of one of the carrying packs.

"How so?"

She tugged the tunic over her head before replying, then combed out her hair and began rebraiding it. "You've surprising insights for an alien species from another galaxy. At times, you seem more like us than unlike us. It makes no sense."

"No, I suppose it doesn't," Rand agreed. "And I have no knowledge of a past, for myself or any of my kind, to explain it. The collective consciousness of the Mother Ship never allowed for any free thought, or memories, or heritage."

Raina finished her braid and deftly tied it off. She flung it over her shoulder and rose. "Well, just as Teague and I won't solve the problems of our past or future this night, neither will you. But it's past time we all take our rest. I'm going to get Teague."

"A wise decision, femina. Just remember. Don't let your fear hold you back from being the person you were meant to be."

"Indeed." Raina gave a wry laugh and strode across the tent to the entranceway.

Teague stood outside a long while, his hands fisted at his sides, his eyes clenched shut. Gods, ah, gods, he silently, repeatedly flung his tormented cry to the heavens. She trusted him. Trusted him, now of all times, when he was the least trustworthy of all.

What was he to do? *What was he to do?*

Time passed. Teague lost track of how long he'd stood there waiting, giving Raina the opportunity to bathe. Finally, a soft voice intruded on his miserable reverie. "Teague?"

He wheeled. She stood there, her face freshly scrubbed, her hair woven once more into the single neat braid down her back. "Finished, are you?" he croaked.

She smiled. "Yes. Would you like to trade places, so that you might have your time of 'privacy'?"

"No." He shook his head with a sharp, definitive motion. "On the morrow. I'll wash on the morrow."

"Then come inside." Raina stepped back and held the tent flap up for him. "It's cold. Besides, I need to talk with you."

There was something in the tone of her voice, gone suddenly tense, something in the way she held her eyes, staring yet not quite looking at him, that gave Teague pause. "Indeed?" he asked, forcing a casual lightness to his voice he certainly didn't feel. He entered the tent, walked over to the pallet and, taking one of the larger cushions, tossed it a meter or so away and sat.

Raina followed him in, ambled over to the pallet, and sank to her knees, facing him. "Najirah is my friend from my girlhood days here on Incendra," she began without preamble. "She lived with me in Ksathra, in the court of Malam Vorax. Both our fathers had fought for him against the old king. Both were rewarded by positions of power in Vorax's court. Najirah's father, however, had also once held a position of power under the old king. Though they didn't live at court then, they made frequent visits. Najirah was fourteen at the time of the rebellion, three cycles older than me."

"And your point in all this, femina?"

Raina hesitated, agonizing over the best way to broach the next revelation. Finally, with an exasperated breath, she forged on. "Najirah thinks you're the crown prince Tarik Shatrevar." She paused expectantly, dreading what she already knew in her heart was the answer. Paused, waited.

When Teague didn't reply, she bluntly pressed on. "Are you?"

A muscle worked frantically in the strong expanse of Teague's jaw. The lines on either side of his mouth deepened. His eyes glinted silver and hard. His breathing became harsh, erratic.

"Are you, Teague?" Raina softly prodded.

"What I was is in the past," he snarled. He climbed to his feet to tower over her. "I suggest you leave it that way. I have."

"If you're the king's son, we can't just 'leave it that way.' " She gazed up at him, met his thunderous glare calmly, and gestured to a spot on the pallet beside her. "Come. Sit by me. It's best we not raise our voices."

"There's nothing to discuss, Raina." He shoved a hand roughly through his hair, setting the long strands awry. "I'm a monk of the Monastery of Exsul. That's all I'll ever be."

"Najirah will tell Bahir."

Teague went still. As full comprehension dawned, horror widened his eyes. He flung back his head, the cords of his neck stretching tautly. *"Gods!"*

"What will he do, once he knows?"

Teague threw himself back down on the cushion he'd been using a few minutes before. He cradled his head in his hands, his blond hair threading through his long, strong fingers. "Ah, gods . . ."

"What will he do, Teague?"

With a shuddering sigh, he lifted a hollow, haunted gaze to hers. "I don't know. He seems to imagine he fights against Vorax in my name, until the day I return."

"And you don't want to 'return,' do you?"

Compassion, understanding, and acceptance gleamed in Raina's striking green eyes. Something strong and good arced between them, piercing Teague clear through to his soul. The barriers he'd fought so long and hard to maintain wavered, began to tumble down. The old fear, the spiraling panic, filled him. He dragged in a shuddering breath.

"No, I don't . . . want to 'return.' I-I'm afraid, Raina. And I don't know what to do."

At his anguished admission, Raina gave a soft cry. On hands and knees, she scooted over to him, taking him into her arms. "It's all right, Teague," she crooned, pressing his head to her breast, stroking his hair. "I'll help you. I swear it. We're partners, and partners stand by each other."

He wound his arms about her, clasping her tightly, frantically, as if he feared for more than just his life, as if . . . he feared for his very soul. He dragged in sharp, little gulping breaths. His heart thudded wildly, heavily against her.

"I'm here, Teague," she whispered, recalling the same words she'd spoken to him the night of the thunderstorm. "You're safe. I won't let anything happen to you."

His breaths came rapidly now, loud, labored, as if he were running, or fighting off some terrible attacker. He broke out in a sweat. His fingers knotted in the fabric of her tunic, twisting, and pulling on it.

Fear flooded Raina. What was he remembering, that affected him so? What could she do to help him?

"What did he do, Teague?" she whispered tautly. "What did Vorax do? Tell me. Purge it from yourself once and for all."

"Nooo," he moaned. "I can't. I can't. It was all . . . my . . . fault."

She froze. His fault? But he'd been just a lad of thirteen. How could any of it have been his fault?

"Tell me anyway," she commanded in a firm, no-nonsense voice. She gave him a small shake. "Tell me."

He went still. The sound of his poor, tortured breathing filled the silence of the night, pressing down on Raina with heavy anticipation. Dread found its chill way into her heart, inexorably sliding through her veins. Gods, what had he gone through? And was she truly doing the right thing, demanding he tell her?

"Tell me, Teague," she pleaded. "You treated me with compassion and understanding when you learned what Vorax did to me. Do you think that I would do any less for you? Let it go, once and for all. I won't judge. I swear it."

"What Vorax did to you wasn't your fault," he groaned. "But what I did . . ."

"I stayed in Vorax's court for four years after he took the throne. I was his betrothed, though he already had a wife, and a young child by her. Yet for a time before I finally saw the true man beneath the smooth, deceitful exterior, I admired him, yearned to life-mate with him when I came of age. There's fault enough in that, I'd say."

"You were young, ignorant of men."

"You were young, too." She brushed the sweat-damp hair from his face. "All I know, all I care about right now, is that you not bear this alone anymore."

He looked up at her in wonder, as if he couldn't quite believe what he was hearing. Tears filled his eyes and, as quickly as they appeared, he fiercely blinked them away. Then he sighed and lowered his head back to her breast.

"I-I used to draw," he finally began, his voice thready, quavering. "My father didn't like that. He didn't like much about me that cycle I turned thirteen. I was small, scrawny, and poor at games and warrior's training. I preferred to read, to draw, to take long, solitary walks and explore."

Teague's voice grew stronger, surer, the longer he spoke, almost as if he began to relive the days past. "I was happy, save that no matter what I did, how hard I tried, I couldn't seem to win my father's approval. Then Malam Vorax came, demanded my father abdicate the throne. And nothing was the same ever again."

"Go on," Raina urged, when Teague failed to continue. "How was your father defeated? Some say he was betrayed, that Vorax led his army into the fortress through a secret passage, taking the king's army by surprise."

He went rigid. Ever so slowly, he released her and moved back, almost as if distancing himself from her before she could do it herself. Flat, emotionless eyes met hers. "It's true enough. One of my drawings, that day on the parapet when my father knocked them out of my folder, floated down to Vorax's army. Some soldier must have found it and taken it to Vorax. It was a drawing I'd made one day of a secret passage leading from the back of the mountain into the fortress."

He dragged in a shuddering breath, a faraway look gleaming in his eyes. "It was so beautiful there, the passage well guarded by two giant stone sentinels that looked so much like flames leaping from the mountainside. I named it 'The Tapestry Passage,' because the secret door to the passage was hidden behind a huge tapestry in my father's library."

"And you think Vorax used a boy's drawing to gain entrance into the fortress?" Raina smiled. "You put too much importance on a piece of paper, I think."

"Do I?" Teague tautly demanded. "Vorax easily took the fortress, didn't he? And then, as he sent my father out to be beheaded, he pulled a ragged piece of paper from his pocket. He glanced at it one last time, laughed, then tossed it aside and followed after the guards taking my father to his execution.

"As if in slow motion, that paper floated to the floor," Teague said, his voice raw, hoarse. "I caught a glimpse of what was on it just before one of the guards holding me leaned down and picked it up, stuffing it into his breeches. It was my drawing, Raina. My 'Tapestry Passage.' In my selfish, self-centered need to defy my father, to show him I would do whatever I wished, I had betrayed him. Betrayed him, my mother and sister, my people."

"It was an accident, Teague," she hastened to refute his self-accusation. "An unfortunate accident. You betrayed no one. It was your father, by his foolish decisions and overbearing ways, who betrayed his family and people. *That* was why the rebellion began and ultimately succeeded. But it was never—ever—your fault."

"It doesn't matter whose fault it was in the end." He gave a low, harsh laugh. "I'm no more worthy to rule than my father was. Our blood is tainted, our reign over, as it rightfully should be. And I've no desire to fail the people yet again."

Confusion filled her. Such terrible anguish over a piece of paper? There was more, she feared, experiences that, building upon the trauma of seeing his family die and his life torn asunder, had been even more terrifying and degrading. But Raina also knew he wasn't ready yet to share those.

"But it was never *you* who failed them, Teague." She reached out to him. *"You* never had a chance to fail them."

He jerked back from her touch, a fierce pride and bitter resignation carved into his handsome features. "Don't. I don't need your pity. It's over, Raina. Has been for these past nineteen cycles. I made my decision long ago. I just wanted you to know why I am the way I am, why I don't want anyone ever to know *what* I was. If you truly care as you say you do, if you really mean to offer me compassion and understanding, you won't push me into doing something I reject with every fiber of my being. You'll respect my wishes in this."

Her hand fell to her side. A keen sense of helplessness flooded her. If she truly cared . . .

The realization that she more than cared about the tormented monk swamped Raina in an overwhelming rush of emotion. She more than cared—she loved him. Wonderment filled her. How, when had it happened? And what was she to do about it?

With a fierce inward shake, Raina flung the surprising revelation with its attendant questions aside. Now wasn't the time. What mattered now was Teague— Teague, who, for the first time, had bared his soul and now waited, wondering how she'd react, what she'd do. *If she truly cared . . .*

Raina glanced up, forced a brave smile, and nodded. "It'll be as you ask, Teague Tremayne. I won't push. I'll respect your wishes in this. And I'll stand at your side, no matter what happens."

Fourteen

Najirah settled her sleeping gown in place and began to comb through her hair in preparation for bed. Bahir hadn't yet returned from the habitual last walk he always made about the camp before retiring for the night. He took his responsibilities as leader of the Tuarets very seriously, especially in the past cycles since he'd finally turned against Malam Vorax.

He was an intense man in the best of times. Now, he bordered on obsession, blocking out nearly everything save what impacted on the continued welfare of his tribe. And since he'd come to the acceptance that his own days were numbered, he'd been even more driven. There was little time anymore in his life for tenderness, for compassion—for her.

She sighed and, returning her comb to the small, intricately carved box that held her wedding jewelry and other personal items, closed and latched the lid. Najirah had hoped, in time, that Bahir would come to love her, once the searing pain of Cyra's rejection had healed. Now, she doubted he'd ever have the time to heal.

Sadness welled from that secret place deep within her. A place she never shared with anyone—especially not with Bahir. He was a good man, a decent man, and he deserved a second chance at happiness. Even if it was never meant to be with her. She would sacrifice even that for him. Even that, if only he could be happy again.

The tent flap lifted. A sharp gust of chill air whirled into the tent. Najirah shivered, pulled a fluffy shawl woven from the soft, fuzzy undercoat of the male capra about her, and schooled her features into a welcoming smile. Turning, she looked up at her husband.

"Is all well this night?" she asked.

Bahir had a preoccupied frown on his face and didn't answer immediately. Instead, he shed his cloak and headcloth, then sat beside her on their sleeping pallet and began to pull off his boots.

"Here, let me help you." Najirah scooted to his feet. Grasping first one, then the other, she deftly tugged off his boots. With the edge of her shawl, she wiped them clean of a light layer of dust, then set the boots aside.

He watched her, his gaze steady, thoughtful. "The camp is quiet, the guards all at their posts."

For an instant, Najirah was puzzled, then realized he'd answered her welcoming question. "Good. And now it is time for you to take your rest." She rose up on her knees, bent toward him, and tenderly brushed a dark, wavy lock of hair from his forehead. "I have missed you."

There was no mistaking the sensuous offer in her words. Bahir's blood warmed. His sex thickened. He hadn't tasted of the sweetness of Najirah's body in a long while. He'd neglected her, that he well knew. He wouldn't tonight.

But first, there were other matters to be dealt with, the most important of which was that of Teague Tremayne and Raina. "You were surprised this eve, when you first met Tremayne," Bahir said. "You acted as if you knew him. Do you?"

She lowered her eyes, averted her gaze. She leaned back, drawing away both physically and emotionally. Always, always, the tribe, the political intricacies and machinations, came first with Bahir. "He reminded me of a lad I once met, in the royal city of Ksathra."

"You called him 'lord,' " Bahir persisted. "Was he a son of the nobility?"

Reluctantly, Najirah dragged her gaze back up to his. She well knew the impact her revelation would have on Bahir. He lived for and dreamt of the day the old king's son would return to overthrow Vorax and reclaim the throne. This knowledge of hers could stir things to a fever pitch and send them all down the road to outright rebellion. But she couldn't deny Bahir; he was her husband. She'd stand by him, support him, over all others.

"I could be mistaken," Najirah forced herself to reply, "but I thought he was the crown prince. He looks so much like his father."

Triumph and a fierce exultation sprang to Bahir's eyes, warming them to molten honey. His firm, sensual mouth lifted. He smiled, but the action was one of grim satisfaction, not simple joy. "I suspected as much," he muttered, half to himself. "There was something about him, about the mysterious way he returned. His destiny called him back to us—to *us,* Najirah—no matter how desperately the Imperium might also need him."

"What will you do, now that you know?"

Bahir considered her question for a long moment. "Tremayne won't join us willingly. For whatever his reasons, he doesn't wish to involve himself in our plight again."

Najirah frowned. "He must have suffered greatly, seeing his family die, enduring the tortures Vorax was said to have inflicted upon him, before he was finally freed.

Perhaps he's no longer the right man to reclaim the throne."

"It doesn't matter if he is or isn't." Bahir absentmindedly massaged the site of an old injury to his right shoulder, working the joint with strong, probing fingers as he considered his options. "He's the rallying point, the focus I need to gather the other tribes to our cause. Once Vorax is overthrown, others can rule Farsala through Tremayne. It's been done before. It can be done again."

"And I say that's cruel and ruthless, Bahir." Najirah hated pointing out such a brutal truth, but she'd vowed long ago to be his helpmate in all things. And he seemed always to value that in her. That, and her insights into the hearts and minds of his people. It was why, despite the fact she wasn't Tuaret by birth, despite the fact that she was a woman, he'd named her his second-in-command.

His hand on his shoulder stilled. He cocked a dark brow. "Ruthless? How so?"

"This Teague Tremayne, crown prince of Farsala though he might be, has the right to choose his own course in life."

"Do you truly think so, *mirah?*" Bahir abandoned his ministrations to his shoulder and leaned back on the cushions piled behind him. "And since when have the nobility had much say in what course their life is to take? They were born to rule. They have a sacred responsibility to do so. I don't see that as much of a choice."

"You would force him to accept that mantle of responsibility then? Force him to reveal his true identity?"

Bahir shook his head. "No. Tremayne is too clever to be overtly manipulated. I thought, instead, to slowly compel him to take responsibility for others. To prod him from the safe little shell he's retreated into. To help him rediscover his heritage, and the debt he owes and will always owe his people."

"A tall order." Najirah poured out a cup of cerevisia from the squat little jug that sat nearby and handed it to him. "How do you intend to go about this?"

"The woman, Raina. She is the key." He accepted the cup and drank deeply. "There is something strong between them, something both fear to examine too closely. But something, nonetheless, that will put my plans into action. I must force them to face it as expeditiously as possible."

Puzzlement furrowed Najirah's brow. Unease spiraled within her. "And how do you plan to force them?"

"They claim to be mates, yet I seriously doubt they are truly life-mated. Yet they *must* become mates. It's the only way to compel Tremayne to open his heart to his true destiny. First with one person, then another and another, until finally he is transformed back into the ruler he was fated to be. Until finally he realizes the inescapable debt he owes Farsala."

Horror filled Najirah, brimming over to rise like bitter gall into her throat. By the firestorms, it was bad enough Bahir meant to use Tremayne! It was cruelty beyond belief to coerce Raina into enduring another sexual assault. "You cannot force them to become mates," she heatedly, unthinkingly blurted. "Raina won't stand for another rape. She's been through enough, and—" She caught herself in the unwitting revelation too late.

Bahir's face darkened in anger. He sat up, grasped her by the arms, and roughly pulled her to him. "You knew her as well, did you, *mirah?*" His demand was brittle, harsh. "How long did you plan to keep that additional little secret from me?"

Najirah twisted in his grasp, panic threatening to overwhelm her. Never, *never,* would she betray Bahir in any way, but to hurt Raina . . . "It seemed insignificant, the fact that we were girlhood friends."

His grip tightened. "Nothing is insignificant. Do you hear me? Nothing!"

"I-I beg pardon." She cast her gaze down, inhaled a shuddering breath, then looked back up at him. "What do you want to know about Raina?"

"Who raped her, and when?"

"Malam Vorax raped her, when she refused to wed him. He met her shortly after he usurped the throne, when her father, a man who'd joined forces with him, came to live at the royal palace with his motherless, eleven-cycles-old daughter. Vorax was taken with Raina's beauty even then and demanded her hand. Raina's father agreed to betroth her to him, thinking it would solidify his position of power in the court, but refused to wed her to Vorax until she was fifteen. Malam vowed to take her as his first and primary wife at that time, and set his current one aside. So Raina lived at court for the next four cycles, and we became close friends. I helped her escape after the rape and got her smuggled on a freighter leaving Incendra. I hadn't seen or heard from her until this eve."

"And her father? What did he do when he learned Vorax had assaulted his daughter?"

"Raina's father?" Najirah's soft mouth twisted in derision. "He was too afraid of Vorax, too fearful of losing the man's favor. He told Raina to wed Vorax. She was ruined, at any rate."

"A most doting and compassionate of sires." Bahir

released her and leaned back on the cushions. "Two strangers come to Incendra," he muttered thoughtfully. "Two people of noble birth, who have both been foully treated by Malam Vorax. And fate has delivered them into my hands."

"Have a care, Bahir," his wife cautioned. "These people aren't objects to be manipulated to your will. They are living beings, with needs and desires, and a right to determine their own fates."

He graced her with an irritated look. "I know that. I'm not a heartless, manipulative monster. In most cases, I'd honor their right to choose their own destinies. But not this time. Not with the fate of Farsala, even Incendra, hanging in the balance. Tremayne owes Farsala far more than he wishes to give, which is presently nothing. And as far as Raina goes,"—he sighed—"well, I'm sorry if she must be a pawn in all this, but if she must, she must."

"Bahir, please. I—"

"No, *mirah.*" He held up a silencing hand. "You've given me your advice, and it is duly noted. But it changes nothing. I need your support in this. Will you help me?"

She hesitated for the span of an inhaled breath. As harsh as his plan seemed regarding Teague Tremayne and Raina, Najirah knew she could never refuse Bahir. His decision to use them was cold-blooded and manipulative, but his ultimate intent was good. And he didn't do it for himself. He did it for Farsala.

Never, ever, for himself, she thought with a bittersweet pang. Bahir never took anything for himself. Or at least, not since Cyra had left him.

With a soft sob, she nodded her acquiescence. "Yes,

you know I'll help you. You are my husband. What is it you wish for me to do?"

Bahir studied her for a long moment, imbibing deeply of her sweet face and the brown hair that tumbled in riotous curls about her shoulders and down her back. Through the thin fabric of her sleeping gown and the loosely woven shawl, he could make out the dark mauve of her nipples. Her full breasts strained against the cloth, taunting him, beckoning to him.

A hunger welled within Bahir for a soft, yielding woman in his arms. For a tight, feminine sheath clamped about his rigid sex. For a wild, wanton female crying out her need, her ecstasy, as he thrust hard and passionately into her.

For Cyra.

Pain, fiery and acrid, scorched through him. Savagely, Bahir thrust the traitorous yearning aside. Najirah was his wife, his first and only wife now, though he'd taken her to him solely out of pity when she'd staggered into camp one day, begging for shelter and his protection after Vorax had executed her husband. It was the right, no, the *duty* of a leader to do such a thing.

But Cyra wouldn't, couldn't ever understand. Though she'd never vented her anger against him on sweet, gentle Najirah, she'd also never forgiven him for taking a second wife. And now . . . now all he had was Najirah.

"I have a plan," he rasped, "but it can wait until the morrow. The time is better spent in loving you, *mirah*." He made a sharp gesture with his hand. "Disrobe. I've a need to see your woman's body. It's past time you have a man atop you, inside you again."

A flush heating her body, Najirah did as he'd requested. The shawl fell; the sleeping gown was shoved first off one, then the other shoulder, sliding down to pool at her knees. The chill night air wafted over her, tightening her nipples to pouting, deep-burgundy-colored buds. She shivered, but remained as she was, allowing Bahir to take his fill. He was her husband. She would deny him nothing.

Nothing . . . though she knew he looked at her nakedness and wished she was another.

The next two days passed in peace and relative harmony. Bahir insisted that he and his men required a short respite back in camp before setting out once more for the firestorm caves. Though neither Raina nor Teague was pleased with the delay, there wasn't much they could do about it. Bahir might have played the most ingratiating of hosts, but there was always an underlying message to all his hospitable actions and smiling explanations. They weren't leaving without him *or* his consent.

Teague seemed to take the enforced stay better than Raina. She paced the confines of the camp until she knew where each and every guard was situated, and knew as well that she and Teague could never escape unnoticed. To ease the frustration and restlessness, she took to accompanying Najirah as she went about her seemingly endless round of daily chores.

And chores there were aplenty. In the light of the next day, Raina discovered that the Tuaret camp consisted of only about twenty childbearing females, thirty-five children of various ages, and ten older couples. The rest were men—most of them unwed.

The realization made Raina decidedly uneasy, as did the lustful if well-schooled glances that followed her wherever she went. She recalled Bahir's abiding interest in whether she and Teague were truly life-mated or not. She understood better now the basis for that interest. His men needed mates.

"Where are all the women?" She finally broached the subject the afternoon of the second day in camp, as she helped Najirah dig up the starchy tubers of the asphodel bushes that grew in dense profusion on the desert floor beneath the Tuarets' rocky fortress. "For so many men, there seems a definite dearth of mates."

The brown-haired woman straightened from her bent position over one of the spiny-leafed plants, arched her back to ease her tense muscles, then cast a glance over her shoulder. The men Bahir had set to guard the women in their labors were well out of earshot.

"When Bahir led the Tuarets in rebellion against Vorax," she explained, "many women refused to follow them into exile."

Raina's auburn brow rose a fraction. "Tuaret women refusing to follow their men? Strange behavior, especially for desert people."

"Much has changed, become corrupted, since Vorax took power," Najirah muttered bitterly. "He seeks, with his deceitful, underhanded ways, to undermine the fabric of our society. He knows it to be the surest route to total control. In the guise of granting more rights and privileges to the women, he has slowly eroded the influence of the husbands and the family."

"Incendra has never been particularly generous when it came to the freedom of its women," Raina dryly offered.

"Agreed." Najirah leaned down and began hacking at the tuberous root of yet another asphodel. "But Vorax's motives have never been to help women, or anyone else save himself. He has done nothing but create chaos and dissension among his subjects. The women are only part of the problem."

She looked up and cocked a brow. "Did you know the Incendarian attraction was always a fabrication, fostered by Vorax and the many rulers before him as just another ploy to keep us from co-mingling with off planet visitors? To keep us from learning more of their worlds, and wanting what they had?"

Raina frowned. "I don't understand."

"Think about it. Bahir fell in love, wed and mated with an off planet woman. When Vorax found out, he ordered Bahir to give Cyra up. Bahir refused. It was the start of the feud between them and the cause of Bahir finally turning outlaw."

"This is most upsetting," Raina murmured.

"What? The reason for Bahir turning outlaw?"

"Y-yes," Raina stammered, distracted with her own thoughts. She hadn't been thinking about Bahir at all, but about the Incendarian attraction. If it couldn't be blamed for her sudden and intense affinity for Teague, not to mention for her recent discovery of her love for him, what could? And just when she'd managed to justify her strange emotions as yet another manifestation of that archaic but long accepted sexual magnetism.

"Vorax also stirs ancient blood feuds among the desert tribes, to keep them constantly at odds," Najirah continued, blithely unaware of the unsettling questions she'd stirred anew in her friend. "It is why Bahir is having such difficulty uniting the twelve tribes."

"And why Vorax remains in power," Raina finished for her, grateful for the diversion from her troubled thoughts.

Najirah nodded. "The Katebs are the worst offenders of all. In the best of times, they were the laziest of the desert tribes, preferring raiding over hard work to obtain whatever they needed. Now Vorax keeps them in his pay and sends them out whenever needed to stir the feuds anew. Of late, the Katebs disguise themselves as Tuarets, so the blame is laid at our feet. Thus, though Bahir has fought tirelessly to dispute the accusations, most tribes still don't trust him. Vorax has been that good at manipulating the hearts and minds of the people."

"It seems a hopeless cause," Raina murmured. She paused to drop a plump tuber into the woven reed basket. "Why does Bahir fight on?"

"Because he's a man of honor." Her friend leaned back and shot her a fiercely defiant glance. "But he needs help, desperately so. Will your mate help him, or not?"

Taken aback by the sudden, vehement demand, Raina stared at Najirah for a long moment. "Bahir knows about Teague, I take it?"

Najirah tossed a sweat-damp lock of hair out of her eyes. "Of course he does. I still believe in loyalty to one's mate."

"As do I, to mine," Raina dutifully replied. "But I also will not ask Teague to do what he doesn't wish to do."

"But our people need him!" the other woman cried. "Bahir hasn't long to live. Someone must take up the cause when he is gone!"

"What *is* wrong with Bahir?" Raina asked, suddenly uncomfortable with the issue of Teague and grateful for the opportunity to divert the course of the conversation. "Except for the strange illness he had back at the oasis, he seems quite healthy."

Najirah shot her an anguished look. "His line is

cursed with a wasting brain disease that eventually destroys the mind and severely damages the brain, while leaving the rest of the body perfectly healthy and intact. Bahir had hoped he'd escaped the curse—both his father and grandfather died of old age without sign of the illness—but in the past five cycles . . ." She inhaled a tremulous breath and lowered her head. "He worsens of late. The spells visit him more and more frequently now."

"How long? How much longer does he have?"

Najirah lifted tear-filled eyes. "It's difficult to estimate. Perhaps a few more weeks to a month or two."

"I'm sorry." Raina reached out and grasped her friend's hand. "I'll admit I don't particularly like Bahir, but I don't wish him harm. And most of all, I don't want you to be sad."

"Then help him, Raina!" The brown-haired woman dropped the small hand spade she'd been using and turned toward her. "Find some way to convince your mate to join with Bahir to reclaim his throne. That's all Bahir wants. That's all he's ever wanted."

"Vorax's overthrow is Bahir's dream, not Teague's. Bahir has no right to force that decision or burden onto anyone else. Teague has been through enough. Besides, it's a hopeless cause. The sooner Bahir realizes that, the sooner he can get on with fully living whatever time is left him. The sooner he'll wake up to the fact that he has a mate who loves and needs him."

Najirah reared back, her eyes wide and moisture-bright. "What are you implying? Bahir is a good husband."

"Is he, Najirah?" Raina laughed disparagingly. "I've watched him with you in camp. He treats you like one of his men. Never once have I seen him touch you, hold you, or even spare you an affectionate glance."

"Bahir isn't a man to parade his affections in public!"

Nor in private, either, Raina thought sourly, noting the embarrassed flush that colored her friend's cheeks. "Then why do you follow his every move with such heartbreaking longing? Why is any and every scrap of attention he deigns to cast your way snatched up with such hunger? Tell me that, Najirah."

"Is it that obvious?" She hung her head, her long brown locks tumbling down into her face. "Ah, gods, what must all the others in camp think of me?" Her hands fisted. She slammed them down on her bent thighs. "Ah, the shame. The shame!"

Raina hesitated, not certain what to say or do. She had no experience with love, or how to navigate the complex courses of the heart. She could barely admit to her own feelings for Teague, much less advise another. But Najirah was in pain. Somehow, in some way, she must help her.

"The shame lies with Bahir," she said flatly. "Not with you, Najirah. He's your mate, yet in all ways that matter, he has betrayed you."

"B-betrayed me?" Bright blue eyes, swimming with tears, lifted to hers. "How can that be?"

"Bahir has abandoned you emotionally. He cares for nothing save this hopeless quest to defeat Vorax. He sees nothing save what is expedient to achieve that goal. And because of that, people—you—will be hurt."

"He cannot help it!" Najirah cried, rushing once more to her husband's defense. "At least he cares, at least he tries to do something to remedy the sorry state the realm has fallen into."

"But what of you, in the meantime? What of your

life together? Your love?" Raina shook her head, exasperated. "It's wasted on Bahir."

"No, Raina, it isn't." A soft, knowing smile slowly lifted Najirah's lips. It illuminated her countenance, making her beautiful. "It isn't wasted. I give my love freely, without expectation of recompense, because Bahir is a good, honorable man, because I cannot do otherwise. Love isn't something you can measure, something you only dole out in equal parts to what you receive. It must be given because to do any less is to not live fully, to not be the person you were meant to be."

Raina was tempted to tell her friend of the message Bahir's first wife had given her to deliver to him. That might well have shattered the idealistic little world she seemed to live in. But that also would have been pointless, and unnecessarily cruel. Instead, Raina gave a disdainful snort. "Well, I, for one, have no wish to pine over a man who doesn't love me."

"Bahir loves me in his own way. It's enough until the day he finally comes to terms with his first wife's betrayal, and his own part in that betrayal. Only then can he finally heal and go on with his life—with loving." She cocked her head in a sad, considering gesture. "Would you desert *your* mate in his hour of need, just because he turned from you for a time?"

The question startled Raina. How could she truthfully answer it? She and Teague didn't even have the bonds of a life-mating to link them. And he was vowed to his Order. Though she loved him, was determined to support him in every way on this mission, she entertained little hope of ever becoming his mate.

If the truth be known, she wasn't all that certain she *wanted* to be his mate. But then, she wryly admitted, when it came to the enigmatic Teague Tremayne, there wasn't a whole lot she *was* certain of.

"No, I wouldn't desert him," she finally replied. "But I'd also have to know that he still loved me through it all. I suppose I haven't your courage, and I certainly don't have your trust—especially in men."

Najirah picked up her spade and turned back to her work. "A strange thing to say, when you're life-mated," she said, casting Raina a sideways glance.

The fine hairs stood out on the back of Raina's neck. Gods, how was she to extricate herself from that careless statement? She wagered that Bahir had shared his suspicions regarding their life mating with his wife. Had he also set her to searching out the truth?

"I haven't had your more pleasant experiences with men," she forced herself to reply. No answer would've been more incriminating than any excuse she might devise. "Though I trust Teague above all others, there's still—and may always be—a part of me that remains wary around him." To avoid direct eye contact, Raina resumed her own work of digging up another asphodel tuber. "It may sound hard to you, Najirah, but it's the best I can manage."

"The old pain goes deep, doesn't it, my friend?"

"I don't know what you mean." Raina refused to look at her.

"You speak always of Vorax, and what he did to you," her friend said softly, "but I think the true betrayal was what your father did. I think that is why the pain, the wounding, lies deeper, lasts longer."

Raina's head jerked up. She riveted a furious pair of eyes on her friend. "Leave my father out of this. He's beneath contempt, or any caring or concern on my part."

"Yes, he was beneath contempt." Najirah paused once more in her work. "He traded you for a position of power with Vorax. And then, when Vorax misused you, your father was so fearful for his life, he sacrificed you once again. He was a pitiful, weak man."

A tight little knot formed in the center of Raina's chest. "You speak of him as if he no longer lived."

"Didn't you know?" Compassion gleamed in Najirah's eyes. "I guess you wouldn't have. He killed himself a few months after you left Incendra. I suppose his conscience, whatever there was left of it, finally gained the upper hand." She sighed. "Poor, unfortunate man. He was never able to summon the courage to overcome his weaknesses until it was too late. Until he'd lost his daughter, and what little was left of his self-respect."

"Don't waste your pity on him!" Raina spat out the words, angry and frustrated that she'd lost the opportunity to avenge herself against her father. One of the two men who'd harmed her had already slipped from her grasp. Vile, sniveling little coward. He couldn't even be man enough to live until she returned to kill him!

"Now, you'll never have the chance to meet him," Najirah murmured sympathetically, "to perhaps share your pain, and come to some kind of peace with him."

"I'd no intention of sharing anything with the man but the hilt of my dagger!" Raina viciously stabbed at the ground with her spade, inadvertently slicing a tuber in half. With a savage curse, she flung the spade aside and climbed to her feet, trembling with fury. "Forgive me, but I need time to compose myself."

Eyes wide, Najirah silently nodded.

Turning on her heel, Raina stomped off toward a nearby ravine and its tiny little stream. Najirah watched her walk away, a heavy sense of futility swelling within her. "Poor Raina," she murmured sadly. "You said Bahir betrays me, but what of you? How much worse has been your betrayal? First your father, then Vorax. And perhaps soon, all too soon, the man you claim you trust above all others."

Fifteen

That evening after supper, they sat around the campfire before Bahir's tent. As time passed, the conversation waned and a sense of tension rose in the air. Najirah cast her husband several imploring looks—none of which was lost on Raina—looks met with an implacable glance and taut jaw. Finally, Bahir rose.

"It's time we all took our rest," he said, glancing down at Teague and Raina. "Come, I'll accompany you both to your tent."

Teague slanted Raina a puzzled look. Since that first night of their arrival, the Tuaret leader had never walked them to their tent. She arched her brow in reply, then, along with Teague, climbed to her feet.

Once they reached the opening to their tent, Bahir halted. "With your permission," he began, rendering them the expected desert courtesy, "I'd like a few moments to speak with you. Privately," he added, "in the seclusion of your tent."

Teague nodded. "As you wish." Stepping aside, he opened the flap. "After you, Bahir."

The nomad entered the tent, then waited for Teague and Raina to follow. He turned and shot Teague a piercing look. "What I have to say isn't pleasant or particularly hospitable. I'm sorry for that, but it's past time it be said, and acted upon."

Raina moved to stand beside Teague. "And what might that be, Bahir?"

His glance skittered to hers, then moved back to lock with Teague's. "You and the *mirah* are not and never have been mates." He raised a silencing hand when the monk made a move to protest. "Play no games with me, Tremayne. You've not lain together in the past days, even within the privacy of your own tent. There are other signs, less overt, but there nonetheless. The charade is over."

Teague exchanged a troubled glance with Raina.

"All suppositions," she muttered darkly, glaring back at Bahir. "It's your word against ours."

Bahir smiled, but the smile never quite reached his eyes. "True enough, but in my camp, my word rules."

"What do you plan to do about it, one way or another?" The first tendrils of apprehension twined through Teague. What was Bahir's game? "And why should it matter? It has nothing to do with our mission."

"Indeed," the Tuaret calmly agreed. "It has nothing to do with your mission. But it has everything to do with my tribe, my men. The *mirah* is an unmated female. Most of my men need mates. She serves a greater good taking one to mate, bearing us children, than accompanying you further. You have our support now to retrieve the stone. Her presence on the mission isn't essential anymore. Give her over to me for one of my men."

Raina's hand snaked to her dagger. "Why, you slime-ridden sand worm! How dare you decide how we choose to carry out this mission? And despite your arrogant, archaic, self-serving outlook on things, I'm no piece of property to be traded back and forth. I'm a free woman, a warrior on my planet. And I'll kill any man who dares lay a hand on me."

"You may well be a warrior somewhere else, but you are, first and foremost, an Incendarian," Bahir calmly replied, eyeing her hand, clenched about the dagger. "As such, you are bound to our laws." He turned back to Teague. "You've made it more than evident you've no intention of mating with her. It would be a generous gesture on your part to give her to one of my men. And fair payment, shall we say, for our continued support to retrieve the stone?"

The mission, Teague thought. The mission, in the end, was what mattered, not their individual lives or needs. And Bahir's assistance in reaching the caves and getting the stone back to the spy ship would be invaluable, if not essential.

But to give Raina to Bahir, to force her into a life she had no desire for, to condemn her to what she would most certainly view as another rape . . . He shook his head. "I'm sorry, Bahir. Though I value your offer of assistance, your terms are unacceptable. Raina and I will not impose on your 'hospitality' a day longer. On the morrow, we'll set out on our own."

The Tuaret's mouth quirked. "And did I say there was a choice in this? One way or another, before the next night wanes, the *mirah* will have a mate." He shrugged. "It can be you, or another, but she *will* have a mate."

"It cannot be me, curse you!" Teague rasped. "I-I'm a monk. I've taken vows of perpetual chastity."

"Indeed?" Bahir cocked his head, a faintly amused smile glimmering on his lips. "How inconvenient for you, and unfortunate for her." He looked at Raina. "I could be mistaken, but I think she'd vastly prefer you over one of my men."

"Curse you, Bahir!" Raina snarled.

His smile died. "You're too late, *mirah*. I was cursed long before you returned to Incendra. And now, I've nothing to lose." He turned back to Teague. "By moonrise on the morrow, I'll know your answer."

Teague dragged in an unsteady breath. "You already have it. I cannot mate with her."

Bahir's teeth flashed white in a lazy, disbelieving grin. "By moonrise, Tremayne." He strode past him then, leaving Teague and Raina standing there in shock. The tent flap, cracking back in place, at last wrenched them from their mutual misery.

Raina turned, grasping Teague by the arm. "You would let him do that, then? You'd give me over to one of his men?"

He jerked away, anguish burning in his eyes. "What would you have me do?" he cried. "We cannot escape this place. Bahir has it too well guarded."

"And your precious vows forbid you sullying yourself, even for a time, with the flesh of a woman. Is that it, Tremayne?"

"It's not like that at all," he hissed furiously. "I gave my word. I cannot go back on it."

"And are your vows of more import than what will happen to me?" Her voice rose on a thread of hysteria. With an effort, Raina mastered herself. She wouldn't beg. She'd vowed never again to beg, after that time with Vorax. "They're but words, and noble intent," she forced herself to continue. "I'm flesh and blood, a living being with feelings and pride and needs."

Teague turned and strode away to stand before the center tent post. "And why would mating with me be any better than doing so with one of Bahir's men?" He flung the statement over his shoulder. "All there has ever been between us is that Incendarian attraction anyway. And you're still being forced to mate against your will."

He glanced back, his gaze slamming into hers. "That *is* what you're suggesting, isn't it? Mating with me instead of with one of Bahir's men?"

Stunned, Raina said nothing.

"Well," Teague prodded ruthlessly, his silver-blue eyes flashing. "Isn't it?"

"There's more than the Incendarian attraction between us. That's only a myth at any rate. No exclusive planetary attraction kept Bahir from taking Cyra to wife, did it? No, it's far more than that," she said, her voice gone soft and infinitely sad. "I know you, Teague. I respect and care for you. I-I trust you. It would indeed be different."

He stared back at her, a myriad of emotions flashing across his face. Shock and surprise, a fleeting pleasure, desire, then fear. "Ah, gods!" With a harsh cry, Teague buried his face in his hands. "I can't, Raina. I just can't. It'll destroy me. *You'll* destroy me!"

"No, Teague," she achingly refuted his words. "You'll destroy yourself, if you let the fear claim you. In the end, whether you live or die, if you allow the horrors of your past to continue to influence you, you've allowed Vorax ultimately to triumph. But it's always been your right to choose. And it always will, until there's nothing left and you die an impotent, futile, despairing man."

Just like my father, she thought. He, too, had lacked the courage to face life and its challenges as they must be faced. Just like Bahir, who chose to fling himself into a hopeless cause rather than deal with his own shortcomings and failings, leaving Najirah to sorrow

and yearn. As were all the men, Raina realized, who
had ever played any significant part in her life.

"I'll die first," she told him, "before I allow myself
ever to be taken again against my will. Just know that,
Teague Tremayne. For what it's worth to you."

She turned then, hurt, confused, and embittered to the
depths of her soul, and strode out of the tent, leaving
Teague behind.

Teague climbed up the narrow trail leading to the
highest vantage point above the Tuaret camp. He carried
Rand with him, intending on a talk with the Volan once
they were out of earshot of the guards. Teague desperately needed a voice of reason and sanity, and his past
experiences with Rand had certainly provided that.

It was a cloudy, overcast day, rare for the desert, bod-
ing rain if the thunderheads churning ominously on the
horizon were any indication. A cool breeze blew down
from the sky, musty and moist. Teague shoved a wind-
whipped lock out of his eyes, chose a flat outcropping
of rock to sit upon, and laid Rand's carrying case on
the ground beside him.

The view provided by his high perch above the camp
was breathtaking. Dry cliffs, purpling in the dimming
light of the approaching storm, rose from a floor of soft
pink sand. Deep ravines slashed the land, vicious scars
that were sure to bleed torrents of muddy water with
heavy rain. As they'd bleed this night, once the storm
broke.

As *he'd* bleed this night, not from any surface harm,
but from the wound that would be indelibly carved on
his soul when he stood by and let Raina go to another
man. Yet what other choice was left him?

"Rand?" The single word, rusty with pain, forced its way past a throat gone tight and dry. "Are you there?"

"Yes, Teague Tremayne," came the Volan's reply. "As I was last night, when the Tuaret came to you and Raina."

A tone of disapproval emanated from the carrying pack. It only deepened Teague's misery. "I didn't bring you up here to listen to more recriminations. Raina has said it all, and most eloquently."

"Then what do you wish of me? Your mind is evidently made. No one can sway you, can they?"

"Is that what you, too, would do? I thought you always deemed the mission of more import than Raina."

Rand made a sound of disgust. "Don't try to turn the problem back on me. What matters here is that she cares for you and you care for her. Would you hurt her, cast her aside, just because you fear intimacy? Just because to have her, you must face your inner demons and amend your life once more?"

"And how many times have you had to amend your life?" Teague snapped.

"Only a time or two in the past hundred cycles," Rand muttered dryly. "But it doesn't matter, at any rate. When the time comes, if it ever does again, for me to claim another body, I, too, will have to rebuild a life of a sorts. I'll be frightened, I'm sure. I always was before. It's a lot safer and easier to remain within my biosphere. Not much is expected of me within this protective shell. But I would still go where my destiny called me. Just as you must answer the call of your destiny."

"You begin to sound like Bahir," Teague growled. "Have you perhaps been talking with him?"

"No, he hasn't," a new voice joined the conversation. "But I find the idea most intriguing."

Teague whirled around. Bahir had silently come up behind him. The monk cursed his inattention. If the Tuaret had been an enemy, he would've been dead.

"How long have you been listening?" Teague demanded, scowling fiercely.

The Tuaret leader shrugged. "Not too long. Just long enough to find I agree with the Volan. The *mirah* cares for you. Any fool can see that."

"Then that makes me a fool."

Bahir laughed. "Most men are, when it comes to realizing that a woman loves him. The biggest fool of all, though, is the one who runs from that love, and the great happiness it can bring."

As he spoke, a haunted look flared fleetingly in the Tuaret's eyes. Teague frowned. What secret memory had Bahir's words elicited? "You sound as if you speak from experience," he said, attempting to divert the conversation from himself.

It didn't work. *"My* love is in the past," Bahir growled. *"Yours* is before you. Will you be a coward and turn from it?"

Teague shot up from his perch on the boulder and stalked over to him. He halted but a half meter away and met his gaze, eye-to-eye. "And what do you care? I'd think you'd prefer it if one of your men took Raina. Why waste her on me?"

"Why, indeed?" Bahir eyed him narrowly, then turned and strode over to the edge of the stone precipice that overlooked the desert. He stared off into the distance for a time, then shrugged. "Perhaps I was wrong about you. Perhaps you truly aren't the man we need."

"I never said I was, curse you!"

Bahir turned. "No, you didn't. But if you aren't, it's past time you saw yourself for what you truly are, without the shield of pious utterances and oaths that allow you to live in a world of falsehood and foolish, futile illusions. Face yourself once and for all, Tremayne. You might be pleasantly surprised. And if you don't, then Vorax has won once more."

With that, the Tuaret walked back the way he'd come. Teague gazed after him, his fists clenching in seething frustration. As he stood there, the stormclouds raced overhead, bringing with them chill air and fierce winds.

"He speaks true, my friend." Rand's voice rose above the intensifying wail of the wind. "Vorax will triumph if you don't face yourself. And with that victory, he destroys not only you, but Raina and Bahir and all the others. He destroys them all."

The storm broke at sunset, pouring down from the leaden sky, sending all scurrying for their tents. Though an invitation was sent by Najirah to join her and Bahir for the evening meal, it was tersely refused by both Raina and Teague.

They sat in their tent, never speaking, both wrestling with their private anguish. Overhead, thunder cracked. The wind battered the tent, setting the tautly stretched sides to flapping. The natural waterproofing of the woven capra hair held, however.

Sometime during the storm's unrelenting fury, the evening slunk into night. The tension rose, becoming a palpable entity. Finally, Teague shot Raina a seething glance.

"Is that what you want, then?" he demanded. "To mate with me over any of the others?"

Her gaze, lowered in pensive contemplation of her tunic, lifted. "Wh-what?" She stopped short. "Are you saying you'll mate with me?"

"Yes. But I don't want you ever throwing it in my face once we're back on the trail. Not then, or ever again."

Raina managed a wan smile. "Does it promise to be such an unpleasant experience, then?"

That query startled him. "I-I don't know. I just thought . . ."

"That I didn't want you? That I find you repulsive?" she gently supplied. A most becoming flush stole into her cheeks. "Well, I do want you, and I find you *most* attractive. I believe I thought that from the first moment I saw you." An image of him, stripped to his red loincloth, sweat slicked and clasping that long blade in his hands, rose in her mind's eyes. "Yes," she murmured. "Most definitely from the first moment I saw you."

It was his turn to flush. "I didn't know, didn't dare let myself wonder . . ." He swallowed hard. "I must tell you true, Raina. I know nothing, save for the technicalities, of the mating act. I . . . I am a—"

"I know. For all practical purposes, so am I." She gave a bitter laugh. "And I certainly don't know what to teach you. I hope, though, that this time the mating act will be more gentle and pleasurable than what I once experienced."

Teague smiled, the look in his eyes tender, compassionate. "I would be gentle with you, Raina. I would try, to the best of my ability, to please you."

"Would you, Teague?" She rose and scooted over to him. Ever so gently, she stroked his face. "As would I with you."

Fire leaped through his veins. His mouth went dry.

His pulse pounded. With a superhuman effort, Teague pulled away. "I must go to Bahir," he said thickly. "Tell him of my decision."

Raina leaned back. "Yes, I suppose that would be wise. Before he makes the decision for you. One, I'm certain," she said with a crooked grin, "would disappoint me greatly."

Teague climbed to his feet and smiled down at her. "As it would me, sweet femina. As it would me."

He made a motion to turn and leave, when Raina halted him. "Teague."

"Yes?" He glanced back at her.

She held his cloak out to him. "Take this. It'll keep at least some of the rain off you."

For the first time in the past few minutes, he became aware, once more, of the storm. He accepted the cloak, surprisingly pleased at her concern for him. "Well, I'll wear it, for what it's worth, but don't be upset if I still return soaked to the skin."

"As long as you return." She managed a tentative smile. "That's all that matters."

He slung the cloak over his shoulders, turned, and wordlessly strode from the tent.

A deluge of chill water slammed into him the moment he stepped outside. Gritting his teeth against the cold and rain, Teague sloughed through the ankle-deep mud to Bahir's tent. He rapped on the tent flap. "Bahir, may I enter?" The shout was all but drowned in the tumult of the storm.

Bahir, however, either heard him or was expecting him, for he stood at the tent opening in but a few seconds. He eyed Teague wryly. "It must be important, for you to come out in such a storm."

Teague graced him with a withering look. "May I come in?"

The Tuaret leader stepped aside. "Please."

The interior of Bahir and Najirah's tent was brightly lit by several hanging oil lamps. Long, gaily colored rugs covered the ground. A big wooden chest and a low table stacked with cooking and eating utensils stood against one tent wall; a bulging water bag, moist with condensation, dangled from a hook on the center tent post.

The sleeping pallet, piled with cushions, sat off to one corner. Bahir walked over to it, picked up two cushions, and tossed them onto a rug that lay directly below one of the oil lamps. Najirah shot Teague a nervous, uncertain glance, then took her place nearby on the sleeping pallet.

The monk strode over and lowered himself to one of the cushions. Bahir sat on the other. "Would you care for a cup of cerevisia, or a plate of palmas fruit?" he asked, suddenly the solicitous host. "Najirah can fetch us—"

"No." The reply was curt. "Thank you, but no." Teague impassively met his gaze. "I didn't come here to pay a social visit, and you know it."

"You've made your decision, then, I take it?"

"Raina will stay with me."

"And you'll make her your mate in all ways?"

"That was the point of this, wasn't it?"

Bahir smiled. "Yes. Yes, it was." He hesitated. "May I ask what made you change your mind? You seemed quite determined last night and earlier today."

Teague subjected him to a long, cold scrutiny. "No, you may not. My decisions are my own. You got what you want, though I've yet to fathom what your true motives were. Let that suffice."

"And suffice it will, for the time being."

A frown creased the monk's brow. What exactly did *that* mean? he wondered. Briefly, he considered confronting Bahir about this cryptic statement, then thought better of it.

At this moment, Teague wanted to get as far away from Bahir as he could. He didn't like being manipulated, and that was exactly what the Tuaret had done. No one used him. No one.

No one . . . but Malam Vorax.

Raina's words last night returned with an unnerving impact. . . . *If you allow the horrors of your past to continue to influence you, you've allowed Vorax ultimately to triumph. But it's always been your right to choose . . .*

And then Rand's blunt statement today. . . . *Vorax will triumph if you don't face yourself . . .*

As much as he'd managed to accomplish as a monk, as much personal satisfaction as he'd found in that life, there was still some truth in their words. Though Vorax had feared killing him, thanks to the strange utterances of some ancient prophecy, he had done the next best thing. He had tortured him, both mentally and physically, in the hopes of breaking his spirit and crippling his mind. And though Teague had lived, Vorax had strived to ensure that he'd never be the same, never be fit to rule.

Anger swelled within Teague. He'd thought he'd escaped Vorax and the horrors of his rule when he'd left Incendra, begun a new life. But he hadn't. The horror had followed him, because he'd failed to overcome the lasting effects of the man's shrewdly wrought tortures. In the end, though Vorax had spared his life, he'd sent him out to a living death. A lifelong one.

The realization pressed down on Teague. The old panic rose; it encompassed and smothered him. He couldn't breathe. His heart thundered in his chest. Get away . . . he *had* to get away.

"Your leave," he choked out. "Have I your leave to return to Raina?"

"Yes, most certainly." Bahir halted him when Teague turned to leave. "One thing more, Tremayne. Play no further games with me. Your mate will be examined on the morrow. A mating will occur this night, or she is lost to you forever."

"It won't be necessary, I tell you," Teague gritted.

"Nonetheless, I—"

"No! Do you hear me, Bahir? No!" Teague took a threatening step toward him, his hands fisted at his sides. "What you force on Raina in coercing me to mate with her is torment enough. I won't permit her to be degraded by some . . . some examination afterward. I give you my word. If that isn't enough—"

"It's enough." Bahir cut him off, a hard, taut expression to his face. He motioned toward the door. "Go. No more games."

"No more games." Teague wheeled about and bolted, desperately needing the open space, freedom from the suffocating confines of the tent.

Outside, the storm swirled around him. The wind plucked at his cloak, tugging it open and flinging the ends up into the air. The rain fell, drenching him, until his hair clung to his face and neck in lank, sodden cords and his clothing molded wetly to his body. Teague slipped and fell in the mud, his hands sinking deep into the oozing muck.

He crouched there on his hands and knees for a long moment, taking the full brunt of the storm. It felt good.

The realization surprised him. It was almost as if he was being cleansed, purified, however crude the ritual might be. Cleansed and purified as he'd been so many times before by his monkish rituals.

But this time it was different. This time he needed nothing but the fresh rain and strong, clean wind. The rain and wind of Incendra . . . his land, his home.

Sixteen

He returned to Raina drenched, muddy to his knees, and shivering. At the sound of his entry, she wheeled from her position kneeling on the floor. One glance at Teague and she hastily put aside a pottery plate of cooked grains and roasted fowl and vegetables she was carefully warming over a small, coal-stoked brazier. Najirah had sent the food earlier, when they'd refused her and Bahir's supper invitation, but Raina had hoped Teague's appetite might have improved.

Grabbing a drying cloth from the small chest sitting by the sleeping pallet, she rose and hurried over to him. "By the five moons," she exclaimed, "I expected you to be a bit wet, but not soaked to the skin and filthy to boot!"

"Th-the camp is treacherously s-slippery," he said, his teeth chattering. Teague glanced down at himself, then began to shrug out of his cloak. "I am a mess, th-though."

Raina stepped up. "Here, let me help you." She flung the drying cloth over her shoulder, and began to tug off his cloak. The sodden garment fell at his feet. Next, she pulled off Teague's tunic and tossed it aside.

The cool night air gusted over his bare, damp torso. His nipples tightened. His pectorals quivered, flexing the claws tattooed across his chest. A thin stream of water dribbled from the wet hair lying on his shoulder, trickling down the powerful expanse of bulging muscle, around his chill-tautened nipple, until it finally descended to his hardened belly and disappeared into the waistband of his breeches.

Fleetingly, Raina's gaze followed the errant rivulet, mesmerized by its slow, sensuous passage down Teague's body. A crazed impulse, to follow that bold little stream with her tongue, filled her. She flushed and dragged her attention back up to him.

He watched her, his silver-blue eyes glittering, wary, and waiting. They stood there for a long moment, their glances locked, silent and tension-fraught. Then another errant breeze gusted Teague's skin. He shivered again.

The action broke the spell, something Raina was deeply grateful for. She grabbed the drying cloth off her shoulder and began fiercely to towel him dry. The cloth rasped across his chest and abdomen, then up and down his arms. Next, she used it to squeeze out as much moisture from his hair as she could.

"Turn around," Raina then ordered.

Teague's mouth quirked at the slight quaver in her voice, but he did as she'd asked. She was already as stirred, as anxious as he, he thought, reveling in the rough chafe of the drying cloth across his shoulders and back. But who could blame her? The moment they'd both desired yet feared and fought so hard against would soon be upon them.

When her efforts to dry him ceased, Teague turned. Her glance dropped down his body to his breeches and mud-covered boots. "Do you have anything on beneath them?" She choked out the query on an unsteady breath, gesturing to the lower half of his body.

Teague looked down. "No."

Raina forced her gaze back up to his. "Well, sit and I'll help you with your boots. Then I'll fetch you some blankets to cover yourself while you take off your breeches."

He managed a ragged breath. "Not quite ready to see me naked yet, are you?"

Her eyes widened. She swallowed convulsively, then nodded, the action jerky, nervous. "No, I don't suppose I am."

His mouth twitched wryly. "Well, I suppose I'm not all that ready to stand naked before you, either. I'll tell you this now, though. The pace of the night is yours to choose." Teague reached up tentatively to stroke the side of her face. "We can go as fast or as slow as you wish."

She trembled at his touch, pulled away, too moved, too stimulated by the feel of his fingers on her skin and the anticipation of what was to come. "And what of you? How fast or slow would *you* like it?"

The query seemed to take Teague aback. "I really don't know." He laughed again, sheepishly this time. "I suppose I'll have to learn that as I go."

With that honest, self-conscious remark, the spiraling tension between them eased a bit. Raina joined in the nervous, uncertain laughter. "Well, we've the whole night to discover the answers to such exalted quandaries, don't we? In the meanwhile, let's get your boots and breeches off, warm you a bit, and have some supper." She quirked a slender, auburn brow. "You *are* hungry, aren't you?"

Teague pondered that question but an instant, then nodded. "As a matter of fact, yes, I am."

"Then sit. First the boots and breeches, then the food."

He did as he was told, tugging off his wet breeches

as Raina went for the blankets. By the time she returned, he stood there quite naked, save for the soggy wad of cloth he held over his groin. At the sight of him, for all practical purposes as unclothed as that night at the hermitage on Bellator, Raina's heart did a little flip-flop.

She shoved one blanket toward him. "Here, put this on." As he dropped his breeches and took the blanket from her, she averted her gaze.

Wordlessly, Teague wrapped the covering around his waist, knotting the ends snugly. Raina handed him the other, which he slung about his shoulders. He subjected her to an amused scrutiny. "Am I decently attired now?"

Still mesmerized by the fleeting image of him, bare of chest and arms, the sculpted sides of his hips and iron-thewed thighs gleaming damply in the lamplight, Raina was slow to reply. "What?" she murmured distractedly.

"Am I decently attired?"

"Oh, yes," she muttered, not at all happy with her flustered response. Turning on her heel, Raina strode over to the rug where the brazier sat, smoking away. She pulled over an extra cushion and motioned to it. "Come. Sit. The meal is almost ready."

Teague took his place across from Raina, unsettled by her uncharacteristic behavior. She seemed rattled, off balance, and most definitely nervous.

A niggling worry insinuated itself into his mind. Perhaps Raina regretted her earlier insistence that he mate with her. She was, at the very least, fearful of the act. She couldn't help but be.

He silently accepted the cup of cerevisia she offered him. Lowering his gaze, he stared down at the rich, amber-colored liquid, preoccupied with his own tumult of thoughts. He was fearful himself of what the night would bring, but it was more a fear of hurting Raina, or failing adequately to pleasure her. What he turned his back on in breaking his vows he blocked firmly from his mind. The morrow was soon enough to pick up the pieces of what remained of his monastic life.

Fervently, desperately, Teague wished for a male friend whom he could talk with, from whom he might learn at least some of the rudiments of loving a woman. But there was no one—not before, in the days of his monastic life, and not now. He didn't trust Bahir, and he doubted Rand had had the opportunity for such an experience even when he had possessed a body.

It was too late now, at any rate. He must try the best he could and hope that sooner or later, those fabled primal instincts took over. In the meantime, he would try to alleviate as many of Raina's fears as he could, and hope his concentration on her would ease his fears as well.

Raina placed the plate of grains, fowl, and vegetables between them. Teague smiled. "It looks quite tasty."

She shot him a startled look. "Er, yes, I suppose it does." She gestured to the big platter. "Take some, please."

Teague did just that, scooping up a generous portion with his fingers and lifting it to his lips. Raina's gaze followed, coming to rest on his mouth. Suddenly, he was acutely conscious of what he did, of his own fingers upon his lips, of their fullness, softness. Soft, sensitive, aching for something far more delectable than food.

With an effort, Teague forced the crunchy grains and tender bit of fowl down a throat gone dry. He took a big swallow of his cerevisia to wash the food down, then instantly regretted it as the fiery liquor seared his throat. It made him cough, choke.

Raina leaned forward, immediately solicitous. "Are you all right? Is there anything—"

He silenced her with an upraised hand. "N-no. I'm f-fine," he sputtered. "J-just give me a m-minute."

She reared back and shot him an uncertain glance then to distract herself from her rising anxiety, dug into the plate of food. Gods, Raina thought, this was sure to go down as one of the most miserable, tension-fraught meals of her life.

Shoving a morsel of meat into her mouth, Raina forced herself to swallow it. The fowl tasted like a piece of dry clay. She drained her cup of cerevisia, then poured herself another and emptied it as well, thinking the potent spirits might relax her. The liquor did little more than upset her stomach.

There was nothing to be done, Raina decided, falling back on her warrior's training, but face the inevitable with courage and get it over with. The mating shouldn't take but a few unpleasant minutes, if memory of the one and only other time served her correctly. She glanced expectantly at Teague, who was still gamely, but equally unenthusiastically, trying to eat more of the meal.

She scooted over to kneel beside him. He paused, a tidbit of grain and vegetables halfway to his mouth. Gently, smilingly, she took his hand and guided it to her, taking the food from him with her lips. Teague's eyes widened, then narrowed, his pupils dilating until they took up the full span of his irises. He went very still.

"Why did you do that?" he asked warily, when she was done.

She met his gaze with a direct one of her own. "Because neither of us is all that hungry. Because we both wish for this to be over. And, I say, let us begin."

He considered her statement briefly. "Yes, I suppose that would be best." His glance skittered to the pallet, then back to her. "Would you like to lie on the pallet, or the rug, or what?"

Raina cocked her head, a soft smile playing about her lips. "I think first, Teague Tremayne, I'd like you to kiss me."

Teague stared at her until Raina felt the first telltale warmth flood her face. Gods, had she offended him with her boldness? Had she been too forward for his masculine sensitivities? Frustration filled her. Must they play games, then? She, the shy maiden, and he, the aggressive hunter?

Then a lazy grin stole across Teague's face. "I think I'd like that, too. Very much so."

He shoved to his knees and turned, grasping Raina by the shoulders. He leaned toward her until their mouths were but a hairsbreadth apart, lingering there for long, agonizing seconds. Raina thought her heart would burst from the pounding it took against her breast, thought she would scream aloud if he didn't close the space between them and kiss her. Yet still he hesitated.

"I . . . I don't know how well I can do this," he finally spoke, his voice harsh with his own anxiety. "I think you should—"

Raina leaned forward and pressed her mouth to his. Teague went rigid. His grip on her shoulders tightened, compressing the flesh and bone in a bruising clasp. Then, with an inarticulate sound, he encircled her in the clasp of his arms, pulled her to him, and opened his mouth hungrily over hers.

She gasped with startled pleasure. His tongue, in a wild frenzy of escalating greed and excitement, inadvertently plunged into her mouth. Both froze, neither quite certain of where this might lead, or if it was even acceptable. Tentatively, Teague probed the velvety warmth of her, rasping gently over her tongue, teasing and tantalizing her.

Sharp bursts of fire shot through Raina's veins. Her tongue arched forward to meet his, touching, teasing, twining. She shoved off the blanket covering his shoulders, running her hands over his upper arms and chest, reveling in his sleek, smooth skin and bulge of muscle. He trembled at her touch, groaned.

Fearful she'd harmed him in some way, Raina pulled back. There was no sign of pain in his eyes or contorting his features. Only a dark, heated, wanting look. She smiled. "Do you know you talk too much? You do much better when you just give things a try."

A puzzled expression flashed across his face. His finely chiseled, sensual mouth twitched. "Do I? Then I'll try to do just that." He hesitated, a sudden look of doubt in his eyes. "How was the kiss?"

Her smile widened. "Wonderful for a first kiss, but I think a bit more practice is in order. Could we perhaps try it again?"

"Most certainly," Teague rasped. "This night is yours, sweet one, for whatever and however you want it." He grinned. "Of course, you'll have to tell me what and how you want it."

"As will you. This is *our* mating, not just mine."

Her statement gave him pause. She didn't understand. He'd give her what she wished to ease the eventual coupling, but the mating was for her, not him. Though his body would ultimately join with hers, he must and would withhold his heart.

He'd given his word, made his vows. He might violate them in the flesh, but never, ever, in the spirit. He mated with Raina, Teague fiercely told himself, out of an act of charity, of kindness and compassion, to do penance for the man who'd sinned against her, a man who would never know or care about the harm he'd wrought. But never, ever, for himself. In this way, and only in this way, could he keep himself pure and maintain the spirit, if not the letter, of his vows.

Raina didn't need to know that, though. Perhaps if she imagined he did this for himself as much as for her, it might help ease her discomfort and add to her pleasure. And he'd do anything to make her happy.

The realization startled Teague. He truly cared to make her happy. Raina deserved it, after all she'd been through on this mission as well as in her life.

Yet he wanted that and even more, he realized. He wanted . . . wanted to share that happiness with her, to be her mate, to live out his life with her. He wanted to . . . love her.

That reluctant admission brought him nothing but pain. He wanted, yet couldn't have. Was there anything more frustrating, more tormenting? It was why he'd shut his heart and life off from others, from any deep or committed caring, after the agony of seeing his sister and parents die, his land and people wrenched from him. He'd wanted so much then, too, and had lost it anyway.

That was why he should slam the gates of his heart shut. Before he risked it all.

Yet gazing down at her as she knelt before him with eyes shining with the same trust and affection that he felt for her, Teague found he couldn't shut himself off. Not tonight at least, and perhaps, though he shied from facing it just now, not ever again.

"Yes," he softly, achingly replied, "it *is* our mating." His grip tightened on her shoulders and he leaned toward her once more.

Raina lifted her mouth to his. She closed her eyes, ready, willing, and eagerly expectant.

Teague gazed down at her for a fleeting instant, moved by her sweetness and almost girlish enthusiasm. She truly was a maiden in all things that mattered. In all ways that truly mattered, this was the first time for both of them. Then he bent the last few millimeters and kissed her, long and slow and deep.

As the seconds passed, a rising tension thrummed through Teague. The blood pounded through his heart, coursing out to heat his skin until it prickled with need. Filling his groin, until his hardening mouth was echoed throughout the length and breadth of his body. His manhood swelled. His hands began, of their own accord, to explore her body.

Raina's long tunic was lifted over her head and cast aside. Soft, full breasts, shimmering like ivory in the lamplight, like the inside of a rare chamma shell, were topped by delicately pink nipples. She bowed her head at her nakedness, flushing crimson, and wrapped her arms across her chest.

"No, sweet one," Teague growled. His voice went deep and husky from the surge of desire the sight of her naked breasts stirred within him. He took her arms and ever so gently pulled them away to expose her fully to his view. "Don't hide yourself from me. You are beautiful. Let me see you. Please."

She couldn't resist the insistent strength of his hands,

nor his ardently couched plea. "Look, then," she whispered, letting her arms fall to her sides. "But be willing to pay the price."

"The price?" Teague reached out and ran a long, strong finger along the side of one breast, slowly, languorously bringing it around until it reached a pouting nipple. He circled it with his fingertip, decreasing the distance with each revolution until the gentle stimulation tightened the tip to a taut little bud. Raina shuddered, drew in a ragged breath.

Teague's gaze lifted to hers. "Does this please you then, sweet one?"

"Y-yes," she managed to choke out the reply.

He smiled, then took his other hand and subjected her other breast to the same sweetly torturing treatment. Her breasts finally too sensitive, her nipples erect and aching for what she knew not, Raina grabbed his hands to stay them. "It . . . it's your turn now," she said, her voice gone hoarse. "Your turn to pay the price."

"Indeed?" Teague cocked a dark blond brow. "And do you now wish to stroke my chest as I did yours?"

His offer was indeed tempting, Raina thought, gazing at his flat, male nipples, the tattooed claws reaching down his bulging pectorals as if to sink the talons into the soft, yielding flesh. She wondered how Teague's nipples would feel at the tip of her tongue, how his skin would taste. Yet a more primal urge beckoned, calling her to a bold demand.

"Yes, I wish to touch you, but first, I've a greater wish to see you naked."

He stared back at her, stunned. Then he forced an unsteady laugh. "Well, I suppose that was inevitable." His hands went to the knot of his blanket. With a few deft moves, the blanket was free and fell to his sides.

Raina glanced down, saw the huge, thick shaft straining, only millimeters away, toward her belly. A strange mixture of fear and fascination, revulsion and excitement, flooded her. Her gaze jerked up to his. "You certainly seem a bit, er, prematurely stimulated."

"Prematurely?" Teague gave a husky laugh. "I may not be overly experienced in lovemaking, but I'd wager most men would find you quite stimulating. Especially," he added, his voice dropping a notch, as he lustily eyed her breasts, "as delightfully unclothed as you are."

He meant to unsettle her, regain the upper hand, Raina thought. Well, this little game could just as well have two winners as one. "Perhaps I was unfair to taunt you so," she began. "This, er, 'state' of yours might be insignificant to how you'll become once you're truly excited." She ran a short fingernail from the light brown nest of hair covering the lower part of his abdomen up the length of his hardened, jutting shaft.

"G-gods!" Teague gasped and jerked back.

Raina arched a brow, an impish light in her eyes. "Is something wrong? Was I too rough with you? Here, let me make it up to you." She reached out once again, this time to clasp him.

He grabbed her hand before she could touch him. "You know as well as I what you meant to do," he rasped thickly. "Would you shame me by having me spew my seed here and now?"

"No," Raina said darkly, "but soon enough. Soon enough." She stood and, in a few quick movements, had freed the fastening of her breeches and slipped them down her hips and legs. Stepping out of them, she extended her hand to Teague. "Come. It's cold. The pallet will be warmer."

Teague glanced up, impaling her with his ice-blue

stare. Silently, he took her hand and stood. "Yes, the pallet and the sweet comfort of your body will be far warmer than anything I've ever experienced." *Or will ever hope to experience again,* he silently added.

When they reached the pallet, Teague knelt, swept back the blankets, then climbed in. Raina hesitated but an instant, then followed, tugging the blanket back up to cover them. They lay there in the flickering lamplight, a scant meter apart, facing each other, the blanket lying loosely about Teague's hips and pulled up to Raina's breasts.

Finally, Teague smiled. "I'm afraid we'll get little accomplished so far apart. Would it bother you if I moved closer, took you in my arms?"

She forced a little smile. "Better still, what if we met in the middle?"

His smile widened into a grin. "A man couldn't ask for more."

Together, they scooted toward each other. Teague slid an arm beneath her head and wrapped the other around her, drawing Raina close. Momentarily, she stiffened, then with a sigh, relaxed and laid her head upon his chest.

Teague's heart, powerful, reassuring, thudded against Raina's ear. Its solid, steady rhythm soothed her. His scent of man and rich cedra wood wafted up to her. He smelled good, felt good, his skin sleek and warm. She nuzzled her cheek against his firm but resilient chest. She sighed again.

"Feeling a bit more comfortable with me, are you?" Teague's deep voice rumbled against her ear.

"Yes. How about you?"

"I like holding you very much."

Raina turned her head, her lips grazing his chest. Her

head lowered to his nipple. "And do you like this as well?" she murmured, her tongue flicking out to lick his soft, flat bud.

He dragged in a sharp breath through clenched teeth. "Y-yes. Please, I don't know—"

"Do you want me to continue?"

"I . . . Yes, I do."

Emboldened by his admission and the husky catch in his voice, Raina turned her fullest efforts to Teague's nipple. She laved him with long, languorous strokes, circling it over and over. Then she took him in her mouth, suckling gently at first, then harder and harder.

He began to move restlessly beneath her, his hands gripping her arms. After a time, he arched toward her, urging her to take him even more deeply, more roughly. His breath became ragged and uneven.

A fierce sense of triumph, of primitive female power, filled Raina. She moved to his other nipple, working it just as avidly until it, too, stood out from the hard swell of his chest, taut, turgid, and straining.

Finally, with a shuddering effort, Teague pushed her away. "Enough," he panted. "I can't take any more." He reared up and forced her over onto her back. "Now, it's your turn," he growled, a savage light in his eyes. "Now, you'll suffer as I have."

For a fleeting instant, fear rocketed through Raina. He was so big, so much more powerful than her. He could hurt her, or force himself on her. Naked and un-armed, there would be little she could do. Teague wasn't some ordinary man. He was a warrior, expertly trained and as fit as she.

Then there wasn't any time left for fear or doubts. His long, blond hair cascading around him, he lowered his head and took one of Raina's nipples into his mouth.

Like her earlier efforts on him, the strokes of his tongue were deft, knowing, eliciting the most exquisite sensations that began at her nipples and shot down to the very core of her womanhood.

Raina writhed beneath him, whimpering soft, inarticulate sounds. Her eyes clenched shut. Her fingers dug into the muscles of his upper arms. And still he worked her, first one then the other, until both breasts tingled and ached so badly Raina could barely contain her cry of pain—and need.

"T-Teague," she breathed. "I-I—"

"Yes, sweet one," he replied, lifting his head to nuzzle the velvety cleft between her breasts, then moving upward to kiss and lave her neck. "What is it you want? Tell me, and I will give it to you . . ."

She clung to him, panting, so confused she could hardly speak. "I want . . . I want . . . Ah, gods, Teague, all I know is, I want you!"

Her anguished admission plucked at his heart. A fierce male pride filled him. Ever so carefully, he slid up her body, dragging his passion-thickened sex along her thighs and belly. "Is this what you want, sweet one?" he asked hoarsely, taking her hand and wrapping it around his throbbing organ. "Or is it something else?"

Raina thought she'd go mad, holding him in her hand, so big and hard, the essence of all that was male. Her aching breasts crushed against the rock-hardness of his body. She felt on fire, trembling with a wet heat between her legs that she'd never experienced before. All she knew was that she wanted him in the most elemental of ways, as a woman joined in intimate union with a man.

"Yes," she breathed on a soft, broken sigh. "I want you . . . this . . . inside me. Please, Teague. Please!"

"Help me, then." He glanced down to where their bodies were meant to join. "Help me, for I can hardly think, much less act."

Raina smiled. She stroked his cheek in the most ineffably tender of motions. "We'll help each other, won't we, my love?"

He nodded.

She drew up her legs, spreading herself wide. "You must move there to position yourself between my legs."

Teague did as she said. "Do you know what to do next?" she then asked.

Once more he nodded, moving forward until his big shaft lay, hot and heavy, upon her belly. For a few strokes, he rubbed himself against her. Then he groaned, pulled back, and grasping himself, lowered the tip of his glans against her slick cleft. Awkwardly, he probed for the opening to her sheath. Yet even those hard little jabs excited Raina. She arched up to meet him, knowing, sensing, that he was near . . . so very near.

Then Teague found her. In his passion, he thrust halfway into her before he could stop himself. Raina gasped, startled by his size and the snugness of her sheath.

"Gods, Raina," Teague groaned, "I didn't mean to hurt you." He rested his sweat-damp head on her shoulder. "I'm sorry. I didn't realize—"

"Hush." She pressed a finger against his lips. "It's fine. Truly it is. Just wait a moment or two, until I get used . . . to you." She lay there a few seconds more, then gently rocked her hips to meet him. "Now, carefully, enter me all the way."

Teague eased his organ into her. Once he was fully impaled, he sighed and gathered Raina to him. They lay there, savoring the sweet ecstasy of penetration for a time. Finally, though, Teague began to kiss her, all the while pushing his throbbing sex a bit in, then dragging it out of her.

The friction and tugging action of his big glans excited Raina. She rose to meet his thrusts. The tempo of their union increased, becoming fast and deep and hard. Raina was stunned at the heat and length and fullness of him. She rocked madly against Teague, greedy for the feel of him, for the deepest penetration. A hot, agonizing tension built within her, threatening release.

She panted. She moaned. She writhed in uncaring abandon, her hands grasping wildly at him. As he drove into her in an ever increasing frenzy, Raina felt his mouth on her nipple, felt his teeth. And it was that sweet pain, on top of everything else, that sent her over the edge.

With a keening cry, Raina arched from the pallet, her eyes clenched, her head thrown back, her slender body trembling with her release. She clawed at Teague, raking his skin, clinging to his massive shoulders, calling out his name. Crying out her love for him.

All the while Teague watched her, filled with a savage, bittersweet joy. For the first time in his life, he knew what it was truly, fully, to be a man. Knew the power, the passion, and the fulfillment. Saw the fire that had built between them finally burst into a conflagration of ardent, passionate union and release. And saw it, as well, tear down their walls and fill their empty, aching hearts with trust and joy and love.

But even as Teague watched Raina's climax finally ebb, he knew the pain of a need that would remain even after this night. A need he might indulge in for a short while longer, but not forever. It was forbidden to one such as him. It had to be. He'd given his word.

Holy vow notwithstanding, however, this night was theirs. And he meant to find the same fulfillment in Raina's arms as she had found in his. It was indeed their night, their mating. For once in his life, he'd not be denied.

He began to thrust into her once more, savoring the slick heat of her, the velvety tug of her sheath over his glans and shaft. The tension grew within him; the fire roared to uncontrollable heights. The pressure mounted, making him so hard it was exquisite agony.

He groaned. He panted. He gripped her lush buttocks, lifting her higher, tighter.

Then the release came, shooting from him in rhythmic, pulsing spurts. Teague went rigid, shook with the ferocity of his climax, his body arched as taut as a bow. Guttural sounds emanated from his throat, sounds of pure, elemental pleasure.

The heavens opened. A bright, blinding light shone down. Happiness, a peace and surety such as he'd never known before, filled him. Then the strength left him in one giant surge. Teague collapsed atop Raina with a soft sigh.

She gathered him to her, cradling his head on her chest, crooning to him. They lay there for a time, their passion-heated bodies pressed tightly together, until the sweet, bone-deep exhaustion of their release finally claimed them.

They dragged him, bound and bleeding, to the base of the dais where the usurper sat, gloating like some big, shiny scarabus bug. One of the two soldiers holding the boy grabbed his head, snaring his gloved fingers in the thick length of golden blond hair, and cruelly wrenched it back. Only then, from the unearthly vantage hovering above and beyond the throne, did she finally see his face.

A boy on the verge of manhood, she mused from the dreamy perspective of her sleeping mind, hardly more than thirteen cycles old. Straight of nose, firm of jaw, with the most unsettling silver-blue eyes. A comely lad, certain to grow into a man of great size and splendor, if the broad sweep of his shoulders and long, coltish legs were any indication. If they allowed him to live past this day . . .

"I cannot kill you," the usurper complained fretfully from his perch on the edge of his throne, plucking endlessly at his shiny new robes as if he couldn't quite get them arranged properly. "That cursed prophecy forbids . . ."

He paused to nervously lick his thin lips, his tongue darting out like that of some slimy reptilian lacerta. "But I am now your king and can prevent you from ever spawning an heir or remaining on Incendra," the corpulent man forced himself to continue with renewed bluster and bravado. "With you far from your planet and people, with little hope of return, I shall live out my reign, prophecy or no."

The boy struggled fiercely in the two guards' grasp, but the cruel bonds and the hand locked in his hair held him fast. "I w-will return," he managed to choke out his reply. "Someday, somehow."

At the boy's childish bravado, a smile of pure malevolence twisted his adversary's face. He toyed with the large aureum signet ring on his finger, not bothering even to look back at the boy. Light from hundreds of perpetual torches placed along the length of the great hall reflected off the gold-colored metal. "When I'm done with you, there'll be nothing left worth bringing back to Incendra. You have my word on that. My torturers are just that good."

"You w-wouldn't. You can't!" the boy gasped, as the guard jerked hard on his hair. "Th-the prophecy—"

"Concerns only your life, my pretty princeling," the usurper finished smugly, once more meeting the boy's tortured gaze. "It has never applied to anything else, such as your mind or pride or ability to rule."

"Curse your soul to the depths of perdition!" the boy cried, and tried anew to get free of his captors. The effort did little but twist the ropes binding him, sending them deeper into his already scored and bleeding wrists. For his futile efforts, he was rewarded with yet another vicious tug on his hair. His head snapped back, exposing the strong young column of his throat. Yet still he fought on, unbowed and defiant.

All the while, the usurper watched with glittering eyes and undisguised pleasure. Finally, exhausted, the boy gave up the struggle. His chest heaved with his exertions. His body shook.

With an unsettling surety, she knew he battled to hold back the tears. Her heart went out to him in his moment of deepest shame and despair. She wanted desperately to aid him. Yet her limbs wouldn't move; her mouth refused to open. There was nothing left her but to watch and await the final outcome.

The realization angered her. She was as much a pawn in this brutal drama as was the boy. As much a pawn as the man he slowly became before her eyes—the man she knew as Teague Tremayne. She railed impotently against that knowledge, fearing the consequences of

*ever having joined forces with him, of ever returning to
a planet and land that had cast her out as heartlessly,
as brutally as it had seemed to reject him.*

For ever having allowed herself to love him.

*Fear curled about her heart, squeezing it painfully.
She fought back, gulping for breath.*

*"N-no," she cried in her fitful, tormented slumber. "I
cannot. I will not!"*

*Someone screamed from a long distance away, hor-
rible and heart-rending. Teague? She turned back to the
scene of throne and prisoner, but a mist now swirled
before her eyes. She could barely make out the form of
the man, slumped over on the floor at the feet of the
usurper, blood gushing from his body.*

*Panic stabbed through her. Was this how it was all
fated to end then? Teague, once more in Vorax's hands,
tortured this time until death? Teague, the man she
loved, lost to her once and for all?*

*"N-no!" Her arms flailed wildly as she sought to
sweep away the black, roiling mist. "Gods, no! No!"*

Raina woke, bolting upright in bed, her heart pounding, drenched in sweat. The oil lamps had burned away
long ago. The darkened tent was quiet, save for the
sound of her harsh, ragged breaths. Outside some night
bird called, its song haunting, melancholy.

Someone moved beside her in the dark. She jerked
back, grasping wildly for the dagger she kept tucked
beneath the pallet.

"Raina?" Teague's voice, deep and resonant, strangely
comforting, rose from the blackness beside her. "What
is it, sweet one? A bad dream?"

"Nothing," she muttered fiercely, the memory of
Teague, sprawled bleeding and beaten before Vorax's
throne, filling her with renewed horror. Gods, she

prayed to any benevolent entity that might hear her, don't let it be true. *Please,* don't let it happen. "It was nothing."

The bedcovers rustled. Teague scooted close and pulled her to him. She shuddered and, clasping her arms tightly about her, crept into the warm, solid haven that he offered. She buried her face against his strong chest, willing the horror to pass. Willing herself to forget, once and for all, and finally be at peace. She'd long ago put aside the memories of her own abuse and humiliation at the hands of her fellow Incendarians. Why couldn't she do the same for a simple dream?

With a despairing sigh, Raina shoved back from Teague. She needed some distance from him, from the intensity, the immediacy of it all. From the heavy sense of certitude that this dream presaged his eventual fate. She needed some air. "Let me go. Please."

He released her without protest or demand for an explanation. She grabbed her cloak lying beside the pallet and rose. Wrapping it about her, Raina padded across the tent to the door.

Raising the flap, she gazed out into the star-studded night. The storm had passed sometime during the darkest hours, leaving behind only a sharp tang of dampness on the brisk wind. The rocky fortress was drenched in moisture, from the standing puddles in the muddy pathways between the tents to the water still dripping slowly from the high stone walls.

Raina's glance lifted and, for long, poignant minutes, she stared up at the peaceful sky. Far out on the horizon, a faint glow smudged the blackness to gray. Dawn would come in another hour or two, she thought. Not soon enough, though, to spare her from the tenacious memories and haunting questions once again stirred to

life by the dream. Not soon enough to dispel the ugly
sense of presentiment and helplessness that twined like
the coils of some deadly serpent about her heart.

"Raina, come back to bed," Teague said suddenly
from behind her. His hands settled on her shoulders,
strong, capable, and comforting. "The night is cold. Let
me hold you, warm you."

With a small, heartfelt sigh, Raina forced a wan smile
and turned. Yes, she thought, let him hold her, warm
her while there was still a time of peace for them. The
future, on this night of joyous discovery and aching intimacy, might soon beckon them to where they no
longer wished to go. A future that wasn't nearly enough,
not after what they'd so recently shared.

Not nearly enough, when she wanted a lifetime.

Taking his hand, Raina led Teague back to bed—and
what remained of the shattered tranquillity of the night.

Seventeen

Teague tried everything he could to soothe her nightmare-ravaged nerves, including another bout of exquisitely tender lovemaking, but it only intensified Raina's distress. As he finally fell into an exhausted slumber beside her, she lay there, her thoughts roiling chaotically.

Though a confusing tumult of issues bombarded her, some things were abundantly clear. Vorax would be furious if and when he learned of Teague's return to Incendra. This time, Raina was certain, he'd seek somehow to have Teague killed.

Stirred by her dream the ancient prophecy, a cryptic jumble of long-forgotten lines, came back to her now. Raina recognized them for the truth they were—and for their hauntingly precise application to Teague. Just like the prophecy had promised, he'd suffered greatly in the rebellion. He'd died to himself and the world when he'd renounced his former life and heritage upon leaving Incendra, as well as when he'd become a monk. And he had, in that cauldron of suffering and renunciation, exorcised the evil of his ancestors.

Teague was a good, moral man, a courageous and thoughtful man. He would make an excellent leader. *If* he chose to assume the reins of power once more. *If* he chose to join with Bahir. But as the prophecy also said, it was his right to search, to choose.

Yet what chance did Incendra have if Teague decided against following his true destiny? And if he did, what impact would that have on their mission, and the fate of the Imperium? Once they'd harvested the stone, she *could* go back to Bellator alone, leave Teague behind if he wished to carry on the fight against Vorax.

As much as the thought of giving up her own plans for vengeance angered her, as much as she hated leaving Teague, there seemed little other choice. Her own needs could never hold the priority that the Volan threat to the Imperium held.

Frustration rose in Raina. From the beginning, nothing had gone as planned. Now, on top of most likely having to renounce her long-dreamt-of revenge, she might well lose the man she loved in the bargain.

But then, she sadly reminded herself, there'd been little hope of anything ever coming of their undeniable, if forbidden, attraction for each other. Teague was still a monk, and he'd made no promises to her, not even in the most passionate throes of their mating. No, if the truth be told, all he'd really done was temporarily renounce his vow of chastity. And he had done so, most likely, only out of kindness to her.

She glanced at him, lying beside her, naked save for the blanket that lay curled below his knees. Sleeping on his stomach, he presented a most delectable sight in the rising light of dawn. The lithe brawn of his upper torso gradually merged with the sensuous indentation of his lower back before curving out once more into the most delightfully rounded, tautly muscled buttocks. Darker, hair-roughened thighs joined with the smooth-skinned, paler buttocks, before skimming yet further downward in a sleekly masculine, muscular way to the vulnerable curve behind his knees and the juncture of the blanket.

Even as her glance caressed his body, Raina felt the desire thrum through her, her skin tauten, the blood pound more swiftly, more heatedly through her veins. Never, in her wildest imaginings, had she realized the sharp, sweet pleasures to be found in loving a man. And to think that the one vile act of Malam Vorax had nearly and permanently deterred her from ever knowing the true joys between a man and a woman.

As she gazed at Teague, a tender smile lifted her mouth. He was such a wonderful lover, even when one considered that last night had been but his first time. He cared for her pleasure, indeed, was exquisitely sensitive to her every need. Though he'd been gentle, beneath his tight control, Raina sensed he was a man of deep strength and passion.

He couldn't help but be, she realized, to have survived, much less totally rebuilt his life after what Vorax had done to him. Most monks never reached the level of a Grandmaster even after a lifetime of effort. Teague had attained it in less than nineteen cycles.

It meant so much to him, his standing in his Order. She'd heard the pride in his words, seen it in the way he comported himself. No matter what she thought of his motives in adhering to the monastic life, it was evident Teague had found a certain peace and satisfaction in it. He'd assuredly gained a well-earned reputation in his tireless service to the Imperium as one of Exsul's renowned warrior monks.

Raina wondered if even the needs of his people would be enough to lure him from the monastic life. One thing was certain: there was little hope that his affection and desire for her would ever be that powerful an inducement.

Yet against all the cautions of her usually practical,

highly disciplined mind, Raina still hoped against hope. She would do anything for Teague: remain on Incendra and fight at his side for his kingdom; leave, and make a life back on Bellator or wherever he wished to go . . . If only she could be with him . . .

With an effort, Raina caught herself in her maudlin, lovestruck dreaming. Anger welled within her. She was a fool to place such import on the whims of a man. Such fatuous considerations would surely doom her to an eventual—and heartbreaking—disaster. Yet hadn't Marissa taken such a chance when she'd accepted Brace as her mate? And hadn't she, because of that, been deliriously happy all these cycles?

Teague was as fine a man as Brace Ardane. She was as deserving of happiness as Marissa was. Yet what was right, what was fair in life, wasn't always the way things turned out. And she would never, ever, no matter how ardently, how deeply she wanted Teague, beg him to accept what he'd not come to desire for himself.

Raina rose from the pallet and dressed. Teague slept on, unaware of her departure as she slipped out of the tent and into the fresh air and morning sunlight. Many of the Tuarets were already up and about, some building cookfires to prepare breakfast, others hurrying down to draw water from the artesian well that lay at the base of the rocky fortress. She grabbed up a empty jug sitting outside the tent and set out, intent on fetching fresh water for her and Teague to use that day.

"You seem no worse for wear, *mirah*," Bahir's voice caught her as she passed his tent. "Have you inadvertently found that mating with the man of your choosing isn't as odious an act as you'd once imagined?"

Raina wheeled, her jug clenched tightly to her, her eyes blazing. Curse his smug, arrogant hide! "And what of you, Bahir?" she spat, glaring down at him. He sat there outside his tent, sharpening his long, curved war blade. "Pleased that your machinations have finally gained you what you wished? *Whatever* that might be."

He had the good grace to flush. "I meant no harm to either of you. It was evident you both wanted each other. I but hastened the inevitable."

"So now, on top of all your other duties, you see yourself as matchmaker?" Raina laughed disparagingly. "It'll do no good. You may temporarily command our bodies, but you'll never command our minds. Never!"

Bahir shot her an angry, congested look, then glanced away. "I only want your mate to do what he knows he must do. Is that so terrible?"

Her anger cooled as quickly as it had flared. She couldn't, in all fairness, fault Bahir for his devotion to Incendra, no matter how much she personally despised the man. "No, it isn't terrible," Raina replied, moderating her tone. "Your intent is commendable. Your methods of achieving that intent, though, aren't."

"Then tell me how to convince him." Bahir swung back to Raina, betraying a surprising eagerness. "If, especially after last night, you don't know his will and how to bend it, no one does."

"So you can use Teague to your personal ends?" Raina's anger swelled anew. "That's all I've ever been in your eyes—a pawn to be manipulated to gain the greater prize, Teague's cooperation in this hopeless, fatal quest of yours."

"What if you have?" he muttered, his jaw going taut. "You've gained in the bargain as well. You're his mate, his woman now. If he should regain the throne, you could well rule beside him. Enough advancement for any woman, I'd say, for sharing her bed."

"And where do love, respect, and honesty enter into all this, Bahir?" She stepped closer, her voice trembling with rage. "Or is that how you view all women, then, as opportunistic bloodsuckers?"

"How should *I* know?" Bahir flung down his sword and shoved to his feet. He walked up to confront her. "I've yet to see much of anything else in a woman, save hard-hearted disregard and callous betrayal. Nor am I now ever likely to, it seems."

As he stood there towering over her, his face gone red and fury emanating from every pore of his body, Raina realized she'd struck a nerve. He spoke of Cyra, the wife who had left him.

An impulse to tell Bahir of Cyra's message filled her, but she refused to give in to it. The fact that in his admission he'd totally discounted Najirah and all she had been to him only stoked the fires of Raina's resolve. By the five moons, the hard-hearted, callous man didn't deserve whatever solace Cyra's message would give him!

"Foolish, pitiful man," she snarled. "The truth of that lies just at the end of your nose, if you ever find the courage to drag yourself out of the self-pitying quagmire you cast yourself into when your first wife deserted you. Then you might finally be able to fathom the real reasons she probably left you. Then, at long last, you might finally see the woman who is still here for you and will always be. Not that you're worthy of her love and respect and honesty. Not that it'll ever—"

"That's enough, Raina."

At the sound of Najirah's quiet but intense voice, Raina turned. Bahir's wife had, from the looks of the sweating pottery jug clasped on her hip, just now returned from the well. She eyed her friend sternly. "You

intrude where you've no right. What Bahir and I share
is no concern of yours."

Heat flooded Raina's face. Gods, she hadn't meant
for Najirah to overhear. She'd suffered enough as it was.

Raina glanced from Najirah to Bahir, then back to
Najirah. "I-I beg pardon," she mumbled. "I meant no
harm. Your husband, however, has a definite talent for
goading me beyond the limits of my control." Raina
stepped back. "I'll be on my way. I'd meant to draw
water for our breakfast meal."

"Wait." Najirah walked over to a black metal cauldron and poured the contents of her jug into it. "I need
more water. I'll walk back to the well with you."

The warrior woman hesitated. What was the harm in
Najirah's company? Besides, a more in-depth apology
was in order. "Fine," she muttered. "Suit yourself."

Which Najirah did, promptly joining her. Raina eyed
her narrowly, then started off down the trail to the well.

Bahir watched them go. Then, with a weary sigh, he
turned back to the blade he'd been sharpening. He'd
never understand Raina, he thought sourly, as he ran the
porous sharpening stone up and down the gleaming
length of metal. At one instant she was cold and calculating, a lethal warrior through and through. The next,
she was ardently defending her mate, or standing up for
Najirah.

Najirah . . . at the thought of his gentle wife, guilt
twisted Bahir's gut. Raina had said some hard words to
him about her. Of the fact that she loved him. That he
was unable to recognize or appreciate that love because
he was still drowning in his grief over losing Cyra. And
that *he* was the one at fault in Cyra's leaving him.

That last accusation pierced to his very soul. Foolish,
arrogant female! How little she knew of the true cir-

cumstances! His hand clenched, knuckle white, about
his sword. He'd given Cyra everything. Everything!

But Raina didn't know that and never would. He'd be
damned if he'd parade his pain and humiliation for all
to see. And especially not before that heartless bitch!
No, especially not her, who was so very like his Cyra.

Footsteps intruded on his anguished musings. Bahir
glanced up. Teague Tremayne was, even then, halting
before him. The look in the other man's eyes, however,
was far from friendly. Well, Bahir wryly asked himself,
what did he expect from either of them after last night?

He motioned with his sword to a spot before him.
"Sit. I don't particularly like staring up at a man."

Teague gave a snort of disgust and lowered himself
to sit in the place Bahir had indicated. "The deed is
done," he began without preamble. "We are now mates
and have fulfilled our part of the bargain. I'd like to
start out for the caves on the morrow."

"Eager to be free of me, are you?" Bahir resumed
his sharpening of his sword. "Well, in this case, I con-
cur. It's a two-day journey there, then about another day
or two to mine sufficient quantities of the crystal. How
many days' journey is it from the oasis where we first
met to your spaceship?"

"With equs, less than a day."

"Good. If all goes well, we'll be back at your ship
in a week." Bahir looked up. "Does this ship require
more than one pilot to get it through the electromagnetic
field and back to Bellator?"

Teague went still. "And why would you ask that? Do
you intend on forcing one of us to stay behind on Incendra?"

"I haven't yet decided. But then, I've yet to be convinced if this mission of yours is truly what you say it

is." The Tuaret leader's mouth quirked. "Volan mind-slavers. It stretches the limits of credibility."

"I tire of the games, Bahir," Teague growled. "Though we've held information back from you in the past, what we told you about the purpose of our mission is true. What other possible reason could induce us to risk Incendra's electromagnetic storm? It nearly killed Raina as it was."

"What else, indeed?" The Tuaret's eyes went hard, calculating. "You care for her, don't you?"

The unexpected turn in the conversation gave Teague pause. Where was Bahir headed now? "What I feel or don't feel for Raina isn't the issue," he gritted.

"Ah, but it is." Bahir went back to work on his sword. He ground a final razor-sharp edge, then set the stone aside. Taking up a soft cloth, he slowly, lovingly, began to polish the blade. "How deep does your love for her go, Teague Tremayne? Deep enough to send her away and stay behind? Deep enough to sacrifice your own will and desires for that of the good of many?"

Teague considered the Tuaret's words and their underlying implications carefully. Was Bahir offering to barter Raina's freedom in exchange for his commitment to join him in the fight against Vorax? Or did the Tuaret really plan to keep them both on Incendra and hold Raina hostage to ensure his continued cooperation? Considering Bahir's earlier words that he doubted the Volan threat, Teague feared it might be the latter.

Bahir was a supremely clever man, a master strategist. Already, he'd begun to manipulate Teague's emotions in forcing him to mate with Raina. Already, Teague would fight to the death to protect her. Already, he didn't want ever to let her go.

Soon it all might be a moot point, at any rate. If

Bahir decided to prevent them from leaving Incendra, there was little they could do about it. Little they could do about anything, for that matter, as long as they remained with him and his band.

The wisest course, Teague resolved, was to devise a plan to escape Bahir once they'd retrieved the special stone. No purpose was served, meanwhile, by raising his suspicions unnecessarily. Bahir already knew where they were headed. To attempt an escape now was pointless. Teague just didn't like the rapidly worsening predicament Bahir was forcing them into.

"So, even after all your earlier promises," he ground out bitterly, "you now require even more from us? You are a cold-hearted, treacherous man."

Bahir shrugged. "I but prod you into doing what you know, in your heart of hearts, to be right. Besides, I promised you nothing, Tremayne, save that I'd give the *mirah* over to one of my men if you didn't take her as yours. I promised nothing save safe escort to the firestorm caves and the return trip to your ship. And I also promised that no harm would come to you by our hands. But that is *all* I promised."

Promises, Teague thought. Vows. It seemed Bahir tossed them aside whenever it was convenient, and then made new ones as the situation warranted. Yet, how really different was he from the Tuaret leader?

Teague had told himself over and over as he'd mated with Raina that he gave her only of his body, not his heart; that he broke none of his monkish vows in what he did. Yet each time he'd taken Raina last night, he'd shattered each of his vows, one by one.

She was a real, living, loving being of flesh and bone. Coming to know Raina had turned everything he'd once believed inside out. Coming to know Raina had forced him to question what he'd never questioned before. And the answers, hard as they were to accept, had found him and his former life lacking.

Perhaps he *had,* to a certain extent, hidden behind the safety of his vows and the monastic life. For him, the monastery, as hard, as demanding as it was, had always been a sanctuary. But perhaps it had also shielded him from facing his deepest fears, from growing fully into the man he was destined to be.

And perhaps he must now set that life aside and make a new one. *As the situation warranted . . .*

No, Teague thought sadly, he wasn't so very different from Bahir, after all.

Whatever course his life took henceforth, though, he vowed not to destroy Raina in the process. She deserved a chance at happiness, and Teague doubted there was any hope of a lasting happiness to be found on Incendra. Bahir was set on a course of certain destruction in going up against Vorax. *If* the Tuaret even lived much longer, Teague thought, recalling the tale he'd learned from Raina soon after Najirah had revealed the truth of Bahir's illness—and his ultimate fate.

Once Bahir was dead, his fine and noble crusade to destroy Vorax would be over. There seemed no one of sufficient stature in the tribe to take his place. The Tuarets would surely scatter, assimilating into other tribes in order to escape Vorax's wrath.

No, all he had to do was bide his time, Teague resolved. And if it was ultimately necessary to sacrifice his own freedom to save Raina, he'd do it, and gladly. If only he could convince Bahir to allow her to leave . . .

But that required convincing Bahir of the veracity of his claims as to the true purpose of their mission. Perhaps it was time to utilize Rand's particular skills of wisdom and diplomacy, Teague thought. After all, who else but a Volan could substantiate the true threat of the alien mind-slavers?

A grim smile twitched the corner of Teague's mouth. The battle for their lives and freedom had only begun. Bahir had yet to go up against the clever, intuitive Rand. Bahir had yet to discover that he had seriously miscalculated if he'd imagined the victory was already his.

They didn't leave the next day, as planned. In the middle of the night, Bahir relapsed, once more, into a coma. This time, the coma lasted five days. As time passed, Najirah became more and more distraught. Though Raina tried her best to comfort her friend, she was inconsolable.

"I n-never told him that I l-loved him," Najirah sobbed, on the afternoon of the fifth day of Bahir's stupor. "And now . . . now it m-may well be t-too late."

Raina, in an effort to distract Najirah from her grief, had taken her down to the muddy river to gather some of the nutritious green blanket weed growing in profusion in the shallows along the bank. The dense algae-like plant, when washed clean of dirt, then boiled and slathered with capra milk butter, was as tasty a vegetable dish as one could ever find in the desert. Yet though they'd managed to garner a plentiful amount in just the span of a half hour, Najirah's mood had failed to improve.

"Najirah," Raina tried again, "it doesn't matter what you said or didn't say. Bahir is so caught up in himself and his need to defeat Vorax before he dies that I doubt the words would have meant much to him anyway."

Her friend looked up from the blanket weed she'd

just pulled out of the river. Water and mud dripped from the thick green wad she held in her hand. In her indignation, her tears abated. "If you're trying to comfort me, I suggest you stop."

Raina paused, reconsidered her words, then grinned sheepishly. "I suppose you're right. That wasn't the kindest or smartest way to put it."

"No, it wasn't."

"I guess what I really meant is that Bahir is in no state of mind to hear much of what anyone would say, no matter who it is, unless it directly applies to his quest." Raina sighed. "I'm sure, though, if he'd the luxury of considering anything else, he'd—"

"Well, it doesn't really matter, does it?" Her friend bluntly cut her off. "I don't even know if he'll survive this attack. It's said that in most cases, when the incidents of coma lengthen to longer than four days, the end is very near. Even if he survives this attack, it'll surely be the last time." She dragged in a tremulous breath. "Ah, gods, Raina! My Bahir is d-dying!"

Najirah stood, brushed off her skirt, then stooped and gathered up her basket of blanket weed. "I-I really shouldn't be away so long. I need to be there for Bahir, in case . . . in case . . ."

Raina took up her own basket and rose. "He's a strong, stubborn man, Najirah. Bahir won't give up life easily."

Gratitude gleamed in Najirah's bright blue eyes. "I realize that. I just want him to know I love him, that's all. All these cycles, I've been so afraid to tell him. First, because he was so hurt and angry over Cyra's departure—he risked much in going against Incendarian beliefs, however archaic and inaccurate they were, in mating with an off planet woman, you know?—that I knew my words would mean little to him. And then later . . ."

She sighed. "Later, when I realized that he'd never truly get over Cyra, I was afraid he'd pity me for my hopeless love and say the words just because he knew I wanted to hear them. But I refuse to beg for his love, or accept it because it's his duty to make me happy." Her small chin lifted and a resolute light gleamed in her eyes. "I would earn it, or not have it at all!"

"And now, Najirah?" Raina asked softly, filled with the surety of her knowledge—a knowledge that she had truly lacked until two nights ago. "Now you don't care, do you? Your pride is of small consequence in light of Bahir's fate. What matters—all that matters—is that you love him."

"Yes." A soft, wondering smile lifted her mouth. "What matters is that Bahir know that I love him so much that nothing can ever come between us. Nothing, not even death."

"Well, there's some consolation to be had in the fact that he agreed to let you come with us to the firestorm caves."

"Yes," Najirah agreed, "there is consolation in that. If he survives this attack." She made a motion with her basket, indicating the trail leading up to camp. "Let's head back, shall we? The day draws on and the blanket weed takes a good hour to cook."

Raina nodded and stepped out at her side. "And you want to get back to Bahir."

"Yes," Najirah whispered, a sad little smile trembling on her lips, "I want to get back to Bahir. Whether he knows it or not," she softly added, "he needs me. And I would be with him to the end."

* * *

By early that evening, Bahir began to come out of his coma. Najirah was overjoyed and threw herself into the wifely task of cooking up a nourishing soup, rich with bits of blanket weed and succulent capra meat. Bahir took half a bowlful, then fell back in an exhausted slumber. Najirah never left his side the entire night.

The next morning, though too weak to inspect the camp, as was his wont first thing every day, Bahir left his bed and, unsteadily and with Najirah's help, walked outside. He spent the rest of the morning propped up against a blanket-covered saddle, meeting with several of his men. Teague came by at midday, Rand's carrying pack in his hand.

Bahir cocked a black brow. "Brought me a visitor, have you?"

Teague laid the pack on the ground beside him. "You said you found the idea of speaking with Rand intriguing. I thought perhaps he could keep you company during your convalescence. He certainly gets lonely, cooped up in his pack inside our tent."

"So he's a gift of sorts for the invalid, is he?"

Teague shrugged. "Call it what you wish. I also thought Rand might be able to convince you of the Volan threat where I had failed."

Amusement danced in Bahir's amber-colored eyes. "Ah, so now we get closer to the truth. I suspected a more subtle motive to your actions than concern for my, or Rand's, welfare."

"We're cut of the same cloth, Bahir." Teague grinned. "Neither of us does anything without a more 'subtle' motive."

The Tuaret smiled. "Already we begin to understand

each other. Could it perhaps be the start of a partnership?"

Teague's grin faded. "Perhaps. And perhaps not."
Without farewell or a by-your-leave, he turned and
strode away.

The early afternoon sun beat down on Bahir. He noticed for the first time how stifling hot it had become.
"Najirah?" he called, glancing around for her.

She was instantly at his side. "Yes, husband? What
is it you desire?"

He swiped an annoying trickle of sweat from his
brow. "I'd like to take my midday meal inside the tent.
Can you help me to my feet?"

"Of course, husband." She squatted and, slipping an
arm beneath his, helped him to stand.

Once he was on his feet, Bahir freed himself from
her tight clasp. "I can make it to the tent on my own.
Would you bring Tremayne's carrying case along?"

Without awaiting her reply, Bahir headed toward the
tent. In the heat of the day, the tent front and back were
tied up to allow cooling breezes to blow through. Today,
fortunately, it was windy. Bahir lowered himself to the
pallet with a sigh of relief, inordinately grateful for the
breeze.

Najirah was at his side an instant later. She placed
the carrying pack next to him, then busied herself
plumping the cushions and arranging them behind his
back. Next, she brought him a dipperful of cool water.
Leaning back on her haunches, Najirah watched as he
drained the dipper.

"Is there anything else you need, husband?" she
asked when he was done. "If not, I'll set about preparing your meal."

"No, I'm quite content, *mirah*." Bahir handed back

the dipper, tamping down on the surge of irritation her oversolicitous actions stirred. Najirah was most likely just overreacting to his recent relapse, he well knew, but by the firestorms, he had yet to become a doddering, helpless invalid!

She hesitated. "A moment more of your time, husband."

"What is it, Najirah?" This time, Bahir couldn't quite hide the tinge of weary annoyance.

It wasn't lost on her. Najirah's eyes clouded. Her lips tightened. She still looked, however, determined to say what she meant to say.

"I thought I would lose you this time, Bahir," she softly began. "You were ill for so long . . ."

He stared up at her, silent, expectant. When she didn't continue, Bahir made an impatient motion of his hand. "Yes, and your point? Obviously, I'm far more resilient than you expected."

She hesitated again, then inhaled a deep breath. "I never told you this before, but I vowed that I would, if you recovered. In the past, I never thought the time was right and, in my fear that I might offend you, I almost lost the opportunity ever to tell you." She took his hand in hers, covering it with the other. "So now I will, but know that it requires nothing of you that you don't wish to give back. Do you understand me, Bahir?"

"Yes," he warily replied. "I think so."

"Fine." Najirah's little chin lifted and she fixed him with a steady look. "I love you, Bahir. I will always love you. And I will always be there for you, in whatever way you want or need me."

Stunned, Bahir looked away for a long moment, then forced himself to meet her gaze. He must say something, he told himself, frantically searching for the right words that were both truthful and kind. She expected *some* sort of a response from him. He was her husband, after all.

"I deeply appreciate the sentiments," he said, knowing even as he struggled to reply that it would never be enough, never be what she wanted to hear. Savagely, he cursed Cyra, whose betrayal had destroyed any chance he'd ever had of loving again. "You have been a good and loyal wife to me, Najirah. A man couldn't hope for a better one."

She smiled, yet the brave effort failed to hide the pain and disappointment that flared briefly in her eyes. "I just wanted you to know, Bahir. That's all." She rose. "I'll go prepare your meal now, if you've no further need of me."

"No, no further need at the present." For her benefit, he forced a faint smile.

Najirah turned and left the tent, making her way over to the cookfire. There she sat. Taking up a long wooden spoon, she began to stir the contents of the pot, never once glancing in his direction.

Bahir watched her for a time. Then, heaving a sigh of regret at his failings when it came to Najirah, he scooted down more comfortably onto the pillows. It was too much for him to consider right now, on top of his rapidly nearing death, the work still left to do to convince Teague Tremayne to accept his destiny, and the impending journey to the firestorm caves. Later, if there ever *was* a later for him, he'd think more about what she'd said.

Later . . . but not today . . . His lids lowered and he gave himself up to the rare pleasure of a warm, lazy afternoon.

"You're a man of *many* failings," a voice unexpectedly rose from the carrying case lying beside him, jerking Bahir back to full wakefulness and astounded outrage. "But the saddest failing of all," Rand ruthlessly continued, "is your inability to confront those failings, and your lack of courage in fighting to overcome them."

Eighteen

Bahir riveted a blistering gaze on the carrying pack. "You presume much, Volan, to dare to speak to me that way. Don't imagine that the hospitality I offer your two compatriots necessarily extends to you, an entity in a box."

"If your 'hospitality' to Teague and Raina to date is any indication, I hardly think I'll languish over its loss," Rand muttered dryly. "But all that aside, you haven't much time left, Bahir, and *no* time whatsoever for those around you to mince words."

"No, I suppose I don't." The Tuaret leader leaned back against his pillows and shot the carrying pack a considering look. "I don't recall, though, asking for your advice."

"No, I don't suppose you did," the Volan admitted. "I've found with those of your species, however, that you rarely know when you need the input. And my heart—figuratively at least—went out to your mate. You totally discount her, you know?"

Bahir's anger stirred anew. "Najirah isn't a topic of discussion."

"Why? Because you feel guilty over how you treat her?"

"She is my wife. I treat her with the utmost respect!"

"I think she'd prefer a bit more passion than respect. It gets rather lonely up there on that pedestal."

Rand's words gave Bahir pause. He *had* put a barrier between them all these cycles. Cyra. And if it wasn't her, something else always seemed to stand in the way. Perhaps it was the lack of time left him and the more pressing importance of all the other tasks he'd yet to see accomplished, or perhaps, just perhaps, it *was* a lack of courage.

But a lack of courage for what? Bahir wondered. He shoved the question aside before its insidious talons could sink into his heart and soul and lay them both open. The answer was there, that he well knew, but he didn't want to, and couldn't, face it. It was far easier, Bahir ruefully admitted, to run.

"I thought Tremayne brought you here to convince me of the Volan threat," he said, smoothly changing the subject. "You waste precious time pleading your cause. You also risk losing your audience with your insistence on discussing a subject that isn't any of your affair."

"I beg pardon," the Volan said, sounding not at all contrite. "The mission to retrieve the crystal from the firestorm caves is, of necessity, of the greatest import. I must confess to a certain fascination and attraction to helping you humanoids solve your problems, though."

"Well, find some other subject to foist your misguided efforts on." Bahir's mouth tightened and he looked away. "I neither need nor want them."

"I'll respect your wishes." Rand sighed. "What is it you desire to know about the Volan threat?"

"Quite simply, I don't believe in it."

"Yet you wish for me to convince you of it?"

"Yes."

There was a long pause. "I think there is more to

this than your concern over the threat to the Imperium. You don't really care what happens to it, do you? Your first concern is and has always been Incendra. And you want me to help you convince Teague to join forces with you."

"How did you know? Has Tremayne told you of my efforts to win him over?"

"No. I hear things and piece them all together. One does that when one has nothing but time and little else to do with it. Something you're lacking in altogether, eh, Bahir?"

Bahir stared at the carrying pack, then gave a low laugh. "Very clever, Volan. Once more you've diverted the topic of discussion back to me."

"Even in your waning days, you are still the focal point of so many lives, aren't you? Najirah's. Teague and Raina's, and, by association, mine. And, most possibly, the fate of an entire Imperium's worth of people."

"Just because of my dedication to seeing Malam Vorax overthrown?" Once again Bahir laughed. "You lay too much power at my feet, Volan."

"No, Bahir," Rand softly contradicted him, "you take the power and wield it like some weapon to punish others. Almost as if, in the wielding, you exorcise your lack of power over someone you couldn't control."

The accusation struck Bahir with the force of a storm wind slamming down from the mountains. Hard, brutal, and so very, very cold. For a long moment he couldn't say anything, his thoughts caught up in a maelstrom of self-doubt and recrimination and pain.

Cyra.

Was it possible? Had he let his loss of her twist him into some bitter, grasping, frustrated man? Yet the need to see Vorax destroyed *was* good. Surely there was no sin, no malice in that?

"I won't give up my battle against Vorax," he rasped thickly. He gripped the blanket that lay upon the pallet, twisting it in his hand, hard and punishingly. "No matter what you say, what you accuse me of!"

"And you shouldn't, Bahir. The man has taken what wasn't his to take."

Hope sprang in the Tuaret's breast. "Your friend, Tremayne. He's the heir to the throne of Farsala. Has he told you of that?"

"No, but I sensed there was some terrible secret behind his exile from Incendra."

"Will you help me convince him to stay, to fight for his throne?"

"The decision must be his, Bahir."

"Even though it's his duty? Even though his people languish under the rule of a brutally oppressive ruler? Or am I the only one who cares?"

"The decision must be his. Give him time."

Bahir stared at the carrying pack, struggling to hold back the surge of savage fury and frustration. "Well, in case you've forgotten, I don't have much time left, Volan! What will happen if he doesn't make up his mind before I'm gone? Answer me that."

"And what will happen if he's manipulated, or forced into joining you against his will?" Rand countered with quiet emphasis. "Is that the kind of man you want leading your people, or ruling Farsala?"

"Ah, gods!" Bahir lowered his head, covering his face with his hands. An agonized hopelessness seared through him. "Then what am I to do? I'm only one man. I'm only one man!"

"Follow your heart. Face what must be faced, but

give yourself permission to fail, to grieve, to surrender one dream to find another. Then get on with what is left of loving and living. Do it now, Bahir. Before it's too late."

Bahir lifted his gaze. Dreams? he thought. In a life that, in the end, threatened to have nothing to show for itself, he couldn't give up the one dream that remained. "It's already too late, Volan," he ground out, feeling as despairing as his words. "My vengeance against Vorax is all I have left."

"Then I pity you," Rand softly said. "For you're already dead."

They set out three days later for the firestorm caves at the base of the Barakah Mountains, almost four weeks since Teague and Raina had first arrived on Incendra. Besides Najirah and Aban, Bahir took a contingent of about twenty men. Any larger a force might draw undue attention, attention that could lead to fatal consequences as they neared the royal city of Ksathra. To keep from drawing unnecessary notice, Bahir insisted they all put away their distinctive curved swords and dress in the more nondescript clothing of the people of the region, in drab browns, blacks, and tans.

The first day's travel was uneventful, if hot and dirty. No oasis lay between the Tuaret hideout and the firestorm caves, so camp that night was made in a dry riverbed. Supper was simple, more journey bread, dehydrated meat sticks, some palmas fruit, and a hurriedly prepared pot of mentha tea. Then, despite how gritty and uncomfortable they all felt, exhaustion soon claimed them.

The next morn dawned as hot and bright as the day

before. They reached the sparse foothills of the Barakah Mountains about midday, then carefully skirted the various small villages that had sprung up wherever there was a water source.

By dusk, the eerie red glow signaling the firestorm caves lit the sky. Bahir insisted they make camp in a stand of scraggly sempervivus high up on a plateau overlooking the desert, about five kilometers from the entrance to the caves. The turbulence and heat from the firestorms precluded camping any closer, he said.

Raina set up her and Teague's bedding beneath the shelter of a low overhang of rock, then went to join Najirah in preparing a cold supper. This close to the mountains, Bahir refused to allow campfires for fear of giving away their position. Raina could well understand his caution. Only fifty kilometers beyond the firestorm caves sat the royal city of Ksathra, proudly perched on a huge outcropping of mountainside, and Vorax's spies were rampant in the area.

They were in dangerous territory, this close to Malam Vorax and his army. Bahir risked much in bringing them here. Raina was tempted to ask him why he did so. He stood to gain little if they were successful in retrieving the crystal. It would do nothing to further his own goals of destroying Vorax. Or at least, nothing Raina could see, at any rate.

He was a complex, enigmatic man, to say the least. And a cold-hearted manipulator at the worst. She only wondered where he really stood in all this.

After seeing to the equs, Bahir and Teague joined them for the supper meal. Preoccupied with thoughts of the day to come and the culmination of the mission, Raina was taciturn, contenting herself with her food. Teague was equally quiet. Bahir ate sparingly, his gaze sharp and assessing. Najirah watched them all with anxious eyes.

The rest of the men camped further away, their voices low and muted in the silence of the night. A night bird called from its perch high above them. Another answered, the sound haunting, sad. A cool breeze swirled down from the mountain.

Raina pulled her cloak more snugly to her and thought longingly of her bed beneath the overhang of rock. With Teague's big body pressed to hers, she knew she'd be warm. Though they lacked the privacy for more intimate pursuits, the thought of cuddling close to him was a most pleasant consolation. If the looks he'd sent her the past two days were any indication, he, too, would welcome the first opportunity for a bit more physical contact.

She'd never thought to so eagerly anticipate bedding down for the night. But then, Raina thought wryly, she'd never been in love before, either. It made for quite a bit of uncertainty and surprises.

"What are your plans for the morrow?" Bahir, finished first with his meal, finally intruded into the silence and Raina's thoughts.

Teague glanced at Raina, then met the Tuaret leader's inquiring gaze. "We mean to enter the caves with Rand, use him to discern the specific stone we need, then remove a large enough quantity to fill the special transport sacks we brought."

"And how do you plan to get inside? The intense heat of the firestorms burning before the caves keeps everyone at least a half kilometer back."

Teague smiled. "We brought special heat-protective suits. And Rand's carrying pack is made of the same material."

"You've thought of almost everything, I see," the Tuaret said. *"Almost* everything. I plan on entering the caves with you. Which of you will give up your protective suit and stay behind?"

Once more, Teague and Raina exchanged glances. "Why do you wish to enter the caves with us, Bahir?" Teague asked. "There's no way out but the way we go in. We can't escape."

Bahir shrugged. "Oh, I'd no fear of you escaping. It's just that I've yet to be totally convinced mining the crystal is your true motive for being here. And I don't intend to let you out of my sight until I am convinced of why you truly came back to Incendra."

"Bahir," Raina snarled, setting down her cup of cerevisia. "I tire of your suspicions and intrusions into everything we do. Teague and I were specially trained in the identification and proper mining techniques of this stone. If you force one of us to remain behind, it'll slow the mining significantly. And the longer we linger in Vorax's territory, the greater the danger. I must go in with Teague. There's no other option."

"There are always other options," the Tuaret softly said. "And I *will* go in with you. But your comments on your special training and not lingering overlong here have merit. We'll just take another, far safer route."

"A safer route?" Teague leaned forward, his eyes narrowing. "And what exactly would that be, Bahir?"

"The firestorms guard the entrance of the caves. They're no danger at the top of the caves, especially as far back as we'll go before we reach the crawl space."

Raina cocked her head. "A crawl space? There's another way in, then?"

Bahir nodded. "Yes. When I was a lad, we used to make our winter camp near the caves. I spent countless hours exploring these mountains. I know secret paths and ancient tunnels and ways into places that few have ever imagined, much less found. And I know a way past the firestorms that'll take us into the caves."

"Then take us to that spot, Bahir," Teague said. "I've no problem with you coming along." He looked over at Raina. "Have you, femina?"

She considered his query for a long moment. "No, I suppose not. Just as long as you don't interfere with what we must do, once we're inside the caves."

"Fair enough." Bahir rose and offered his hand to Najirah. When she accepted it, he pulled her to her feet. "We'll set out before dawn, so few will notice our passing or destination. In the meanwhile, it's time we all took our rest."

Teague nodded and rose. He glanced down at Raina. "Are you ready to come to bed, femina?"

At his softly couched query, a thrill coursed through Raina. She climbed to her feet. "Yes, more than ready."

They headed off into the darkness toward their little shelter, the light of a full moon illuminating their way. After shedding her boots and removing the sheathed dagger fastened to her thigh, Raina climbed onto the pallet. She shoved the dagger under her makeshift pillow of a rolled blanket, then slid beneath the covers. Teague soon joined her.

He lay there beside her, his big frame blocking the moonlight, so near, yet so far away. Raina couldn't make out his face in the shadowed dimness, but she sensed he stared at her in watchful anticipation. "What is it, Teague?" she finally asked. "Is there something you want?"

He hesitated for the span of a heartbeat. "Yes. I'd like to hold you. If you've no objection, that is."

"I'd like that, too." She smiled. "Shall we meet in the middle, like before?"

A low chuckle rumbled in his chest. "Yes, most definitely."

Teague moved toward her. Raina immediately did the same. In an awkward, uncertain tangle of arms and legs, they soon settled into place against each other.

Raina sighed and snuggled close, savoring the soothing, reassuring thud of his heart against her ear. He felt warm, solid, and strong. She liked being held by him, she realized with a pleasurable twinge of surprise—very, very much.

"I could come to require this kind of touching every night," she murmured contentedly.

His head moved. His lips touched her forehead. "As could I, sweet one. As could I. You've given me much in these past weeks, shown me a life I never thought to have, and shared such pleasures of the flesh with me . . . well, they're pleasures I'll never forget."

There was something in his words, some tone, some finality, that plucked at Raina, filling her with unease. "You speak as if it's soon to be over for us. What are you keeping from me, Teague?"

He should've known he couldn't hide his thoughts or plans from Raina for long. Already, she knew him too well. "I don't trust Bahir," he reluctantly admitted. "He's determined to keep me here, to help him in the fight against Vorax. I'd hoped to find some way to escape him, once we'd obtained the crystal, but I begin to think that's a hopeless dream. As you can see from tonight, he means even to follow us into the firestorm caves."

Teague sighed. "He won't let me out of his sight,

Raina. You must prepare yourself for the fact that you may have to return to Bellator without me."

Her fingers clenched in the lightweight fabric of his tunic. "I won't go without you, Teague. Somehow we'll find a way to thwart him!"

"Ah, sweet femina," he murmured, laying his cheek against the top of her head. "Your words stir my heart, but we both know Bahir is too clever to be easily thwarted. And he has the advantage over us. For all purposes, we're his prisoners."

"I still have my dagger, and the other stunner. Bahir doesn't know about the other stunner."

"Would you use it on him and all his men?"

"If need be, yes."

"They'd still come after us."

"Then let's kill Bahir once we're inside the caves, or stun him and take him hostage. Once we're safely within the spy ship, we can let him go. There's nothing they can do to us with their puny weapons, once we're inside the ship."

Teague smiled. Raina was resourceful and determined, and intent upon saving him. Yet he wasn't so sure he deserved to or should be "saved."

Even before he'd set foot again on Incendra, he'd been struck with the realization that perhaps there was something left undone and he was being called back to finish it. From the start, the land had beckoned to him, filling him with a bittersweet longing for a time long ago. Farsala was in his blood, ground in as indelibly as the wind and sand that blasted the desert rocks, until they were all one and the same.

No, though he'd tried hard to ignore the stirrings of the land and its people, they'd never ceased to call.

Never, he realized now, even in all those cycles of his exile.

As much as he wanted to hate Bahir, to blame the man for forcing him into something he'd no wish to do, the Tuaret leader had never been more than the relentless voice of his own conscience. Bahir had been nothing more than the voice beckoning him to his final test, to that living cauldron of fire and pain wherein he would at long last fully die to himself and the world. Wherein he'd finally be purified. Wherein he'd finally be found worthy . . . in the final confrontation with Malam Vorax.

Perhaps the ancient prophecy *did* apply to him. The consideration was scant consolation, even if it did. When all its fine verbiage was stripped away, the prophecy had still promised nothing. Nothing save the surety of searching and hard choices to be made and suffering. Never had it guaranteed victory, at least not in the physical sense of assuring Vorax's overthrow. Bahir might hope and dream that it had, but it hadn't.

Yet in the total scheme of things, even the prophecy's ambiguity mattered little. What mattered was that he'd been called back to Incendra for a reason. What mattered was that he couldn't run anymore.

"Your loyalty is most heartwarming," Teague forced himself to say, knowing they'd be the hardest, potentially cruelest words he'd ever spoken. "I, however, have made my decision. I need to stay behind, Raina. It's my duty. You told me once that I chose to avoid my responsibilities, that I fled from myself. Well, I've finally decided to stop running."

On a certain level, Teague knew he lied—he, who had always prided himself on telling the truth. But if it would save Raina, send her back to a life with far more chance of happiness than she could ever hope to have here, he'd swallow his pride and stoop to that. For Raina, he would do anything.

He had turned her words against her, Raina thought in an anguished surge of frustration and despair. She'd meant for him to stop running and face life—and loving—not to sacrifice himself on the altar of some hopeless cause. A cause some fatally ill man had pinned all his hopes to in order to die with some purpose to his life. Ah, curse Bahir. Curse him to the depths of perdition!

"You've listened too long to Bahir," Raina said, grasping for some way, the right words, that would change Teague's mind. "But he's dying and desperate. Most likely, he won't even live to see his futile dream come to fruition. No," she muttered bitterly, "he'll never see the death and destruction his wretched, reckless dreams have wrought. But *you* will, Teague. You will, and will suffer horribly for it."

"Still, it's my choice to make, and I have made it."

"And what of your monastery back on Bellator?" she whispered savagely, her fingers twisting his tunic, gouging into his chest. "What of the vows you made to serve the Imperium as a warrior monk? You're needed on Bellator, too, Teague. Perhaps even more so, now that the Volans threaten us all."

"The Imperium has more warrior monks. It also has men the caliber of Teran Ardane and his brother to draw upon. But I'm the only crown prince of Farsala."

His hand settled on her shoulder, then slid down to gently stroke her back. "I must do this, sweet one. I failed so long ago. Failed my family, my people, myself. Despite all I've achieved, all I've done to serve the Imperium, deep in my heart, I've still felt so unworthy . . . ever since that day Vorax marched into Ksathra. Always felt that I'd failed my father . . ."

He dragged in a shuddering breath. "But no more. If I join with Bahir, if I fight with him against Vorax, I'll have finally redeemed myself in his memory. He always wanted me to be a warrior. I'll be the one he wanted me to be at last, in defense of Farsala, our home."

"And *die* in his memory, too," Raina added bitterly. "For all he would care. If he didn't accept you as a boy, as his son and heir, he and his cursed memory aren't worthy of you now. Yet you'll sacrifice your life in the memory of a man who was never a worthy father to you."

"Just as you've sacrificed yours because of what Vorax did to you?"

Yes, she thought, *and in the memory of the man who was never a worthy father to me.*

Tears filled Raina's eyes. *Will you throw it all away?* Marissa had once asked her. *Killing them won't heal you. Only you can do that.*

Raina knew now that even their deaths wouldn't heal her. Her father was already gone, pitiful, tormented man that he'd been, and the pain of his rejection and betrayal was no less acute.

Pitiful . . . A sad smile twisted her mouth. Pitiful . . . not hated. Not anymore.

He was to be pitied, not hated, for he was never able to summon the courage to overcome his weaknesses. To stand up for his brutalized daughter, to love her enough to fight for her honor, much less care enough even to be outraged. But she wouldn't sacrifice what was left of her life and happiness because of him anymore.

Strangely, even the hunger to avenge herself on Malam Vorax had paled. Raina pondered that new revelation, wondering when that seething rage against him had eased. It had happened sometime in the past weeks, as she'd come to know and love Teague. Perhaps it was because Teague had, in a sense, returned what Vorax had taken—her self-esteem as a woman, the power over her own body to give it as she chose.

Or perhaps it was something else altogether. She hated Vorax, would never forgive him for what he'd done, but there were more important issues in her life now. She hadn't time to allow herself to sink into the seductive and ultimately destructive quagmire of hatred and unrequited need for revenge. She had a mission of Imperium-wide import to carry out—and a man whom she loved to live and fight for.

Yet the cruelest irony of it all was that just when she'd finally been able to free herself of the cycles of seething hatred and anger and opened herself to love once more, that love, and the man who had revealed it to her, might soon be lost. It didn't seem fair. It *wasn't* fair.

"Not anymore," she whispered, in answer to his challenge. "I won't sacrifice my life anymore. I love you, Teague. I want to spend my life with you, no matter where it is or what the conditions. But you have to come back with me to do that. It's the only way we can be together."

The words, spoken with such tender conviction, were like talons stabbing into Teague's heart. She loved him? Gods, never in his wildest dreams had he entertained the hope that Raina would come to love him! He was hardly worthy of redemption for all his past blunders. And never, ever, worthy of her love.

Her sweet admission thrilled him nonetheless. Almost from the start, he'd felt her to be a kindred spirit. Almost from the start, he'd sensed her compassion for him, her concern, her caring. And it had felt so very, very good. Until now, Teague hadn't fully realized how lonely he'd been, or how he'd longed for that sense of soul-deep union with another.

But that longing now warred with duty—a duty to Farsala and to Incendra that overshadowed his freshly roused and most elemental of human needs.

One's petty concerns are as naught. One's fears are groundless. All that matters is the unceasing flow of the universe.

The *Litany of Union*. Its sacred, healing words flowed over Teague, stirring him once more to the deepest recesses of his being. They spoke of a greater truth, a higher calling, yet this time not to the tenets of monasticism, but to the needs of living beings. And in light of those holy words, his own needs, even to his very existence, meant nothing. As he'd once wholeheartedly served the Imperium, it was now time to serve Farsala and Incendra. And in the process, think of Raina as well.

"I say again," Teague forced himself to reply, his heart ripping asunder to spill out all his pain and regret even as he spoke. "You must return to Bellator with the crystal. I must remain here. Never forget that we came back to do our duty, a duty that will finally near its culmination on the morrow. But as your duty is to return to Bellator, mine is now to stay behind. That is all that matters. That is all, in the end, that can *ever* matter."

He released her then to lie there, physically distancing himself even as he verbally cut the fragile bonds that had so recently bound them. "Though I deeply appreciate your kind words to me," Teague whispered hoarsely, achingly, into the heavy stillness of the night, "love has never been part of the bargain between us. Not now, nor can it ever be."

Nineteen

An inferno of great size and force ascended toward the heavens, blazing before a series of huge, cavernous openings in the base of the mountain. Fed by strong, inrushing winds from all sides, the firestorm roared like a mighty, enraged beast, scorching all plant life from the area and setting pools of molten rock to shimmer in the light of the rising sun.

It was a terrifying sight, a sight intensified by the crimson and gold rays of the sunrise inundating the land, until not only the mountain and caves but the world around them appeared set afire, and it seemed they were the only beings left on the planet. Those strange, disembodied feelings, Teague thought, gazing up at the towering inferno, hadn't changed from the days of his youth. The firestorm caves still held an awful power and fascination, were an awesome symbol of Incendra and its harsh and volatile history.

He glanced at Raina. Her gaze, guarded and unreadable, met his. She'd said not another word to him after he'd flatly told her last night there was no hope for them or their love. She'd just pulled back from him, turned on her side, and lain there until exhaustion had finally claimed them both.

And she wouldn't say anything more. Raina was proud; she'd never beg him for his love.

Teague turned to Bahir, who stood on his other side, along with Aban. Bahir's big, burly compatriot had insisted on coming along. Teague wondered if his motivation arose from a desire to protect Bahir from them or from a quite understandable concern that his leader not overwork himself. "Let's get on with this expedition, shall we?" he growled, motioning to the mountain that loomed before them.

The Tuaret leader smiled thinly. "A wise plan." He lifted his arm, indicating a particularly steep and winding path high on the mountainside. "That's where we must go."

If Bahir hadn't pointed it out, Teague would never have noticed it, as well hidden as it was among the rocks and scraggly vegetation. "Come," Bahir said. "The beginning of the trail is several kilometers down from the caves."

They followed him without comment and soon reached the trailhead. The trek up the mountain was strenuous. However, Bahir maintained a strong, steady pace and, by midmorn, they'd reached a small, boulder-strewn ridge about a third of the way up the mountainside.

Bahir led them to a large stand of rocks, climbed over the top, and disappeared. Raina and Teague exchanged a puzzled look with Aban. A few minutes later, Bahir appeared once more.

"Are you coming or not? The crawl space lies behind these boulders."

Teague, Raina, and Aban scrambled up the rock pile to join the Tuaret. Next to his left foot was a black hole big enough for a man with supplies to slide through. Warm, musty air spewed from the opening, rife with ancient smells and decay.

"How tight is this crawl space?" Teague asked. "I'm

not particularly fond of holes in the ground, especially narrow ones."

"Neither am I," Bahir admitted, "though when I was a lad, this hole seemed quite large. It goes on like this for about five meters, then opens into a quite adequate tunnel for the rest of the way into the caves. Can you manage it for five meters?"

"If I have to," Teague muttered. He gestured to the hole. "Why don't you lead the way?"

Bahir nodded, then shed his headcloth, cloak, and long tunic. Aban did the same. Clothed only in their breeches, short under tunics and boots, they shoved their curved daggers beneath their belts. Then Bahir flipped on a perpetual light torch and, dropping to his knees, climbed into the crawl space. As Aban followed suit, Raina and Teague quickly removed their outer, more cumbersome clothing, shouldered their backpacks—one of which contained Rand's metal shielding receptacle— illuminated their torches, and followed.

True to Bahir's word, the crawl space did open to a quite adequate tunnel where they could stand in but five meters. The journey back toward the firestorm caves took nearly as long as the trek up the trail to the crawl space. By Teague's calculations, it was midday by the time they reached the first of the myriad caves.

The torch beams reflected off the walls of crystaline rock, sending blinding shards of light ricocheting into their eyes if the perpetual light torches weren't angled properly. Teague paused, slung his pack off his back, and extracted Rand's shielding receptacle. Bahir walked over.

"Time for the Volan to perform, is it?" the Tuaret inquired.

Teague flipped open the latches of the shielding receptacle, opened the box, and pulled out a membranous sphere about the size of a human head. Attached to the sphere's top was a set of three tubes. As Teague moved the sphere slightly in taking it from the box, a green luminescence suddenly appeared inside it.

"What's that?" Bahir asked suspiciously.

"Nothing more than life forms within the biosphere that help maintain the Volan spirit entities. I disturbed them when I jostled the sphere." Teague looked down at the now glowing globe. "Can you hear me, Rand?"

"Yes, Teague. We're within the caves, aren't we?"

"In the first crystaline cave, to be exact. Feel any unusual resonance within this chamber?"

"No."

Teague glanced at Bahir. "Well, let's get on with it, then. If memory serves, there are over twenty caves within this part of the mountain behind the firestorms."

"Twenty-three," the Tuaret corrected him. "I've counted and explored them all."

"I only hope you remember the way back through them all," Raina muttered, speaking up for the first time since they'd entered the crawl space.

Bahir shot her a wry grin. "So do I, *mirah*. So do I."

Raina gave a disgusted snort. "Well, it's your life and Aban's if you don't. We still have the protective clothing to get us through the firestorms. You two, on the other hand, might be relegated to wandering the caves for the rest of your days, until you finally die of thirst or go mad."

"A fate," he drawled, unperturbed by her grisly tale, "I'd wager you wouldn't shed a single tear over."

She finally smiled, a grim, tight upturning of the corners of her mouth. "I wouldn't wish that on Aban, but as far as you go, you'd win that wager hands down."

"Er, shall we get on with this?" Teague growled irritably. "You two have all the time in the world to continue this pleasant little conversation later. I, for one, have no inclination to remain within these caves any longer than necessary."

Bahir cocked a dark brow, then shrugged and set off across the cave toward the tunnel leading to the next chamber. They spent the next two hours traversing a total of sixteen rooms, the temperature gradually rising as they drew nearer and nearer to the firestorms blazing outside. The air grew stifling. Moisture, seeping through the mountain, wept from the ceilings. The clothing soon clung to their bodies in a mixture of dripping water and sweat.

Then, when they entered the seventeenth cavern, a chamber even hotter than the last, Rand suddenly groaned. Teague looked down at the biosphere. The green luminescence swirled wildly, as if suddenly agitated.

"What's wrong, Rand?"

"Th-the vibrations. They p-pain me. I-I can hardly think."

Teague swung his torch up and around the room. Irregular chunks of crimson crystals, piercing in their brilliance, lined the walls. Stalagmites thrust from the floor in this particular room, lending it its otherworldly feel. Though the stone was similar in appearance to many other rooms they'd traversed, the luster of the crystal was slightly different—more shimmering, and of a richer, deeper color and greater fire. A fire that seemed, when the torch light struck it just right, to mirror the leaping tongues of the firestorm that had so long guarded it.

"Is this the first time you've felt the pain and vibrations?" Teague asked. Raina stepped close to listen.

"Y-yes," Rand gasped. "This is the correct crystal, my friend. How long must I . . . remain exposed to it?"

"Not much longer." Teague could only guess what the high-frequency vibrations the correct crystal sent out were doing to the Volan. "A minute or two more, just to identify accurately which areas are truly the resonating crystal and which are not. This room could easily contain more than one form."

"I-I understand. Just hurry. There's something unusual about this stone. Almost as if . . . as if it's malevolent."

Unease filled Teague. Malevolent? A stone? But why not? The Knowing Crystal was reputed to be evil, for all the tales of its wondrous powers. It was why Teran's brother, Brace Ardane, had finally been forced to destroy it in the pools of Cambrai. But surely an unworked crystal from an entirely different source couldn't possess the sentient abilities of that former stone of power. Or could it?

It didn't matter. Their task was to bring some of the Incendarian stone back to Bellator. Others could determine later what its true properties were and how to utilize it.

Teague headed toward the nearest stand of stalagmites, in themselves a rich store of crystal if they were indeed of the proper kind. He held out Rand's biosphere to them. "Is this the right kind?" he asked.

"Y-yes," Rand groaned.

Forcing himself to ignore the Volan's pain, Teague moved off to another stand of stalagmites. The entire success of the mission hinged on them bringing back an adequate supply of the crystal. "And these?"

"Y-yes. Yes!"

The Volan's voice strained with anguish. Teague clamped down on his surge of compassion and forced himself to stride toward the nearest wall. Great chunks of gleaming crystal protruded from the wall in a rich mass of misshapen stone. "And these, Rand. What of these?" he asked, strangely compelled now to continue to search out more and more stone.

"The same," he whispered. "Teague . . . I can't . . . bear it . . . much longer."

Not true, a tiny voice inside Teague's head cried. The Volan could bear that and more. He wheeled, intent on examining yet another wall, when a strong grip settled on his arm. "Put him away, Tremayne," Bahir commanded, his angry amber gaze knifing into his. "Now, before you kill him."

"Yes," Raina called from the farthest stalagmite as she dug the mining tools out of her pack. She stared back at him, puzzled and concerned. "You've identified more than we can carry back out or need. Put Rand away."

As if snapping out of a trance, Teague opened the lid of the shielding receptacle and shoved the biosphere back within it. He slammed the lid shut and refastened the latches.

Bahir released him. "What did you intend? To take the Volan to his furthest limits and beyond?"

Bemused by the anger in the other man's voice, Teague stared back at him. "I don't understand. It was Rand's job to identify the stone. I but used him to—"

The Tuaret shot him a wary, considering look, then

sighed. "Never mind. He's well protected inside that box, isn't he?"

Teague glanced down at the shielding receptacle. "Yes." He paused. "Are you all right, Rand?"

"Better," the Volan whispered. "Teague, there's something wrong with this stone. It not only . . . has terrible resonating qualities . . . but it can kill. It was trying to kill me."

"Are you certain, Rand?" Raina walked over. "The intensity of its vibrations against your neural network may have seemed like it was more vicious than it truly was. Your perceptions might well have been so disrupted that it seemed—"

"Perhaps, femina," the Volan gently interrupted. "Perhaps. But I don't think so."

"Well, that isn't an issue we can resolve here," Teague said. "Let the scientists delve into all this deeper. We've got a lot of work ahead of us, and I'd like to be off that treacherous mountain trail and back in camp before nightfall."

Raina eyed him closely, then nodded. "Yes, so would I." She turned and walked back to where her pack lay. Picking up a hand held laser stone-cutting device, she turned it on and went to work on the nearest stalagmite.

Teague watched her for a moment. Then, setting down Rand's shielding receptacle, he dug out another stone-cutting tool from his backpack. He glanced back at Bahir. "There's a lot of stone to cut. Do you think you and Aban could help by loading the crystal into the transport sacks?"

The Tuaret nodded. "Most certainly." Teague made a move to turn and walk away. "Tremayne?"

Teague paused. He glanced back. "Yes?"

"I-I beg pardon for doubting you and your mission."

Concern darkened the Tuaret's eyes. "Your words about the Volan were true as well. I think, though, that there is more, far more to this, than even you and your compatriots on Bellator yet realize. But I do believe you now." He paused as if suddenly at a loss for words. "I just wanted you to know."

"And do you finally understand," Teague asked, "why it's vital that we take the stone back to Bellator?"

"Yes." Bahir nodded, his brow furrowing in thought. "I see now that the Imperium needs you even more than Farsala or Incendra. Because of that, I can no longer in good conscience keep you here against your will. No matter what I want, what I believe."

Teague looked deeply into Bahir's eyes and saw his sincerity. Saw his regret, as well, for a cause lost. Saw the courage it took for a man to relinquish his dreams for the sake of many. The very last dream Bahir had to cling to in the waning days of his life.

Sadness welled within him. Sadness, and a profound respect. Misguided and exasperatingly single-minded as Bahir was at times, he lived by his own set of unwavering principles. He would die by those same principles, too.

Though he chose not to tell Bahir of his decision to stay behind and help him in his battle against Vorax just now, the Tuaret would at least die knowing the man he'd waited so long and fought so hard for had finally joined him. Bahir deserved at least that much. And so did his people. No, Teague quickly corrected himself. So did *their* people.

It might not be enough, ultimately, to save Farsala, but he would at least have tried. And in the end, the fact that he'd tried would be enough. He'd at last be found worthy. In his own heart, his soul . . . where it counted the most.

"What I choose to do from here on out *will* be of my own free will, Bahir," Teague said, extending his arm to the Tuaret leader who clasped it. "I just wanted you to know."

"Bahir? Bahir, wake up!"

With a great effort, Bahir wrenched himself from a deep slumber. For a moment he lay there, disoriented and confused. It was dark, that deep, rich darkness that came in those last hours before dawn, when the stars had faded and the moon had rotated past the edge of the horizon. It was also far too early to awaken, after the past two days of backbreaking labor in the firestorm caves.

"Bahir," the urgent voice—Aban's voice—came. "An army—Vorax's army—marches on us from Ksathra even as you lie there. We must be up and on our way immediately!"

The Tuaret leader levered to one elbow. "Vorax?" he croaked groggily. He knew he should be concerned, but the ramifications seemed as distant, as unreal, as the message.

Najirah moved beside him, sat up, and flipped the blankets back. "How many, and how close?" she tersely demanded of Aban.

The big Tuaret shot Bahir a puzzled look, then turned to Najirah. "Three hundred or more. And they're but two hours away. If it hadn't been for a friendly Vastitian tribesman who lives at the base of the royal city's mountain . . ."

Bahir forced the lingering, strangely tenacious cobwebs from his mind. He shoved to a sitting position, then slowly climbed to his feet. "We must be away . . ."

He paused, his mind working. The four pack equs carrying the stone would slow them down considerably. Yet if they left them behind, it seemed unlikely that they would ever be able safely to return to the firestorm caves and mine more of the crystal. Conversely, though, if they didn't abandon the stone, Vorax's army would surely catch up to them in a very short time.

Bahir helped Najirah to stand, then turned to Aban. "Fetch Teague Tremayne and Raina. We must talk."

Najirah watched Aban walk away. "What do you plan to do?" she asked then, turning back to Bahir and gripping his arm. "And what is wrong with you? You look ill, and you woke very slowly to Aban's summons. Is it the—"

"I'm fine, *mirah*," he said, even as an unpleasant premonition that he wasn't fine threaded through him. "I'm just overtired from the mining of the past two days." He forced a lopsided grin. "I'll admit to the fact that I'm unused to such hard labor. I must be getting soft."

"You're one of the most fit men I've ever known," his wife fiercely rose to his defense.

"And you're the most loyal mate a man could ever hope to have." Bahir leaned down and kissed her forehead. "Now, we've other issues of greater import to deal with," he said, noting Teague and Raina's approach. "And one way or another, I'm wide awake and fine now."

Najirah knew when she was defeated. "So you say." She released his arm and stepped back. Still the horrible feelings wouldn't subside, the inexplicable certainty that there was more to Bahir's slowed response on waking than just exhaustion.

She eyed him furtively as he walked up and extended his arm to Teague. He did indeed look strong and decisive, the consummate leader once more. Perhaps she *had* let her ongoing worry over him influence the accuracy of her perceptions. Najirah hoped and prayed that was all there was to it. But it was also said that, in rare cases, the last days of those who died of the brain illness were heralded by a gradual weakening, with moments of lucidity up to the very end, before the mind was finally snuffed out.

There was nothing to be done about it, though, one way or another, Najirah thought, as she joined Bahir and the others. Bahir's time would come when it did. In the meantime, as he said, there were issues of greater import to deal with.

Raina met her gaze as she came to stand beside Bahir, the look in her eyes questioning, wary. Najirah tried to give her a reassuring smile and knew it failed miserably when worry flared in her friend's eyes.

"What's wrong, Bahir?" Teague asked, his words cutting through the rising anxiety. Around them, Tuarets scrambled to pack their bedding and saddle their equs. "Aren't we breaking camp a bit prematurely?"

"Vorax's army has decided to pay us an unexpected visit. Seems some opportunistic Farsalan decided to betray our presence for the price of a few coins."

Teague frowned. "With the pack equs loaded down with the crystal, it's doubtful we can outdistance them for long."

"Indeed."

"Do you have a plan, then?"

The Tuaret leader hesitated a moment, his glance meeting Najirah's, then skittering away. "Yes. We'll break into two parties. You, Raina, and the pack equs will head out by a secret path through the mountains. It'll cut off a full day from your journey back to your spaceship. It'll also," he added, "steer you clear of Vorax's army. The rest of the men will ride out across the desert with a great show of noise and force. Our pursuers will never know they follow only part of our band."

"Who will lead us through the mountains, Bahir?" Teague asked, as Aban, apparently finished with rousing the camp, drew up beside him.

Bahir shrugged. "There's little choice. It has to be me. I'm the only one who knows the secret way through the mountains."

"Then who will lead the rest of the men?" A rising apprehension filled Najirah.

He looked directly at her, his face an expressionless mask. "You will, *mirah*. You're as brave and resourceful as any of my men. And you're my second-in-command."

"No, Bahir. Please, no." He meant to send her away, didn't want her to see him die. She knew that. She just *knew* that. "Let Aban lead the others. I want to go with you. Please."

His keen eyes knifed into hers. "Aban must go with me. That leaves only you, Najirah."

He wouldn't order her or beg, not now in front of the others, or later. But he also knew he didn't have to.

For a fleeting instant, anger flared in Najirah, searing clear through to her soul. Curse Bahir! He knew, had always known, of her love and loyalty—if not consciously, then on some subconscious level. He was so sure of it that he never doubted her eventual acquiescence to his every desire.

Yet what had it gotten her in the end? Nothing. Absolutely nothing. When all she'd wanted, more than anything else, was to be with him in his last days, to hold him in her arms when he died.

Cyra, on the other hand, she thought bitterly, had flouted Tuaret customs and tossed Bahir's appeals to try a little longer and work harder on their marriage back into his face. Then she'd turned and walked away, out of his life and off Incendra. Yet she still had, for all her defiance and ultimate betrayal, won and kept his undying love.

Bahir must have seen her inner battle. A dark brow rose and an indulgent smile quirked one corner of his mouth. " 'In whatever way I might need you,' " he said, harking back to her words to him that day she'd finally told him of her love.

I love you, Bahir. I will always love you.

The words, so bravely spoken, had come back to betray her. Words she'd shared with the man she loved had now been used by that very man, without guilt or remorse, against her.

But Bahir didn't comprehend the inherent cruelty of what he did, Najirah realized, gazing up at him with eyes of love. He was too proud to die in front of her or his people if he had any choice. And she knew as well as he, gazing deep into his beautiful, amber-colored eyes, that his end was very, very near.

Najirah's shoulders slumped. All the fight drained from her. For the sake of her love, she'd give him this last gift. "It'll be as you ask, then," she whispered. "Where do you want me to lead the men?"

"Across the Ar Rimal, due east and as far away as you can from the Blandira oasis and the region where the spaceship is hidden. If possible, lead them on the chase for at least five days. Then circle around and head back to the Tuaret encampment. Aban and I will meet you there."

If you make it back, she thought sadly. A huge lump swelled in her throat and she couldn't speak. Instead, she nodded.

"I would go with Najirah."

As one, all eyes swung to Teague. "What did you say?" Bahir asked hoarsely.

"I would go with Najirah," he repeated. "I'd planned to wait until we'd reached the spaceship, but Vorax has inadvertently changed my plans. I'm staying behind on Incendra. I'll help Najirah in leading Vorax's army away and, when you return, I'll fight with you against him."

The Tuaret leader's eyes narrowed to slits. "You truly mean it? You'll join the fight against Vorax?"

"Yes."

"But what of the stone?" Bahir made a motion toward Raina. "What of your mate?"

Teague's glance locked with Raina's. Something arced between them, something ardent, yet anguished. "Raina will return to Bellator with the stone. She already knows of my decision. She accepts it."

Najirah turned to Raina and grasped her arm. "Raina, no! You cannot mean to leave him. You're life-mated. You love—"

"It's decided, Najirah!" Raina cried, twisting free of her grip, a tortured resolve burning in her eyes. "Just as Bahir has decided to shut you out of his life, so has Teague closed me out of his. So be it, I say. I'll not stay where I'm not wanted. Perhaps you'd be wise to do the same."

Bahir glowered at Raina, then looked to Teague. "Perhaps you and your mate would like a few minutes to discuss this privately. Then we must be on our way."

Teague's jaw clenched. "She has the right to say—" He caught himself, then nodded stiffly. "Yes, perhaps that would be best." He took a step toward Raina.

"No." She lifted her hand to him in a halting gesture. "I'm not some foolish child who must be taken out before she embarrasses her elders. I've said all I want to say, at any rate. We must *all* make our choices," Raina added fiercely, her glance taking in both Teague and Bahir, "and live with the consequences."

"That we must, *mirah*," Bahir softly concurred. He held out his hand. "Come, it's time we completed the final preparations. You wish to take the Volan back with us, don't you?"

She cocked her head and visually challenged Teague. "His chances of someday finding a body of his own are a lot better back on Bellator. But it's up to Teague and Rand. What do you think, Tremayne? Do you wish to keep him here with you?"

"No." He shook his head, his eyes glittering. "Take Rand back to Bellator. He serves no further purpose staying behind, and he deserves his chance at happiness. Just as you do."

"Happiness?" Raina laughed unsteadily. "When every man of any importance in my life has betrayed me?" She hesitated and had opened her mouth to say more when her eyes filled with tears. Without another word, she turned and stalked away.

Bahir hesitated. His mouth quirked at Teague in wry apology. "I'm sorry if I . . . came between you. I never believed in the seriousness of your mission, so I hoped you two would both remain here . . . to help me."

"It was never meant to be." Teague sighed. "She deserves better."

"Does she, Teague Tremayne?" Najirah softly asked.

"Or do you just look for an excuse to run away once more?"

"Najirah, that's enough," her husband warned. "Go, prepare yourself for the journey."

"Just like that, Bahir?" She turned to him, her eyes luminous, bright with tears. "I'll never see you again, and you'll dismiss me *just like that?*"

He sighed. "By the firestorms, Najirah! What do you want of me? I'm sorry there's no time for us, but . . . but there just isn't. We must be off."

"Will you at least hold me for a moment? Before we part?"

Bahir bit his lip and smiled awkwardly at Teague and Aban. "Aban, see to Raina's preparations. Teague . . ."

Teague smiled, then turned and walked away. Aban did the same. Bahir glanced back at Najirah. "Come here, *mirah.*" He held out his arms.

With a low cry, she ran to him and flung her hands around his neck. "Ah, Bahir. Bahir," Najirah sobbed, the tears flowing unchecked. "I-I'm so sorry if I shamed you before them, but . . . but I'm never going to see you, or hold you, or be able to take care of you again!"

"Hush, *mirah,*" he soothed, stroking her long hair. "You don't know that. You can't be sure."

She leaned back and glared at him through her tears. "Don't lie to me, Bahir Husam al Nur. Not now. You owe me that much."

"I owe you that and so much more, Najirah," Bahir sighed. "I just never gave us a chance, did I?"

"It doesn't matter." She put her finger to his lips. "Life never gave us a chance, but I never stopped loving you. And I do this *because* I love you more than life itself. Remember that . . . always."

Najirah leaned up on tiptoe and touched her lips to

his. Bahir groaned, took her face in his hands, and kissed her back, long and fierce and deep. Time slowed, intensified with their poignant, bittersweet farewell but, finally, they parted.

Stepping back, Najirah forced a brave smile. "Farewell, my dearest love," she whispered. "Until we meet again."

With a flurry of long dress and cloak, Najirah wheeled and ran away. Bahir watched her go, a myriad of anguished, confusing emotions tangling and twisting beneath his breast. High overhead, the night bird called once more, his cry bewildered, desolate.

Twenty

They rode through what was left of the night, Bahir leading the way, followed by Raina, the four pack equs, and then Aban, who brought up the rear. Rand's carrying pack was tied to the back of Bahir's saddle. Raina couldn't even bear the Volan's nearness just now.

She couldn't bear much of anything. All her efforts, all her concentration, had to be focused on getting to the spy ship, loading the crystal, and then safely breaking through Incendra's electromagnetic field once more. It was enough to deal with. She dared not look back or consider what she'd left behind.

The wind began to blow, bringing with it the redolent tang of rain. Clouds churned overhead, stooping low to capture the peaks in heavy swirls of murky whiteness. The temperature dropped. Raina shivered, pulled up the collar of her cloak, and hunkered down in its warmth.

Up ahead Bahir rode on, seemingly impervious to the sudden change in the weather, taking them up steep trails, around hairpin turns, drawing farther and farther from Vorax's army and the rest of his band. Did he care what he left behind? Raina wondered. Did he wonder if he'd ever see Najirah again?

She doubted it. The Tuaret leader had always been focused on the next challenge to be overcome. No time to spare for tenderness or love, for regrets, or to desire the life of a normal man. Bahir was a man on the run, from himself, from love, from ever letting himself be hurt again.

Teague was like that in many ways, but where Bahir had once been happy and had chosen to put such opportunities aside forever, Teague had determined that he simply wasn't deserving of such things. Though he'd come a long way in the past weeks, he still searched, still wasn't certain. She should be happy he'd found some purpose and peace in staying to fight for his people. At least in that way he'd opened his heart and allowed himself to care again.

But he didn't care enough for her. Not enough to ask her to stay, even if both knew that one of them would still have to return to Bellator. But at least if he'd told her he loved her, and that he wished they could be together . . .

Raina tossed the futile wish aside. It didn't matter. He didn't want her, and that was that. There was nothing left but to go on, to look ahead. She must go on with her life. Go on . . . as she always had before.

In the end, as she'd always known it had to be, all that truly mattered was survival.

Bahir drove them through the night and into dawn. As the day broke, they reached the cloud-shrouded peaks. Rain fell, pummeling them with frigid droplets, soaking them to the skin. And still Bahir pushed them on.

The trail became slick, the rocky terrain treacherous. Bahir was forced to slow their pace, but still he pushed them on. Najirah . . . he wanted to get back to her. He didn't want to die out there in the desert. He didn't want to die without seeing her one last time. But he feared . . . he feared . . .

"How long?" Rand asked from his carrying pack, hanging behind Bahir. "How many days' journey to the spaceship?"

The Tuaret shrugged. "Five days. Maybe a bit less, if we push ourselves and the equs. Eager to be gone from Incendra, are you?"

"It was inevitable," the Volan replied. "But I worry about Teague and Najirah and the others. Three hundred soldiers . . . If they should become trapped . . ."

"Najirah is well trained in evasive tactics. And she knows that area well. She grew up there, you know."

"Yet if something should happen to them, all your fine plans would be destroyed. All your fine machinations would ultimately be of little consequence."

"And your point, Volan?" Bahir snarled. "Before I terminate communications?"

"What would you have then, Bahir? To show for all your efforts?"

"I'd have nothing, curse you. Just as I soon will at any rate." He smiled grimly. "But at least I'll have experienced life with a body. I'll have felt the warm sun, seen the majesty of a sunset, and known the comfort of a warm and willing woman in my arms. What will *you* have, Volan, for all your efforts?"

"We're both living lives that in many ways are woefully incomplete," Rand admitted. "I had a body not so long ago, you know," he said, his voice going low, pensive.

"Did you, now? Then you were a fool to give it up. To be relegated for the rest of your days to a biosphere . . ." Bahir shuddered in revulsion. "I'd rather be dead."

"It can indeed be a form of living death, especially after knowing the agony and ecstasy of being whole. But it wasn't my body. I took it from another. And that man deserved to have it back."

"So you gave it back to him?"

"Yes."

"How?" In spite of himself, Bahir's curiosity was stirred. "How did you do it?"

"My biosphere can serve as a transport medium either into a body or out of it. As long as my Volan entity is willing . . ."

Bahir pondered that for a long moment. In spite of Rand's earlier harsh words to him, admiration filled him. "It was a noble thing you did, giving the man back his body."

"It was the right thing to do. It made the decision no less hard, though. I'm not that noble."

"Do you regret it sometimes? Giving up the body?"

It was Rand's turn to pause. "In some ways, yes," he finally replied. "But I want always to live my life with honor and courage, no matter how difficult that might be. Even if that decision relegates me to this biosphere for the rest of my days. Even if it's the last choice I ever have the chance to make."

"Well, you've got more courage than I, Volan." A sense of defeat, of burgeoning despair, rose in Bahir. At the end of his life, he'd finally realized how dismally he'd failed in so many ways. He wasn't even half the man this entity in a globe was.

"Do I, Bahir?" came Rand's soft reply. "Do I?"

They made camp the next morn in a forested area in the foothills of the Barakah Mountains. Bahir could

barely stay astride his equs. His exhaustion weighed him
down like some heavy burden, a burden he now wondered if he'd ever again be able to shed. He slept
through the entire day and only Aban's most determined
efforts finally woke him at sunset.

"Bahir, what's wrong?" his friend demanded, worry
darkening his eyes. "Are you ill again? Is it the sickness?"

The Tuaret leader groaned and shoved to one elbow,
only to fall back again. "It-it's nothing. I'll be fine."
He extended a hand. "Just help me up. My head will
soon clear." .

Aban pulled Bahir to a sitting position, then rose and
went off to retrieve a water bag. Returning, he squatted
once more beside Bahir and offered him a cup of water.
"Here, drink this. We must leave soon if we're to make
good time this night."

Bahir took the cup and drank deeply. "Yes. The
sooner we make it to the spaceship, the better." He
handed the cup back to Aban. When his compatriot took
it, Bahir captured his wrist in an iron grip.

"If I grow too weak to travel, don't call a halt to the
journey. Do you understand, Aban?" Bahir locked gazes
with his friend. "Even if you have to sling me across
the beast and tie me to it. You can't save me this next
time, no matter what you do."

"Bahir . . . I . . ." Aban's eyes filled with tears.
"Najirah . . . ?"

"She knows. She has her mission, and so do I. Help
me in this, my friend. I want to die knowing at least
that I had some effect on something. And this quest to
save the Imperium . . . well, in the end it might well
be all I'll ever accomplish."

"No!" Aban whispered fiercely. "You were our

leader. You kept us alive and free. In all those years of our war against Vorax, against overwhelming odds, he never bested us. And now . . . now you've managed to convince the king's son to join with us. Now, at long last, Vorax is certain to fall."

Bahir released him and cocked his head to stare up at the big Tuaret. "You knew? About Tremayne?"

Aban smiled. "I, too, recognized him almost immediately as the king's son. I'd have told you, but I wasn't sure how to. And then, when Najirah recognized him, I knew it was no longer my responsibility. She never kept anything from you, except the secret of her love."

"By the firestorms!" Bahir looked away. "Did everyone know but me?"

"You would've known, if you'd cared to," Aban said sadly. "But you didn't. And now . . ."

"And now it's too late," Bahir snarled, riveting a furious countenance on his friend. "Is that what you meant to say? Eh, Aban?"

The burly Tuaret leaned back. "So it seems, if you're determined to die out here on the desert."

"I cannot choose the time and place for this cursed illness to take me! If I could—" Bahir's voice broke. "Ah, what does it matter?" He motioned Aban away. "Go, put away the water bag and finish packing the equs. I'll be up and about in a few minutes."

The dismissal was evident in both Bahir's words and the way he drew into himself, leaving Aban once more alone. The big man rose, hesitated a moment longer, then turned and walked back to his equs. Bahir sat there until his thoughts grew too painful to bear. Then he awkwardly shoved to his feet and made his faltering way over to join him.

* * *

Bahir markedly weakened as the days went on. By
the time they reached the Blandira oasis, he was so frail
that he had to be assisted to and from his equs. That
night's camp was somber and subdued. The next day,
they tied him upright on his equs. Two days later, as
they neared where Teague had hidden the spy ship, the
Tuaret leader was barely alive, fading in and out of consciousness for increasingly longer intervals.

"R-Rand," Bahir whispered, as they set out that last
morning of their journey. He'd roused out of his stupor
just as they'd tied him onto his equs in preparation to
leave. Aban now led the party, with Raina bringing up
the rear with the pack equs.

"Yes, Bahir?" the Volan replied from his spot tied to
the Tuaret leader's saddle.

"I-I haven't much time left," he gasped. "I want you
to do one thing for me, if you will."

"If it's within my power, I'll be happy to help."

"C-Cyra." Bahir dragged in an unsteady breath, fighting the encroaching mists that threatened to pull him
back into oblivion. He *must* say this, before it was too
late. "My first wife. The one who left me."

"Yes?" Rand prodded gently, when Bahir failed to go
on. "What about her?"

The reminder jerked Bahir from his rising confusion.
"Cyra . . ." He clenched his eyes shut and threw back
his head, fighting, fighting . . . "She never knew I had
the brain illness, though I discovered it shortly before
she left me."

"Then why didn't you tell her? Perhaps she would
have stayed if she'd known."

The Tuaret gave a disparaging snort. "And have her

stay . . . out of pity . . . rather than love?" He shook his head. "Would any man's pride let him stoop that low?"

"I suppose not." Rand paused. "Is that what you meant to tell me, then? And if so, how does that require anything from me?"

"That requires nothing. I just wanted you . . . to understand," Bahir rasped. "What I ask is that you carry a message."

"A message?"

"Yes. If you ever see my wife again, tell her . . . tell her I love her, have always loved her. And tell her . . . I finally understand . . . who betrayed whom. It wasn't her fault. I expected her to do all the changing, to adapt totally to me and our customs. I was . . . arrogant, thoughtless. Tell her . . . though the knowledge comes too late for either of us . . . at least I finally understand."

"You are brave to say these things." Rand sighed. "It must be hard . . . especially now. But the message would come better from Raina. I'm rather limited. In my biosphere and all."

"No . . ." the Tuaret leader groaned. "Raina hates me. She's hated me from the start. And especially now that I've taken Teague from her. She wouldn't carry my message. You . . . you must do it. Please!"

"You must talk to Raina. You must share your needs and concerns with her. She's hurting as much as you are, Bahir. It's past time for a healing between the two of you."

The Tuaret shook his head. "No. I can't . . . I won't beg. Even now, I still have my pride." He grimaced. "What little is left of me *to* be proud of."

"You've bared your soul, surrendered your pride in tendering that message to your first wife. The same

courage that drove you to that admission can now help
you extend the hand of friendship to Raina."

"She should stay behind, Rand. Teague needs her."

"Yes, she should," the Volan admitted. "But there's
no one else who can pilot the spacecraft."

Bahir sighed. He was so weary, so tired of fighting.
If only he could hold out until he reached the spaceship,
know that the mission was complete . . . If only . . .
"I'll think on your words, but I make no promises . . .
about Raina, I mean."

"Just don't wait too long, my friend."

"No, I won't. I dare not . . ." With that, the stupor-
ous mists of his illness claimed him once more. Bahir
gave himself up to the darkness. It was too hard to fight
it for long anymore . . .

If not for the strange array of rocks Teague had
placed over the site of the buried spaceship, Raina
would never have found it in the ever-changing pano-
rama of the desert. As it was, the shifting sands had
buried it under an additional meter of fine grit. With
Aban's help, Raina spent the better part of an hour digging the front of the ship out in order to reach the bur-
rowing mechanism. She activated the delayed timer, then
ordered Aban to stand well clear of the ship.

As they watched, the Volan spy ship gave a lurch,
then, with a low hum, began slowly to lift itself out of
the sand. Eyes wide, Aban stood stock still until the
spacecraft once more sat fully atop the desert floor. With
the remaining sand streaming down its sleek sides, the
ship seemed foreign and strangely out of place.

He turned to Raina, wonder in his eyes. "It was all
true. Everything you and Tremayne said."

"Yes." She smiled and gestured to the ship. "Would you like to come inside and look around while I turn on the systems and prepare the craft for takeoff?"

His glance strayed to Bahir, his head bowed in stupor, sitting silently atop his equs. "First, I should get him out of the sun. It's horrendously hot today."

"I suppose you should," Raina muttered, casting the Tuaret leader a seething look. Try as she might, she found it difficult to feel much sympathy for Bahir's increasingly pitiful plight. He'd been such a consistently selfish, self-centered man, manipulating her and Teague, all but ignoring Najirah, caring little for anything but his own ambitions. No wonder Cyra had left him.

At the memory of Bahir's first wife, guilt plucked at Raina. She'd promised Cyra to give her message to her husband if she should happen to run across him. Yet she'd purposely withheld the message, at first as a potential bargaining piece, and later, out of spite for the man. Even now, though Bahir didn't deserve the potential comfort the message might give him, Raina knew her honor would allow no less. She'd given her word to deliver Cyra's message. She'd do so at long last.

"Come." She motioned toward Bahir. "Let's get him inside and out of the sun."

They carried Bahir into the cockpit of the spaceship and laid him on the floor. Raina activated the onboard computer, life support systems, and engines. Then she headed back outside to tether the equs and retrieve Rand's carrying pack.

By the time she returned, the cool air had begun to flow through the ship. Aban had laid his rolled up cloak under the head of his unconscious leader. Bahir looked quite comfortable lying there, as if he'd decided suddenly to lie down for a nap.

Raina spared Bahir a brief glance, then met Aban's tortured gaze. "There's nothing more we can do for him just now, and I could use some help unloading the sacks of crystal into the hold."

Aban looked back at Bahir one last time. "No, I suppose you're right. Until he regains consciousness, he'll be comfortable in here." He climbed to his feet and forced a wan smile. "Lead on, femina. Let's finish this and get you off toward your own home."

Your own home. The big Tuaret's words struck a bittersweet chord within her. Once, she'd have agreed. Her home was no longer on Incendra. But in the past weeks, she'd discovered so much here—renewed friendships, shocking revelations, and the brief joy of loving a man and the physical expression of that love.

She'd watched the heartstopping glory of the desert sunsets. Savored the clean, dry air, the sweet scents of the plants and trees and vegetation that were unique to Incendra, and viewed once again the pristine beauty of her unspoiled land. A land that had been indelibly impressed into her blood, her heart, and her soul, no matter how long and hard she'd tried to deny it.

But she couldn't stay now, whether she wished it or not. Her first loyalty lay with the Imperium. Besides, Teague didn't want her. He simply didn't want her.

"Yes, let's get it over with, shall we?" Raina growled, so full of bitterness she thought her heart would shatter.

They worked for the next four hours, unloading sack after sack of the stone and carrying it down into the hold. Each sack was placed into a lidded, shielded receptacle on one of the shelved compartments. They worked steadily, taking only one short break for some water, before heading back outside for more sacks.

The day wore on. In the late afternoon, Bahir woke once more. "A-Aban," he called weakly. "Raina."

Aban took the sack Raina was carrying and slung it over his other shoulder. "Go to him," he said. "I'll put these last two sacks away, then join you."

Reluctantly, Raina nodded. She didn't particularly like the idea of spending any additional time alone with the dying Bahir, but knew she'd have to face him sooner or later. And now was as good a time as any to get the unfortunate task of sharing Cyra's message with him over with. He didn't look like he'd much time left.

She walked over to him and sat. "What is it, Bahir?"

"I-I haven't been kind to you," he gasped. Despite the relative coolness of the ship's interior, sweat beaded his brow and his skin had taken on a sickly gray, waxen appearance. "I beg pardon."

Raina stared down at him, bemused and unexpectedly speechless. "Let me get this straight, Bahir. Are you apologizing for the way you treated me all this time?"

He managed a feeble nod. "Yes, *mirah,* I am. I was wrong. My motives were good, my methods weren't. I . . . I made a lot of mistakes. With so many people . . ."

"Yes, you did, Bahir." Though he was dying, Raina refused to temper her words. Yet despite his high-handed techniques, one truth still stood out from all the rest: he'd engendered love and loyalty from those who knew him. Aban, Najirah, Cyra . . .

She wet her lips. "I've a message for you. One I should've delivered long ago, but you angered me so . . ." She paused. "Well, the reasons don't matter now, do they? Since we're finally being so forthright with each other, I mean?"

He managed a tremulous smile. "No, I don't suppose they do."

Something flared in the depths of his amber-colored eyes. Something warm and open, revealing at last the heart of the man. Regret plucked at Raina's heart. Perhaps if she'd given Bahir a chance . . .

She shook that futile consideration aside. There'd been no time—for either of them. "I met your first wife, Cyra, just before I left for Incendra. She was one of the Bellatorian scientists working on the project to create a deterrent device against the Volans."

A joyous light flared in his eyes. "Cyra? You saw Cyra? How was she? Did she—" He let the questions die. "She was well and happy, I hope?" Bahir continued in a tightly controlled voice.

"She was well enough."

"Had she taken another mate? I'd have understood, mind you. After so long a separation, she'd have been within her rights to have applied for an Imperial divorce."

Raina locked gazes with him, saw the anguish and guarded hope in his eyes—a hope that in spite of it all, Cyra hadn't divorced him. "No, Bahir," she softly replied, glad, for his sake, at least, that the truth would please him. "Cyra hadn't taken another mate. She claimed to have only one—you."

"She still called me husband?" He levered himself to one elbow.

"Yes. She said to tell you, if ever I should find you, that in spite of it all, she loved you still—and always would."

With a weary sigh, Bahir fell back. "By the firestorms, it's more than I ever dared hope. I'll at least die happy now, knowing that." He smiled up at her. "I thank you for delivering her message."

He'd die happy, knowing Cyra still loved him? But what of Najirah and her love? Had she never been, then, of any consequence to him?

"And what of Najirah?" Raina demanded, renewed anger filling her. Gods, would this man never see past his loss to the true damage his frustrated need for Cyra had wrought? To the hurt he'd caused? "Will you die happy knowing *she* loved you as well?"

He frowned. "That is none of your affair."

"And I say it is. Najirah's my friend. She'd never do or say anything against you, but someone has to speak for her." Raina leaned back and pounded her thigh in frustration. "Gods, but you're the most complex, exasperating of men! One moment I find myself almost liking you, and the other, well, I hate you for your selfishness!"

For a long moment, Bahir said nothing. "It's easier to be selfish than to face the truths of your heart, to risk hurt again," he finally whispered. "And perhaps that is my greatest failing."

Pain twisted his handsome features, but whether it was from an emotional pain or a physical one, Raina couldn't tell. "You can't make yourself love someone, Bahir," she forced herself to say, wishing, for Najirah's sake, that it wasn't true, but knowing Bahir didn't deserve the full blame for what had happened. "Yet you can and should tender her the respect of recognizing it and sharing that knowledge with her."

"I didn't want to . . . to hurt Najirah."

"So instead, you discounted her love and pretended it never existed. But that was a greater hurt to her, in the end, than never talking about it. She deserved better than that, Bahir, even if you never loved her."

"But I *do* love her."

The words were spoken so softly that Raina thought for an instant that she'd misunderstood. She leaned forward. "What did you say, Bahir?"

He wouldn't look at her, riveting his gaze instead on the cockpit ceiling. "I d-do love her." He closed his eyes. "Ah, curse it all, I do love her!" Bahir turned and locked gazes with her. "Tell her that, *mirah*. Tell her I came too late to the realization, but I do love her. She was always there for me—always. I was a fool, but no more."

"Too late indeed," Raina muttered. "I'll never see Najirah again, either. You forget. I'm returning to Bellator. Best you give the message to Aban."

A sad smile lifted the Tuaret leader's lips. "And if I make it so you don't have to return, will you still persist in making the same mistake as I? Will you allow your pride and stubbornness to keep you from the love that is there for you, if only you would summon the courage to fight for it? Don't do it, Raina. Don't wait until it's too late. Don't be a fool . . ."

Aban, finished with stowing the sacks in the hold, walked back into the cockpit just then. Bahir turned to him. "Aban," he said weakly, motioning him over. "Bring Rand's carrying pack to me."

The big Tuaret cocked a quizzical brow but did as requested. The carrying pack was set beside Bahir's head. "Open it," he ordered Aban, "and take out the shielding receptacle."

"Bahir, what do you intend?" Raina asked, unease winding through her.

"To talk with Rand. I've yet one thing more that

needs completing." He turned back to Aban as he pulled the square metal case from the pack. "Rand?"

"Yes, Bahir."

"I asked you to carry my message back to Cyra. I still wish you to do so. But now, I would also like you to take something more back with you."

"As you wish, my friend."

Bahir struggled to his elbows, panting heavily. Raina moved to help, scooting behind him to prop him on her bent thighs. He shot her a grateful glance, then turned back to stare at Rand's shielding receptacle. "Th-this is a fine body. It has . . . many cycles of life still left in it. It would serve you well, I'd wager. But first it needs a fully functioning and healthy mind."

The Tuaret leader coughed and choked. His eyes closed in an apparent battle against the approaching stupor. Finally, after a time heavy with hushed anticipation, he spoke again. "I want you . . . to take . . . my body for your own. Fill it with your essence, your goodness. Use it to help others."

"Bahir," Rand softly said, "I don't know—"

"Can you enter my body, Volan?" Bahir fiercely cut him off. "Can you take over where my mind has fled?"

"Yes."

"Then why the hesitation? Are you suddenly too proud to accept the body of a man who has managed to make such a horrible muddle of his life?"

"No." Rand's voice was deep, intense, as if driven now by some savage emotion. "I'm not too proud, Bahir. I would deem it an honor. But I've come to see you as a friend. And it seems self-serving for me to—"

"The honor is m-mine, Volan! *Mine,* do you hear me?" The Tuaret arched back in Raina's lap, his whole body going rigid, taut as a bowstring. "Do it now, before the disease kills not only what is left of my mind, but damages my brain beyond use as well. I . . . give you . . . leave . . . to do it!"

Raina glanced at the shielding receptacle. "How, Rand? *How* should we do it?"

The Volan was silent for a long moment. "Remove my biosphere from the box," he finally said, reluctance deepening the timbre of his voice. "Disconnect the life support system. Then sit Bahir up, shake the biosphere to activate the temeritas, and press the biosphere to the base of the back of his neck. I'll do the rest."

"Aban," Raina said, shoving Bahir up and toward the other man. "Take Bahir. Hold him."

The burly Tuaret shook his head, the tears running down his cheeks. "I-I can't. It isn't right. I . . . just . . . can't."

"It *is* right," Bahir whispered, his breathing coming in ragged, shallow pants now. "Do this for me . . . my friend . . . Please, before it's t-too late."

Anguished eyes met those of his leader's. Then Aban nodded. "If that is what you wish." He reached out, grasped Bahir by the shoulders, and pulled him to him.

Raina turned to the shielding receptacle. With fingers gone suddenly weak and unsteady, she flipped open the latches, lifted the lid, and pulled out Rand's biosphere. A few seconds more, and she had the life support and communications wires and tubes disconnected. Holding the large, membranous globe before her, Raina brought it up to the back of Bahir's neck.

She shook the biosphere gently. A green, luminescent glow filled the thin, heretofore invisible, outer layer. "It's ready, Bahir," she said.

"D-do it," he wheezed. "I c-can't hold back the . . .

the final stupor much longer. You need an undamaged brain as well as a healthy body. Do it. N-now!"

Raina locked gazes with Aban. The Tuaret managed a tremulous smile, nodded, then glanced down at Bahir. "Farewell, my friend. May we meet again in the infinite cosmos, on another plane."

"That we will, Aban," Bahir whispered, grasping his compatriot's arms to hold himself steady. "That we will."

Raina pressed the biosphere against the base of the Tuaret leader's neck. "Rand. It's time."

The green luminescence flared in intensity. The membranous globe began to soften, mold to the back of Bahir's neck. The luminescent temeritas swirled, churned wildly.

Bahir stiffened. "N-Najirah. Ah, Najirah . . ." he cried. Fierce spasms wracked him.

In her fear and confusion, Raina tried to pull the biosphere free. She couldn't. The globe seemed to have adhered to Bahir's spine.

He opened his mouth. His face contorted in agony. Deep in his throat, death rattles rose. As she watched, the luminescent glow slowly dissipated. Rand, Raina thought. Even now, he was entering Bahir.

Terror filled her. What if it was too late? What if Bahir's mind died before Rand could fully assimilate into him? If he entered a damaged brain, would both of them be lost?

Gradually, the spasms that had wracked Bahir's body lessened. He went slack, falling limply forward into Aban's arms. The biosphere deflated, then fell away.

Over the Tuaret leader's bowed head, Raina's and Aban's gazes met. A question burned in Aban's eyes, but Raina had no answer. "Here, let's lay him down."

She slid out from beneath Bahir's body. "Only time will tell if Rand made it safely into Bahir before . . . before his mind went."

Once more, Bahir was laid on the floor of the cockpit, and Aban's rolled cloak was placed beneath his head. Raina and Aban sat beside him, watching, waiting. The minutes ticked by, the heavy silence broken only by the resonant thrum of the engines. Anticipation and a strange dread rose, tightening Raina's throat and turning her mouth dry.

Bahir. Rand. Had she lost them both, then?

With a low groan, the man lying before them stirred. His head turned. Dark lashes lifted and amber-colored eyes stared back at Raina.

Confusion clouded his gaze. He blinked once, twice, as if struggling to clear his vision. Then, recognition seemed to bloom. He smiled.

"It is done, femina. Bahir's body is now mine."

Raina eyed him warily. "Indeed?"

He shoved to a sitting position and looked down at his body. Tentatively at first, he touched himself. First a hand on an arm, then on a leg, then he lifted both hands to his face. As he ran his fingers over the strong blade of a nose and dark, high-bred features, wonderment and a wild joy filled his eyes. "At last," Rand murmured. "At last."

Aban made a tortured, choking noise.

Rand swung to the sobbing Tuaret. "I am sorry for your loss." He reached out a hand to the man, hesitated, then pulled back, not knowing what comfort his touch would give. "I am sorry to have been the beneficiary of your friend's death. But if it's any consolation, Bahir's mind died just seconds before I entered it. I waited outside his brain until he did. I refused to profit until he, as the man we knew, truly *was* dead."

"I appreciate your kindness and respect for him in that." Aban wiped his tear-streaked cheeks with the back of his sleeve, then climbed to his feet. "I ask only that you treat his body with the same respect it deserves. For all his failings, he was still a good, brave man and our beloved leader."

Rand rose to meet Aban eye-to-eye. "I'll always treat this body with the utmost respect, my friend. I swear it."

He extended his arm in the Imperial greeting. After a moment's hesitation, Aban took it. The two men stood there, clasped arm to arm, until Raina finally rose and walked over.

"It's time we headed back to Bellator," she said, meeting the Volan's steady gaze.

"Are you still of a mind to go?"

Surprise widened her eyes. "What do you mean? Of course I am!"

He smiled in gentle understanding. "Bahir paid a terrible price for betraying the calling of his heart. Will you now do the same?"

Anger flooded Raina, spilling out into her voice and words. "You don't know of what you speak, Volan. Teague doesn't want me, never has. Why should I risk all to go after him?"

"There are few assurances in life, femina. And the choices at times are daunting, if not terrifying." He lifted his hands in a wryly self-conscious gesture. "I'll have many of my own to make now. But I have time. You don't."

"Do you think you can pilot the spy ship back to Bellator on your own?" She managed a taut smile.

"I listened to all the same instructions you did when you and Teague were being trained. Besides, this is a Volan ship. How different can it be from the ones I've piloted before?"

"Your words have merit, Volan," Raina grudgingly admitted.

"Rand."

"What?" She frowned up at him, puzzled.

"My name is Rand. Won't you please call me by it? I'm as human as you now, Raina."

She gave a wry laugh. "Yes, I suppose you are. It'll just take some time to adjust to the changes."

"But you haven't much time left, do you?"

Her glance dropped to the dusty toe of her boot. "No." She looked up. "I need a few minutes to think."

"You have it, femina."

"I'll be outside."

Rand nodded.

Raina wheeled and quickly headed toward the exit. Though she sensed Rand somehow understood her dilemma, she couldn't bear to stand another moment with him or Aban. Too much had changed, and far too quickly.

Now, thanks to the gift of Bahir's body, the choice—whether to leave or stay—was once more hers. She stepped outside and back onto the desert. The sun had begun its fading trajectory toward the distant horizon. Brilliant beams of red-orange light emanated from the dying orb, bathing the land of sand dunes and rocks with a soft, gentle glow.

Incendra, Raina thought. Her beautiful, fiery land. Her land . . . and Teague's.

But did she possess the courage to stay? To fight for her love? Once Rand lifted off in the spy ship, there

was no way to leave Incendra. Her fate would be irrevocably sealed.

And there was still no guarantee that Teague would
want her. No assurance that sending her away, though
at the time an unavoidable necessity, hadn't been but a
convenient excuse for turning her out of his life. Perhaps
it wasn't so much that he didn't feel worthy of her love.
Perhaps it was just the plain fact he didn't want it.

Yet what other reason was there for remaining on Incendra? True, the land called to her, but she had been
quite content with her life with the Sodalitas on Moraca.
She could just as easily find fulfillment there as on
Incendra.

No, she'd only stay for Teague. Though she still despised the man, her need for vengeance against Vorax
had faded. And her father, already gone from this existence, had punished himself far more savagely than
she'd have ever done.

Her initial motivations for remaining on Incendra after the mission was complete were no more. But now,
where once the cruelties of men had driven her away,
the love for one called her back. That much she'd
learned, and would always cherish, from having met and
known Bahir and his wife, Najirah.

What had Najirah once said? Raina's thoughts flew
back to that day they'd dug asphodel tubers together. *I
give my love freely,* Bahir's wife had gently told her,
*without expectation of recompense . . . because I can-
not do otherwise . . . to do any less is to not fully live,
to not be the person you were meant to be . . .*

The sun slid behind the horizon in an explosion of
riotous color. From all sides, the sky began to darken,
deepening to blue-violet. It was time for Rand to be
off, Raina thought. Time for her and Aban to head back

across the desert. Back to Tuaret lands, back to join a battle against a usurper whose downfall had finally begun. Back to stand at the side of the man she loved.

She couldn't do otherwise. To do any less was not to be the person she'd always been meant to be.

Twenty-one

In the deepening twilight, the last rays of the sun barely smudging the sky, Raina stood with Aban and the equs and watched the Volan spy ship lift off. The earth rumbled, the rear thrusters fired in a burst of flame, and the ship soared into the heavens. Raina watched until the spacecraft was swallowed in the blackening maw of night, then turned to Aban.

"Let's be off. The sooner we reunite with Najirah and Teague and the others, the better I'll feel."

The big Tuaret nodded. "Best we head to our hidden encampment, then. Bahir told them to meet us there." At the mention of his former leader's name, his face fell. "By the firestorms," Aban groaned. "He's gone, femina. It's hard enough losing him, but to see his body rise again, ruled by another mind . . ."

She grasped his thick-muscled arm. "I know, Aban. But at least you're the only one to see it happen, the only one who knows Bahir's real fate. Perhaps it would be better if no one else learned the truth. Even Najirah. It's best that she think Bahir dead—in every way."

He nodded. "It would be the kindest solution. To know some man is out there, in the body of her husband . . ." He shook his head and sighed. "I vow not to tell her, femina."

"And neither will I. It's enough that she know he

loved her, and that he spoke her name with his dying breath." She released his arm and stepped back. "Now, come. It's time we left this place."

They rode long into the night, the events of the past day stirring such restless thoughts and painful memories that they couldn't have slept if they'd tried. Only when dawn's first light washed the sky did Raina call a halt—at the oasis where she'd first met Bahir. That place, too, was filled with many memories, but after being awake almost twenty-four hours, they were both exhausted and fell asleep as soon as their heads hit the blankets.

Pushing themselves hard, they reached the Tuaret encampment in the middle of the third day after they had left the oasis. Najirah's band, however, had yet to arrive.

"I don't like it, Aban," Raina grumbled, over a cup of mentha tea that evening. "It's been over eight days now since we parted at the Barakah Mountains. They should've been back by now. There's something wrong. I can feel it."

The Tuaret contemplated the contents of his cup. "I, too, feel great unease." He looked up at her over the campfire, his expression grim and worried. Flames licked at the blackness between them, sending blazing motes of red swirling into the night. "I suppose we could send out a search party . . ."

"And if they've been captured by Vorax's army?" At the man's ineffectual suggestion, frustration filled Raina. "What then?"

"We cannot hope to prevail against an army the size of Vorax's."

"No, *we* can't, but if we could get the other desert tribes to join with us, well, then we'd have an army to be reckoned with."

Puzzlement furrowed Aban's brow. "But even Bahir

couldn't get the other tribes to join with him. And now he's gone. How do you hope to succeed where he failed?"

Aban wasn't the stuff of leaders, Raina realized. It answered a lot of questions as to why Bahir, as close friends as he was with Aban, had instead chosen his wife to be his second-in-command. But she could still use him and his standing in the tribe to her advantage, Raina knew. If she could just get him to support her plan.

"I mean to succeed," Raina patiently explained, "because I but carry on where Bahir's plan left off. Teague is more than just another man who decided to join with Bahir against Vorax. Teague is the man Bahir was waiting for all these cycles—the heir to the royal throne of Farsala."

"Yes, that's true enough," Aban nodded his agreement. "I recognized him from the start as the old king's son." His bushy black brows dipped in great concentration. He scratched the large black mole peeking through the beard on the left side of his jaw. "But how can we use that knowledge to our advantage?"

"Can you send out messengers to the rest of the tribes, at least, the ones who we can trust to value the message and its implications? Ask them to join us at some hidden spot on the way to Ksathra for a secret meeting? The news of Teague's true heritage will spread fast once we send out the messengers. Time will be crucial then, if we're to strike against Vorax with some element of surprise."

Aban considered her suggestions for several minutes, then nodded. "Yes, it seems the best of all plans. The messengers will go out on the morrow." He grimaced. "We'll omit sending a messenger to the Katebs, though.

They, of all the tribes, will never support anything the Tuarets lead. The tribal rivalry has been too long and too fierce for us ever to hope for their support."

"Then so be it." Raina met Aban's gaze squarely. "And on the morrow, we must head out to find Najirah's band, with you as our leader. Agreed?"

Aban smiled. "Agreed. The men will best follow me until we reach Najirah. But you'll advise me along the way. Agreed?"

Raina smiled. "I suppose that could be arranged. I had some experience as a warrior leader in my former life on Moraca."

He grinned. "I thought as much. You're a worthy mate for the king's son. You'll rule well at his side."

She lowered her gaze once more to the fire. Aban already had her crowned queen of Farsala. Though her doubts were many that that day would ever come, it served her purposes now to let him think it would. He'd support her and her plans as the future queen. So would the others, if the need arose.

If the need arose. Despite the warmth of the campfire, Raina shivered. She feared that need had already arisen. Teague and Najirah hadn't returned. And that didn't bode well. Not well at all.

They found Najirah and her men two days later, their mutilated, lifeless bodies sprawled about in the end of a long ravine. The exit of the steep, rain-washed gully had been purposely filled with a pile of boulders and debris, blocking escape. Strewn among the carnage of Tuarets and Vorax's soldiers were the bodies of many Kateb warriors. It had obviously been a trap set by the Katebs, whom the Tuarets had pursued into the blocked ravine, only to be caught there when Vorax's army had drawn up behind them.

Raina discovered Najirah's body high on the pile of rubble blocking their escape. She'd evidently been climbing up to safety when a Kateb dagger had snuffed out her life. Teague, however, was nowhere to be found among the dead. Had he, Raina wondered, managed to make it up and over the barricade?

She helped Aban take Najirah down, her heart full of a bittersweet pain. Najirah would never hear the message Raina had hoped to give her, that Bahir had finally admitted to his love for her, that he'd called out to her with his final breath. But, small consolation that it was, her girlhood friend was at last eternally joined with the man she loved.

Perhaps, in that afterlife where they would always be together, she was even now hearing the words from Bahir's own lips. And, perhaps, just perhaps, that was the way it was meant to be.

With the other Tuarets, Raina buried Najirah and her unfortunate warriors in a mass grave. There was no time for anything more. Teague's life might well be at stake, and Bahir's hopes and dreams lay with him. The Tuaret leader's men understood. In his memory, they would do their best to see that dream of his came to fruition.

The trail of Vorax's army and the large group of accompanying Katebs led straight back across the desert to the Barakah Mountains. If Teague was their prisoner, he would soon lie in the torture caverns of the royal city of Ksathra.

That thought only stirred Raina to a faster pace. Vorax had taken her, as his bride-to-be, down into the dank, dark depths of that cavernous hole in the moun-

tains only once. The horrors she'd seen there had filled
her with nightmares for months to come.

But what exactly would Vorax do with Teague this
time? Raina wondered. Did the evil man still fear the
prophecy, or had the cycles of total power dimmed the
terrible promise of those ancient words?

Somehow, she doubted Vorax would dare set Teague
free again. He was a man now, powerful of mind and
body—the image of his dead father. And the people,
though most not of the courage to confront Vorax's
might, as Bahir had, were said to be almost universally
unhappy with his reign.

No, there was no time to be wasted. Sooner or later,
Vorax would see Teague dead. She only hoped the man
would hesitate long enough for her to get Ksathra.

As they rode across the desert, large groups of nomad
warriors from the twelve tribes began to join them. Bahir had been right: all they'd needed was a rallying
point. The tale of Teague's return had been the answer
all along.

"We must draw up soon," Raina said, on the second
day of their journey across the Ar Rimal. In the distance, the Barakah Mountains shimmered deep purple
through the desert heat. "Our army grows larger each
day. An overt attack on Ksathra, however, would only
assure Teague's immediate execution. And the city is too
well fortified to take it quickly, no matter how large our
army grows."

"What do you suggest, then, domina?" Aban, riding at
her side, asked, bestowing upon her the term of ultimate
respect as their new leader. Once Najirah had been found
dead, the Tuarets had again been without a chief. Aban
had then proposed that Raina lead them, both as a proven
warrior in her own right and as the heir's mate. There'd

been some minor grumbling, the Tuarets recalling Raina's constant battling with Bahir, but Aban had finally calmed the malcontents. Raina had then stepped forward and sealed the decision in an impassioned speech demanding the desert right, as Teague's mate, to avenge him.

"There's only one plan that'll work," she said, forcing her thoughts back to the present. "Teague once told me of a secret passage into the palace through the back of the mountain. If we're fortunate, though it may now be sealed, with some time and effort, we might be able to reopen it. From there, it'll be a simple enough task to bring the entire army into Ksathra."

She smiled grimly, recalling Teague's anguish over his drawing of the tapestry passage being used to destroy his family and lose Farsala. Even that terrible pain would finally be set to rest—*if* her plan worked. "It's only fair that the means that gained Vorax his victory all those cycles ago," she added, "should now be the instrument of his downfall."

Aban nodded, smiling in turn. "A wise plan, indeed. We'll need some men inside, though, to guide us in and unlock any doors between the passage and the palace."

"That's where the rest of my plan comes in. Until Vorax hears of our army's approach, it'll still be a simple task to gain entry into Ksathra with the usual daily parade of visitors and tradesmen. I'll enter the city alone. Once there, I know a way that should win me a chance to regain Vorax's confidence. When that is accomplished, I should have free run of the palace and an opportunity to get to Teague."

"I don't like it." The big Tuaret shook his head. "It's too dangerous. Better you stay as far from that man as possible. He has an insatiable taste for comely women, whom I hear he treats cruelly. There must be some other way to—"

"We must all take risks if we're to save the king's heir and finally rid Farsala of Malam Vorax," Raina firmly interjected. She'd little taste for what she must do, but Teague's life was all that mattered. And she'd do anything for him—even surrender her life and body once again to Malam Vorax. "Trust me in this, Aban. I know Vorax better than you might ever guess. And I say again, it's the only way."

"As you wish, domina." Aban sighed and glanced back toward the mountains. "I see now why you and Bahir were always so much at odds. You're both headstrong and proud—and demand your own way in everything."

"Someone must make the decisions," she said, chuckling at his frustrated expression. He was right, though. Bahir and she *had* been very much alike. "I ask you, isn't that what a leader must do?"

"Yes, I suppose so, domina," he grumbled, "but that doesn't mean I always have to like it."

"No, you don't, but you do have to obey."

"And I will." Aban swung back to her, a fierce resolve gleaming in his dark eyes. "For Bahir, for Najirah, and for the king's heir, I *will* obey."

"For them all," she said, filled with a sudden rush of emotion that was both pride and pain. Raina lifted her gaze then, seeking out the spot where the army would hide until the call came to enter Ksathra and rescue the king's heir. And fervently prayed, even as she did, that Teague would still be alive when that day came.

The entrance to the tapestry passage was indeed closed, filled with such a mass of boulders and brush that if Teague hadn't told her of the two flame-shaped stone sentinels that marked the tunnel's opening, Raina would never have been able to find it. The passage could be cleared, but the effort would require a large number of men and around-the-clock work for at least the next two to three days.

Raina immediately set the men who'd come with her and Aban to work. She then dispatched a messenger back to where the rest of the army camped in a deep ravine at the edge of the Ar Rimal, with orders for a good hundred more men to return to help in the job.

"Once the clearing of the passage nears completion," she then said to Aban, gazing down at him from the back of her equs, "send for the rest of the army. Have half approach Ksathra from the front. Bring the other half around and into the passage. When Vorax sees the army at his front gates, I'll know it's time to rescue Teague. Once he's free, we'll come through the palace and unlock the secret door to the tapestry passage. If we take them by surprise, it should be an easy enough task to sweep through the city and open the gates to the rest of the army."

Aban's swarthy smile was feral and foreboding. "Vorax won't know what happened until it's too late."

"Indeed." Raina smiled down at him. "The success of this all rests on timing, though. Don't send the army to the city gates until the passage is clear. Do you understand me, Aban?"

He nodded solemnly. "It'll be as you ask, domina. I may not be the stuff of leaders, but I take orders well. I never failed Bahir. I won't fail you, either."

She reined in her mount. "I know you won't, my friend. Farewell, then, until we meet again—inside Ksathra." With that, Raina turned her equs and headed the beast down the steep and treacherous trail that had led up to the tapestry passage.

As she rode along, myriad thoughts and realizations assailed her. Though she'd led Aban to believe she was certain that her plan to infiltrate Vorax's palace would be successful, Raina knew there were many potential pitfalls along the way. Getting into the city and palace should be easy enough. Gaining an audience with Vorax would be a bit more difficult, but she still felt confident she could manage that as well.

What she planned to do and say to convince Vorax to take her back as a mistress, if not a mate, however, she wasn't all that certain of. She'd just have to fall back on instinct when the time came, Raina decided, and respond to Vorax's lead. Her ability to think fast on her feet had served her well in the past. She only hoped it would serve her well this time, too.

The thought of letting Vorax get near her, much less touch her again, filled Raina with loathing. Curiously, though, the sense of impotent rage wasn't there anymore. It was strange how one's experiences, both positive and negative, could color one's perceptions. The past weeks had changed so much for her.

Not that she didn't still hate Malam Vorax and wish him dead. Raina knew herself too well ever to imagine she'd forgiven the man or would ever accept what he'd done. It just wasn't imperative anymore that *she* be the one to kill him. Not if it risked the success of her mission. Not if Teague was the one to suffer for it in the end.

She wondered where he was now. In Vorax's torture caverns, most likely. She *had* to believe he was still alive. To risk herself, to give herself up to Vorax, and then discover Teague was already dead . . .

With a savage effort, Raina cast that consideration aside. Teague couldn't be dead. She'd know it, feel it, if he were. No, he was still alive, but he suffered . . . suffered greatly.

The memory of that horrible dream the night she and Teague had first mated plucked at her. The impact of seeing him, sprawled bloody and beaten, before Vorax's throne, still left her shaky and breathless. Even then she'd feared that the dream was a presentiment of what was to come.

And it *had* come true, at least in part. Teague was a prisoner of Malam Vorax, the man who stood to lose everything if Teague lived.

Despite the awful intensity of the dream, though, it didn't mean Teague must suffer that same fate, Raina fiercely resolved. She wouldn't let that happen. She chose to believe the prophecy instead. The prophecy that spoke of the possibility of life over death, of triumph instead of obliteration.

She had to trust that good would prevail. She just *had* to. To do otherwise would doom them all.

The pain. Gods, never had he known such pain! Teague shifted slightly in the metal shackles that bound him, spread-eagled, to the rough stone wall, attempting to ease the throbbing agony of the unnatural position of his arms and shoulders. It did little but scrape raw the already abraded flesh of his back.

He willed himself to block out the pain. It worked for a time, the old monastic mental discipline blessedly muting the worst of the battering he'd received during his capture and subsequent journey to Ksathra. Then the memories crept back in.

Memories of Najirah, casting herself before the dagger aimed at him as they climbed the wall of rocks blocking the ravine. Of her dying in his arms, smiling, Bahir's name trembling on her lips. Of being surrounded by Kateb warriors, ready to deliver the death blow, when the officer in charge of Vorax's army had stepped forward, his eyes wide in horrified recognition. And then the brutal march across the Ar Rimal with him bound and forced to walk behind the equs, without food or water, until he could walk no more.

The officer had been clever and calculating, taking great care not to reveal Teague's true identity. He correctly anticipated Vorax's desires. Teague had been brought into Ksathra under cover of darkness and immediately taken to the torture caverns. There he'd hung for hours, stripped naked, save for the meager cover of his red loincloth, awaiting—dreading—the moment Malam Vorax would deign to visit. Visit . . . and determine his fate.

He didn't cherish much hope of rescue. By now, Raina and Rand had reached the spy ship and taken off, headed through the blackness of space back toward Bellator. Bahir's days, if he still lived, were numbered. No, there would soon be no one on Incendra who cared if he lived or died.

The realization seized him in the claws of a remorseless, all-too-familiar terror. No one cared, no purpose would be served by his living—or his dying. He was alone. Alone and at the mercy, once again, of a man who had always been his worst nightmare.

With a groan, Teague strained against the unyielding bonds of his shackles. The muscles of his arms bulged, his chest heaved, and he twisted and fought to break free. He must get away. He *must*.

Now, before Vorax came down to him. Now, while he still possessed some shred of pride and dignity. He didn't know what he'd do if Vorax broke him again.

Overhead, a thick, wooden door opened, then closed. Footsteps sounded on the stone stairs. Voices, low and masculine, rose, reverberating against the cavernous chamber of rock.

Teague's heart thundered in his chest. He lunged forward in an attempt to jerk the shackles free of the wall. The metal sliced into his wrists. Blood, warm and sticky, welled to flow down his arms.

Frustration rose. Teague writhed, his body tiring, his breathing coming now in short, painful gasps. Writhed, twisted, and fought—to no avail.

The footsteps came closer, the voices louder. Vorax's voice. He'd never forget that voice to his dying day. Stronger, more forceful now, but still overlaid with a whining petulance. "I care not for your tastes when it comes to torture, Sinon," Vorax said. "They're as depraved as your physical appetites."

"And yours aren't, Father?" the other man replied smoothly. "But how can that be? You have always been the man I idolized in all things."

"Enough!" Vorax snarled. "I tire of the bite of your tongue these days. Your sire though I may be, remember, and remember well, who the ruler of Farsala is."

At that moment, they rounded the bottom curve of the stairs and stepped into Teague's view. Vorax halted. Their gazes locked. Teague's struggles stilled, his pride stung by the sly, pitying smile twisting Vorax's lips. Anger swelled within him, the force of its heat burning away the last remnants of his doubts and fears. His disbelieving glance swung down the other man's body.

Vorax was little more than a fat, white slug that had

slithered out from beneath its stone. The powerful ruler
of Farsala was short and corpulent, pasty of skin, with
thin, stringy gray hair that hung like a fringe from a
bald and shiny pate, his body adorned lavishly with layers of crimson and gold serica cloth. On his heavily
beringed hands gleamed a large aureum signet ring, the
ring of the titular ruler of Farsala.

By the firestorms, Teague thought, looking back into
the eyes of the man who'd stirred such terror in him
all these cycles. Surely the cycles had dimmed his
memories. This wasn't a man to be feared, but instead
one to be squashed like some odious little bug.

A fierce determination flared in Teague. He'd be
damned if he'd let Malam Vorax, *or* his slimy spawn—
he eyed the slight, slender build of the effeminately
dressed younger man—beat him again!

"So, what have we here?" Vorax asked, waddling up
to stand before Teague. "Is it possible? Has the young
Tarik Shatrevar returned after all these cycles?" He
walked to one side of Teague, eyed him closely, then
strode back before him to stand and examine him from
the other. "And where have you been keeping yourself,
princeling?"

Vorax gestured to Teague's chest, coated with a mixture of fresh sweat and grime from the past days of
marching across the desert. "You've acquired some
strange markings in your travels. What is their significance?"

Teague didn't answer, but only glared back at him.

"Perhaps I can help loosen his tongue, Father," Sinon
said, moving to stand directly before Teague. His glance
slid down Teague's body and a covetous, calculating expression flared in his eyes. "You're magnificent," he

breathed, lifting his gaze to Teague's. "One of the most finely wrought males I've ever seen."

He extended a bejeweled finger and touched Teague's chest where the tattooed claws began high up on a bulging pectoral. With a slow, sinuous motion, he traced a path downward until he reached Teague's nipple. Sinon circled it with his finger, sensuously, appreciatively, teasing, then pinching the sensitive flesh until it reflexively tautened.

"Very nice," the younger man purred. "You're very sensitive. I like that."

His smile widened into a predatory grin. Then, in a sudden, unexpected move, he twisted Teague's nipple hard.

Teague gasped in pain and surprise, then clamped down on the revealing response, masking all reaction, all emotion, behind an expression of stoic calm.

Sinon twisted even harder, grinding his nails into Teague's chest. "My father asked you a question, princeling. I suggest you answer him before I tear your teat away."

A tight smile lifted Teague's lips. He looked down at his tormentor, never breaking gaze. With a snarl Sinon reached up with his free hand and, grabbing hold of Teague's hair, brutally wrenched his head back, exposing the strong column of Teague's throat.

"Answer him, princeling," Vorax's son savagely ordered, "before I snap your neck in two!"

"Enough, Sinon," his father commanded. He chuckled low in his throat. "Your power over men is no more effective than your power over females. You waste time soiling your hands on vermin like him, just as you waste every day of that pitiful existence you call a life. Step back and see how a master extracts whatever he desires."

Sinon clenched his teeth, hissed softly. A look of pure hatred and barely contained fury glittered in his eyes. Then he smiled and stepped back, simultaneously releasing Teague's hair and nipple. "As you wish, Father," he said with an oily smirk. "You always know what is best."

"Yes, I do, and it's wise that you never forget that." Vorax half turned and motioned across the room to a shadowed doorway. "Come in, Orcus. It's time to ply your exquisite torments. The princeling has grown bold and arrogant in all the cycles of his exile. Come forth and finish what you began so long ago."

A huge man, beefy arms swinging, cruel, beady eyes gleaming, strode from the darkened doorway. Teague watched his approach and saw horror personified stride toward him. Orcus. Somehow, he'd managed to push the memory of that name into the furthest reaches of his mind, never recalling it until now. Orcus. The half-mad master torturer.

The man had aged well in the past nineteen cycles. Though gray heavily frosted his close-cropped hair and deep lines furrowed his pockmarked face, he had the body of a much younger man: strong, heavily muscled, cruelly powerful. As cruelly powerful as the brutish, eerily astute light glowing in his eyes.

The man knew how to break him if any man did. The realization sent a cold chill rippling down Teague's spine. With all the strength left in his battered, exhausted body, Teague summoned every power he'd ever acquired in his life. He would *not* be broken. Not this time. Not ever again.

This time, he would fight Vorax and his sadistic torturer to the end. There was no hope of escape, no hope of rescue. Just like in his tormented dreams and waking nightmares, he was back in Vorax's hands, this time never to leave. But this time he'd prevail.

This time, Teague resolved, he'd redeem himself, regain his lost honor. For himself, for his family, for his father. Fleetingly, he saw his father's face superimposed over that of the man who approached, a face stern, foreboding, eternally disapproving. Why, he wondered, had he tried so hard to please a man it seemed impossible to please? Why, indeed, was he trying so hard even now?

Because, as harsh and demanding a sire as his father had been, Teague realized at long last, he had made Teague the man he was. A man of faults and self-doubts and fears, but a man who even in the darkest, most despairing moments of his life had never given up. A man who had never purposely done evil, who had tried always to be fair and kind. And a man who had known and won the love of a brave, beautiful woman, however undeserving he might ultimately be.

In his father's name and for the sake of his own honor and self-respect, Teague knew he must face this final testing. It was the unfinished quest he'd been sent back to Incendra to complete. If he must die in this final battle, he would at least die a man—a man who was and had always been the true and rightful heir to the royal throne of Farsala.

Any being who dies creates the cause for a new being . . . The son must suffer, die to himself . . . before the taint can be exorcised, the evil overcome . . .

The holy words of the *Litany of Union* filled his mind, rising to join and entwine with those of the ancient prophecy, until Teague couldn't tell where one began and the other ended. Like some hallowed monastic chant, it reverberated over and over in his mind, soothing him, healing him . . . preparing him.

Then, with a malevolent grin and gleeful chortle, Orcus stepped forward, a double-toothed metal pincer in his hand.

Twenty-two

Ksathra was as she'd always remembered it, loud, crowded, and colorful. Yet as Raina strode through the wide boulevards of garishly painted shops and businesses and past the tenements piled one atop the other in the narrow side streets off the boulevards, on closer inspection, she saw the subtle signs of a city falling into decay.

The cobblestone pavement running through Ksathra had ruts in it and innumerable spots where stones were altogether lacking. The coating of mud, sand, and lime that covered the outsides of all the buildings was chipped and patchy. The whitewash had long ago darkened to a murky yellow. The areas of planned parks to break up the unrelenting white stone, though still green, were overgrown and filled with refuse.

It was the demeanor of the people beneath the distracting facade of noise and activity, though, that gave Raina the greatest pause. A hopeless, helpless look burned in their eyes; the slump to their shoulders was somber, despairing. Women sat in the doorways to their houses, listlessly teasing out thick bunches of lana wool and spinning it onto a spindle. The men talked in hushed voices, or sent sly, furtive looks about them before joining a group on the streets.

She knew she shouldn't be surprised. The effects of

Malam Vorax's harsh rule would be even more evident
in such close proximity to the evil man. Raina sup-
pressed a small shudder. She planned to get closer to
Vorax than even these people. She must be mad.

It would take all her powers of self-discipline to control the reflexive response to his hands on her, Raina
thought grimly, as she moved through the city. But
knowing that was to be forewarned, and it helped to
prepare for the eventual meeting. One thing at a time,
she told herself. First, she had to get to Vorax. She only
wondered how far she'd get before the way to the Farsalan ruler was blocked.

That answer was forthcoming as she approached the
ornately pillared walled enclosure that spread out in a
huge circle from the royal palace. Up ahead, past the
open gate guarded by six stout soldiers, Raina could see
the long expanse of steps, gleaming white and bright in
the midafternoon sun. A young man, dressed in glimmering blue and gold serica-cloth robes and accompanied by several others, descended the steps, apparently
headed in their direction.

Raina eyed him for an instant, then closed off further
consideration of the man from her mind. What mattered
was the palace that beckoned to her from the top of
those steps. A palace, at least temporarily, now inaccessible to her.

"Halt, female," the most heavily decorated of the six
soldiers said, moving to block her way through the
gates. Of medium height, the man resembled a gnarled
and thick-set robur tree, his red-bronze skin the obvious
result of many cycles of living out of doors, his arms
and legs scarred and bulky with muscle. Garbed in the
green and black livery of the royal house, complete with
tall black boots and a black headcloth to shield him

from the intense mountain sun, he stood there before her, his left cheek bulging with some wad he was chewing. Over his shoulder rested a stout Vastitian cudgel.

"And where do you think you're going? Plan to apply for a position of royal courtesan, do you?" The soldier eyed her from head to toe, then glanced toward his compatriots, a leer twisting his lips. The other men chuckled.

Raina felt her anger rise but clamped down on a biting retort. She schooled her face into a bland smile. "I need to see Malam Vorax. I wish for you to announce me to him."

"Do you, now?" The big man smirked. "And so do hundreds of other females since our revered ruler's consort died three cycles ago. All wish for a chance to win a position of power at his side."

He grinned, exposing a perfect pair of aterroot-stained teeth. "One as pretty as you just might be able to turn his head. Not that I'm recommending it, you can be sure. It's rumored the royal consort left this life under suspicious circumstances." He paused to spew a thin stream of dark brown fluid from his mouth. Then, stepping forward, the soldier reached out toward Raina as if intent on touching her.

She leaped back. "I'll take my chances with Vorax." She eyed his extended hand with a jaundiced eye. "Will you notify him or not?"

"Perhaps, and perhaps not." The soldier's eyes narrowed. "What's in it for me?"

"Vorax's gratitude, if you get me to him, and his enmity, if you don't." Raina smiled grimly. "We go back a long while, Malam and I. I think he'll be quite pleased to see me again." She shrugged. "But if you're insistent on refusing me entrance, it's your head."

"And exactly what *is* your relationship to my father?" a voice asked from behind the soldiers.

At the sound of the voice, the men standing before Raina froze. As one they parted, then turned, rendering the man standing behind them a deep bow. "We didn't hear your approach, Royal Majesty," the highest-ranking soldier hurried to explain. "This . . . this impertinent female distracted us, I'm sorry to say, with her demands and outlandish claims to know your father. I-I beg pardon for our oversight."

The young man who Raina had seen descending the stairs smiled thinly. "Your conduct was both dismal and reprehensible. But we'll deal with that later." His glance skimmed Raina, mildly curious but with none of the hot, hungry intensity of the soldiers. "And you, femina? You were saying you and my father go back a long while. Please explain."

Raina met his steady, skeptical gaze. Vorax's son. This was indeed an opportune moment. If she played it very carefully, he could well be the chance she needed to get to Vorax.

She smiled sweetly, taking in the man even as she did. He was slight of build, shorter than her by several centimeters, his pale blond hair falling to his shoulders in carefully formed curls. His eyes were a watered-down blue. His skin was as pale as his hair, and it gave him a sallow, colorless appearance.

What he lacked in natural coloring, however, he made up for in dress and jewels. His undertunic, falling to his delicately sandaled feet, was of the finest gold serica cloth. His trim waist was belted with a heavily jeweled band of thin, flexible aureum metal. Over his long tunic he wore a long-sleeved open robe of the most brilliant cerulean blue, made as well from serica cloth. Rings of varying sizes and stones sparkled on all his fingers, and a chunk of jadeite stone, set in yet more aureum, gleamed from his left earlobe.

A fop, to be sure, Raina thought, but the sly gleam in his eyes belied his more self-absorbed outward appearance. This son of Vorax would have to be handled very circumspectly.

Her smile softened. "I knew your father when I was but a child. My father was one of his most loyal supporters, and I grew up in the palace. If your name is Sinon, you were just a babe then and I saw you grow to a chubby toddler before I left. Your father had a . . . special affection for me then." She lowered her lashes in an intentionally demure gesture. "The rest is personal. I'd prefer not to share it before these soldiers."

Vorax's son held out his hand. "Then come, femina. My name is indeed Sinon, and we can speak further of this in a more private spot—say, the royal gardens? My father is engaged in meetings for the next hour or so. I'd be honored if you'd spend that interim visiting with me."

Raina took his hand and managed some semblance of a deferential bow. It had been so long, and she loathed such affectations, but for Teague, she was willing to do even worse. Which she soon might, she reminded herself grimly, thinking ahead to the eventual meeting with Malam Vorax. In the meantime, it remained to be seen what this strange son of his wanted from her. And want something he did. If all went well, perhaps both of them might benefit from this little interchange.

"I thank you for your kindness, my lord," she murmured, her smile never wavering. "I would be honored to spend the time visiting with you." She took his hand

and stepped past the soldiers, casting their leader a triumphant look.

Then she was inside the gates and, hand still clasped in Sinon's, walking around the base of the stairs toward the side of the palace and a cunning stone wall that enclosed a large garden. At the little garden gate, Sinon turned to his retainers. "We won't be needing your assistance further." He made an airy, dismissing motion with his hand. "Go. Get on with you. I'll call for your services later."

The retainers bowed low and scurried away, apparently as eager to get away from Vorax's son as the soldiers were to see him leave. Raina took in that bit of information and filed it away. So, Sinon Vorax was no more loved than his father.

He led her through the gate and into the garden. Lush with drooping shade trees and tall, aromatic cedra hedges, the royal garden was a cool, intimate hideaway. Water splashed from several fountains, to one of which Sinon led her.

A fine mist filled the air, setting Raina's sun-heated skin tingling. The water felt good. She smiled and flung back her head to catch the invigorating spray on her face.

"You're an exquisitely beautiful woman," Sinon said, jerking her from her momentary enjoyment of the refreshing mist. "Why do you want to sacrifice yourself to my father?"

Raina's head jerked down. Her smile died; her lips clamped tightly. She locked gazes with him, wary, assessing. There was no light of lust in Sinon's eyes. He but asked the obvious.

"Strange words, coming from the man's son," Raina

replied, carefully choosing her own words. "One would think you view your sire as some kind of monster."

Sinon smirked and, walking over to a stone bench beside the fountain, sat. "And if *you* don't, you're either singularly naive or a fool, or you have some hidden agenda in getting close to my father." He arched a slender blond brow. "Are you some assassin then, sent to kill my father?"

Raina, startled, took a moment to answer. "And if I were, do you think I'd admit it to you?"

He shrugged. "Most likely not. I wouldn't care if you did kill him, though. It would just open the way for my rise to the throne."

"Well, I haven't come back to kill your father." Strange, Raina thought, how that original plan had indeed changed. It was the truth nonetheless. "I . . . I left him cycles ago with great anger and pain still unresolved between us. I've had a long time to reconsider things. Now, I'd like to make amends, if Malam will accept my apologies."

"You're the girl he meant to wed and cast aside my mother for, aren't you?"

She steadily returned his curious gaze. "Yes, I was that girl, but that was many cycles ago."

"Well, I think you make a grave error in returning. If Father deigns to take you back into his favor, he will, I'd wager," Sinon said, "accept—no, *demand*—a lot more than apologies from you. Father has always had a peculiarly violent aberration for the feminas." He gave a disparaging snort. "Not that you'll find him particularly appealing these days, the disgusting old sand slug."

"I remember him as a great leader and a virile man."

"And those glorious memories are what brought you back, then, eh?" Sinon's lips curled derisively.

"My reasons are for your father's ears only." Raina smiled thinly. "I mean no offense, but I hope you'll understand."

He eyed her for a long moment. "As you wish, femina. You won't mention to Father, will you, what I said to you? It's our little secret, isn't it?"

At his cajoling, whining tone, Raina gritted her teeth. Gods, what a simpering little weakling! And he wanted to rule in his father's place? As despicable as Malam Vorax was, he at least had the strength and force of personality to command fear and obedience. But Sinon . . . Sinon must be an embarrassment and disgrace.

Satisfaction filled Raina. It was a sweet kind of retribution that Vorax was incapable of siring a good, decent man for a son. His empire crumbling around him, he wouldn't even have the comfort of knowing he had a competent offspring to carry on his name.

The irony was that the son who really *was* worthy to rule—Teague—might not have the chance he deserved. Two sons unappreciated by two fathers, yet one had never, *ever,* deserved the humiliation and abuse heaped upon him. A fierce determination swelled within Raina. If there was any way to do it, she *would* see Teague back on the throne that had always been his.

"Well, femina?" Sinon took up her hand and patted it between his two hands. "You *will* keep our little secret, won't you?"

Raina jerked her attention back to him. The look in his eyes was both pleading and shrewd. He tested her, she realized. Though the thought of allying herself with Sinon, however temporarily, filled her with distaste, Raina was no fool. She needed to get to Vorax, and Sinon, whatever his personal motives, seemed willing to help her. It could be no worse, she decided, than what she must endure to regain her place again at Vorax's side.

"Of course." She forced a smile. "It's our little secret."

"Good, good." He released her hand and stood. "Come. My father will be finished with his meeting soon. Let's return to the palace and I will introduce you to him."

Raina rose. Together, they left the safe, pleasant environs of the fountain and headed back to the steps leading up to the palace. A strange foreboding filled Raina, but whether it was for the meeting to come, or the unsettling alliance she'd just made with Sinon Vorax, she didn't know.

Already, events were beginning to take twists and turns she hadn't anticipated. There wasn't much she could do but adapt as situations arose, and buy time for both her and Teague until Aban and the others had the Tapestry Passage cleared. She didn't have to like it, though. She didn't have to like anything—just as long as, in the end, Teague survived.

The interior of the royal palace was even more lavishly furbished than Raina remembered it. Rich carpets covered the stone floors. Tapestries of every imaginable hue and historical depiction hung from the walls. Sensuously curved vases sat on low, dark-red robur-wood tables. Long-legged servant women and strongly built young men walked to and fro, carrying armloads of linens, or pitchers of drink and platters of sweet meats. It looked to Raina like a grand and lavish party was in the offing.

She turned to Sinon, who had halted in the middle

of the great entrance hall. "Does your father plan some celebration?"

The younger man smiled. "Yes, as a matter of fact. He has recently come into the possession of a man who has been a long-term threat to the stability of his reign. The men he even now meets with will be witness to this particular person's execution on the morrow. Then we'll all celebrate with a gala feast."

Raina went rigid. "And who could possibly, after all these cycles, threaten the reign of a man as powerful as Malam Vorax?"

Sinon cast her a wry look. "Don't you know, femina?"

The blood pounded through her veins. Her mouth went dry. "And why would I know? I just now arrived in Ksathra."

"Why, indeed?" Sinon shrugged. "My mistake." He offered his hand. "Come, let me escort you to my father's private reception chambers. We'll await him there."

Raina accepted his proffered hand. "As you wish, my lord."

He led her down a long, carpeted and heavily tapestried corridor off to the right. Raina remembered it well. The hallway led to the formal rooms of several private reception chambers and the large banquet hall. Beyond that lay the huge palace kitchens with their underground food storage pits.

For an instant, Raina was overcome by a poignant if bittersweet nostalgia. At any moment she half expected to see Najirah come running down the hall, or her father, tall and broad-shouldered, with a smile of welcome on his face. But they were just specters now, of a time and life never to be again.

A harsher, more desperate purpose drove her now.

And there was no one here anymore who cared about her. No one but Teague, and he was helpless to assist her. It was all up to her: Teague's continued existence, as well as the ultimate success of the upcoming attack upon Ksathra.

They reached the door Raina knew led to a private reception chamber. Sinon halted, opened the door, and motioned her in. When he didn't follow, Raina cocked a questioning brow.

"I go to fetch my father," he replied to her unspoken question. "There are fresh ewers of uva wine and a locally brewed cerevisia, plus a plate of fresh palmas fruit and other delicacies. Feel free to imbibe. I'll return shortly."

Raina nodded, then turned and walked farther into the room. Behind her, the door shut softly. She glanced around. The chamber was empty, save for a long table filled with food and drink and a high-backed chair set before a cluster of soft lounging couches. Tapestries covered three of the four walls. The wall opposite the door was of glass, inset with a framed glass door that appeared to open onto a broad balcony overlooking the palace gardens.

Nervous with anticipation, Raina strode to the long table and poured out a cup of uva wine which she quickly downed. Then she walked over to the glass wall, opened the door, and stepped out onto the balcony. Enclosed by the palace walls on the right and across the back, the garden's final barrier was the mountain on the left. It was there, Raina knew, that the Tapestry Passage led from the royal library through to the far side of the mountain. How she longed to head for it even now.

First, though, she must get to Teague and free him. First, the passage must be cleared by Aban and his men.

First, the signal must be given. There were many firsts, but the most important of all was first to win Vorax's confidence.

The door opened behind her. Raina wheeled, the now empty cup of uva wine clenched in her hand. Sinon walked in, then a shorter, far more heavy-set man. Though the cycles had failed to treat him kindly, Raina recognized him immediately.

Malam Vorax stepped into the room. As he caught sight of her, he stopped dead. Surprise, confusion, then dawning recognition flashed across his pasty-complected, heavy-jowled face. He shot his son a seething glance.

"Where did you find her?"

Sinon shrugged, glancing casually down to straighten one of his many rings. "She was at the gate, demanding to be let in. She said she once knew you, so I decided to discover if her tale was true." He lifted his gaze, innocent inquiry in his eyes. *"Do* you know her, Father?"

"Yes," Vorax muttered. "I do. Call in the guards. I'll not stay in any room alone with her."

"Indeed?" his son purred. "And since when has a mere female been a threat to the mighty ruler of Farsala? Strange, isn't it," he mused, "that in the course of a few days, two people appear whom you seem to fear above all others? I find this turn of events most intriguing."

"The guards, Sinon!"

The young man nodded curtly, then turned and exited the room. A minute later, four guards accompanied him back. "Your 'protection' has returned, Father," Sinon said. "Would you like for them to seize the femina?"

Vorax hesitated, seeming to consider that for a moment. "No," he said finally. "I'm sure Raina's motives for coming back now are quite reasonable and friendly. And if they aren't, well, the presence of my guards will be enough to discourage her from trying anything foolish."

She strode out across the room toward him, drawing up midway. Her hands rose to a position of exasperation on her hips. "I'm not a child anymore, Malam. And I'd be a fool to return like this if I meant you harm."

He eyed her narrowly. "Then why *did* you return? Unless I misinterpreted your actions, you were none too pleased with me the last time we were together."

"No, I wasn't too happy," Raina calmly agreed. "Your . . . passion . . . was too much for me then. But that was fifteen cycles ago. I've learned much since then, have thought long about what there used to be between us, and decided that, now that my mate is dead, I'd return and see if we couldn't make amends."

"Indeed?" Vorax arched a graying brow. "And why, after all these cycles, do you think I'd care to 'make amends'?"

"I don't know what you'd want or not want. I but thought it was worth a try." She smiled thinly. "Perhaps we could make some sort of an arrangement? Between two mature adults, I mean."

"An arrangement, eh? And what do you offer as *your* part of the bargain?" His skeptical glance took in her tunic and cloak-covered body. "Do you hope to insinuate yourself back into my heart? Perhaps even regain the position you once held as my betrothed and future consort?"

Beside him, Sinon hissed softly in triumph. Raina quickly calculated the possible advantages versus disadvantages of an affirmative answer. Vorax, however, had always been a practical if very vain man. She doubted the cycles of total power had changed that. It seemed the best course was to make this appear as some sort of mutually agreeable pact.

"You wanted my body once. I've always wanted the comforts your power can bring," Raina boldly replied. At the hard look that sprang to his eyes, she quickly softened her proposition. "It's not just a matter of money and flesh, though. At least not for me. I-I missed you all these cycles, Malam. You always treated me so well . . ."

"And your deceased mate didn't?"

As she brushed a nonexistent speck of dirt from her cloak, Raina made a great show of quirking her mouth in distaste. "He was a big, lumbering equs trader. He treated me well enough, but we never had anything more than our desert tent and a few pots and plates. I quickly grew weary of the hardships and wanted desperately to return to you, but you know how binding a desert life mating can be. If I'd run from him, the other men of his tribe would've helped him hunt me down."

She sighed and shook her head. "So, his death became my only hope of freedom."

"And why should I believe any of this?" Vorax walked over to stand before her. "Do you think me still so smitten with your beauty that I'd leap at the chance to have you again?"

"If you still find me pleasing," Raina said with an arch little smile, "I certainly hope so. I've little else to offer. I realize that now."

"Do you?" A closed, calculating look glittered in his eyes. "And how far will you go to prove that you want me again? How deep does your loyalty lie?"

Here it comes now, Raina thought with an anticipatory shiver. Now he'll offer to take me back to his bed. "I'll do anything to come back to you, Malam. Anything."

Vorax cast Sinon a hooded glance. Then he turned back to Raina. "Come with me, femina." He extended a pudgy, berringed hand. "There's someone I want you to meet first, before you swear that oath of allegiance. The price I demand is high, but if you do what I ask, you'll have proved your loyalty beyond a shadow of a doubt."

Unease curled within Raina, but she forced herself to take Vorax's hand. Silently, he turned and led her out of the reception chamber and back down the hall. Through the palace they walked, followed by a narrow-eyed Sinon and the four guards. They passed through the main entry hall, then down the corridor to the library—and the staircase that led to the torture caverns.

There Vorax paused, casting her a questioning glance. "Once before I took you down there," he said, gesturing to the door that opened onto that special place of terror. "You ran screaming from it. Will you be so squeamish this time?"

"No." Raina bit back a wild surge of hope. No matter Vorax's intent once he got her down there—and she began to suspect it just might be to test her response to Teague—she welcomed it. If the journey provided her with the opportunity to ascertain his condition and give him warning of what was to come, it would be well worth it. "I'm a woman now, Malam. Such things don't disturb me anymore. Whoever is down there deserves to be, has been disloyal to you. I'll rejoice in his punishment."

A secret smile lifted his lips. "Indeed, he *does* deserve to be there, until the day he dies." He tugged on her hand, almost impatiently. "Come, femina. See the price I ask you to pay."

She followed him down the long expanse of stone stairs, their footsteps echoing hollowly off the high ceiling of the cavernous room. As they rounded the last curving swell of steps, however, Raina saw a sight that took her breath away.

Head bowed so that his long blond hair tumbled down and hid his face, Teague hung shackled, hands and feet, to the stone wall. His meager red loincloth was his only clothing; his nearly naked body gleamed in the dim light of flickering oil lamps. He was covered with sores and cruelly wrought wounds, as if someone had methodically worked his torturous way over Teague's body.

It took every bit of Raina's strength not to cry out and run to him. It was equally as difficult not to withdraw the dagger sheathed to her thigh and plunge it into Malam Vorax's heart. But she did neither. The time wasn't right, their cause surely lost before it had barely begun if she attempted such a foolhardy act.

So instead, she forced a bland smile and turned to Vorax. "Is this what you brought me down here to see? A man tortured nearly to death? I'm not impressed, Malam."

"Then come closer, femina," he said with a hoarse chuckle, "and see if you recognize him. Then you'll begin to understand the enormity of what I ask of you."

Vorax pulled Raina over to stand before Teague. As he lifted his hand to grasp Teague by the hair, Sinon stepped up to his father's side. "Will you permit me to do the honors?" he said, an eager, almost feral look in his eyes. "I do so like handling this one."

Raina's glance shot from Vorax to Sinon. There was something ugly, perverse in the young man's eyes, as if . . . as if he . . . *desired* Teague. Recognition flared. Each in his own way, father and son had fallen to the depths of depravity.

Her gorge rose and it was all she could do to keep from slapping that smug, possessive look off Sinon's face. The disgusting young fool! If he thought ever to equal, much less win, a man like Teague Tremayne, he was sadly mistaken.

Glancing back at Teague, her heart swelled with compassion. Gods, what had he suffered in the past days? If Sinon had laid one hand on him in some carnal way, she'd make certain—

She stopped short. Emotions, however justified, would only confuse the issue at hand and threaten the success of this mission. Later, there might be time for the luxury of revenge. For now, though, she must take great pains not to antagonize either man.

"I grow impatient, Malam," Raina forced herself to say, her tone utterly bored. "What has this man to do with the issue of my devotion to you?"

Vorax nodded to his son. "Lift his head. Show her his face. Then she may finally discern the importance of this man." He grinned malevolently. "And understand the price she must pay."

Sinon smiled, stepped close to Teague, and slid his hands up both sides of his face in an appreciative, almost caressing gesture. "So pretty," he murmured, as he lifted Teague's head. "So strong."

His face, swollen and bruised, slowly came into view. His lips were cracked, bleeding. His nose was broken.

Rage flooded Raina. She ground her teeth and fisted her hands. Control . . . she *must* maintain control.

"Yes?" she asked, swinging her gaze back to Vorax's.

"You don't recognize him?" Incredulity deepened his voice.

She made an imperious gesture in Teague's direction. "How could anyone recognize him, as beaten beyond any possible remembrance as he is? I tire of this game, Malam. I came to you in good faith, to lay my heart and life at your feet. Just tell me what it is you want."

He considered her for a long moment, his arms crossed over his chest. "Well, you were young then, and he is a bit mangled." Vorax gestured at Teague. "This is Tarik Shatrevar, the crown prince of the former dynasty. I'd thought to be rid of him, but he now returns, fool that he is. This time, however, I cannot be as merciful as I was all those cycles ago when he was a lad. This time, he is a man, and a considerable threat to my reign."

"And I ask again. What has all this to do with me?" Even as she spoke, a dreadful presentiment coiled within her.

"What has this to do with you, femina?" Vorax smiled, a flat, emotionless gesture that did little more than lift the corners of his mouth. "Why, everything, of course. The prince must die, on the morrow, in the main courtyard before all the people of Ksathra. And you, my lovely femina, to prove your loyalty and devotion to me, have been the one chosen to kill him."

Twenty-three

Raina stared at Vorax dumbfounded. Teague groaned. She swung back to him. Bleary, bloodshot eyes met hers.

"No," he croaked, his voice rusty with disuse and pain. "Don't ask such a thing . . . of her."

"And why should you care, princeling?" Vorax's brow arched in inquiry. "Do you imagine she's too weak to do it?"

He motioned to a large, heavily muscled older man who, until now, had stood unnoticed by Raina in the shadows. At Vorax's signal, the man walked forward, lifted a beefy fist, and slammed it into Teague's jaw. Teague grunted, then went limp.

It was all Raina could do to choke back a gasp and keep from going for the big man's throat.

Vorax eyed Teague's unconscious form briefly, then turned back to Raina. "Well, femina? *Are* you, too weak to thrust a dagger into him, to kill this man, this enemy of mine?"

She locked gazes with the fat little man even as her mind raced to find some way—any way—out of this unforeseen dilemma. "I can kill him." Raina forced her voice to sound calm, sure, her glance to remain steady. "But if he truly *is* who you claim he is, what of the prophecy? Doesn't it forbid his death?"

At mention of the ancient words, Vorax's already pale complexion went a shade paler. "The prophecy promises woe to any who harm him. But I, sweet femina, won't be the one to harm him. You will."

So, he meant for the prophetic consequences to fall on her head, not his, Raina thought. How clever. In one brutal act, he'd rid himself of the greatest threat to his rule *and* test her loyalty in the surest way he knew how. She only wondered if he wouldn't kill her just as soon as she finally freed him of the protracted encumbrance of the curse, to expunge any lingering taint if for nothing else.

"Why didn't you kill him long ago?" Raina hedged, desperately seeking some way out of this increasingly worsening situation. There seemed none. "Why wait until now?"

Vorax shrugged. "He wasn't any danger as a lad. I thought to destroy him mentally then, so even if he lived, he'd be unable to lead others against me, much less ever rule. It solved the problem of the prophecy, yet eliminated him as any potential threat. Obviously," he added dryly, "my plan failed."

Yes, Raina thought, it *had* failed, but only because Vorax hadn't bargained on the resiliency and courage of a lad who'd grown into an equally strong and resilient man. Though she'd time and again disparaged Teague's monastic training, perhaps it *had* helped to hold all the shattered remnants of his tormented mind together long enough for his heart and soul to mend. Perhaps it had, in the bargain, provided him with the psychic strength to go on.

Provided him with powers that even now might be his salvation.

A wild hope flared within her. Powers . . . powers

that could be used, even as she "killed" him, to mislead others into thinking he was dead. Powers such as she'd seen that night in the monkish enclosure high up on the face of the Carus Mountains on Bellator.

But how to warn Teague beforehand? Raina wondered. And, in his present condition, was he even capable of performing such a feat? There was no way of knowing until she talked with him. *If* she could indeed find some way to talk with him before they must meet again on the morrow.

She managed a grim little smile. "So, now you ask me to finish what someone else left undone?"

"Precisely." Vorax returned her smile. "Will you do it?"

"Yes," Raina softly said, forcing out the lie that nearly choked her. "For you, Malam, and no other, will I do it."

The night grayed to dawn before Raina's eyes, eyes that burned, felt as gritty as the Ar Rimal from lack of sleep. She'd stayed awake all night, watching and waiting for her chance to slip down from her room in the royal suite and pay Teague a nocturnal visit. Yet though Vorax had chosen not to test her willingness to bed him this night, he'd made certain sufficient guards patrolled the palace interior. Enough guards to prevent Raina from daring a trip to the torture caverns.

She knew she could chance it anyway. She knew as well that if she was caught, Vorax's punishment would be swift and fatal. So instead, Raina had decided to bide her time and wait until the right opportunity presented itself.

Until Aban and the others broke through to the secret

library door, no purpose was served in taking any unnecessary risks, at any rate. Raina only hoped they'd
finish the clearing of the tunnel in time. Even if she
succeeded this day in saving Teague from a certain
death, their ruse would last only so long. Though from
her girlhood days she recalled many nooks and crannies
in the palace to hide in, it would still be but a matter
of time before they were found.

The maidservants came in midmorn, bathed her in
warm water scented with arosa petals, patted her dry with
soft cloths, then offered Raina her choice of gowns. She
cast a longing look at her tunic, boots, and breeches, then
chose an emerald green gown of shimmering serica cloth.
The servants clasped armlets of hammered aureum about
her upper arms and a circlet of thinner-hammered aureum
around her neck. Her thick auburn hair was then piled
atop her head and bound with fine cords shot with
aureum threads.

The chief maid stepped back to admire their handi-
work. "You look lovely, domina. Our king will be
pleased." She gestured to the door. "If you will, he
awaits you even now."

Raina eyed the door. She wasn't ready just yet to
depart. "I'll be along shortly. You may all go."

The maidservants looked at each other, confusion in
their eyes. "It's quite all right. Really," Raina said, smiling reassuringly. "I'll only be a minute or two. Why
don't you just wait for me outside?"

They silently turned and exited the room. Raina
strode over to the bed, dug out her Nadrygean dagger
and sheath, and the stunner she'd successfully managed
to hide in a wide crack in the bed frame. Lifting her
skirt, she quickly fastened the sheath to her left thigh,

replaced the dagger, then slid the stunner snugly beneath the sheath strap.

That task complete, she dropped her skirt back in place and examined her silhouette in the floor-length mirror. No suspicious bulges were evident. Raina smiled grimly. If her plan to rescue Teague was discovered, she'd not be taken alive.

As requested, the maids awaited her outside her sleeping chamber. In a flurry of excited feminine voices, delicate floral scents, and swishing gowns, they followed Raina down the stairs. Malam Vorax, accompanied by Sinon, several guards, and an ornately cloaked man holding what appeared to be a ceremonial dagger on a finely wrought argentum tray, gazed up at her from the foot of the stairs. At the sight of her, a hot, hungry light leaped to life in Vorax's eyes.

"You look exquisite in that gown," he purred. He extended his hand. "My anticipation of bedding you grows with each passing moment."

Raina placed her hand in his and watched as his pale, pudgy fingers closed over hers. She swallowed back a surge of bile and smiled brightly down at him. "As does mine for you, Malam. But first, there is one task more to prove my devotion."

"Yes, there is indeed." A fiendish eagerness flared in his eyes, effectively dampening his rising lust. He squeezed her hand hard. "And the sight of you driving the dagger deep into the prince's gut will only rouse my desire for you to even greater heights." His smile widened, lending an evil, predatory cast to his face. "There's just something about death . . ."

"Yes," Raina muttered, fervently wishing it could be Malam Vorax on the receiving end of her dagger rather than Teague. "There *is* something about death."

He tugged on her hand. "Then come. The people await the official ceremony, and all this talk of killing threatens my control. The sooner I take you, the better for both of us."

She followed him then, out of the palace, down the long expanse of steps, and through the gate. An armed escort of gaudily liveried guards joined them there, forming an impressively colorful and intimidating escort around the aureum-gilded robur-wood open sedan chair set on poles. The conveyance consisted of two rows of plush, cushioned seats and was carried by eight brawny men.

At their approach, the sedan chair was lowered to the ground. Malam escorted Raina into the front row of seats. Sinon and the dagger-bearing servant took up the seats behind them. Once all were settled, the eight men, in a surprisingly smooth and well-coordinated effort, lifted the sedan chair to their shoulders.

Crowds of people, unsmiling and somber, lined the boulevard leading to the great courtyard just inside the city walls. There, in the center of the great courtyard, was a large stone platform built into one of the walls, thrusting from it in a huge half-circle of coarse gray stone. The entire populace of Ksathra appeared to be assembled about its base.

The mood in the courtyard was tense, the people restless, and the looks many sent them in their open sedan chair were angry and mutinous. The people of Ksathra, at the very least, were primed for a rebellion, Raina thought. Primed for a new leader. If only she could save Teague. If only she could reach the door to the secret passage and let Aban and the others through.

With a fierce wrench, Raina marshaled her attention back to the most immediate problem at hand—how to find a minute or two to speak with Teague without being overheard or having her motives for conversing with him found suspect. Raina only hoped, when the time came, he'd be able to marshal those special powers of his quickly enough.

What had Marisa said? . . . *A man of his high training, in the proper meditative state, is impervious to pain or injury . . .*

In the proper meditative state. Gods, why hadn't she ever asked him about that strange ritual of his? Or how long it took to reach the "proper meditative state"?

She would just have to buy Teague the time he required before she stabbed him. Somehow, in some way, or all would be lost. But what if she still managed inadvertently to kill him?

Malam Vorax would die; of that there was no doubt. The only question remaining was would she turn on him then and kill him, or wait for the ensuing attack of the Tuarets and the other desert tribes to do it for her. At that moment, Raina honestly didn't know what she'd do, though logic told her the latter course would ultimately be the better one. But the thought of watching Teague die at Vorax's feet, if all went awry, and do nothing about it, was more than Raina could deal with just then. And if that horrible dream of hers should ultimately come true . . .

The chair bearers halted a few meters from the base of the stone porch and its steps. A hush settled over the restlessly milling crowd. A door, high up on the wall that backed the platform, opened with a groan of ancient hinges. Teague, escorted by four armed guards, stepped out of the blackness.

His arms bound tightly behind his back, he stood there for a moment, bare-chested but dressed once more

in breeches and boots, blinking in the bright glare of
sunlight. Then, with a brutal jerk, the two guards holding him by the arms urged him forward. Across the
broad stone porch they walked, drawing up only when
they reached two stone pillars that thrust from the floor
about ten meters from a dais set with an aureum and
purple cloth draped over the throne chair.

The guards forced Teague to his knees. Taking up a
thick chain attached on one end to each of the pillars,
they threaded the metal links around his upper arms
several times before fastening the other end snugly back
onto the pillars. With the chains pulled tight about his
arms, Teague was forced to kneel upright between the
two pillars, facing the throne.

Vorax led Raina up the steps and to the dais. Sinon
and the dagger bearer followed. Climbing onto the
raised wooden platform, Vorax walked over to his chair
and sat. He motioned Raina to join him at his side.
Sinon came to stand on his other side, with the dagger
bearer waiting a respectful distance away until he was
summoned.

"He is truly pitiful, is he not, femina?" Vorax asked,
gesturing in Teague's direction. "No matter the tortures,
he never said a word until he protested your killing him.
As if it truly mattered who the giver of his death was."
He smirked. "Sad, impotent, pitiful fool. He never, ever,
had a chance."

"If you feel such pity for him, Father," Sinon said,
leaning close, "spare him a few days longer. The people
will revere you for your mercy, and I'll have a time
more with him." As if in anticipation of the pleasures
to come, he licked his lips. "He's the most magnificent
male specimen I've ever seen."

Vorax shot his son a disgusted look. "Spare him?

Why? So you can use him for more of your revolting carnality?"

Sinon glanced back, unruffled by his sire's disdain. "And what do you care what I use him for? I'd think you'd find pleasure in his total degradation and humiliation. Perhaps, in the end, I could loosen his tongue where all your torturers failed. You'd then get what you wanted and, in the bargain, so would I."

"He won't talk, no matter what either of us does to him," Vorax snarled. "I wonder, even now, if he hasn't always been half-mad."

"Perhaps he is. It matters not to me, at any rate. I can use his body with or without his consent."

With the greatest effort, Raina contained her impulse to slap the lecherous look off Sinon's face. Though the price might well be high, sparing Teague's life even another day might buy her the time she needed. Aban and the others should have the tunnel through the mountain cleared soon, perhaps even this very day. But would it be soon enough?

She didn't know how long Teague could feign death, even if their plan worked. Gods, Raina thought. So many unanswered questions, so much that depended on the speed with which the tunnel could be opened.

Yet she didn't dare interfere in the two men's conversation. To show too much concern one way or another . . .

"It matters not to me, either," Vorax continued, "whether you do or don't satisfy your unnatural cravings. Already, you're the laughingstock of the palace. Do you wish to spread the ugly truth of your depravity yet further? You'll never be permitted to rule, once news of your perversions reaches the desert tribes. They, of all the peoples of Farsala, won't tolerate it."

"I can handle the desert tribes," Sinon hissed, anger purpling his thin, effeminate face. "They'll never come together into any force of power. Their tribal feuds will always keep them apart."

"Perhaps. But perhaps not. They may but need the right cause to rally them. If you aren't careful, you could well be that cause, Sinon."

"Curse them all! I'm not concerned with their moral judgments of me."

"And that will someday be your greatest undoing," his father said. "One way or another, though, the prince will die this day. I want no further problems from him."

The resolve—and the finality of his decision—was evident in Vorax's tone. As his father turned once more to Raina, Sinon shot him a venomous look, then stepped back, defeated. "As you wish, my lord," he gritted.

"I will speak to the people," Vorax said to Raina. "Once I am finished, the dagger bearer will step over to us. You will take the blade, leave the dais, and walk over to the prince. Grasp his hair and pull back until you have him leaning far enough backward to provide ample angle for your dagger thrust. If you wish to spare both of you unnecessary pain, stab him just below the breastbone, then quickly slice—"

"I think I have the idea." Raina hastened to interrupt his sickening fascination with the finer details of Teague's execution. "Let's just get on with it, shall we?"

"Not so eager for his death anymore, are you?" Vorax cocked a quizzical brow. "And why is that, femina?"

"I do this for your sake, Malam," Raina retorted. "Not mine. I've little stomach for killing."

He eyed her for a long moment, then shrugged. "Well, that's probably for the best. I like my women soft and gentle." He paused. "You will be soft and gentle with me, won't you, femina?"

"I'll be whatever you want me to be, Malam." Raina's nerves were strung so taut she could barely control the impulse to reach out and throttle him. Gods, why was he dragging this out so long?

"I'll hold you to that." Vorax stood and lifted his arms to the crowd. His long sleeves fell back, exposing white, flaccid arms. The renewed mumblings and shufflings of feet stilled once more. He waited for a long, tension-fraught moment, allowing the anticipation to build. Then, when Raina thought she'd scream from the strain, he finally spoke.

"In my boundless mercy," Vorax cried, his voice echoing off the natural arc of the walls and mountain that formed the perfect acoustical backdrop, "I have foregone official executions for a long while now. Yet despite my warnings, despite the fact that I once most mercifully spared his life, a man has returned who cannot be permitted to live. For the sake of Farsala, for its continuing reign of peace and prosperity, I am even willing now to risk the dire words of the prophecy."

He slowly turned and pointed to where Teague knelt on the stone platform below him, his head bowed, his long blond hair cascading down about his face. "This man is the last of the Royal House of Shatrevar. He is the prince whom I spared so many cycles ago and sent away to begin a new life in atonement for the greed and stupid ambition of his forefathers. To his shame, he chose to let that ambition and greed lead him back here. Of his own volition, he has risked much—and lost."

Vorax swung to Raina. "This woman, in the name of us all, will kill the prince. This woman, in the name of us all, will put an end at last to the prophecy. This woman, as she plunges the sacred dagger into this man, will free Farsala, once and for all, from the taint of a royal line that long ago rotted from within."

Raina stared back at Vorax, seeing that very taint he spoke of, the corruption that was such an inherent part of his being, emanating from him and his spawn. At that moment, all the hatred, all the seething need to see him dead, churned up within her, threatening to spew forth in an explosion of rage and revenge. She fought it, knowing the terrible consequences, the fatal outcome, if she gave in. Fought it, and won.

"Come, sweet femina," Vorax said tenderly, his voice dropping for her ears alone. "Come and prove your love."

As if guided by some force outside herself, Raina moved toward him. Simultaneously, the servant bearing the tray holding the dagger stepped forward. Both met before Vorax at the same time.

He took the dagger from the tray, extending it, hilt first, to her. Raina accepted the blade, grasping it firmly in her hand. The dagger's weight and heft felt good. It was a finely wrought weapon. She only wished she could plunge it into Vorax's heart.

But she loved Teague too much to assuage her lust for revenge, however justified it might be. Loved him at the expense of her life, her pride, her independence, to the very offering of herself to the man she loathed above all others. And loved him enough to sacrifice even the certainty that, though she risked everything for him, he loved or would ever love her in return.

Najirah. Now, at this most profound, most poignant moment of her life, Raina finally understood. Love ennobled you. Love completed you. Love refined you. And even the pain, the doubt, and the potential loss of that love were not worse than never having experienced it at all.

She turned and walked across the dais to the steps leading down to the stone porch, and the man who awaited her, the fragile essence of his life now resting in her hands. Her heart pounded beneath her breast. Her mouth went dry, her hands clammy. Warrior though she was, Raina feared the upcoming confrontation more than she'd feared any battle in her life.

The journey to the two pillars holding Teague was the longest journey of her life. So much depended on her—Teague's survival, the success of the rebellion, the downfall of Malam Vorax, and salvation of Farsala. Such a heavy, heavy burden for one person to bear.

Yet she made the journey, one resolute step at a time. Just as Teague must go when his turn came. To choose, as the prophecy said, the living death or one of life, to face obliteration—or triumph.

Raina drew to a halt before him. He was sheened in sweat, exhausted, breathing heavily. Furtively, she eased a small skin bladder of capra blood into the palm of her right hand, adjusting it until it lay beneath the hilt of the dagger. Then she grasped his hair in her left hand and gently pulled back his head until his face was up-turned to hers.

"Teague?" she softly said. "Can you hear me? Can you understand?"

"Y-yes," he rasped. "I hear. I-I understand."

"The night before we first met, I sought you out at that hermitage above Rector. I saw you perform some strange monkish ritual where you stabbed yourself in the belly with a dagger, yet lived."

His lids slowly lifted. Ice-blue eyes stared up at her. "You saw . . . saw me perform the blade ritual?"

"Yes." Raina nodded tersely. "You must prepare yourself—and quickly—that same way. Then, when I stab you in the belly—"

"No," he groaned. She didn't understand. He'd lost those powers when he'd opened himself to caring for her, in loving her. The startling admission gave him pause.

Loving her.

He *did* love her, with every fiber of his being. With all the strength and power and depth that he possessed. But it was too late.

"I cannot perform the blade ritual anymore, Raina. I began to lose those powers, powers only a chaste man is worthy to possess, when I let myself begin to want you. And, after that night we mated . . ." He sighed. "Well, they're surely gone."

"Chastity has nothing to do with it, Teague Tremayne!"

In her rising anger and frustration, Raina's fingers clenched in his hair. Teague winced but said nothing.

"You'd give up, then?" she persisted, disbelief threading her voice.

"It doesn't matter. I'm done, spent."

"Be strong for me, Teague," Raina pleaded. "And if not for the sake of our love, then for yourself, for Farsala, for Incendra."

"And why *not* for the sake of our love?" Teague savagely demanded. "Though you deserve better, I tell you true that I love you with all my heart. That I'll do anything for you. Do you hear me? *Anything!*"

"Then prepare yourself one last time in the way you learned as a monk," she whispered, as behind her, the people massed before them began to grumble and mutter among themselves. "One last time, Teague Tremayne."

"Kill him!" Vorax shouted, above the rising roar of the increasingly agitated crowd. "I grow weary of your hesitation. Drive the dagger into him and be done with it."

Raina glanced over her shoulder. The ruler of Farsala had climbed to his feet and was now frowning down at her, his gaze narrowed in distrust.

Fear shot through her. "Quickly now," she urged Teague. "Vorax grows suspicious."

"One thing more. If I fail in this, don't blame yourself. Give me your oath that you won't blame yourself."

"Teague, there isn't any time left for—"

"Your word, Raina!"

She sighed her acquiescence. "My oath, then."

He gazed up at her for a brief moment longer, wanting more, wanting to know she'd live, wanting for them to be together, but he knew that might never be. He hesitated a moment more. "I love you, Raina. Never doubt that."

She managed a wobbly smile. "I won't."

Teague took his fill of her for one final wondrous instant, then closed his eyes. He willed himself to slow his breathing, willed his pulse to slacken, willed all sounds, all feeling, all thought, to subside, save for those of the strengthening, sustaining words of the blade ritual.

And little by little, Teague felt the power swell within him. He fed it by drawing on the physical anguish of his body. *Only in the pinnacle of his torment would he at last be free . . . Free . . .* to attain the final purification. Free to face the final test of all.

"Now," he cried hoarsely. "Do it now!"

At his command, Raina tugged hard on his hair, jerking his head back. Teague's body followed, his chest thrusting forward, his back arching to expose his unprotected abdomen. His bound arms lurched against the chains binding him to the pillars.

He opened his eyes. Sunlight glinted off the blade held high above him, blindingly bright. Then, with lightning-swift speed, the dagger arced downward, plunging deep into his tautly straining belly.

Twenty-four

For a long moment Teague knelt there, his body arched back, rigid in pain, his mouth opened in soundless agony. The crowd roared out its shock and distress, surged forward. Then he went slack and slumped over, the dagger still thrusting from his gut.

Raina waited for the blood to flow, for its sticky, sickening warmth to gush over her hand, fervently, desperately praying it wouldn't. And as the seconds passed, the blood didn't come. Teague's heart continued to beat; he breathed, if very slowly and shallowly.

Relief flooded Raina. It had worked. Teague's blade ritual powers had worked!

Bending over him to hide the act, she squeezed the bladder of capra blood hard in her hand, rupturing it. The blood squirted onto the blade, spraying a copious amount of the red liquid onto Teague's belly and down the front of his breeches. Then, with a dramatic flourish, Raina withdrew the dagger. Climbing to her feet, she held it high over her head.

The crowd went silent and still, staring up at her dumbfounded. Out of the corner of her eye, Raina caught the movement of Vorax's hand, motioning to the head guard, who immediately signaled to those of his men spread out in strategic positions throughout the crowd. With a few surreptitious jabs to the ribs and blows to the heads of the unfortunate people standing in their vicinity, the guards prodded the crowd to a feeble cheer.

There was nothing they could do, however, to force an enthusiasm that was lacking. Raina turned, strode over to the dais, and climbed the steps. "It is done, then," she said, as she halted before Vorax. "I've killed him as you asked."

A wary admiration gleamed in his eyes. "Yes, you have."

He motioned for the dagger bearer to take the bloody weapon from her. Once she'd surrendered the dagger, the servant offered her a damp cloth. Raina wiped her hands and lower arms clean of the blood, then accepted the drying cloth. Only when she'd returned that cloth did Vorax extend his hand.

"Come," he said. "Let us go to the banquet hall for the great feast. You have justly won my esteem and that of all Farsala. You will be honored as we'd honor any great warrior."

Raina feigned hesitation. "The prince." She cast a distressed look in Teague's direction. Already four guards were removing the chains that bound him and readying a litter to place his body upon. "What will they do with him now?"

Vorax glance briefly followed hers. "We'll abide by the standard sanitary practices. His body will be prepared for burial in the embalming chamber down in the torture caverns. Then, after dark, he'll be taken outside the city and secretly buried in an unmarked grave. We can't risks the rebels exhuming him and claiming he lives still. I want the tales and false hopes put to rest once and for all."

"A wise decision." Raina took his hand.

"I take great pains not to leave any detail undone." Vorax began to lead her back across the dais. "It is the secret of my long and prosperous rule."

Sinon fell into step behind his father, a mocking, bitter smirk on his lips. As they walked back to the sedan chair, the guards laid Teague on the litter, covered him with a large black cloth, and carried him away. Raina watched them, her mind racing.

She had to get to Teague before the embalmer discovered he wasn't truly dead. But how to escape Vorax without him suspecting anything?

Raina's opportunity came as they disembarked from the sedan chair. She tripped climbing down and fell to her knees. Vorax was immediately at her side, grasping her elbow to help her up.

"Are you all right, femina?" he asked anxiously. "Do you feel ill or light-headed?"

"Yes," she said, seizing on the excuse offered. "I-I'm sorry, but the strain of the morn must have been more than I first imagined." Raina covered her eyes with her free hand. "My head . . . it aches so."

She lowered her hand and managed a wan smile. "Perhaps if I took a short rest in my room . . ."

"Yes, yes." He nodded. "Perhaps that would be best. There'll be speeches and toasts for a time, before the feast truly begins. Would an hour be sufficient to ease your headache?"

"I'll make it enough time, Malam." Raina patted the hand that still gripped her arm. "I never want to disappoint you in anything."

He grinned back at her like some besotted lad. "And especially not tonight, eh, femina?"

"No," she agreed with all the enthusiasm she could muster. "Most certainly not tonight."

The big, curved Farsalan trumpets blared just then from the city walls. Vorax turned and frowned. Even as they stood there, the discordant sound of the city gates beginning to grind closed filled the air.

Sinon climbed down from the sedan chair and joined them. "The gates closing in the middle of the day? What can that mean?"

His father's jaw went taut. A terrible rage exploded in his eyes. "One thing and one thing only," he growled. "An enemy approaches."

Raina waited until the guards who'd escorted her back to her room in the palace had left. Then she sent the maidservants away, pleading a need for total privacy to ease her headache. Once she'd made certain the door was locked behind her, she shed her gown and delicate sandals, removed the weapons she'd strapped to her leg, and donned her breeches, boots, and tunic. To cover her old clothing and minimize suspicion, Raina put on a rich cloak of midnight blue, trimmed in fine aureum threads. A gift from Vorax, she thought wryly, that might well be used to hasten his undoing.

The Nadrygean dagger was strapped again to her thigh, the stunner slipped beneath her belt, and she was once more at the door, unlocking it. The approach of Aban and their army at last toward Ksathra had bought her a bit more time, but all could still be lost if she didn't get to Teague soon. If they discovered he truly wasn't dead, and turned on him . . .

The halls were all but deserted, the majority of servants and guards evidently called into service for the feast. Raina was easily able to slip down the corridor leading from the royal bedchambers and to the base of the stairs opening onto the entry hall before her presence was noticed.

One of her maidservants saw her and hurried over. "Domina," she said. "Are you so quickly recovered?"

"I feel much better." Raina glanced about her. She couldn't risk lingering here. She was too open and vulnerable.

She looked back at the maid. "I forgot the wonderful brooch Malam gave me and need it for my cloak. Do you remember it? The aureum one with the jadeite and blue lazule stones?"

The maid servant nodded. "Yes, domina."

"Then fetch it for me. I haven't the energy to climb those stairs again. The brooch is on my bedside table."

She nodded again. "Yes, domina."

Raina watched her climb back up the long flight of stairs and round the corner. Once the woman was out of sight, she turned down the corridor leading to the torture cavern. Blessedly, though she passed a few more servants, none stopped her or questioned her presence. She reached the part of the hall where the door to the torture cavern was located, lingering in rapt admiration before a huge portrait of Malam Vorax on the wall across from the door until the hall was clear. Then she raced across, opened the door, and slipped inside.

As she made her stealthy way down the twisting stone steps, Raina pulled out her stunner. Though the journey this far had been relatively easy, she doubted she'd be able to get Teague out of the torture caverns without a fight. The stunner, though, had the potential of tipping the odds in her favor, with minimal noise or disruption to call unnecessary attention to her.

There was no one in the main cavern. Voices and movement, however, emanated from a room off to one side—two men's voices, one unfamiliar, the other that of the master torturer, Orcus. She'd never forgotten that harsh, rusty voice from the time Vorax had taken her down here as a girl. Even now, the sound of it sent a cold chill rippling down her spine.

Stepping over to the door, Raina eased it open just enough for a full view of the room. Teague lay on a stone slab, naked, his arms unbound and lying at his sides. A thin little man dressed in gray robes, a long, bloodstained domare-hide apron covering his front, dug around in a tray of instruments lying on a table to one side of the slab. Orcus stood at Teague's head, a look of eager anticipation on his otherwise moronic face.

The thin man turned then, two long metal instruments curved at both ends in one hand, a narrow, very sharp knife in the other. He handed Orcus the long, curved instruments. "Here," the embalmer said. "Once I make the incision, I'll need you to insert these and pull the flesh and muscle apart so I can see my work area. Do you understand what you must do?"

Orcus scowled. "It seems simple enough. I'm not an imbecile, you know."

"Fine, fine." The thin little man motioned toward Teague with his knife. "Let's get on with it, then." He moved to Teague's side, placed his other hand on Teague's chest to brace himself, and lifted the knife to make the incision.

Before Raina could react, a strong, long-fingered hand shot up and grabbed the embalmer by the wrist. The man gave a horrified squawk. Orcus, apparently less startled by the unexpected, grunted in anger, then lifted one of the curved instruments to strike Teague.

Raina didn't hesitate. She raised her stunner, pointed it at Orcus, and fired. Orcus grunted again, this time in pain, then collapsed where he stood. The instruments he'd been holding clanked to the floor and skittered across the room.

Still clasping the embalmer's wrist, Teague slowly pulled himself to a sitting position. He smiled—a feral upturning of his lips—right in the man's face. The thin little man paled. His eyes rolled back in his head and, with a gurgle, he fainted.

Teague released the embalmer and watched him plummet to the floor. Then he swung his legs over the side of the table and turned to Raina. "I gather he's not accustomed to someone returning from the dead?"

"Most people aren't." She shoved her stunner back beneath her belt and strode over. Her glance fell to his abdomen. An incision from her earlier dagger thrust still marred the rippling perfection of his belly, but aside from the dried blood, it looked now more like a superficial wound than a fatal injury.

His glance followed hers. "It'll be completely healed in another twenty-four hours."

"Does it hurt?" She couldn't bear to think she'd caused him even the most minor a pain.

"No, not really."

Raina reached out, touched his belly. "I-I was so afraid . . ." She swallowed hard. "So afraid that I'd lose you." Her glance lifted. Her gaze met his.

His mouth quirked. "You couldn't have been more afraid than I at the thought of leaving you in Malam Vorax's clutches."

The mention of the evil man's name wrenched Raina back to reality. "Vorax! Even now he celebrates your death in the banquet hall, along with many of the men still loyal to him. In the meanwhile, Aban holds part of an army at the city gates, while the other half awaits us at the Tapestry Passage."

"The Tapestry Passage?" Teague's forehead furrowed in puzzlement. "But surely that was sealed cycles ago. Vorax is no—"

"I've had men clearing it for the past few days. Aban was ordered not to approach Ksathra until the passage was clear. All we have left to do is reach it and open the hidden door."

He stared down at her, bemusement slowly fading to be replaced by a tender pride. "You orchestrated all this, didn't you? My fierce warrior, always the take-charge leader."

"I couldn't let you die, or allow Vorax to continue his despotic rule, could I?"

Teague smiled and, leaning down, gave her a slow, gentle kiss. "No, you couldn't. You're not that kind of woman."

Once more, her hand moved to his belly, then ever so lightly trailed lower. As her fingers encircled his shaft, Teague gasped in startled pleasure.

Raina smiled. "You've very little idea exactly what kind of woman I really am." Her glance dropped to his rapidly thickening manhood. "But I've every intention of apprising you of it, just as soon as we get the small matter of a palace takeover finished."

As if suddenly remembering himself then, Teague straightened. Raina released him and stepped back. He slid off the stone table, walked over to where his clothes and boots lay, and began to put them on.

"Fine words and sentiments," he muttered thickly. "Ones you can be sure I'll hold you to . . . later. In the meanwhile, it's indeed past time we finish this— once and for all."

"Yes," Raina agreed softly, stirred to the depths of her being by the love and respect and proud possession she saw burning in Teague's ice blue eyes. "It's past time, indeed."

With the boisterous sounds of a celebration echoing throughout the palace even as an army threatened outside the city gates, Raina and Teague made their stealthy way to the library. Unheeded by the servants hurrying to and fro, they slipped inside, found the great tapestry and the secret door hidden behind it, and opened it. The other half of the army swarmed in.

Teague leading the assault with Raina at his side, the desert warriors streamed through the palace, some taking the drunken and unsuspecting revelers totally by surprise, others heading through the city to open the gates to the rest of the army. In the course of but a few hours, Ksathra was taken.

Sinon was one of the first to surrender. Vorax was finally found hiding in one of the large, wooden vats of fermenting uva wine, soaked to the skin and purpled from his neck down. They brought them both down to the torture caverns for safekeeping, as much to protect them from the people as to hold them prisoner.

Once the palace was secured and some semblance of order restored, Teague called for a gathering of the inhabitants of Ksathra. Raina joined him on the royal dais before the milling, excited mass of humanity that packed the Great Hall. Though he'd been uncomfortable assuming the chair of power, Raina had insisted. The rebellion was too new, she'd told him, to weaken it by the lack of a strong figurehead. Whether he wished the role or not, he must accept it at least temporarily.

Before Teague could rise and speak to the people, the royal chamberlain, an ancient man who'd served the royal house of Ksathra and gone into hiding during Vorax's reign, hobbled forward. Behind him came the leaders of the twelve desert tribes. As temporary leader of the Tuarets, Aban led the others, bearing a crown on a padded tray of crimson edged with argentum and aureum metal.

Teague eyed Aban and the object on his tray. His throat went tight. The crown of dominion, his father's crown. "This is premature, Aban," he rasped, gesturing to the contents of the tray. "The people have yet to speak, *or* choose their new ruler."

"And do you think they will not choose you, sire?" the royal chamberlain asked, stepping forward to take the crown from Aban and move up the dais to stand before Teague.

Teague shot Raina an imploring glance, then riveted a steely gaze back on the old man. "More to the point, *I* haven't decided if I—"

The chamberlain turned and lifted the crown high above his head. "Is Tarik Shatrevar worthy to rule Farsala?" he cried, his voice surprisingly strong for so old a man. "What is the will of the people in this?"

"Let him rule," a voice shouted from the depths of the crowd. "He is worthy. The prophecy has been fulfilled, the taint exorcised, the evil overthrown. He is worthy, I say!"

"Yes," another roared. "Crown him. Crown him now!"

As one, the people surged forward, crying out their accord.

Raina leaned close and whispered in his ear. "You *are* worthy, my love. And Farsala needs you."

His glance locked with her. "I'm afraid, Raina."

"It's a terrible responsibility. But you can't run from it. Your destiny always called you back to Farsala."

He sighed. "Yes, I know that well." His mouth tightened and, with a resolute lift of his chin, he turned back to the chamberlain. "I bow to the will of my people. But the coronation must wait a time. First, I have a few other issues to settle. Set the date for the ceremonies for a week from now."

The old man smiled. "It will be as you ask, sire." He turned back to the crowd. "The prince will accept the crown. We'll commence the official ceremonies in a week's time."

The people roared in jubilation and, for a time, bedlam reigned in the Great Hall. Then Teague stood and motioned to the guards standing off to the right, beside a door. At his command, the men opened the door and signaled within. Four Tuarets led the unbound Vorax and Sinon into the hall. At sight of the pair, the crowd went still, save for soft, angry mutterings that arose from various parts of the big room.

Teague glanced at Raina. "What's to be Vorax's fate? After what he did to you, I'd say it's your prerogative to choose."

She shot him an arch look. "And do you discount, then, what he did to you? He had your father and mother murdered, your sister raped and driven to suicide. Not to mention the physical and mental torment he put you through. I'd say you've suffered far, far more than I."

"It's in the past, Raina. I don't want to return to it, even if only to garner the anger necessary to kill him."

"Still, he cannot be allowed to go free."

Teague arched a dark blond brow. "Then it's lifelong imprisonment, is it?"

She considered that for a moment, then slowly nodded. "That seems fair enough, for all the cycles of pain and suffering he put us and everyone else through. He needn't know the full extent of our mercy immediately, though."

"You wish to twist the knife of his submission a bit, do you?" He smiled.

"Exactly. Vorax deserves to squirm for a time." Raina paused. "And what of Sinon?"

He considered that for a moment. "His fate can be determined later. Vorax is who matters right now."

Teague extended his hand and she took it. Together, they turned to face the man who had once been their greatest nemesis.

Vorax drew up before them, fat, wet, and ludicrously colored. His gaze shifted anxiously from one to the other. "You will kill me, then, will you?" he finally forced the words out.

Teague stared down at him, piercing him with a grim look. "You deserve that, and more, for all the cycles of your brutal reign."

The garishly stained man wobbled, then sank to his knees. "I-I beg you. Don't kill me. I-I don't want to die."

"Please. Have some dignity, Father." Sinon stepped closer, a sneer on his face, toying with one of the rings on his hand. "Be a man for once and face at long last the consequences of what you have wrought."

Teague's glance never wavered from the cowering man kneeling before him. "It's indeed time that Vorax faced the consequences of what he has wrought. Look up. Face me, Malam Vorax."

Ever so slowly, Vorax lifted his gaze.

"Why should I show you mercy?" Teague demanded with cold ruthlessness. "Did you show me mercy, either as a lad, or recently, when you held me once more? Did you show my father or mother or sister mercy?"

"Your father, your line, was corrupt." Vorax strained against the hold on his arms and the two men who held him. He was like a cornered animal now, ready to lash out at any and everyone. "I did Farsala a service in destroying him. I served Farsala well in excising a tainted, unwholesome heritage."

"Yet ultimately, you still failed." Raina leaned forward in her chair. "Teague prevailed, just as the prophecy promised. And the taint exorcised, the evil overthrown, was perhaps always as much that of you and your spawn as it ever was the House of Shatrevar's."

"Then let that spawn of his exorcise the evil once and for all!" Before anyone could react, Sinon turned and, grabbing his father's soggy tunic, pulled him around and pressed his fisted hand to his neck. A thorn, protruding from an open-topped ring, sank into the flesh at the base of Vorax's throat.

Vorax screamed in agony and fell to his knees. Then the Tuarets were upon them, pulling Sinon away. The ring, containing the deadly Arborian nexus thorn, was wrenched from his hand.

"Die, you foul-hearted animal!" His face purple with rage, his eyes gleaming with a crazed, triumphant light, Sinon struggled against the men who held him. "You were a failure at everything. At ruling the people, as a husband, and most of all, as a father. You've always been nothing but an old fool . . . a pitiful disappointment."

"Take him . . . take him away," Teague growled

above the rising tumult of the crowd. He motioned for the guards to lead Sinon out of the hall.

Teague sat there for a time, his hands clenching the arms of his chair, his mind awhirl. Sinon had killed his father. Never, even in the darkest of times, had he ever felt that way about his own father.

A fool . . . so disappointed in you.

The words, so long a bitter torment to him, no longer held the same bite. Where Sinon had shriveled beneath the onslaught of an indifferent and callous father, Teague had striven to fight even harder. And ultimately been found worthy, where in many ways his father had been unworthy.

They dragged Sinon away, shrieking in rage. Then Vorax, already convulsing in the final throes of the thorn's fatal nerve toxin, was carried out. The people, stunned at what had just transpired, filed silently out of the room. When the Great Hall was empty once more, Teague rose and offered Raina his hand.

She looked up at him, a questioning light in her eyes.

"Come," he said. "The memories hang heavy about this room. Let us leave it."

Raina stood. "As you wish. Even a ruler needs an occasional reprieve from the hardships of his reign, though he must eventually still sacrifice his will for the good of the many."

Teague smiled and shook his head, his long fingers closing gently, tenderly around hers. "Do you realize how much like Bahir you sound right now?"

"He's dead, you know," she said, suddenly wistful. "He gave his body to Rand at the end."

Any being who dies creates the cause for a new being . . .

At the memory of those sacred words, Teague's smile

faded to a bittersweet, slight upturning of his lips. "And Rand took the crystal back to Bellator?"

"Yes. He thought I should stay behind and be with you."

"I'm so very glad that you did, sweet one." He tugged on her hand. "Come, let's walk out onto the balcony."

She followed him without protest, thankful, after all that had transpired in the past few days, just to be alive and to be with him. Together, they walked out onto a broad stone porch enclosed by a short, pillared railing. Before them spread the city of Ksathra, and beyond, the foothills and lush lands that gently eased, far in the distance, into the barren, undulating expanse of the Ar Rimal.

Behind them the sun set in the mountains, bathing the white buildings and boulevards in a rose-pink light. The streets were quiet now. Oil lamps winked in the windows. Sounds of meals being prepared and families settling down for the evening rose on the twilight-tinged air.

Teague guided Raina over to the balcony railing, then pulled her close. They stood for a long while, content just to watch the peaceful scene.

"It'll be better now," he finally said. "For the people, for Farsala, for both of us. A fresh chance at a new life and a new reign. A reign that promises to be far better than the one we both left cycles ago."

"You'll be a magnificent ruler." Raina snuggled yet closer. "You chose well—and triumphed."

He bent to kiss the top of her head. "Yes, I did," Teague whispered into the soft tumble of her hair. "Yet my greatest victory of all was the prize of your heart, your love."

She leaned back to gaze up at him, wonderment and a wary hope shining in her eyes. "Truly, Teague?"

"Truly." He stared down at her, a myriad of emotions flashing through his eyes. "I love you, Raina. Will you be my life mate? Be my queen and help me rule? I fear I can't do it without you."

Raina chuckled softly.

Teague arched a brow, suddenly suspicious. "Pray, what is so amusing? I just offered you my heart and love, and all you can do is laugh?"

"I was just thinking about some wise words that Najirah once said, and that you're the strangest monk I've ever known."

He took her face in his hands, cupping her cheeks in the hollow of his calloused palms. "But a monk no more, sweet one. That life once served me well, but not now, or ever again."

"Yes, it did indeed serve you well and helped to make you the man you are. I see that now. I see a lot of things more clearly now."

She turned her face into his hand and kissed him over the pulse throbbing at his wrist, her heart so full of joy she thought it might burst at any moment. "And I suppose I *shall* accept your offer of a life-mating," Raina said, smiling up at him, an impish twinkle in her eyes. "What choice does either of us have? The same destiny that first called us together would never permit anything less."

"I suppose you're right," Teague thoughtfully replied. "Yet, despite all that happened finally to bring us together, I don't think I would wish it any other way."

"Nor would I, my love." Raina's eyes brimmed with happy tears. "Nor would I."

Dear Reader,

I hope you enjoyed *FIRESTORM.* I always try to do just a little bit more in each book, to stretch and grow as a writer. Bahir and Najirah's story, as you can well imagine, was something new for me. I really enjoyed including their romance—however bittersweet it may have been—and feel it enhanced not only the story, but Teague and Raina's relationship as well.

My next book for Pinnacle Books is *FIRESONG,* the third and last book in my Volan trilogy (begun with *FIRE-STAR,* which is still available.) It is the tale of Rand, the Volan, who, even though he at long last has the humanoid body he so dearly desires, won't find the way simple or necessarily always pleasant. In *FIRESONG,* he is forced to join with Cyra, Bahir's first wife, and take on the rapidly worsening problems caused by his own kind, an alien race of mindslavers. Cyra, torn with guilt and mixed emotions over her desertion of Bahir five cycles earlier, is none too pleased to learn that Rand, a hated Volan, now possesses her husband's body. As they work together to save the Imperium, however, they cannot long deny their growing attraction. But can a Volan ever hope to win the love of a humanoid woman? And will it even matter, if the unexpected and most deadly threat of all cannot be defeated? *FIRESONG* will be a July 1996 release from Pinnacle Books.

In the meanwhile, I love hearing from my readers. If

you'd like a personal reply and an autographed excerpted flyer for *FIRESTORM* and/or *FIRESONG* (with a list of all my previously published—and mostly still available—books), please send a self-addressed, business-sized, stamped envelope to P.O. Box 62365, Colorado Springs, CO 80962. Happy Reading!

Kathleen Morgan

Kathleen Morgan

FOR THE VERY BEST IN ROMANCE—
DENISE LITTLE PRESENTS!

AMBER, SING SOFTLY   (0038, $4.99)
by Joan Elliott Pickart
Astonished to find a wounded gun-slinger on her doorstep, Amber
Prescott can't decide whether to take him in or put him out of his misery.
Since this lonely frontierswoman can't deny her longing to have a man
of her own, who nurses him back to health, while savoring the glorious
possibilities of the situation. But what Amber doesn't realize is that this
strong, handsome man is full of surprises!

A DEEPER MAGIC   (0039, $4.99)
by Jillian Hunter
From the moment wealthy Margaret Rose and struggling physician Ian
MacNeill meet, they are swept away in an adventure that takes them
from the haunted land of Aberdeen to a primitive, faraway island—and
into a world of danger and irresistible desire. Amid the clash of ancient
magic and new science Margaret and Ian find themselves falling help-
lessly in love.

SWEET AMY JANE   (0050, $4.99)
by Anna Eberhardt
Her horoscope warned her she'd be dealing with the wrong sort of man.
And private eye Amy Jane Chadwick was used to dealing with the wrong
kind of man, due to her profession. But nothing prepared her for the
gorgeously handsome Max, a former professional athlete who is being
stalked by an obsessive fan. And from the moment they meet, sparks
fly and danger follows!

MORE THAN MAGIC   (0049, $4.99)
by Olga Bicos
This classic romance is a thrilling tale of two adventurers who set out
for the wilds of the Arizona territory in the year 1878. Seeking treasure,
an archaeologist and an astronomer find the greatest prize of all—love.

*Available wherever paperbacks are sold, or order direct from the
Publisher. Send cover price plus 50¢ per copy for mailing and
handling Penguin USA, P.O. Box 999, c/o Dept. 17109, Bergen-
field, NJ 07621. Residents of New York and Tennessee must include sales tax. DO NOT SEND CASH.*